Praise for

THE OTHER LADY VANISHES

"Between the novel's cleverly conceived and brilliantly executed plot and Quick's signature delicious dash of dry humor, *The Other Lady Vanishes* is the perfect cup of literary tea for both historical romance readers and historical mystery mavens."　　—*Booklist* (starred review)

"With humorous repartee, a diabolical plot, and characters that make the 1930s spring to life, Quick's lively story of murder, intrigue, and romance keeps its secrets until the very end."

—*Library Journal* (starred review)

THE
OTHER LADY
VANISHES

❧

AMANDA
QUICK

BERKLEY
NEW YORK

BERKLEY
An imprint of Penguin Random House LLC
1745 Broadway, New York, NY 10019

BERKLEY and the BERKLEY & B colophon are registered trademarks of
Penguin Random House LLC.

ISBN: 9780399585357

The Library of Congress has catalogued the Berkley hardcover edition of this book as follows:

Names: Quick, Amanda, author.
Title: The other lady vanishes / Amanda Quick.
Description: First edition. | New York : Berkley, 2018.
Identifiers: LCCN 2017057658 | ISBN 9780399585326 (hardback) | ISBN 9780399585333 (ebook)
Subjects: | BISAC: FICTION / Romance / Suspense. | GSAFD: Romantic suspense fiction. |
Mystery fiction.
Classification: LCC PS3561.R44 O84 2018 | DDC 813/.54—dc23
LC record available at https://lccn.loc.gov/2017057658

Berkley hardcover edition / May 2018
Berkley trade edition / January 2019

Printed in the United States of America
1   3   5   7   9   10   8   6   4   2

Cover design by Eileen Carey
Cover photo by Lee Avison/Trevillion Images
Book design by Laura K. Corless

For Frank, with love

THE
OTHER LADY
VANISHES

Chapter 1

The screams of the patients on ward five told Adelaide Blake that time had run out.

She stopped searching for the key to the file cabinet and went to stand at the door of the small office. She had not dared to turn on any lights in the laboratory. There was enough moonlight spilling through the high, arched windows to illuminate the long workbenches and create ominous silhouettes of the equipment and instruments.

The wails and shrieks and howls from the floor below were escalating rapidly. Something or, more likely, someone was agitating the patients. The ward on the fifth floor was reserved for the most hopelessly mad and insane. The locked rooms housed those who were forever lost in their own private hells. Some of the patients were afflicted with violent, paranoid visions and hallucinations. Others battled fearsome monsters that only they could see.

Soon after she had been locked in one of the cell-like rooms on ward five, she had learned that the patients provided an excellent alarm system, especially at night. Nights were always the worst.

The nerve-shattering chorus of the damned echoed up the stone staircase. There was no one around to calm the inmates. The orderlies on the locked ward had been given the night off.

She could not delay any longer. If she did not escape now, she might not make it at all. She would have to leave the file behind.

She left the doorway of the office and started to make her way cautiously through the maze of workbenches. She had plotted her exit strategy down to the smallest detail, but the last-minute decision to look for the file had put the plan in jeopardy. She had to get out of the laboratory immediately or she might not escape.

Originally, the Rushbrook Sanitarium was the private mansion of a wealthy, eccentric industrialist who had intended to entertain on a grand scale. The result was a Gothic nightmare of a house with five floors, endless hallways, and the tower room that now served as a laboratory. The single redeeming architectural virtue as far as Adelaide was concerned was that there were a number of discreetly concealed staircases intended for the use of a large staff.

Most of the servants' stairs had been permanently closed and sealed long ago. Others had disappeared under various waves of renovations and remodeling projects. But a few were still accessible. She had the key to one of the little-used staircases.

She was halfway across the lab when she heard panicky footsteps on the tower stairs. Someone was coming up to the laboratory. Whoever it was would see her as soon as he turned on the lights.

There was nowhere to hide except behind Ormsby's desk. Discovery spelled doom. Dr. Gill would order increased security for her. She might never have another chance to escape.

A cold sense of certainty sliced through the fear. If necessary, she would try to fight her way out of the sanitarium. She could not—would not—go back to the cell on the fifth floor. She would rather die.

She turned quickly, searching the shadows for something that could function as a weapon. She knew the lab all too well because it was where they had brought her when Gill and Dr. Ormsby decided to give her another dose of the drug. In her desperate attempt to hold on to her sanity by focusing on an escape plan, she had memorized every inch of the tower room.

She went to the nearest cabinet, yanked open the door, and pulled a couple of glass jars off the shelf. She had no idea what she grabbed—it was too dark to read the labels—but she had seen Ormsby take a variety of chemicals out of the cabinet. Many were flammable. Some were highly acidic.

With the two jars in hand she hurried back into the office. Ormsby's desk was neat and tidy. He was a fussy little man who was obsessed with his research, but orderliness was high on his list of priorities.

Aside from the usual desk accessories—telephone, blotter, and inkwells—there was one other object on the desk. The black velvet box looked as if it had been made to hold a woman's collection of jewelry. But Adelaide knew there were no necklaces, rings, or bracelets inside. The velvet box contained a dozen elegantly cut crystal perfume bottles.

She made it behind the desk with the jars of chemicals just as Dr. Harold Ormsby staggered into the darkened laboratory. It sounded as if he was gasping for air. He did not turn on any lights.

"Get away from me," he shrieked. "Don't touch me."

Adelaide heard other footsteps on the stone staircase, the slow, steady, determined tread of a predator stalking prey.

Ormsby wasn't trying to catch his breath, Adelaide realized. The doctor was in the grip of raw panic.

His pursuer did not respond, at least not verbally. Crouched behind the desk, Adelaide removed the tops of the jars. The acrid odors that wafted out made her gasp and turn her head away. She hoped the screams of the patients covered the small sounds she made.

She tried to keep her breathing as light and shallow as possible, but it wasn't easy. Ice-cold perspiration dampened her skin. She shivered and her pulse skittered wildly.

Ormsby screamed again, louder this time. The high, unnatural screech affected Adelaide like a bolt of lightning. For a few seconds she wondered if it had stopped her heart.

And then she wondered if lightning actually had struck the laboratory. A narrow beam of fire blazed in the darkness. Peering around the corner of Ormsby's desk, she watched the glow move past the office doorway.

Ormsby's piercing screams rose above the cacophony from the fifth-floor patients, the cries of a man being sent into hell.

Running footsteps reverberated in the tower room. Heavy glass shattered. Night air flowed into the laboratory.

Ormsby's hopeless cries echoed in the night for another second or two. The suddenness with which they were cut off told its own story.

Adelaide froze as she realized what had just happened. Dr. Harold Ormsby had leaped straight through one of the high, arched windows. No one could survive such a fall.

In the shadows of the lab the fiery light winked out. It dawned on Adelaide that someone had lit a Bunsen burner and used the flame to drive Ormsby out the window. That didn't make sense. He had obviously been terrified, but she knew something of the man. It was easy to imagine him pleading for his life or cowering in a corner, but jumping to his death seemed oddly out of character. Then again, she was not the best judge of character. She had learned that lesson the hard way.

The screaming from the fifth-floor ward got louder. The patients sensed that something terrible had happened.

Adelaide heard rapid, purposeful footsteps crossing the tile floor, coming toward the office. She gripped the containers of chemicals and waited, aware that the only thing protecting her now was the noise from the inmates down below. The shrieks and cries would make it difficult if not impossible for the killer to hear the sound of her breathing.

The intruder stopped directly in front of the desk. A flashlight came on briefly. Adelaide prepared to fight for her life.

But the intruder turned and hurried quickly out of the office. A few seconds later, footsteps sounded on the stairs.

The keening of the agitated patients rose and fell, but there were more shouts now. They came from the courtyard below the broken window. Someone had found Ormsby's body and was sounding the alarm.

Adelaide waited a few heartbeats and then got to her feet. She was shaking so badly she had a hard time keeping her balance. She thought briefly of trying once again to find the key to the file cabinet, but common sense prevailed. Escape from the sanitarium was the first priority.

She reached up to adjust the nurse's cap pinned to her tightly knotted hair. When she glanced down at the desk, she saw that the black velvet box containing the perfume bottles was gone. The intruder had taken it.

She selected one of the two open jars of chemicals to use as a weapon and left the other one behind on the desk. She picked her way through the moonlit lab. When she got to the staircase, she descended cautiously.

At the foot of the stairs, she paused in the stairwell and looked around the edge of the door.

The inmates continued to howl and scream through the grills set into the locked doors, but the hallway was empty. There was no sign of the intruder.

Her room was located at the far end of an intersecting hallway. There were no other patients in that corridor. Earlier she had arranged the pillows and blankets on her bed in an attempt to approximate the outline of a sleeping figure, but it looked as if the ruse had been unnecessary. The agitation of the other inmates and the commotion in the courtyard were sufficient to conceal her movements. The white cap and the long blue cloak, familiar elements of a nurse's uniform, would do the rest. With luck, anyone who chanced to see her from a distance would assume she was a member of the hospital staff.

The entrance to the old servants' stairs was in a storage closet on the opposite side of the hall. She was edging out of the stairwell doorway, preparing to make a dash for the closet, when the patients' screams rose in another hellish crescendo. It was all the warning she got. It was just barely enough to save her.

She retreated to the shadows of the stairwell and waited. When the screams faded a little, she risked a peek around the doorway.

A man dressed in a doctor's coat, a white cap, and a surgical mask emerged from the hallway that led to her room. The black velvet box was in his left hand. In his right he gripped a syringe.

The only thing that saved her from being seen was that the masked doctor was intent on rushing down the hall in the opposite direction. He disappeared through the locked doors just beyond the nurses' station.

She did not think it was possible to be any more terrified, but the sight of the masked doctor leaving the corridor that led to her room sent another shock of horror across her nerves. Maybe he had intended to kill her, too.

With an effort of will, she pulled herself together. She certainly could not continue to dither in the stairwell indefinitely. She had to act or all was lost.

She took a deep breath, clutched the jar in one hand, and rushed across the hallway. She opened the door of the storage closet.

A bearded face appeared at the steel grill set into a nearby door. The insane man stared at her with wild, otherworldly eyes.

"You're a ghost now, aren't you?" he said in a voice that was hoarse from endless keening and wailing. "It was just a matter of time before they killed you, just like they did the other one."

"Good-bye, Mr. Hawkins," she said gently.

"You're lucky to be dead. You're better off now because you can leave this place."

"Yes, I know."

She slipped into the storage closet, closed the door, and turned on the overhead fixture. The door to the service stairs was at the back. It was locked. To her overwhelming relief, one of the keys she had been given worked.

By the time she made it downstairs to the darkened kitchen on the ground floor, she could hear sirens in the distance. Someone had telephoned the local authorities. The sanitarium was located a couple of miles outside the small town of Rushbrook. It would take the police and the ambulance several minutes to arrive on the scene.

There was no one around to see her when she slipped out of the kitchen. She inserted another key into the lock on the massive wrought iron gate that the delivery vehicles used.

And then she was free, hurrying down a rutted lane with only the light of the moon to guide her.

She was not at all sorry that Ormsby was dead, but his death could complicate her already desperate situation. It would be so easy for the authorities to conclude that the patient who had escaped the secure grounds of the Rushbrook Sanitarium on the night of the doctor's mysterious demise was, in fact, a crazed killer.

She had to get as far away as possible from the asylum before the orderlies realized she was gone.

It occurred to her that one person already knew she had disappeared—the doctor in the surgical mask who had gone to her room with the syringe.

She wanted to run but she did not dare. If, in the darkness, she stumbled over a rock or a fallen tree limb, she could twist an ankle or worse.

The emergency vehicles passed her a short time later. They never noticed her hiding behind the heavy shrubbery at the side of the lane.

❧

Dawn found her standing on the side of a highway, hoping that a passing motorist would take pity on a nurse whose car had run out of gas in the middle of nowhere.

She raised her hand to wave down a truck. The gold wedding ring on her finger gleamed malevolently in the morning light.

Chapter 2

Burning Cove, California
Two months later

"Your new neighbor is back," Florence Darley said in a low voice. She plucked the kettle off the stove and poured hot water over the leaves in the teapot. "That makes eight days in a row except for Sunday."

Adelaide did not look up from the small scale she was using to measure a quarter pound of Tranquility tea. "We're closed on Sundays."

"Which only goes to prove my point. Mr. Truett has become a regular. I see he's reading the morning edition of the *Herald*, as usual. Five will get you ten he'll order the same thing—a pot of that very expensive blend of green tea you convinced me to order from the San Francisco dealer, no sugar, no tea cakes, no scones, no cookies."

"Mr. Truett does seem to be a man who likes to keep to a routine," Adelaide said.

She did not add that Truett's apparent preference for keeping to a schedule made it easy to time his morning walks on the beach. He never failed to show up at seven thirty. He always walked for precisely thirty minutes. It was June and there was often fog in the morning at this time of year, but that did not stop him.

She was the one who was annoyed by the fog, she thought. It meant that she could only catch fleeting glimpses of him taking his daily walk. And she had to admit she had come to look forward to watching Jake Truett in the mornings. He might be a man of strict habits, but he did not move like a man who was a stickler for rules and regulations. He did not march across the sand like a martinet. Instead he prowled the beach with the easy physical power of a large hunting cat.

Florence chuckled knowingly. "I don't think he's here every day because of your fancy tea. And he doesn't come in because we're fashionable these days. He's not the type to care one bit if the customer at the next table is a celebrity or a garbage collector. Got a hunch you're the reason our Mr. Truett has developed the habit of stopping by."

Adelaide flushed. She was very fond of her new boss, not to mention extremely grateful for the job, but Florence's newfound determination to play matchmaker made her uneasy.

After two months in Burning Cove, she was just starting to breathe more easily. No manhunt had been launched to recapture an escaped mental patient. In fact, there had been no mention in the press of her late-night departure from the Rushbrook Sanitarium.

As far as she could tell, no one was looking for her. Nevertheless, she was not yet ready to take the risk of dating. At least, that's what she told herself every day when Jake Truett walked into the tearoom carrying a leather briefcase, sat down at the same table, and asked for green tea, no sugar, no tea cakes, no scones, no cookies.

Florence had other ideas. She was a plump, comfortably proportioned woman in her late sixties. She had opened the tearoom nearly a decade earlier in the wake of the crash and somehow managed to keep it going during the worst of the hard times.

The tearoom had survived because the exclusive town of Burning Cove was a retreat for the rich and the famous, two groups that were largely insulated from the financial disaster that had shaken the rest of the country. But even in such a wealthy community it took fortitude and sound business instincts to stay profitable. Florence possessed plenty of both qualities. Adelaide was learning a lot from her.

In addition to hiring a waitress with no restaurant experience and no references, Florence had helped her find an inexpensive place to live, a cottage on the bluffs above Crescent Beach. When Adelaide had explained that she could not come up with the first month's rent, Florence had waved off the problem. *Don't worry, I'll take care of it and you can repay me later. Something tells me you'll earn your keep.*

Adelaide was pleased that she had, indeed, begun to earn her keep. She badly wanted to repay the debt. When she suggested that Refresh start creating and marketing specialized teas and herbal tisanes, Florence was dubious but she agreed to let the experiment take place. Within a month, the Refresh Tearoom, which had enjoyed a quiet but steady business for years, moved up to an entirely new level of prosperity.

Recently, a few of the celebrities, socialites, and tycoons who used Burning Cove as a vacation playground had begun requesting exclusive blends designed for specific personal needs. In the past few weeks Adelaide had concocted teas and herbal tisanes to treat a variety of complaints—insomnia, anxiety, and lack of energy. One of her most popular teas was the one she had created to alleviate the symptoms of a hangover—a common problem for the Hollywood set who tended to party until dawn.

Business had picked up so much that Florence was thinking of hiring another waitress so Adelaide could concentrate on creating and packaging the special blends.

All of which made it more difficult to come up with excuses for a failure to show an appropriate interest in an apparently eligible male. Jake Truett did not wear a wedding ring, but Adelaide reminded herself that that didn't mean much. She didn't wear a wedding ring, either.

She filled the small sack with the quarter pound of Tranquility tea blend that she had just measured. "I really don't think Mr. Truett is interested in me, Flo. We're two very different people. He's a wealthy businessman who has traveled the world. I'm a tearoom waitress. I've never been out of California. It's not as if we have a great deal in common."

"I think Mr. Truett is just shy," Florence said. "He's trying to work up his nerve to ask you out. You should give him some encouragement."

"Trust me, the man is not the shy type. I'm very sure that if he wanted something, he would go after it."

"I told you, I heard that he was widowed a few months ago. That means he's out of practice when it comes to dating."

"He's probably still grieving," Adelaide said. "That would explain why he never smiles."

"Maybe he just needs a reason to smile." Florence winked, picked up the pot of tea she had just prepared, and bustled out of the kitchen.

There was no point arguing with her. Adelaide suppressed a sigh, dusted tea off her hands, folded the top of the sack, and went out of the kitchen. The customer, a harried-looking young woman dressed in a business suit, was waiting anxiously at the counter.

"Here you are, Miss Moss," Adelaide said. "Miss Westlake's special blend, Tranquility."

Vera Westlake was the latest Hollywood celebrity to discover Refresh. Florence, who followed the celebrity gossip magazines with great enthusiasm, had been thrilled when the star the press had labeled the most beautiful woman in Hollywood became a customer.

"Thank you." Miss Moss opened her handbag and took out her wallet. "Miss Westlake will be very happy to get this. She ran out this morning while she was studying her new script. She insisted that her driver bring me into town immediately to get some more. She says that drinking the special blend you made up for her helps her maintain her focus."

"Always happy to be of service," Adelaide said.

Miss Moss paid for the tea and scurried out of the lightly crowded tearoom. A limousine was waiting for her. She climbed into the rear seat. The driver motored off down the tree-lined street.

Adelaide picked up a pad and pencil. It was time to take Jake Truett's order. Green tea. No sugar. No tea cakes. No scones. No cookies.

Truett had become a regular shortly after arriving in town eight days earlier. Florence had immediately made a few inquiries. She had returned with the news that Truett was a businessman who, until recently, had owned an import-export business headquartered in Los Angeles. After the death of his wife, he had sold his business and retired.

According to Florence, there were rumors that Truett had some health problems—something to do with exhausted nerves. Evidently his doctor had ordered him to spend a couple of months at the seaside in the hope that the ocean air and long walks on the beach would help him recover.

His nerves aside, Truett certainly appeared physically fit. Unlike so many of the celebrities and socialites who vacationed in Burning Cove, he lacked the snaky-thin body that was the Hollywood ideal, a look that was generally achieved through chain-smoking and the frequent consumption of cocktails. Truett was lean but he was sleekly muscled.

She found the rest of him equally intriguing. He was tall but not exceptionally so. He didn't tower over her the way Conrad had done. His dark hair was cut short and parted on the side. He was not unhandsome, but his ascetic features were too austere to be labeled handsome. His eyes were an arresting shade of amber brown—cool, watchful, and intelligent, but very hard to read. She sensed that he was always aware of what was going on around him, but she could not tell what he was thinking. He was the watcher in the shadows, not an actor on the stage.

There was something implacable and forbidding about him. She had the feeling that he would be slow to anger, but if you pushed him over the edge, he would make a formidable enemy. His revenge would be cold and thorough.

There was nothing about him that suggested he suffered from exhausted nerves.

She reminded herself that those who suffered from afflictions of the nerves often appeared quite normal. She was a case in point. She had been successfully passing for normal in Burning Cove for two months. No one had guessed that she had spent nearly two months locked up in the Rushbrook Sanitarium.

Order pad and pencil in hand, she whisked around the end of the counter and crossed the tearoom to the table where Jake Truett sat reading the *Burning Cove Herald*. His leather briefcase was on the floor beside his chair. She knew from eight days of personal observation that there was a yellow legal pad and four perfectly sharpened pencils inside. She also knew that after he finished reading the *Herald* from first page to last, he would open the briefcase, take out the yellow pad, and make notes.

He wore his customary uniform, a crisply pressed white shirt, an elegantly knotted tie, a cream-colored jacket, and dark brown trousers.

She knew that he was aware that she was approaching his table, but he waited until she came to a halt, pencil hovering over the order pad, before he looked up from the newspaper. She braced herself as she always did for the little electric thrill that crackled through her whenever she was this close to him.

He nodded once, gravely polite. "Good morning, Miss Brockton."

"Good morning, Mr. Truett." She gave him her bright, customer-friendly smile. "Will you be having the usual today?"

"Yes, please. The green tea. No sugar. No tea cakes. No scones. No cookies."

His voice, low, resonant, and so very masculine, sent another whisper of excitement through her.

"Right," she said. "Will that be all, then?"

He glanced at the pencil and pad she was holding. "You didn't write down my order."

"No need." She tapped the side of her waitress cap with the tip of the pencil. "I've got a pretty good memory."

"And I am nothing if not boringly predictable."

She was horrified. "I didn't mean to imply that you were boring. Not at all. I'm very sorry."

"No need to apologize. I *am* boringly predictable. In fact, you could say I am going out of my way to be boring and predictable. My doctor suggested I stick to a strict routine, you see. Supposedly it's good for exhausted nerves."

Adelaide cleared her throat. "In my experience the so-called experts don't always know what's best for exhausted nerves."

"I'm inclined to agree with you. The green tea you serve here at Refresh has done me more good than any nerve tonic."

She frowned. "You take a tonic for your nerves?"

"Well, no. The doctor prescribed one but I'm not taking it. Promise you won't tell him?"

For a moment she wondered if he was trying to make a small joke. But she could not be certain so she played it safe.

"Of course I won't tell him," she said.

"Thank you. It occurs to me that I should mention your special teas and herbal blends to my doctor. He might be interested in offering them to his other patients."

"*No.*" Panic flashed through her. The very last thing she wanted was to draw the attention of a doctor who was in the business of treating disorders of the nervous system. She recovered her poise with an effort of will. "I mean, I don't think that it would be a good idea to tell your doctor about the blends we serve here at Refresh. They aren't anything special, just traditional herbs and a variety of imported teas. No modern-thinking doctor would approve of using them to treat problems associated with the nerves."

"I see." Mr. Truett assumed a politely interested air. "You obviously know a lot about the subject. Do you mind if I ask where you received your training in herbs and teas?"

She hesitated. There was only one person in town who knew something about her past. Raina Kirk was another newcomer to Burning Cove, and it was clear that she was also concealing a lot about her own personal history. In addition to the knowledge that they were both trying to reinvent themselves in Burning Cove, the understanding that they each had things to hide had produced an unusual bond between them.

But not even Raina knew about the Rushbrook Sanitarium and the wedding ring that was now concealed in the floor safe under Adelaide's bed.

"You could say I grew up in the business," she said. "My mother was a botanist."

"And your father?"

"A chemist." This was getting dangerous. It was past time to change the subject. "Thanks for your order, Mr. Truett. I'll be right back."

"Good. I need the tea to take the edge off the three cups of coffee I had for breakfast."

Shocked, she stared at him. "You had three cups of coffee this morning?"

"I like coffee in the mornings."

"Mr. Truett, I realize this is none of my business, but if you're having trouble with your nerves, the last thing you should drink is a lot of coffee."

"Call me Jake. I'm supposed to be relaxing by the seaside, remember? When you call me Mr. Truett, you make me think of business. The doctor instructed me not to concern myself with business matters."

She cleared her throat. "I was under the impression that you had sold your business in L.A."

Something that might have been amusement briefly came and went in Jake's eyes. "I've always heard that rumors get around quickly in small towns like Burning Cove."

She flushed. "Sorry. I didn't mean to pry."

"Don't worry about it. The rumors are true. Like you, I grew up in a family business. In my case it was an import-export firm. Three generations of Truetts operated the company. I inherited the firm after my father died. I was nineteen. It's the only business I've ever known."

"And now you're out of that business?"

"Apparently."

"Because it wasn't good for your nerves."

"Right."

"What will you do now?" she blurted out before she could stop herself.

"I have no idea. That's one of the things I'm not supposed to think about."

"Until your nerves recover?"

"I suppose so. Meanwhile I won't starve. The import-export business was good to me. Now that you know my life story, I hope you will do me the favor of calling me by my first name. Jake."

She was very sure she did not know his life story. But he did not know hers, either. Fair enough. She considered briefly and came to a decision.

"All right," she said. "Jake."

"That sounds much better. Friendlier. We're neighbors, after all."

So he knew she lived in one of the cottages on the bluff above Crescent Beach. That should not have come as a surprise but for some reason it did. The realization that he had been paying some attention to her was oddly thrilling but it also made her deeply uneasy. Then again, maybe she was overreacting. In recent months she had learned that it was often difficult to determine the fine line between caution and paranoia.

Jake was watching her with a look of mild expectation. It dawned on her that she had not given him her first name. For some reason it seemed like a very big step.

"Adelaide," she said. "My name is Adelaide Brockton."

It was probably not a good idea to embark on a new relationship with a lie, but it wasn't as if she had a lot of options. In any event, it was highly unlikely that this was the start of an acquaintanceship that would ever, even remotely, metamorphose into a real relationship.

"Adelaide," he repeated. He seemed pleased with the sound. "Nice name. It suits you."

She knew she ought to go back to the kitchen and prepare Jake's tea, but she found herself hesitating. She wanted to linger at his table.

"Are you enjoying your stay in Burning Cove?" she asked.

"You want the truth? I cannot be absolutely certain but I believe that I am starting to go out of my mind."

She stared at him. "Uh, that doesn't sound good—"

"With boredom."

She relaxed. "Perfectly understandable. You're obviously a fit and healthy man who needs to remain active and engaged with the world. If you're bored, it's probably time for you to start planning for a new career, in spite of what the doctor told you."

"Do you think so?"

"It's entirely possible that your doctor was right when he said you required a temporary change of scene. But it doesn't necessarily follow that an extended period of outright boredom and strict routine are good for you."

"Do you give advice a lot?"

"Advice seems to go hand in hand with the tea business. People are always asking me about teas and herbs for various conditions. Weight control. Insomnia. Anxiety. Lack of—"

She managed to stop herself just in time.

"Lack of . . . ?" he prompted.

She took a deep breath. "Lack of interest in various . . . activities."

"Activities."

"Sometimes people find that they lack the energy or desire to engage in certain activities of an intimate nature. Activities that are quite ... natural."

"I see." Jake nodded wisely. "Activities that at one time they found stimulating."

She had the awful feeling that she was turning very red. The conversation was deteriorating rapidly. She cast about desperately for inspiration.

"Exactly," she said, striving for a brisk, clinical air. "Activities such as taking long walks on the beach or swimming in the ocean."

"I often walk on the beach and sometimes I swim."

"Precisely."

"Perhaps I should cease doing those things," Jake said.

"Why would you want to stop? Those are very healthy and invigorating forms of exercise."

"They are also stimulating," Jake said. "My doctor said I should try to refrain from anything that stimulates my nerves."

"My mother believed that certain types of stimulation are good for a person."

"What therapy do you recommend?"

She went blank for a beat. Then a thought occurred.

"There is a very nice art museum in town," she said. "The new exhibition featuring local artists got excellent reviews in the *Herald*."

"Don't you think that an art exhibition might be too stimulating for my delicate nerves?"

He was teasing her, she thought. Florence was wrong. Jake Truett was not interested in her, not in a romantic way. He was simply bored. He could find someone else to amuse and entertain him.

"Sorry," she said coldly. "I thought you were serious. I'll get your tea."

She started to turn away.

"Wait," Jake said quickly. "I thought you were joking."

"When it comes to the subject of strong, healthy nerves, I never joke."

"I understand. I apologize. About the art exhibition. Would you perhaps care to—"

"Don't worry, Mr. Truett, you won't get any more advice from me." She gave him her sharpest, iciest smile. "I'll get your tea. You're right. You are very predictable. You are also bored. I'm sure that if you put your mind to it, you can find something stimulating to do in Burning Cove, but I can assure you that you won't find it here at the Refresh Tearoom."

His eyes tightened a little at the corners. He was no longer amused. She got the feeling that he was startled by her response. He hadn't expected her to snap at him. It was dawning on him that he had miscalculated. Evidently he was not accustomed to making mistakes of that sort.

Chapter 3

"It's been two months," Conrad Massey raged on the other end of the phone. "How could you lose her for two damned months? You said you'd find her within hours. You said she couldn't get more than a mile or two away from Rushbrook. But she vanished."

Ethan Gill clenched his hand very tightly around the phone and reminded himself that above all he had to keep his composure; he had to sound soothing and reassuring. He was a doctor according to the fake diploma on the wall. He knew how to deal with an anxious patient. Above all, he must not give Massey any reason to think that the situation was spinning out of control.

"I do apologize for the delay," he said, using the plummy tones he used with the wealthy people who brought their crazy relatives to the Rushbrook Sanitarium to have them committed. It was a voice that assured them that they were doing the right thing by their relations and that he would take the burden off their shoulders—for a price. "I'm afraid a small problem has arisen, but there is nothing to worry about. Matters will be sorted out very soon."

"You told me that everything was under control." Massey's voice was sharp with frustration, anger, and something else, something akin to panic. "You said you had a lead on her whereabouts. You said it was only a matter of time before you had her safely back in her room there at Rushbrook. I can't cover up her disappearance indefinitely. Sooner or later someone connected to the estate will start asking questions. What the hell is going on, Gill?"

"There have been . . . complications," Gill said, striving to keep his voice calm. The truth was, Massey was not the only one who was on the verge of panic. "But nothing that can't be dealt with soon. I assure you the situation is in hand."

"Complications? What complications?"

"The patient has gone into hiding. She is a very ill woman, Mr. Massey, prone to extreme paranoia."

"How can she hide?" Massey snapped. "She has no money. No family. No resources. If she goes to the police—"

"It's difficult to say precisely how she is surviving financially but I'm positive she won't go to the police. She knows that if the authorities discover that she is an escaped mental patient, she will be sent back here to Rushbrook immediately. Relax, Mr. Massey. I will contact you as soon as I have more information."

"I can't believe you let her disappear like this."

Gill struggled to suppress his own anger and fear. He was not about to tell Massey that Patient B had been located two weeks ago. She was living under the name of Adelaide Brockton and working as a tearoom waitress in the exclusive seaside resort town of Burning Cove, California. Massey was a desperate man. He had to be handled with great care. If he found out where the research subject was currently residing, he would very likely try to take matters into his own hands. If that happened, he would put the entire plan in jeopardy.

At the moment Massey was a necessary nuisance. Not only was he a source of badly needed cash, he had every reason to keep his mouth shut.

"I assure you, the matter will be resolved quite soon," Gill said.

"Do you have any idea how much money I've got riding on this?"

Not nearly as much as I have. Gill wanted to shout the words down the phone line. But he could not let the panic and the rage take control.

"I told you, I'll take care of the situation," he said in the firm, authoritative voice he had cultivated to use with agitated patients.

It didn't have any noticeable effect.

"We've got to get her back to Rushbrook immediately," Massey said. "Sooner or later she's going to try to get access to her inheritance. Who knows what the estate lawyers will do if she contacts them. If they discover the truth about the marriage—"

"I told you, the patient won't dare contact the police or the estate. The situation is under control. It won't be long before we find her. I must hang up now, Mr. Massey. I've got another appointment."

"Let me know as soon as you have any news."

"Don't worry, you'll be the first person I call."

Gill forced himself to replace the receiver very gently into the cradle. Silence fell on his elegantly appointed office. He sat behind the big wooden desk for a time, contemplating the disaster that had befallen him. He was fairly certain that Massey had believed him, but that did not solve all of the problems.

He glanced at his watch. It was time to call his associate in Burning Cove. He picked up the receiver. When the operator came on the line, he gave her the number.

Calvin Paxton answered on the first ring.

"This is Dr. Paxton."

Gill grunted. Paxton's voice was even richer and more resonant than his own. They had known each other since their days in medical school. Neither of them had started out with the upper-class voices. They were both the products of small towns in northern California, and they had arrived at medical school with the accents that reflected their origins.

Their similar upbringings and the fact that both of them were struggling in medical school had established a loose connection between them back at the start. But it was another shared quality that had forged a long-lasting business partnership—ambition.

They had dropped out of medical school because it had soon become obvious that there were easier ways to make a lot of money. The MD behind their names was useful, however—people trusted doctors—so they had paid a guy who printed counterfeit bills for the mob to create a couple of very authentic-looking diplomas. No one had ever questioned them.

For a time he and Paxton had gone separate ways. Gill had dabbled in the quack cure business before landing the position of director of the Rushbrook Sanitarium. Once in charge he had discovered there was a great deal of money to be made operating a high-class sanitarium for wealthy families who wanted to conceal their crazy relatives in a discreet asylum. "Out of sight, out of mind" was the unspoken motto of the Rushbrook Sanitarium.

The sanitarium had been in business since the turn of the century. When the last owner died, his family wanted no part of the operation. They had sold it to Gill for a song. His first step had been to double the fees charged to the families of the patients. When no one complained, he tripled the charges. It soon became apparent that wealthy people would pay any price to keep their crazy relatives locked up.

Paxton had used his Hollywood looks and style to take a different route to financial success. He had headed for Los Angeles, where he soon discovered that celebrities would pay any price to stay thin and beautiful. When the gossip magazines informed the general public that the secret to looking like a Hollywood star was Dr. Paxton's Diet Tonic, business had boomed.

Paxton had been the smart one, Gill thought. He was not only making a lot of money, he lived in the glittering world of Hollywood.

He rubbed shoulders with celebrities. He went to the best parties and spent his nights at the most exclusive nightclubs.

Rushbrook Sanitarium made money but it was situated outside the small, rural town of Rushbrook on the California coast. The remote location meant that very few people were aware of the asylum's existence. That certainly pleased the families of the patients. But he was trapped in a hick town. If he didn't find a way out, he was the one who would go crazy.

Three years ago he had been seriously thinking of selling the asylum and moving to San Francisco or L.A. And then Paxton had contacted him with a fascinating proposal. There was, according to Paxton, excellent money to be made marketing drugs to the Hollywood set. Gill had jumped at the opportunity.

The drug business had gone very well, indeed, but it had not freed him to leave Rushbrook. In order to prosper they had needed a laboratory, one that would not draw the attention of the FBI. The obvious place to install a fully equipped lab had been at Rushbrook. No one questioned a laboratory in a mental hospital. But it meant that, for most of the time, Gill was still trapped in his role as the director of the sanitarium, still imprisoned in the isolated, rural community.

Everything had changed the day he had learned about the drug called Daydream. He and Paxton understood immediately that the possibilities were breathtaking. Yes, there was a fortune to be made, but the drug held the promise of something even more alluring—power. Once Daydream was perfected, it could be used to control anyone, from mobsters to presidents.

Patient B's escape had put the entire plan in jeopardy.

"We're running out of time," he said. "Massey is getting impatient. If we can't recover the subject soon, the experiment will have to be terminated."

"It's not that easy," Paxton said. "Patient B has had time to establish herself in the community. She's got friends here. If she goes missing, there are people who will ask questions. That's the last thing we want."

"You said she is working as a waitress in a tearoom. Who would look for a missing waitress?"

"Her closest friend here in Burning Cove happens to be a lady private investigator."

"*What?* How the hell did she get involved with a private detective?"

"I have no idea but that's the situation."

"Damn it," Gill hissed. "You've got to deal with this mess. We can't risk the subject going to the cops or the FBI with information about Daydream. They probably wouldn't believe her but if the press gets hold of the story—"

"I'm well aware of that," Paxton said.

"We need to get control of the situation now. Things are deteriorating, in case you haven't noticed. First Ormsby accidentally ingests some of the drug and jumps out a window, and then the new research subject escapes. You said you would take care of everything."

"I told you, things are more complicated than they first appeared," Paxton said. "But I've got a new plan. I can't carry it out alone, though. I need your help. You'll have to come to Burning Cove."

Gill glanced at the wall clock. "It's a three-hour drive. I can be there early this evening. Make a reservation for me at a hotel."

"I'd suggest the Burning Cove Hotel. That's where I'm staying. But under the circumstances I don't think it would be a good idea for us to be seen together. I'll find a smaller, more secluded place for you to stay."

"All right."

Gill tossed the receiver back into the cradle. He would probably end up at a cheap auto court that wouldn't have room service or decent plumbing.

Paxton, on the other hand, was staying at the Burning Cove, a legendary hotel that catered to the rich and famous. Not only that, he was fucking Vera Westlake, the actress the press had dubbed the most beautiful woman in Hollywood.

Somehow, Paxton always seemed to get the better end of every deal they had ever done together.

Gill glanced at his watch. Time to go home and pack. But first he had to come up with a reasonable excuse to give to his staff to explain his absence.

Once again he found himself wondering whether Ormsby's death truly had been the result of an accident. But what other explanation could there be? Paxton had no reason to kill the chemist who concocted the drugs.

Chapter 4

Calvin Paxton tossed the phone down onto the cradle. Gill was a problem. Eventually he would have to be removed, but Patient B was a higher priority at the moment.

He crossed the villa's living room to where the French doors stood open. He looked out at the private patio where the most beautiful woman in Hollywood was reclining on a shaded lounger.

Vera Westlake was studying a script with an earnest air. A bottle of Dr. Paxton's Diet Tonic stood on the table beside the lounger. A glass of ice sat next to it.

Vera was not staying at the Burning Cove Hotel. She had just dropped by to spend the afternoon with him. Her studio had rented a private villa in another part of town for her. Vera's public image was that of an aloof, untouchable star who longed for privacy. Her publicist had determined that to maintain the impression, she should not stay at one of the most famous hotels in California.

Although celebrities claimed they came to the exclusive Burning Cove Hotel to escape the demands of Hollywood, the truth was they

chose the hotel precisely because of its reputation as a celebrity en-
clave. Their publicists made certain that they were photographed arriving and departing through the ornate front gates. On the grounds
they were always highly visible poolside or in the bar. The guest villas,
like the one Paxton was staying in, provided temporary sanctuary because they included private, enclosed patios. Vera was protected while
she was visiting him, but when she left she would walk through the
elegant Spanish-colonial-revival-style lobby. She would draw the attention of anyone who was in the vicinity. Her driver would whisk her
out through the grand front gates where the photographers and report-
ers lurked, cameras at the ready. Vera's publicist would make certain of
it. Nothing sold the gossip magazines like photos of the most beautiful
woman in Hollywood trying to evade the press.

He gave himself a moment to admire the stunning sight of Vera on
the lounger. She wore a pair of green shorts with narrow cuffs that
showed off her long, elegant legs. The halter top matched the shorts. A
wide-brimmed sun hat protected her lovely face from the warm California sun.

Paxton smiled to himself. He had come a long way from the small
farm town where he'd grown up. These days he not only partied with
the stars, he was fucking the most beautiful woman in Hollywood. Her
first film, *Dark Road*, had made her an overnight sensation. The studio
had moved quickly after that hit, casting Vera as the lead in two more
films. The most recent one, *Lady in the Shadows*, had been out for only
two months, and she was scheduled to start shooting her fourth picture
in a few weeks.

Not only was she making money for her studio, she was pulling in
a lot of cash for him. He made sure that, as often as possible, the cameras caught her with a bottle of Dr. Paxton's Diet Tonic in her hand.

Vera noticed him and looked up with a concerned expression. Not
for the first time he marveled that her beautiful brown eyes—eyes that

could reflect any emotion that a director demanded for the camera—had such a remarkably vapid quality in real life.

"Did you solve your business problem?" she asked.

She had the voice to go with the face—warm, husky, sensuous. It was a voice that thrilled audiences from coast to coast.

"I think so." He walked forward and sat down on the lounger adjacent to Vera's. "The bottling plant is overwhelmed. I'm going to have to expand the facility. I told the manager to go ahead and have the architect draw up the plans."

"That means that business is good, doesn't it?"

He chuckled. "Business is excellent, thanks to you, sweetheart."

"After all you've done for me, I'm just glad I can do something for you, darling."

The press often speculated about why Vera was not romantically linked with one of Hollywood's leading men. But Paxton understood. Liaisons between powerful stars were fraught. The two people involved in such a relationship were fundamentally rivals, after all. They competed for the same publicity opportunities—the covers of the gossip magazines and the front pages of the nation's newspapers.

Career jealousy was an ever-present acid that ate away any hope of a long-lasting relationship. Hollywood was a jungle, Paxton reflected. Only those who were willing to claw their way to the top stood a chance of survival. Love and friendship were the first casualties along the way.

But unlike a leading man, he was not a direct career threat, Paxton thought. Vera felt safe with him. He had done a very good job of convincing her that she needed him in order to feel emotionally secure.

In a few years her looks would start to fade, of course. The press would bestow the title of the most beautiful woman in Hollywood on another, younger actress. He would no longer have any use for her. But for now she trusted him. He was her closest confidant. That made her very useful, indeed.

There was another bonus for him in the relationship. He got an amazing erection every time he thought about the fact that he was the man who was fucking the most beautiful woman in Hollywood.

On impulse he leaned forward and kissed her. He would smudge her carefully applied maroon red lipstick but she could repair her makeup before she walked back through the hotel lobby.

She dropped the script beside the lounger. The anxiety in her eyes told him just how much she needed him.

"Calvin," she whispered urgently, "promise me you will never leave me alone. I don't know what I'd do without you."

He slipped one hand between her warm thighs. "Don't worry, sweetheart. I'll always be here to take care of you."

She believed him, he thought. The most beautiful woman in Hollywood would never win the title of the smartest woman in Hollywood.

Chapter 5

Adelaide went briskly back across the tearoom. The encounter with Jake Truett had left her feeling oddly energized. It occurred to her that she had been living a lie for so long—first at Rushbrook Sanitarium and now, for the last two months, in Burning Cove—that she had forgotten how it felt to allow her real emotions to surface. The short burst of temper a moment ago had felt real, and it was nothing short of *stimulating*.

Florence, who had evidently watched the entire scene from the other side of the counter, rolled her eyes. Adelaide pretended not to notice.

She was halfway to her goal when she heard the rumble of a heavy car engine. She glanced out the window and saw a familiar green Packard limousine come to a halt on the street in front of the tearoom. Madam Zolanda had become a regular customer shortly after her arrival in Burning Cove two weeks earlier.

The driver jumped out from behind the steering wheel. As usual, Thelma Leggett was nattily attired in a chauffeur's livery. Having a female driver added yet another exotic touch to Madam Zolanda's allure. Thelma reached out with a gloved hand and opened the rear door with a flourish.

Madam Zolanda—the woman the press had labeled the psychic to the stars—emerged. She walked to the front door as though she were walking onstage. Thelma sprang forward to open the door. Zolanda made her entrance and masterfully succeeded in turning every head in the tearoom.

She was as flamboyant as any of her film star clients and, whenever she was in public at least, she stayed in character. She was in her late twenties and unusually tall for a woman. She was also very pretty with vivid blue eyes and a wealth of blond hair that billowed around her shoulders in deep waves. Her eyebrows had been plucked to a fare-thee-well and redrawn with a pencil to create elegantly arched curves. Her lipstick was the latest, most fashionable shade of red.

As usual, she was dressed for her chosen role in a long, flowing, exotically printed red and orange caftan that looked as if it had been created from an assortment of fantastically patterned silk scarves. Gold-toned bangles were stacked halfway up her arms.

The small crowd in the tearoom watched, fascinated, as Zolanda came to a stop just inside the entrance, closed her eyes, and appeared to go into a trance.

"There is such good energy in this place," she intoned.

Adelaide changed course instantly and rushed to greet her. "May I show you to your usual table, madam?"

Zolanda opened her heavily made-up eyes and bestowed a beatific smile on Adelaide.

"Thank you, my dear," she said. "I am in need of some of my special tea. I am preparing for a performance here in town tomorrow evening. Perhaps you are aware of it?"

"Yes, of course," Adelaide said. She was no actress but she was a waitress, and a good waitress knew how to respond to a customer's cue. "You'll be appearing onstage at the Palace."

"At seven thirty," Zolanda clarified in a voice meant to carry across the tearoom. "The performance is almost sold out."

"I'm not at all surprised," Adelaide said. "This way, please."

Zolanda spoke to the chauffeur without looking at her. "That will be all for now, Miss Leggett. I'll send someone to notify you when I'm ready to leave."

"Yes, ma'am."

Thelma tugged at the bill of her cap and let herself out the door. She retreated to the long, green Packard.

Adelaide escorted Zolanda to a small table near a window.

"You'd better bring a large pot of my Enlightenment tea," Zolanda said. "I'll need two cups today. Oh, and I'll also have one or two of those lovely little tea cakes."

"Of course," Adelaide said. She made a mental note to make sure there were three tea cakes on Zolanda's plate.

"Your Enlightenment tea helps me fortify myself for the stress involved in opening the psychic door to the other dimension," Zolanda said.

"Happy to be of service," Adelaide said. "I'll be right back with a large pot of Enlightenment."

"Thank you, Miss Brockton."

Adelaide went around the end of the counter and selected a teapot. She exchanged a glance with Florence, who bobbed her thin brows up and down a few times. They both knew that Madam Zolanda was good for business. She was not a film star, but her clients were. The press and the public were well aware of it.

Normal conversation resumed in the tearoom. Adelaide arranged the pot of Enlightenment and a cup and saucer on a tray. She added three dainty tea cakes and carried the tray to Zolanda's table.

"Thank you," Zolanda said. "By the way, I have a small surprise for you."

Adelaide set the tea things down and straightened. Her first thought was that Zolanda was about to offer her a free psychic reading. She tried to think of a polite way to decline.

"That's not necessary—" she began.

Zolanda interrupted, raising her voice so that everyone in the tearoom could hear her. "As I said a moment ago, I will be giving a performance at the Palace Theater tomorrow night. I would love for you to attend."

Adelaide struggled to come up with an excuse. She was living on a strict budget these days. It allowed for the occasional dinner and a movie with her friend, Raina Kirk, but she was not keen on springing for an expensive ticket to attend one of Madam Zolanda's performances.

"That would be wonderful," she managed weakly. "But I'm sure the performance will be sold out—"

"Of course it will be sold out," Zolanda said. She waved one hand in a grand gesture that set the bangles on her arms clashing. "I always play to a full house. But that does not mean that I don't save a few special seats for special people. There will be a ticket waiting for you at the box office tomorrow night. Remember, the show starts at seven thirty sharp."

"That's very kind of you but I expect tomorrow will be a very busy day here at the tearoom. I'll probably be too tired to go out."

"Bring a friend." Zolanda made another sweeping gesture. "There will be *two* tickets waiting at the box office. Surely you know someone who might be thrilled to attend the performance with you?"

Another hush had fallen over the tearoom. Adelaide realized that this time she was the center of attention. Everyone, including Jake, was waiting to see if she would take the generous offer. There was no graceful way out.

"Thank you," she said in low tones. "I'll look forward to it."

"Excellent," Zolanda said, delighted. "I'm so glad. I sense that my connection to the spirit world will be especially strong tomorrow night. The moon is almost full, you know. A full or nearly full moon always enhances the experience."

"Really?" Adelaide said, somewhat weakly. "How interesting."

The Rushbrook Sanitarium staff had maintained that the patients got crazier than usual on nights when the moon was full. There had been a full moon the night she escaped.

"I hope you and your lucky friend enjoy the performance," Zolanda said.

Adelaide went back across the room. Florence bobbed her eyebrows again.

"Who are you going to take with you?" she asked.

"I don't know. Haven't had a chance to think about it. Do you want to come?"

"Nope. You should ask Truett."

"Are you kidding?"

"No, I am not kidding. Ask him."

"I'm sure he's got better things to do than watch a fake psychic pretend to commune with the spirit world," Adelaide whispered.

"No," Jake said quietly behind her. "I don't have anything better to do."

Startled, Adelaide whipped around. Jake was lounging against the counter looking like a man who was waiting to pay his bill. Adelaide glared at him.

"You must be *really* bored if you want to attend Madam Zolanda's show with me," she said, careful to keep her voice to a near whisper.

"I was planning to invite you to go to the art museum with me, but Zolanda's show sounds more interesting."

Florence beamed approvingly. "I'm sure it will be a lot more entertaining."

What the heck, Adelaide thought. According to Florence, Jake Truett would only be around for a few weeks, if that long. He had made it clear that he was already bored. When he'd had enough of resting his nerves by the seaside, he would head back to Los Angeles. She would never see him again. There was no risk of a long-term relationship. No risk that he would ask too many questions that she would have trouble answering. All in all, he was the ideal date.

Besides, she was tired of spending most of her evenings alone.

She fixed Jake with a level look. "All right, Mr. Truett. You can have my second ticket to the show tomorrow evening. I'll meet you at the box office."

"It's Jake, remember? And there's no need to take two cars," Jake said. "I'll pick you up."

She hesitated but couldn't think of a reason to refuse. She wasn't even sure she wanted to refuse. Her car was a used Ford that was quite capable of breaking down and leaving her stranded by the side of the road.

"Fine," she said. "I'll be ready by seven. Now, will you kindly return to your table before people start to wonder what is going on?"

"Good idea," he said. He smiled politely but there was a calculating gleam in his eyes. "I could use that cup of tea I ordered. I think my nerves are exhibiting unmistakable signs of overstimulation."

"Wouldn't want that to happen," Adelaide shot back.

"Of course not. No telling where it might lead."

He turned, moving with his usual prowling grace, and made his way back to his table.

Florence looked at Adelaide. "His nerves are overstimulated? What was he talking about?"

"I have no idea, and you can bet I'm not going to ask him. Call me psychic, but something tells me I wouldn't like the answer."

Chapter 6

"Well?" Thelma asked as she fired up the Packard's heavy engine. "Did she take the bait?"

Zolanda, ensconced on the elegantly tufted leather seat, met Thelma's eyes in the rearview mirror. They had been a team for three years. Their partnership had been formed when she was still Dorothy Higgins, an aspiring actress who had never managed to land a role. She knew that she had the talent and she was pretty enough, but she lacked the magical quality that transformed an actress like Vera Westlake into a radiant beauty on the silver screen.

At the time, Thelma had been a secretary at one of the studios and a regular at the lunch counter where Zolanda worked. Thelma, too, had once had dreams of becoming a star, but working for an executive inside the business had given her a more realistic approach to life. It was Thelma who had observed that actors were a superstitious lot. They spent an amazing amount of money on palm readers, fortune-tellers, mystics, and psychics.

Thelma had pointed out the business potential over a turkey sandwich that Dorothy had just put in front of her on the counter. *You're a damn good actress,* she'd said. *You would just need to get into the role.*

Exclusivity had been the key, of course. Celebrities did not patronize psychics who worked out of shabby storefront fortune-teller shops. Thelma had selected their first client, a neurotic actress who was easily persuaded that she needed career advice from a psychic. The initial consultation had been a huge success. Zolanda looked back on that first performance as a psychic advisor to the stars with pride. It had been nothing short of brilliant.

A week later the neurotic actress had requested another session. Within the month she had a handful of new clients. Thelma arranged for the consultations to take place in the privacy of the clients' own homes.

Within two months *Hollywood Whispers* and *Silver Screen Secrets* had bestowed the title "Psychic to the Stars" on Madam Zolanda. Once the word got out that the stars were consulting Zolanda, everyone who was anyone in L.A. was calling for an appointment. Thelma was careful to keep the client list limited.

It took another few months for Zolanda and Thelma to realize that, as lucrative as the fashionable psychic business was, the real money was in collecting their clients' secrets. Blackmail was an inherently dangerous pursuit, but it could be astonishingly profitable.

Some of the secrets were time sensitive and had to be cashed in immediately. Others would become more valuable in the future. She and Thelma had always referred to those secrets as their pension plan.

"Adelaide Brockton agreed to attend the performance tomorrow night," Zolanda said, "but she was not exactly enthusiastic. I had to cough up an extra ticket and convince her to bring a friend."

"So what? All we care about is that she shows up at the Palace Theater tomorrow night."

"She'll be there," Zolanda said. "But we may have another problem." Thelma glanced into the rearview mirror again. "Truett?"

"He seems to have taken an interest in Adelaide."

"It's got to be a coincidence," Thelma said.

But she looked uneasy.

"I don't like the fact that he just happened to show up here in Burning Cove eight days ago," Zolanda said.

"Where else does a rich businessman from L.A. go for some rest and relaxation? I'm telling you, his being here is sheer coincidence."

Zolanda snorted softly. "A real psychic would tell you that there is no such thing as a coincidence."

Thelma smiled. "But you aren't a real psychic, are you? You're just a damn good actress."

Zolanda looked out the window. The morning fog had burned off. The golden light of the California sun flashed and sparkled on the Pacific. She thought about the day that she and her best friend had gotten off the train in Los Angeles with a couple of battered grips that contained all their worldly possessions.

Her dreams of stardom had kept her going for a time. She had worked the lunch-counter job and slept with too many sleazy bastards who claimed to be talent scouts or studio executives. But the guys had all been liars and cheats. She had never even managed to land a screen test. It was all so unfair because she possessed real talent.

Her best friend, however, had gotten lucky. In Hollywood, a woman's face was her fortune, and Vera Westlake had a face the camera and the audience loved.

Zolanda tightened one hand into a fist. The rage welled up deep inside, as hot as ever. She did not try to suppress it. She savored it. The anger gave her strength. But she was very careful to keep her jealousy concealed behind the mask of Madam Zolanda, psychic to the stars.

She might not be the most beautiful woman in Hollywood, but she was a very talented actress. Tomorrow night she would prove it.

She realized that Thelma was watching her in the rearview mirror again. There was no way she could know what was scheduled to happen tomorrow night. No possible way.

But one thing had become clear. Thelma would be a problem in the very near future. She knew too much, not just about the value of the secrets they had collected, but also about the past. Thelma knew everything. It was time for her to quietly disappear.

Chapter 7

The dream opened the way it often did . . .

She was walking through the deceptively serene gardens of the Rush-brook Sanitarium. She wore a hospital gown. The Duchess was with her, dressed in a style that had gone out of fashion for wealthy, well-bred ladies three decades earlier. The long skirts of her pale pink tea gown brushed the graveled path.

They spoke in low tones because the Duchess worried that the servants might be listening. Adelaide knew that was a very real possibility.

"I've told you before, dear, you should not return to this place," the Duchess said. "You're not like me. You don't belong here."

"I don't want to return," Adelaide said, "but I left something behind."

"I strongly advise you not to come back. I no longer trust any of the servants."

"Neither do I," Adelaide said.

"You understand why you don't belong here, don't you?" the Duchess said. "You're not crazy like the rest of us."

"Gill and Ormsby told me that I had a nervous breakdown. What if it's true?"

"Nonsense. I've been here since my eighteenth birthday. There's no question but that I am crazy. So are all of the houseguests, except you."

"Are you certain?"

"You are not like the rest of us. Trust me, I know the difference between sane and insane."

"Do you want to leave, madam?"

"Of course not, dear." The Duchess gave an airy wave with one gloved hand. "I have a responsibility to remain here, away from the view of polite society. One must not embarrass the family, after all. If I were to go out into the world, there would soon be rumors that the bloodline was tainted by a streak of insanity. Can't have that, now, can we?"

Adelaide woke in a cold sweat, the way she always did after a dream about Rushbrook. She sat up on the side of the bed and waited for her pulse and breathing to slow to a more normal pace.

After a while she pulled on a robe, went downstairs, and made herself some tea. She used the special blend she kept on hand for the bad nights.

She'd had a lot of bad nights since she had first awakened to the nightmare that was the Rushbrook Sanitarium.

It was still dark outside but she knew she would not be able to go back to sleep. She took the freshly brewed tea into the living room, turned on a floor lamp, and picked up the new book she had purchased two days earlier. She curled up in the big, padded leather chair and started to read.

In the dream she had told the Duchess the truth. She had escaped the Rushbrook Sanitarium but she was not yet free. She had left something behind.

Chapter 8

"You do realize that Madam Zolanda is a fraud." Raina Kirk picked up a pencil and tapped it gently on the desktop blotter. "A complete charlatan who has found a very lucrative market—rich celebrities who are also silly enough to believe in the occult."

Adelaide paused in her survey of the newly opened office of Kirk Investigations to glare at her friend. "Of course I know she's a fake. Anyone who claims paranormal powers is a fraud."

She and Raina had met several weeks earlier when Raina had stopped in at Refresh for tea. They had immediately recognized each other as kindred spirits—two women on their own in the world, both newcomers in Burning Cove who were determined to reinvent themselves.

One of the things they had in common was that, by unspoken mutual agreement, neither of them talked much about the past. Little by little they were starting to confide in each other, but neither of them was ready to lower all the barriers. Their mutual respect for each other's secrets was, in itself, a strong bond, Adelaide thought.

Although they were careful not to spend too much time talking about the past, they were comfortable with each other. Their friendship had taken root when Raina had come by Refresh to quietly ask for a recommendation for a tea or tisane that would improve her sleep. Adelaide had prepared one of her mother's favorite remedies for insomnia, a blend that included valerian, lemon balm, and other herbs. Raina had found it helpful.

In return, Raina had made the hundred-mile trip to L.A. with her to help her purchase a small gun and some ammunition. On the way home they had stopped at a deserted beach where Raina had given her some basic instructions on the use and care of the weapon. There had been a few more clandestine visits to the secluded strip of sand.

Some friends went shopping or had lunch together, Adelaide thought. Some went out for target practice.

She knew that Raina had concluded that Adelaide was running from a man. That was true enough, she thought. For her part, she had not asked Raina to explain why she had left a secretarial post with a New York law firm to move across the country to Burning Cove. Nor had she inquired about Raina's familiarity with firearms.

Raina was an attractive, polished woman in her mid-thirties with an innate sense of style and an air of cool, professional reserve. She was always fashionably dressed and she drove a flashy new speedster. Her investigation business had opened in an exclusive business plaza. Adelaide had taken care not to inquire about the source of the money.

"Madam Zolanda put me in an awkward position," Adelaide said. "I didn't want to appear rude. She's been a great customer. Florence is thrilled because Zolanda has brought a lot of celebrity business into the tearoom."

"Zolanda is currently very fashionable with the Hollywood set," Raina said.

"Yes, I know," Adelaide said.

She crossed the room, admiring the leather chairs and the handsome floor tiles along the way. Raina's new office was classy, like Raina herself. It looked more like the office of an expensive lawyer than one that belonged to a private investigator.

She stopped at the window and looked out at the shady plaza. Every shop and office in the vicinity, including Raina's, was done in the Spanish colonial revival style that Adelaide had learned was de rigueur for Burning Cove. The city council wielded a lot of authority when it came to enforcing the strict rules that covered construction and remodeling. The vast majority of structures—from clothing stores to gas stations and everything in between, including the public library, the hospital, and the grand Burning Cove Hotel—featured red tile roofs, white plaster walls, palm-studded courtyards, and a lot of breezy, covered walkways.

The whole town looked like it had been copied from a picture postcard illustration of a Mediterranean village. But Burning Cove was very real, Adelaide thought. She was starting to hope that it was a place she could call home.

"Just promise me you won't leave Zolanda's performance convinced that she really does have paranormal powers," Raina said.

"Not likely." Adelaide turned around. "Don't worry about me, Raina."

"Why do I have the feeling that there is something you haven't told me about your plans for tomorrow evening?"

Adelaide smiled. "Maybe you're the one who is psychic. Probably a useful quality in a private investigator. As a matter of fact, there is something I haven't told you. I have a date for Zolanda's show."

Raina's elegantly arched brows rose. "Well, well, well. That certainly makes things more interesting. Congratulations. Who's the lucky guy?"

"His name is Jake Truett. He's my neighbor out on Crescent Beach. He's here in Burning Cove because his doctor told him he needs an extended stay by the seaside."

"He's got health problems?"

"Evidently his nerves have been badly stressed because he has been working too hard."

"Hmm. Did he ask you to prescribe some herbal blends that will help his nerves?"

"No." Adelaide winced. "I made the mistake of offering him some advice, though. He was clearly annoyed. He made fun of me for being so serious."

"Let me get this straight—you are going to the theater tomorrow night with a gentleman who was rude to you when you offered to help him?"

"To be fair, I think I offended him."

"By offering advice?" Raina's voice rose in disbelief.

"I doubt if any man wants to admit that he has been diagnosed with exhausted nerves. It was obvious he regretted telling me his reason for being in Burning Cove."

"How did you respond when he was rude to you?"

Adelaide considered the question briefly. "I was rather rude myself. I assured Mr. Truett that it would be a cold day in hell before he got any more advice from me."

Raina smiled. "You mean you gave him the edge of your temper?"

"Yep."

"Good for you. And then you agreed to let him accompany you to the theater."

"Yep."

"Hmm."

"What?"

Raina smiled a little. "You enjoyed it, didn't you?"

"Enjoyed what?"

"Losing your temper with the gentleman in question."

"It was," Adelaide said, "refreshing. Especially when he tried to apologize and then practically begged me to let him escort me to the theater."

It made me feel normal, she added to herself. *As if I didn't have to hide my real self.*

Raina looked thoughtful. "You say his name is Jake Truett?"

"Yes. He used to own an import-export business in Los Angeles."

"Hmm," Raina said again.

"I sense suspicion."

"Well, I am in the private investigation business," Raina reminded her. "I'm supposed to be suspicious."

Adelaide sank down on one of the two client chairs in front of the desk. "What is your problem with Mr. Truett? You've never even met him."

"That's one of the problems. The other is that the import-export business has been known to cover a multitude of illegal activities."

"Such as?"

"Smuggling comes to mind, as well as the underground trade in forgeries, stolen art, and illegal drugs. The list of illicit activities that can be concealed in the import-export business is endless."

Adelaide was amused. "You really are the suspicious type."

"I'll tell you what." Raina sat forward and replaced the pencil in the handsome amber plastic tray. "I've got some connections in L.A. I'll make a few phone calls and check out your Mr. Truett. I'll telephone you as soon as I've confirmed that he's a legitimate businessman."

"I appreciate your concern," Adelaide said. She spread her hands. "But what else could he be?"

"You'd be surprised," Raina said.

"Sometimes you scare me, Raina."

"Sometimes I scare myself."

Raina telephoned at five o'clock the following evening. Adelaide was still trying to decide what to wear.

"I don't have a lot of new information on Truett," Raina said. "He appears to be exactly who he says he is, a widower who inherited his family's import-export business. He sold the business shortly after his wife died."

"How did she die?"

"Elizabeth Benton Truett took her own life."

Adelaide tightened her grip on the phone. "How awful for Jake."

"I'm sure it was," Raina said. "Mrs. Truett hanged herself in the basement. Truett found the body."

"That must have been a terrible shock. No wonder his doctor advised him to rest his nerves."

"According to my sources, in the wake of Mrs. Truett's death there were rumors that she may have been involved in an affair. It was all hushed up by her family, of course. The Bentons are a very wealthy, very proud New York clan. I'm told their summer cottage in Bar Harbor is almost as large as the Burning Cove Hotel, and the one in the Hamptons is even larger. They move in exclusive circles and have for several generations."

"I wonder how Elizabeth wound up on the West Coast."

"Good question," Raina said. "Maybe she wanted to be a movie star."

"Her family background certainly explains why the Bentons wanted to keep the cause of death quiet," Adelaide said.

Families, especially those that moved in elevated social circles, went to great lengths to keep suicides out of the press. Their concerns were well-founded. The resulting publicity inevitably led to rumors of scandal or, even more dire, speculation that the bloodline was tainted by mental illness.

"That's all I've got for now," Raina said. "Truett is who he claims to be. I'll let you know if anything else turns up."

"Thanks," Adelaide said.

She hung up the phone and stood quietly for a moment, sorting through the information that Raina had provided. She had sensed from the start that Jake Truett was a man who possessed some closely held secrets. But she had a few secrets of her own. So what if she hadn't known that his dead wife might have been unhappy in her marriage and taken her own life? Jake didn't know that he was dating an escapee from an asylum.

Of the two of them it seemed obvious that she was keeping the darkest secrets. She went back upstairs and got dressed.

Chapter 9

Midway through Madam Zolanda's performance, Jake realized he was enjoying the evening. The pleasure had nothing to do with the psychic's routine and everything to do with the woman sitting beside him.

When he was near Adelaide Brockton, he felt off-balance: intrigued, curious, and very, very aware of her in a way that should probably concern him.

She was attractive but in an unconventional manner, with a striking profile; impossibly big, very serious sea green eyes; and shoulder-length hair the color of darkest amber. He had known women far more beautiful. Hell, he had been married to one for a few months.

For some reason, however, he found himself fascinated by Adelaide in ways that were altogether new and different. She was far more interesting and intriguing than any other woman he had ever known. At seven o'clock that evening when she had opened the front door of her cottage, he concluded that he was in trouble.

Until that moment he had only seen her in a crisply starched blue and white waitress uniform and an apron, her hair tightly rolled and pinned under a perky little cap. But her smile never failed to dazzle him. Temporarily, at least, her smile had the power to distract him from his grim thoughts and the dark reasons for his presence in Burning Cove.

She had dressed for the date in a green and yellow frock with flutter sleeves. Strappy sandals with chunky wooden heels accented her gracefully arched feet. Her hair was parted in the middle and tucked back behind her ears to fall in luxurious waves to her shoulders. The harried tearoom waitress had vanished.

The transformation enchanted him but it had also served to deepen the aura of mystery that swirled in the shadows around Adelaide Brockton.

Onstage Madam Zolanda was ensconced in an ornate throne-like chair. She was draped in a gown composed of several layers of red and gold scarves. There was a matching red velvet and gold turban on her head. Gold glittered at her ears and on her wrists. It was clear that the psychic business paid well, at least when you numbered a lot of celebrities and socialites on your client list.

She put her gloved fingers to her temples and closed her eyes in a dramatic gesture. When she spoke, it was in eerie, otherworldly tones that carried easily across the packed theater.

"I perceive that you chose the queen of hearts. Is that correct, sir?"

The volunteer from the audience, a young man in a slick suit, was standing several feet away on the stage. He looked at the oversized playing card that he had just selected from the pack that Zolanda's assistant had offered. He appeared incredulous.

"Gosh, it's the queen of hearts, all right," he said. "That's amazing, Madam Zolanda."

He handed the card to Zolanda's assistant, who held up the card so that the audience could see it.

Jake had done enough research on Thelma Leggett to know that she had once worked as a secretary at a studio. She was now Zolanda's assistant, driver, and publicist. Leggett was not in her chauffeur's costume tonight. Instead she wore an elegantly tailored tuxedo.

Another round of applause broke out.

"She does give a good performance," Adelaide whispered. "The audience is captivated."

Jake waved that aside. "So far she's just done the usual mind reading tricks."

"Yes, but it's not the actual illusions that matter in this sort of performance," Adelaide said. "The acting talent is the important thing. Zolanda is a certainly a fraud but you have to hand it to her—she's a very good actress."

"What makes you say that?"

"She's always in character, not just on the stage tonight, but whenever she's out in public. She's been a customer at the tearoom almost every day since she arrived in town, and I've never seen her put a foot wrong. She is always Madam Zolanda, psychic to the stars."

Jake gave that some thought. Adelaide was right. The ability to stay in character for an extended length of time required considerable acting talent. It also required a lot of stamina. No one knew that better than him.

"I see what you mean," he said.

"It's very hard to assume a certain persona and maintain it twenty-four hours a day. It takes a toll on the nerves."

The cool certainty in Adelaide's voice sent a flash of knowing through him. He could have sworn that she was speaking from experience.

"That is very . . . insightful," he said.

"For a waitress, do you mean?"

The edge was back in her voice. He had inadvertently offended her again.

"For anyone," he said.

Onstage, Zolanda was giving a demonstration of mind reading, speaking as though in the throes of a deep trance.

"Miss Leggett, I sense that someone in the third row is concerned with financial matters. Something to do with an inheritance . . . Yes, it's coming through quite clearly now. Someone died but he . . . or was it a woman? . . . left something important to a person who did not deserve it . . ."

A woman in the third row shot to her feet. "That's me, Madam Zolanda. My uncle promised to leave his house to me but my sister got it."

Thelma Leggett went to stand at the end of the third row. "Madam Zolanda, do you have any advice for this lady?"

"I see money coming to her very soon from an unexpected source. But wait. I'm getting another message. It's quite murky. Now I understand. She must be cautious because there are those who will seek to take advantage of her improved financial situation."

"That's for sure," the woman said. "My brother and sister will have their hands out. Thanks for the warning, Madam Zolanda."

The audience member sat down quickly.

"Fourth row, near the center, Miss Leggett. And—wait—also the seventh row. I perceive some ladies and gentlemen who suffer from insomnia."

There was an astonished gasp from several members of the audience. Several hands went up in the fourth and seventh rows.

"I can now perceive their auras," Madam Zolanda continued. "There is a great deal of negative energy in each one. That is the cause of their insomnia."

There was another round of applause.

Jake leaned toward Adelaide. He caught her light scent—some delicate perfume spiked with spice and flowers mingled with her indescribably feminine essence. For a beat or two he felt a little light-headed. He wished that he really was in Burning Cove to relax.

"It doesn't take any psychic power to assume that in an audience of this size there will be several people who have trouble sleeping," he said.

"True." Adelaide's mouth tilted up a bit at the corner. "At Refresh I get a lot of requests for blends to treat sleep problems."

Onstage, Thelma fitted Zolanda with a blindfold and then turned to speak to the audience.

"Silence, please," she instructed. "Madam Zolanda will now endeavor to provide a demonstration of astral projection. I must warn you that this is not always possible. It depends on the energy in the atmosphere. Noise from the audience can distort the astral wavelengths."

A hush fell over the crowd. Anticipation gripped the theater. For the first time Jake was mildly impressed. Madam Zolanda was doing literally nothing onstage and yet she had managed to rivet everyone's attention.

Slowly, deliberately, Madam Zolanda began to speak.

"I am floating above the town of Burning Cove. It is bathed in the light of the moon. I can see the Burning Cove Hotel and the Paradise Club. There is a small dog barking at me. The dog can sense my presence. I am being tugged toward a certain location. It is imperative that I go there. I must warn someone. Wait. I am being drawn to this very theater. I don't understand."

There was a collective gasp from the audience. Madam Zolanda continued, her voice rising with alarm.

"Now I am inside the theater looking down from the ceiling. Spirit Guide, tell me why you have summoned me to this place."

By now almost everyone in the audience was looking up at the darkened ceiling. There was a breathless pause . . .

. . . Shattered by a nerve-jangling scream.

Zolanda.

As one the audience turned back to watch, shocked, as Zolanda rose to her feet and tore off the blindfold. There was an expression of raw horror on her face. Her eyes were wild with panic as though she found herself in a hellish nightmare.

"I see blood. Blood and death. Mark my words, someone in this theater will be dead by morning."

The audience was absolutely motionless now. All eyes were on the stage.

Zolanda gave a high, shrill cry and collapsed. Her silk scarves cascaded around her in crimson waves.

Chapter 10

"You'll have to admit it made for a dramatic finish to the act," Adelaide said. She slipped into the buttery-soft leather seats of Jake's dark green speedster. "But why on earth would Zolanda make such a ghastly prediction when it is unlikely to come true?"

"Good question," Jake said.

There was a solid, satisfying *ker-chunk* as he closed the passenger side door.

Adelaide watched him walk around the front of the long hood. He looked very good in an elegantly tailored evening jacket and trousers and a perfectly knotted tie. If human auras really did exist, she was sure that his would radiate strength of will and a deeply passionate nature held in check by ironclad self-control.

She could tell that he had been affected by Zolanda's final act but his interest was of a detached, clinical nature. He was curious, she realized, but, unlike her, he was not disturbed.

Her nerves, on the other hand, had been badly rattled. She would not sleep well tonight, if she slept at all. The mere prediction of bloody death, even if only for dramatic effect, shocked her senses. It hurled her thoughts straight back to the night of her escape. Memories of the laboratory window exploding beneath the weight of Ormsby's body and visions of the killer emerging from the hallway that led to her room would haunt her until dawn.

She suppressed a small sigh. It wouldn't be the first time she had tossed and turned and finally given up on sleep. She had not had a single night of truly sound sleep in months, not since the terrible day when the police had come to her door to inform her that her parents had been killed in an explosion in their lab.

True, the authorities were not searching for a homicidal escapee from an insane asylum, but she was very sure that someone was looking for her.

There were excellent reasons for keeping the news of her escape a secret, of course. As long as she was assumed to be under lock and key at Rushbrook, Conrad Massey could continue to drain her inheritance and Dr. Gill could continue to hope that the FBI would not become aware of his experiments with Daydream. But it also meant that a killer was on the loose and quite likely searching for her.

She was well aware of her own reasons for having been unnerved by Zolanda's prediction, but Jake's odd silence made her wary. Instead of dismissing the final act as the melodramatic finale of a fraudulent psychic, he had gone very quiet after the curtain came down.

She thought about what Raina had said that afternoon when she had telephoned with the news that Jake Truett was evidently exactly who he claimed to be—a successful businessman and a widower who had sold his import-export business in the wake of his wife's tragic death. Under the circumstances it was probably not surprising that he would find such a dire prediction unsettling, even if it had been delivered by a charlatan. Nevertheless, his abrupt lapse into near silence struck her as strange.

He opened the driver's side door, got behind the wheel, and turned the key in the ignition. The powerful engine purred to life. He put the car in gear and pulled away from the curb.

She was very aware of the shadowed intimacy of the front seat of the speedster, but as far as she could tell, Jake was oblivious. He was lost in his own thoughts. Whatever those thoughts were, she had a feeling they were dark. She waited, tense and uncertain, for him to make another comment about Zolanda's prediction. When she could not abide the silence any longer, she tried to restart the conversation.

"This is Burning Cove, after all," she said. "I'm told there is very little serious crime here."

That comment had the effect of hauling Jake up out of some deep place—temporarily, at least.

"A friend informed me that a while back an aspiring actress died in the spa pool at the Burning Cove Hotel under suspicious circumstances," he said.

"I did hear something about that. Still, Florence assured me that was a very unusual situation. Murder is hardly a common crime in this town. This isn't New York or Los Angeles or San Francisco, where a fake psychic could play the odds and assume that somewhere in the city someone might die by violence in any given twenty-four-hour period. As it stands now, everyone will be opening up their copies of the *Burning Cove Herald* first thing in the morning looking for a report of a murder."

"She predicted a bloody death," Jake said. "She did not predict murder."

Adelaide glanced at him in surprise. "You're right. I hadn't considered the exact wording of the prediction. But when you think of a bloody death, murder is the first thing that comes to mind, isn't it?"

"Yes."

"Why would Zolanda risk her reputation by making a prediction that probably won't come true?"

"I don't think Madam Zolanda's reputation will suffer if the prediction fails," Jake said. "That's the interesting thing about the psychic business—it's virtually impossible to kill off a good act. Nobody remembers the predictions that didn't happen. People believe what they want to believe and forget the rest."

"So Zolanda made that horrible prediction just to inspire dark thrills in the audience?"

Jake shot her a quick, searching look and then returned his attention to Cliff Road, a narrow, two-lane strip of pavement that followed the bluffs above the ocean.

"Zolanda's grand finale really upset you, didn't it?" he said, his voice very neutral.

It upset you, too, she thought, but she did not say the words aloud.

She took a deep breath and composed herself. "I admit I was rather startled." She paused, searching for a brighter conversational topic. "You were right about the psychic act. It's just a form of stage magic. A combination of clever tricks and a good story."

"The difference is that when you watch a magician perform, you know it's all clever tricks and a good story," Jake said. He eased the car smoothly into another gear. "The magician invites you to be amazed, and if he's good, you are astonished by his skill. But a psychic wants you to actually believe in the paranormal. Those who fall for the act can be persuaded to do things that they might not otherwise do—things that prove to be harmful or dangerous."

She studied his hard, unyielding profile. Understanding whispered through her.

"Can I assume you know someone who was taken in by a psychic or a fortune-teller?" she asked quietly.

He hesitated and then nodded once. "Yes."

"I see. If your opinion of psychics is so low, may I ask why you wanted to accompany me to the performance tonight?"

For the first time since leaving the theater, a shadow of a smile briefly transformed Jake's stern features.

"Isn't it obvious why I talked you into giving me that second ticket?" he said.

A flash of understanding sparked through her. She clenched her hand around her evening bag. *I should have known he had an ulterior motive,* she thought.

"I see," she said, striving to keep her tone cool.

"What do you see?"

"Madam Zolanda was the psychic who tricked your friend, wasn't she?"

Jake took his eyes off the road just long enough to give her a quick, narrow-eyed glance.

"How the hell did you figure that out?" he asked.

He was annoyed, she decided, but not with her. He had never intended to give himself away. But he probably wasn't accustomed to dealing with paranoid mental patients who were always ready to suspect a plot or a conspiracy.

She gripped her bag with both hands and stared straight ahead at the winding road. So much for the possibility of engaging in a fleeting seaside romance with an interesting businessman from out of town.

"It explains a lot," she said. "You found me and my extra ticket very convenient, didn't you?"

"You are a very smart lady." Jake tightened his hands on the wheel. "But for your information, I already had a ticket to Zolanda's performance tonight. That's not why I wanted to accompany you this evening."

"There's no need for explanations," she said. "You've made yourself clear. You're in Burning Cove because you followed Madam Zolanda here. That's why you've made a habit of showing up at Refresh every day. You know that there's a good chance she'll show up, too. You're watching her."

"Stop jumping to conclusions. I admit that Zolanda is why I'm here, but I asked you for that extra ticket because I wanted to spend the evening with you. Zolanda's performance seemed like the perfect opportunity." Jake paused. "It was either that or the art museum."

The museum crack was an attempt to change the subject, she decided. She was not about to fall for it. He had used her, and she'd had enough of being used by men.

"Let's get back to your real reason for being in town," she said. "What do you hope to do? Prove Zolanda is a fraud? What good will that do? As you've already pointed out, people will believe what they want to believe."

Jake was silent for a few seconds. She knew he was debating how much to tell her.

"I have reason to think that Zolanda is in possession of a diary that does not belong to her," he said. "If the contents of the diary were to become public, there are people whose lives could be destroyed."

Adelaide thought she had been prepared for an alarming turn of events. Nevertheless, she was stunned.

"Are you telling me that Zolanda isn't just a phony psychic?" she said. "She's a blackmailer?"

"Yes."

"I see. So you are in town under false pretenses but for a very good reason."

"Damn it, Adelaide—"

"It's all right. No need to apologize." She waved a hand in what she hoped was an airy gesture of dismissal. "I'll admit I'm irritated that I was under a misunderstanding for most of the evening, but I do appreciate your reasons for the deception. In your shoes I probably would have done the same thing. Maybe."

"Will you listen for a moment? Yes, I am here in Burning Cove because I promised someone that I would do my best to recover the diary. But that is not why I asked you to let me use that second ticket tonight. My reasons for that were personal."

"Sure. And while we're on the subject of your deceptive behavior, there's something that I should mention."

"What?" Jake asked.

She was pleased by the very cautious undertone in the single word. *Call me petty,* she thought. She had a hunch that making Jake a little uneasy was likely the only revenge she would get.

"One of my friends was concerned about my date for tonight," she said, grimly cheerful. "She made some phone calls to Los Angeles and asked about you. She wanted to be sure you were who you claimed to be."

"You had someone investigate me?" Jake sounded nonplussed.

She had actually managed to shock him. She smiled to herself.

"My friend's name is Raina Kirk," she said. "Raina just opened a private investigation agency here in Burning Cove. Congratulations. Looking into your background was her very first case. All right, not exactly her first case."

"What the hell does 'not exactly' mean?"

"I didn't actually pay her. She did it as a favor."

"Damn." Jake was silent for a beat. "I came up clean, I take it?"

"Raina assured me that you are who you say you are."

"That's good to know. I'm very glad to find out for certain that I'm who I've always assumed I was. You can't be too careful these days."

"I just thought you should know that I checked up on you."

"It was an excellent idea." Jake turned serious again. "More women should exercise the same caution."

She thought about Conrad Massey. "You are so right."

Jake took the Crescent Beach turnoff. A short time later he brought the speedster to a halt in front of her cottage. He shut down the engine and climbed out from behind the wheel.

When he reached down to assist her out of the seat, she got another little electric thrill. It took willpower but she managed to suppress the urge to ask him in for a nightcap.

He went up the front steps with her and waited while she got out her key, opened the front door, and turned on a light. She moved into the small hall and turned to face him.

"Good night," she said, determined to hang on to her breezy, devil-may-care attitude at all costs. "It's been an interesting evening."

He gripped the doorjamb and leaned in a little, his eyes very intent. "I just want to make it clear one more time that I did not ask for that second ticket because I found it convenient to accompany you to the performance this evening. I asked for it because I wanted to be with you tonight."

"Is that the truth?"

"Yes. Madam Zolanda is the reason I came to Burning Cove but she is not the reason I went to the theater with you."

"All right."

"That's it? You're accepting my explanation?"

"You don't owe me any explanations. Good night, Jake."

His eyes tightened at the corners. He looked as if he wanted to argue about something, but evidently he couldn't come up with a reasonable excuse.

With obvious reluctance he released his grip on the doorjamb and stepped back.

"Good night," he said.

He waited while she closed and locked the door. She twitched the curtains aside and watched him go down the steps to his car. He drove the short distance to his own cottage. When the lights of the speedster disappeared into the small garage, she turned off the living room lamp and made her way upstairs to the bedroom at the end of the hall.

The drapes were open. She went to the window and stood looking out at Jake's cottage for a time. When she saw the lights come on upstairs in his bedroom, she closed her own drapes, sat down on the little dressing table chair, and unfastened the straps of her sandals.

Shoes in hand, she got up and opened the large wooden wardrobe. She started to put the sandals in their proper place on the shoe rack.

For a few seconds she could only gaze, bewildered, at her brown and beige Oxfords, the shoes she wore for work. They were in the space reserved for the evening sandals.

She spent a full minute trying to remember if, in her excitement about getting dressed for the date, she had forgotten exactly where she had positioned the Oxfords.

She took a closer look at the bottom of the wardrobe. It wasn't just that the Oxfords were in the wrong place. The wooden shoe rack had been moved.

In her head she heard Dr. Gill speaking to her. *Paranoia is a sign of mental instability, Adelaide. This drug will help you recover.*

In a desperate effort to put her mind at ease, she hoisted the shoe rack out of the wardrobe and set it on the floor. Carefully, as if she were opening a box that might contain spiders, she opened the lid of the built-in storage compartment in the base of the wardrobe.

For a moment she stared at the neatly folded spare blankets. The faded patchwork quilt was on top. That was wrong. She was certain that she had left the plaid wool blanket on top.

She was paranoid. So what? She had a right. A woman who had spent two months locked up in a psychiatric asylum had every reason to be paranoid.

She crossed the room and went down on her knees beside the bed. The elderly lady who had rented the cottage to her had told her about the small compartment in the floor. She had explained that it was where she and her husband had hidden what little money and valuables they still possessed after the crash. One certainly couldn't trust the banks.

Adelaide pressed the concealed spring. The trapdoor popped open. She took out the wooden box she had hidden inside and placed it on the bed. She straightened and raised the lid of the box. The gold wedding band caught the lamplight. She ignored it and the handful of newspaper clippings about a mysterious, year-old explosion in a laboratory that had claimed two lives.

She took out the little pistol and made sure it was loaded.

Gun in hand, she left the bedroom, turning on every light along the way. She checked the bathroom and the spare bedroom and then she started downstairs.

It took every ounce of nerve she possessed to conduct the search, but she forced herself to open every closet and every cupboard that was large enough to conceal a person.

No killer garbed in a surgeon's mask leaped out at her.

By the time she reached the kitchen, every light in the house was blazing.

The back door was locked.

The window in the small laundry room was not.

A wave of bone-chilling cold swept through her. She was very certain now that there had been an intruder inside the house. The question was, what had he hoped to find? A transient searching for food or valuables was the most likely explanation, but she could not bring herself to believe it.

Paranoia is a sign of mental instability, Adelaide.

She was concentrating so intently that she nearly screamed aloud when she heard the knock on the front door.

Chapter 11

"What the hell did you think you were doing with that last prediction?" Thelma tossed the black tuxedo jacket across the back of the nearest chair. "Are you crazy? Tomorrow morning this whole town is going to wake up and grab the morning paper to see who got murdered overnight."

"The stage act needed some fresh drama." Zolanda yanked off the heavy turban, dropped it on the coffee table, and went to the liquor cabinet. "I decided to experiment. It worked. The audience loved it."

Thelma's jaw tensed in a stubborn line. "What are you going to do when there's no headline about a bloody death in the *Burning Cove Herald* tomorrow?"

"Who knows? We may get lucky. In a town this size it's entirely possible that someone will die overnight, either by accidental or natural causes."

"And if the paper doesn't report any deaths?"

"It won't matter because it won't be long before people will be talking about the mysterious disappearance of a certain tearoom waitress," Zolanda said, trying for patience. "They won't find a body, at least not right away, so everyone will assume that she was the one who suffered a bloody death. And when I discover the remains using my astonishing paranormal powers, I will be the most famous psychic in the nation."

Thelma stared at her. "Are you out of your mind? When the waitress goes missing and turns up dead, the cops will question you. They'll want to know how you could predict such a thing."

Zolanda shrugged. "I've got the perfect explanation. I possess paranormal powers. Stop worrying, Thelma. The authorities won't look twice at you."

"I can't believe this. You're putting everything we've worked for at risk."

"Stop fretting." Zolanda yanked the stopper out of a decanter, splashed a large measure of whiskey into a glass, and took a fortifying swallow. "I know what I'm doing."

Thelma stalked back and forth across the living room. "What if Adelaide Brockton, or whatever she's calling herself these days, doesn't disappear?"

"She will."

But it wouldn't matter one way or another, Zolanda thought, not if she had been successful tonight. She suppressed a satisfied smile. She had been nothing short of brilliant. The audience was riveted. The note she received in her dressing room after the performance said it all. *Congratulations. You're going to be a star.*

She drank some more whiskey. She had given the performance of her life in that last act but she had lied to Thelma. The dramatic prediction she had used to close the show had nothing to do with the disappearance of the tearoom waitress. Adelaide Brockton was no longer important. She represented the past. Tonight the door to a glorious new future had been opened.

That future did not include Thelma.

"I hope you're right," Thelma said. "I still say you made a huge mistake, one that could backfire on both of us."

"Stop fretting. Why don't you run along and have some fun at the Carousel. In the morning you'll see that everything is going to be just fine."

"Yeah, sure." Thelma shook her head. "I still say you should have talked to me before you pulled that stunt."

She grabbed the limo keys and headed for the door.

Zolanda lit a cigarette and poured more whiskey into her glass. There were times when she envied Thelma. As far as the public was concerned, Thelma was just the psychic's assistant and chauffeur. She got to relax when she wasn't on the job. But for Madam Zolanda there was never a moment when she could be herself in public. The past three years had been exhausting.

It was all worth it, though, because she had been a great success tonight. She had come a long way from the midwestern farm town where she grew up. Wealthy socialites and Hollywood stars begged her for advice and confided their deepest secrets. She had collected a fortune in blackmail material during the past three years. But that was not enough. She had always dreamed of being a star, and soon that dream would come true.

The ornate gold and white enamel phone on the table rang. She picked it up, remembering to use her Zolanda voice. The caller asked one question. Zolanda responded.

"Yes, I'm alone."

She hung up and poured herself another drink. She deserved to celebrate tonight.

A short time later she heard a car coming up the long, secluded drive.

She rushed to open the door. Her future was calling.

Chapter 12

Thoroughly rattled by the unexpected knock on her front door, Adelaide reacted instinctively and hit the light switch. The action plunged the kitchen into darkness. There was, she thought, no sense making a target out of herself.

On the other hand she was probably overreacting. Why would an intruder who had already invaded her home return to knock politely on her door? She could not think of a reasonable answer to that question.

"Adelaide, this is Jake Truett. Are you all right? If you don't respond, I'm coming in."

Relief washed through her in a disorienting wave. She lowered the gun to her side and hurried to open the door. Jake glanced at her with hard, cold eyes and then looked past her, searching the shadows.

"Jake," she said. "You don't know how happy I am to see—" She froze when she caught the glint of metal in his hand. She looked down and saw the gun he was holding alongside his thigh.

Aside from the new accessory, he was still dressed as he had been for the theater, although he had discarded the fashionable drape-cut evening jacket and his tie. His crisp white dress shirt was open at the collar. His hair was tousled. It dawned on her that he had run the distance between his cottage and hers.

"What's wrong?" he demanded.

She realized he was looking at the gun in her hand. She tightened her grip on it and took a step back, raising the weapon as she did so.

"First, get rid of your gun," she ordered.

"All right," he said. Crouching, he set the weapon down on the floor just over the threshold. He straightened slowly but made no move to force his way into the hall. "Sorry. Didn't mean to scare you. I just wanted to be sure you weren't in some sort of trouble."

"What made you think I was?"

His brows rose. "How about the fact that I glanced out my window and noticed that you were going through this place, turning on every light in every room? I'm assuming something scared the living daylights out of you."

She exhaled slowly. "I think someone broke in here while you and I were out tonight."

"Anything stolen?"

"Not as far as I can tell. I haven't done a complete search but nothing important seems to be missing."

"What about food? Transients sometimes break in just to get a bite to eat."

"I thought about that, but I don't believe that whoever broke in was after food. Nothing was disturbed in the kitchen."

He glanced meaningfully at the pistol. "Would you mind pointing that gun in another direction while we sort this out? You're making me nervous. I'm not supposed to allow my nerves to get overstimulated, remember?"

She lowered the pistol. "I apologize. I'm a little nervous myself at the moment."

"Call the police. I'll wait here on the front porch. They'll send an officer out to take a look."

She struggled with that for a few beats. The last thing she wanted to do was draw the attention of the local police. She was new in town, after all. Complaining about a break-in might cause the cops to ask questions about her past. She would have to lie, and that would lead to more lies, and then things could get complicated.

"What would I tell them?" she said. "That I *think* there was an intruder? That nothing was stolen? That all I've got to show for proof is an unlocked window? They'll tell me I most likely forgot to lock it."

"May I come in and take a look around?"

She thought some more. Common sense finally descended. There was no way he could have been the intruder. He had been with her all evening.

"First, tell me why you showed up on my doorstep with a gun," she said.

He gave her a faint, ice-cold smile. "I used to be in the import-export business, remember? I traveled to some dangerous places around the world and met with some dangerous people. Years ago I started carrying a gun for protection when I traveled. It became a habit."

"You consider Burning Cove a potentially dangerous town?"

"I don't think there is any such thing as a crime-free town." He paused a beat and glanced at the pistol in her hand. "I would also point out that you seem to have the same opinion of Burning Cove."

"I'm a woman living alone. It seems sensible to take precautions."

"I won't argue with that. So, what's it going to be? Do you want me to take a look around or leave?"

If he wanted to do her any harm, he'd had ample opportunity earlier in the evening when he had brought her home. She was overreacting.

She stepped back, opening the door wider. "Pick up your gun and come on in. Yes, I would appreciate it if you would take a look at the laundry room window and see if you think it could have been opened from the outside."

"The intruder used a window in the laundry room?"

"That was the only one that was unlocked."

Jake stooped, collected his gun, and moved across the threshold.

Letting him into her home was the biggest risk she had taken since her escape from the Rushbrook Sanitarium, she thought. But it was a calculated risk.

Chapter 13

Zolanda stood at the edge of the roof and looked out over the moonlit ocean. She had never felt so thrillingly alive, so powerful. She was the queen of the night, and soon she would be a star on the silver screen. She spread her arms wide, savoring the euphoric sensations sweeping through her. She was on fire. She could fly.

The wide sleeves of her caftan caught the cool breeze like great wings. Maybe her visitor was right, maybe she really could travel by astral projection. She was in a waking dream now. All she had to do was take one more step off the edge of the roof and she would be floating high above Burning Cove. The experience would be exactly as she had described it in her performance tonight. She would drift above the lights of the gorgeous Burning Cove Hotel and watch the glamorous people drinking their cocktails and making arrangements for illicit encounters. Soon she would be one of them, no longer the psychic to the stars; she would be a star.

But even as the glorious possibilities dazzled her senses, a tiny flicker of doubt intruded. Like a drop of poison in a glass of water, the whisper of uncertainty tainted the vision. She didn't have paranormal powers. There was no such thing as astral projection.

What if she was hallucinating?

She thought about the last glass of whiskey she had finished before climbing the stairs to the roof of the villa.

A drop of poison.

"The drug," she gasped. *"You gave me some of the drug, didn't you?"*

The killer watched her from the shadows, saying nothing.

The horror of what was happening was swept away by a searing rage.

"You lied to me," Zolanda hissed. "You poisoned me with Daydream. I'll kill you."

She tried to lunge toward the killer but the monsters of the night were moving toward her now. Their eyes glittered with a hellish fire.

Some small part of her mind struggled with reality. She was not seeing monsters with eyes of fire—the killer had just lit a cigarette.

But the hallucinations were in control. The dazzling rivers of the night swirled around her in fiery, disorienting waves. She staggered wildly on the parapet.

The monsters advanced, relentless and implacable. The killer told her exactly why she was going to jump off the roof of the villa and quoted the old adage about revenge—a dish that was best served cold.

"No," she said, desperate to save herself. "You don't understand. It was all a mistake. I can explain."

But the killer did not believe her.

Zolanda lost her balance and fell, shrieking, into the night.

The screaming stopped when she landed on the unforgiving concrete patio.

The killer went downstairs, crowbar in hand, walked through the glass-walled conservatory, and stepped outside onto the patio. The psychic to the stars was very dead. There was no need to use the length of heavy metal to finish the job.

The killer went back into the house and began to search for the psychic's stash of blackmail secrets. The drug had hypnotic as well as hallucinogenic properties. In her delirium, Zolanda had talked freely, describing exactly where she had hidden the papers.

Panic set in a short time later. There was no sign of the extortion material. Zolanda had probably not lied—the drug was very powerful—but she had somehow succeeded in taking her secrets to the grave.

Chapter 14

"You're not going to be able to sleep tonight, are you?" Jake asked.

Adelaide looked at him with haunted eyes.

"Probably not," she said. "But that's my problem. Don't worry about me. I appreciate your taking a look around but, as I told you, nothing is missing and every window is locked now."

They were sitting across from each other at the kitchen table. Adelaide had surprised him by brewing coffee instead of one of her unique tea blends. Some situations require coffee, she had explained. He had agreed.

At least she was no longer pointing her little pistol at him. But the gun was currently lying on top of the big, scarred kitchen table, within reach. That made him uneasy because it was obvious that she had not had a lot of experience with it. She seemed to know the basics but she was not comfortable with the weapon. Guns in the hands of professionals were dangerous enough. In the hands of amateurs they were an even greater cause for concern because of the possibility that the trigger would get pulled by accident or impulse.

His own gun was also on the table, also close at hand. He'd left the shoulder holster behind on his nightstand. There had not been time to buckle it on after he'd become alarmed by the lights in Adelaide's cottage.

They had established a cautious truce but were circling each other warily. He knew that Adelaide was not telling him everything but he also sensed that she was not lying to him. Fair enough. She had a right to her secrets. He was keeping a few from her.

All things considered, it had been a very unusual first date.

"I could stay here until morning," he said.

He realized immediately that the offer had not come out quite the way he had intended.

She tensed. "Thank you, but that won't be necessary."

He groaned. "I didn't mean that the way it sounded."

She relaxed a little. A ghost of a smile touched her mouth. "I know. But, really, I'll be all right. To be honest, I'm starting to wonder if I actually did leave the laundry room window open."

"You said you thought the shoe rack in your wardrobe had been moved—as if someone had searched the place for valuables."

"Maybe I was wrong about that, too," Adelaide said, her tone stark. She shook her head. "Maybe I imagined that it had been moved. I . . . get a little nervous after dark."

The possibility that she had let her imagination run away with her common sense disturbed her more than seemed appropriate under the circumstances. After all, she was a woman living alone. She had a right to be extra cautious, especially at night.

He glanced at the gun.

"One question comes to mind," he said.

Her eyes narrowed a little. "What's that?"

"If someone did search your house looking for valuables, why didn't he find the gun?" A thought struck. Now his nerves really were rattled. "Don't tell me you had it in your handbag all evening."

"Of course not," she said.

"I'm relieved to hear that."

"I keep it under my bed."

She slept with a gun under the bed. The lady was running from someone; a man, most likely.

"Can you think of any logical reason why someone would break into a house like this but not take anything?" she asked.

She was serious, he realized. She was searching for an explanation for the break-in that would be less frightening than the one she evidently feared.

"There are some very dangerous people in the world," he said. "It's not inconceivable that someone broke in here tonight because he believed that you were at home and in bed and, therefore, vulnerable."

She lowered the mug and stared at him, her eyes widening in surprise. "Do you think someone broke in here tonight because he intended to assault me?"

It struck him as a very odd reaction, especially coming from a woman who lived alone. The possibility that a rapist might have targeted her should have been the first thing that occurred to her. Instead, it seemed to be the very last thing she had considered.

"That kind of crime does happen," he said, "even in places like Burning Cove."

"Of course. I should have considered that immediately. I suppose I was more focused on . . . other possibilities."

"Such as?"

"Theft, naturally," she said a little too forcefully.

"But nothing was taken."

She winced. "No. That doesn't leave a lot of other logical explanations, does it?"

"There is one other thing you should probably consider."

She eyed him warily. "What?"

"A moment ago I reminded you that there are some dangerous people in the world. There are also some very disturbed people running loose in society. Not all of the crazies are safely locked up in an asylum."

She almost dropped the coffee mug. Her lips parted but no words came out. She just stared at him, stricken.

"Right." He had upset her enough for one night. Reluctantly he pushed himself to his feet. "If you're sure you don't want me to stay—"

"Thank you, but there's no need, really. I'll leave all the lights on until morning. I don't think any intruder will return to a house that is lit up like a movie set, do you?"

She had found her voice again but she was talking much too fast now.

"Probably not," he agreed.

"If he does, I'll be awake and I'll have my gun. Please don't worry about me."

"Tell you what, use the lights as a signal. If you hear anything, anything at all, turn the lights off in whatever room you happen to be in at the time. I'll keep an eye on this house until dawn. If I see even one of the windows go dark, I'll come back to check on you."

She frowned. "But you'll be asleep."

"No," he said. "I won't be asleep."

"You're going to sit up all night watching my windows?"

He smiled. "Not like I've got anything better to do. Told you I was bored."

She studied him for a long moment. She looked torn. Finally she moved one hand in a dismissive gesture.

"If you're going to insist on watching my house for the rest of the night, you might as well stay here. I've got some books and magazines you can read if you don't want to sleep. I'll make more coffee."

"That sounds like an excellent plan."

"You're welcome to nap on the sofa."

"I won't be doing any napping."

"It's going to be a long night," Adelaide warned.

He smiled a little. "Not my first."

She gave him a considering look. "You're not the partying type. If you were, you would spend your evenings at the Burning Cove Hotel or the Paradise Club while you're here in Burning Cove. I'm assuming those other long nights you just mentioned were connected to your import-export business?"

"Good guess."

"Sometime I'd like to hear more about your line of work. It sounds interesting."

"I told you, I've retired from the import-export business."

She nodded. "You're looking for a new job."

"I hadn't given it much thought."

"Nonsense." She gave him a severe look. "You're a healthy man in the prime of life. You need a profession, a career—a job."

He sipped his coffee. "If you say so."

"You're not really interested in talking about this, are you?"

"No, I'm not."

"Why not?"

"I've got other things on my mind at the moment."

She looked as if she wanted to argue, but she managed to beat back her concern for his rather dim employment prospects. She gave him a cool smile, got to her feet, and picked up her little pistol.

"Let's go into the living room," she said. "The chairs are more comfortable there."

She had a point. The wooden kitchen chairs did not invite extended sitting. He collected his own gun and followed her into the living room, enjoying the cozy feel of the small house. The floral upholstery on the sofa and chairs was badly faded and so were the curtains, but it was obvious that Adelaide had repainted. The walls were a smoky shade of green that reminded him of the inside of an avocado. The deep purple trim around the doors and windows could have been stripped off the outside of an eggplant.

A recent issue of *Life* magazine and a novel sat on the coffee table in front of the cushioned sofa. A bookmark was positioned in the middle of the book.

Adelaide came to a halt in the center of the room and looked around. Jake got the impression that she was trying to figure out what to do with him. Her gaze fell on the card table near the bookcase. She brightened.

"We could play cards," she said.

He smiled. "All right. Are you a betting woman?"

"Not if it involves money. I don't have enough to risk. But I've got a box of seashells we can use for wagers."

"That will work." He glanced at the book on the table. "I see you're reading the new Cooper Boone spy novel."

"*Deception Island.* Yes, it just came out. I love the way Cooper Boone travels to mysterious places around the world and confronts dangerous villains. Did you read the first one, *Code Name: Arcane?*"

"I did, as a matter of fact."

"What did you think?"

"All that stuff about villains with secret island fortresses, weird art collections, and strange weapons isn't exactly realistic."

Adelaide gave him a steely smile. "That's probably why they call it fiction."

For the first time in a very long while, he laughed. Adelaide looked as surprised as he was.

Chapter 15

They were both still awake when the first light of dawn seeped into the sky. Jake put down the last hand of cards.

"Gin," he said. "You owe me three shells."

Adelaide pushed the last of her shells across the table. She eyed the large stack on Jake's side.

"You're awfully good at cards," she said.

"Sometimes I get lucky." Jake pushed himself to his feet and stretched in a leisurely manner. He checked the gold watch on his wrist. "Time for me to go."

"Won't you stay for breakfast?" she said quickly. "Eggs and toast? It's the least I can do under the circumstances."

"Thanks, but I should be on my way. Wouldn't want anyone passing by your house to see me leaving at this hour."

"I doubt that anyone would notice. It's not like I have a lot of neighbors. Just you and the summer visitors who rented the cottage at the other end of the beach. They're only here on the weekends."

She realized that at some point during the night she had become

accustomed to his presence. A quiet intimacy had settled on them. Not
that it had been a night of true confessions, she thought. Instead, they
had talked of everything and nothing—the weather, the scandals of the
stars rumored to be vacationing at the Burning Cove Hotel, the clever
names of the teas and tisanes that she had invented to promote her
special blends at Refresh, the rumors of war in Europe—but they had
somehow arrived at a mutual agreement to respect each other's secrets.

It wasn't that they weren't curious about each other, she realized,
but for now, at least, they weren't going to try to push past each other's
boundaries.

"No point causing gossip," he said.

She smiled at that. "In this town people have genuine celebrity
scandals to entertain them. I doubt if anyone would bother to gossip
about us, but I understand the concern. I'll try to find a locksmith today
and see about installing better locks."

She opened the kitchen door for Jake. A thick morning fog was
rolling in off the ocean. It would be gone by noon but for now it cloaked
the world in a weightless mist.

Jake stepped outside, took in the scene, and looked satisfied. "No
one will see me leaving your place, not in this fog."

"Are you sure you won't stay for breakfast?"

He stopped and looked at her. He smiled. "You and the fog just
talked me into it."

"I'll get the eggs going."

"I'll come back inside in a few minutes," he said. "I want to take a
look around the outside of the laundry room window and see if I can
find any signs of the intruder."

She tightened her grip on the doorknob. "And if you don't find any
evidence? Will you conclude that I imagined the whole thing?"

He paused at the edge of the back porch. "Regardless of what I find
or don't find, I believe you had excellent reasons to conclude that someone broke into your house last night. I don't think your imagination got

the better of you. I don't think you were suffering from bad nerves. Are we clear on that?"

She relaxed. "Yes. Thank you."

She stepped back into the kitchen, closed the door, and crossed to the stove. She picked up the cast-iron pan and put it on a burner.

The telephone on the wall rang just as she started cracking eggs into a bowl. Startled, she dropped one of the eggs. It broke on the green tile countertop.

It's just the telephone. Get hold of yourself, woman.

But she could not think of a single person who would call her at such an early hour.

Paranoia is a sign of mental instability.

She reminded herself that she had just spent a sleepless night after discovering evidence that someone had invaded her home. She had a right to be jumpy.

She wiped her hands on her apron and picked up the receiver.

"Hello?" she asked, trying not to reveal her anxiety.

There was a short, startled pause, as if the caller had not expected the phone to be answered.

"Miss Brockton? Is that you?"

"Yes. Who is this?"

"Thelma Leggett, Madam Zolanda's assistant. I realize I probably woke you. Please forgive me but I am absolutely desperate."

Thelma did, indeed, sound frantic.

"What's wrong?" Adelaide said.

"It's Madam Zolanda. She's in a terrible state. I think she's having a nervous breakdown. She won't come out of her room. She's begging for some of the special tea that you blended for her—Enlightenment—but we're out. Refresh doesn't open until nine. I don't dare wait that long. In any event, I'm afraid to leave her alone. In her present mood she might do herself some harm."

"If she's in such a bad way, you should call the doctor."

"No, Madam Zolanda would be furious if I did that. She'd likely fire me. If you wouldn't mind bringing me a fresh batch of her special blend, I would be very grateful. I assure you, I'll make it worth your while. We're staying in the villa at the end of Ocean View Lane. Do you know it?"

"Yes, but I really think you should call the doctor."

"I just can't risk it," Thelma whispered. "It would mean my job. I really do think Madam Zolanda will be fine once she's had a chance to calm down. Your tea works wonders for her. Please say you'll bring some to the villa right away."

Adelaide glanced at the wall clock. It was very early in the morning. She did the blending of the teas and tisanes in her own kitchen so she had everything she needed on hand. There was time to serve breakfast to Jake, prepare a packet of Enlightenment, and drop it off before she had to get dressed for work.

"All right," she said. "I'll be there within the hour."

"Can't you make it sooner?" Thelma pleaded. "This is an emergency."

The phone went dead before Adelaide could say anything else. She replaced the receiver and stood very still, trying to decide how to handle the situation.

The kitchen door opened. Startled yet again, she swung around a little too quickly. The edge of her hand caught a spoon on the counter and sent it clattering onto the brick-red linoleum floor. The lack of sleep was taking a toll. She was on edge today.

Jake walked into the room, looking grim. He was holding something in his right hand.

"What is it?" she asked a little too sharply. "Did you find something?"

He opened his hand to display two cigarette butts and a nearly empty matchbook. "I found these behind the garage. Looks like the bastard smoked at least a couple of cigarettes while he waited last night."

It took a few beats before she grasped the full meaning of his words. "While he *waited*?" she finally managed. "You think there was someone out here *all night*?"

"There's no way to know how long he watched this cottage. We didn't hear a car coming or going during the night, but that isn't surprising, not if he parked some distance away on a side road. The sound of the surf would have covered the noise of an engine. But here's how I read the scene."

She stared at him. "The scene? As in, the scene of a crime?"

He ignored that. "I think he got into the house and had a good look around while you were gone. Then he went outside to wait until you returned. He knew you were with me. He was stuck until I left. I think the plan was to wait until you turned off the lights and went to bed before he went back into the house. But you didn't go to bed. Instead, you turned on all the lights."

"And you came running to see what was wrong and stayed with me the rest of the night," she concluded. "It doesn't make any sense. Why would he enter the house while I was gone and then go back outside to wait for me to go to bed?"

"Got a feeling," Jake said, "that he went into the house to familiarize himself with the layout so that when he went back inside in the dark, he would know exactly where he was going and how he would get out in a hurry. It's a small place so there was nowhere for him to hide inside until you went to bed."

"How can you possibly know that?" she asked.

"Just seems logical."

It was the truth, she thought, but not the whole truth. She was very sure that what Jake had left unsaid was, *It's what I would have done.* Probably best not to press the matter, she decided.

She looked at the damning cigarette butts and the matchbook. "It wasn't some transient who was after food."

"No," Jake said. "I don't think it was a burglar, either. If I'm right—and for now, at least, we had better assume that I am—whoever left these cigarette butts is stalking you the way a predator stalks prey."

Chapter 16

The villa on Ocean View Lane was an extravagant, Hollywood fantasy version of a mansion done in the Spanish colonial revival style. The residence, with its high ceilings and decorative parapets, rose three stories above the walled grounds.

Jake drove through the open wrought iron gates and along a drive that cut through a garden filled with well-kept flowering plants. Orange and grapefruit trees were scattered about the grounds. A decorative grape arbor marched along one wall.

He brought the speedster to a halt at the front of the villa.

"This is some house," he remarked, shutting down the engine.

"Florence told me that it was built by a tycoon just before the crash," Adelaide explained. "The tycoon lost everything when the market plunged. This mansion was neglected for years and then another very wealthy man from L.A. picked it up. He poured a lot of money into it and now rents it out to celebrities who want more privacy than they can get at the Burning Cove Hotel."

Jake opened his door, climbed out from behind the wheel, and walked around to her side of the car to open the door. She got out, bag of tea in hand. Together they went up the front steps. She pressed the doorbell.

"It really wasn't necessary for you to accompany me today," she said, not for the first time.

"I told you, I've got a personal interest in Madam Zolanda."

"Yes," she said. "You did tell me that."

She did not say anything else. They waited in silence for a minute or two.

"I thought the assistant told you that this was an emergency," Jake said.

She pressed the doorbell again. Again there was no response.

"Maybe they're having breakfast out on the patio," she suggested. "It's a big house. They might not hear the bell."

She started walking along a flagstone path that led through the gardens to the rear of the villa. Jake followed without comment. He had been in a grim, somber mood since finding the cigarette butts and the matchbook, but there was a new level of tension in the atmosphere around him now.

"This vacation is not doing a lot for your nerves, is it?" she said. "I'll bet your doctor would be very unhappy if he could see you today."

"I don't plan to tell him."

"That's probably a good idea," she said. She raised her voice. "Miss Leggett? Madam Zolanda? It's Adelaide Brockton. I have your Enlightenment blend."

She and Jake rounded the back of the house and stopped at the edge of the large concrete patio. Some lounge chairs, a table, and an umbrella furnished the garden retreat.

There was also an untidy bundle of what appeared to be vividly colored silk scarves.

Adelaide stopped abruptly.

"No," she said very softly.

Madam Zolanda had been a tall, dramatic figure in life. She looked so much smaller in death.

Chapter 17

"Stay here," Jake said.

He touched Adelaide's shoulder briefly as he moved around her, silently reinforcing the command.

She watched him crouch beside the body. Something about the swift, efficient manner in which he moved told her that this wasn't the first time he had dealt with the dead. She thought about Raina Kirk's opinion of Jake's old line of work. *The import-export business has been known to cover a multitude of illegal activities.* And then she remembered what Raina had said about the death of Jake's wife. *Mrs. Truett hanged herself in the basement. Truett found the body.*

"She's been dead for a while," Jake said. He got to his feet. "Several hours, I think. Her neck is broken." He looked up at the roof of the house. "She must have jumped. Or else someone wants us to believe that's what happened."

Adelaide looked up at the high parapet that decorated the roof of the villa. "*Someone* wants us to believe she jumped?"

"If I'm right about Zolanda, she was collecting blackmail secrets from a lot of people. It's possible that one of her victims tracked her down and silenced her."

"I understand."

It made sense, but dark memories of the night that Dr. Ormsby, hallucinating wildly, had leaped through the arched window at the Rushbrook Sanitarium ghosted through Adelaide's head. *It must be a coincidence,* she thought. *Just a horrible coincidence.*

She realized Jake was watching her.

"Are you all right?" he asked.

"No," she said. "I'm not. But I'm not going to faint, if that's what's worrying you. Jake, this makes no sense. Thelma called me a short time ago. You said Zolanda has been dead for quite a while."

"I think so, yes. I want to take a look around inside before we call the police."

"You're hoping to find that diary that you said Zolanda was using to blackmail your friend."

"It's a long shot, but I have to check it out."

Jake was already moving toward the open doors of the conservatory attached to the back of the mansion.

Unable to think of anything else to do, she trailed after him. The glass room was furnished with green wrought iron benches and a lot of potted plants. Jake took in the surroundings with a quick, assessing glance and kept going.

He opened another door and led the way along a wide, arched hall. At the far end he started up an elegant staircase.

"Stay here," he said. "I'll be down in a few minutes."

He disappeared on the landing.

Adelaide realized she was still clutching the packet of Enlighten-ment tea. She turned slowly on her heel and looked around. From where she stood she had a view of the grand living room with its high ceiling, arched windows, and dark wooden beams.

The interior of the villa was as exotic as the outside. The walls were painted a rich ocher. There was a lot of colorful tile work around the hearth. The furniture was mostly covered in saddle brown leather and accented with throw pillows in jewel-toned fabrics.

The turban that Zolanda had worn during her final performance sat on a coffee table. It looked as if it had been tossed there in a careless manner. A tuxedo coat was draped over the back of a chair. It looked too small for a man. Adelaide concluded it was probably the jacket that Thelma Leggett had worn in her role as Zolanda's assistant.

For some reason Adelaide found herself drawn to the turban. She studied it for a long moment and thought about Zolanda's last prediction. *Mark my words, someone in this theater will be dead by morning.*

There was an empty glass next to the turban, a small residue of what looked like whiskey inside.

She could hear cupboard doors opening and closing overhead. Jake was making his way very quickly through the upstairs rooms.

She wandered around for a time with absolutely no idea what she was looking for.

She was about to give up on the living room and try her luck in the kitchen, when she caught the glitter of what looked like a chunk of broken glass on the floor beneath the bottom shelf of the liquor cabinet. The shard was a deep blue color.

There was a lot of glassware in the cabinet but none of it was cobalt blue.

She took a handkerchief out of her handbag, crouched beside the cabinet, and started to reach for the piece of glass.

She froze when she realized that she was not looking at a shard of blue glass. She had been about to pick up the elegant stopper of a cobalt blue cut crystal perfume bottle.

She stared at the stopper in disbelief. All she could think about in that moment was the black velvet case on Ormsby's office desk, the case containing a dozen cut crystal perfume bottles. She had been trapped at Rushbrook long enough to learn a number of things about the inner workings of the asylum. She knew that Ormsby didn't distill perfumes—he crafted illicit drugs. Some of those drugs ended up in elegant crystal perfume bottles.

She reminded herself to think logically. Zolanda had done very well in the psychic business. She had no doubt owned several bottles of expensive perfume.

She used the handkerchief to pick up the glittering crystal object. She brought the stopper close to her nose and sniffed very cautiously. There was no scent, no trace whatsoever of perfume. How long did the fragrance of a perfume cling to crystal? She had no ready answer. But she knew a lot about the drug called Daydream. It was odorless and tasteless.

She took another look around the living room. There was no sign of the other portion of the perfume bottle. Only the stopper remained.

It could not be one of the bottles in the black velvet case, she told herself. How could a fake Hollywood psychic possibly be linked to the Rushbrook Sanitarium?

She had to get control of her growing paranoia. She was starting to sound a lot like the other inmates on ward five. The blue perfume bottle stopper was just a blue glass object. It had obviously been part of a very expensive bottle of perfume, but there were probably thousands of bottles just like it.

However, if the police concluded that Zolanda had been murdered, and if they discovered a link between the sanitarium and the psychic to the stars, and if they discovered that there was an escaped mental patient working as a tearoom waitress in Burning Cove, said escaped patient would probably become the number one suspect in the murder.

There were a lot of ifs involved, but if they proved to be true, she would have to be prepared to disappear again.

She put the stopper back down on the floor beneath the cabinet where she had found it. The police might notice it but she doubted that they would see it as significant. It was just part of a perfume bottle.

Shaken, she went down the hall to the large kitchen.

There was a half-full sack of Enlightenment on the tiled counter. A teapot and a kettle stood beside it. Zolanda had not run out of her special blend.

"Damn," Adelaide said softly.

A movement in the doorway made her spin around. Jake stood in the opening. He looked at the tea things.

"Can I assume that bag on the counter contains Zolanda's special tea?" he asked.

"Yes," Adelaide said. "What's more, there is plenty of it. Why would Thelma Leggett lie? Why would she call me this morning and insist that I come over here immediately?"

Jake met her eyes. "You know the answer to that as well as I do."

"She was trying to set me up to take the fall for the murder of Madam Zolanda."

"Obviously," Jake said. "And I can think of only one good reason why she would do that."

"She's probably the person who is responsible for Zolanda's death."

"If I were the detective investigating this death, I'd certainly consider Leggett my number one suspect," Jake said. "However, it's possible that she simply got scared when she found the body, and decided to run. Regardless, I think she took Zolanda's secrets with her."

"You didn't find the diary you are after, did you?"

"I didn't find it or anything else that looked like blackmail material."

"Maybe Thelma Leggett murdered Zolanda for her stash of extortion secrets," Adelaide said.

"At the moment Leggett is at the top of my personal list. But if I'm right about Zolanda collecting blackmail secrets, we've got a long list of mostly unidentified suspects. She was playing her psychic games with some of the most powerful people in Hollywood. The studios employ fixers whose job it is to get rid of extortionists like her."

It was probably a measure of her paranoia that his words actually lifted her spirits, Adelaide thought. She was oddly relieved by his analysis. If Zolanda was in the blackmail business, a number of people would have had a motive to murder her. There was no reason to assume that the perfume bottle had contained drugs from the lab at the sanitarium.

"We'd better call the police," she said.

Jake raised his brows at her enthusiasm for summoning the authorities, but he did not comment on it.

"Yes," he said. "The longer we wait, the farther away Thelma Leggett will get."

"What, exactly, are we going to tell the police?"

"The truth." Jake crossed to an end table that held an elegant telephone. "Most of it. We'll tell them that this morning you got a phone call from Thelma Leggett pleading for an emergency delivery of tea. When we got here, we found the body and, good citizens that we are, we immediately called the police."

"We don't mention the missing diary, I take it?"

"No," Jake said. "If that diary ever became part of a police investigation, there would be no way to keep the contents out of the press."

"What about us—you and me? The police will wonder why we're both here at this hour of the morning."

Jake tightened his jaw. "My apologies for the failure of chivalry, but I'm afraid we'll have to tell them the truth about that, too."

"You mean we tell them that we spent the night together. Yes, I understand." Adelaide crossed her arms and shook her head, resigned to the inevitable. "They'll assume the worst, of course."

"The worst?"

She glared at him, flushing a little. "They'll think we're involved in an affair. Don't worry, it's not a problem for me. I told you, I'm not concerned with my reputation. This is Burning Cove, after all. People here are much more interested in which leading lady is sleeping with which leading man at the Burning Cove Hotel. They won't care about the private life of a tearoom waitress."

"Maybe not in other circumstances, but as of this morning that tearoom waitress is one of the people who found the body of the psychic to the stars. Don't kid yourself; that will show up in the afternoon edition of the *Burning Cove Herald*."

"Things might be a little awkward for a while." She brightened. "Probably good for business at Refresh, though. Curiosity is bound to bring a lot of people into the shop. Florence will be thrilled."

"That's the spirit; look at the marketing angle." Jake's eyes got colder. "A small reminder, if this case blows up into a full-scale murder investigation, you're not the only one who will need an alibi."

It took a beat before she got his meaning. When she did, she drew a very deep breath.

"Yes, of course," she said. "I never thought of that. You could be viewed as a potential suspect. After all, you believe that Zolanda was an extortionist."

"In other words, I have a very good motive for killing her."

Adelaide unfolded her arms and spread her hands. "Looks like we're stuck with each other."

"I prefer to think of us as allies."

"Right. Allies."

"By the way," Jake said. "I found this in the other room under the liquor cabinet. Would you mind putting it in your handbag?"

He held out the perfume bottle stopper.

The crystal stopper glittered darkly in the palm of his hand. Adelaide got a little light-headed. Jake obviously thought that the stopper was important. That did not bode well.

Reluctantly she crossed the short distance between them, reached out, and plucked the stopper from his palm.

"Can I assume we're not going to tell the police about this, either?" she asked as she dropped it into her handbag.

His smile was razor sharp. "No, we are not going to tell the police about that perfume bottle stopper."

She swallowed hard. "Why not?"

"I doubt if the cops would think it was important, but it might get dumped into an evidence file where we won't be able to get at it."

"Why would we want to get hold of it again?"

"A couple of reasons. The first is that it's the one thing that looked out of place in the living room."

"Most women have bottles of perfume," Adelaide pointed out.

"But most women keep their perfume on their dressing tables, not in their living rooms."

She could not argue with that logic. "What's the second reason for taking it with us?"

"That stopper looks like it belongs to a very expensive bottle of perfume," Jake said. "If we find the missing portion, we might find the killer."

"You really think Zolanda was murdered, don't you?"

"Yes."

He picked up the elegant telephone and dialed the operator.

Chapter 18

"The police are going to conclude that Zolanda jumped to her death, aren't they?" Adelaide said.

Jake looked at her. She sounded almost hopeful—enthusiastic, even—about the possibility that the cops would call the psychic's death a suicide. He couldn't tell what she was thinking, but he was certain that she had undergone a few changes of mood from the time they had discovered the body until that moment in the kitchen when he had given her the top of the perfume bottle.

At the moment she was standing next to him in the gardens at the edge of the patio. They were watching a handful of uniformed officers and a detective named Brandon from the Burning Cove Police Department. A doctor named Skipton, who evidently served as the local medical examiner when one was needed, had taken charge of the body.

"I'm not so sure," he said. "Detective Brandon doesn't like the fact that Thelma Leggett has disappeared. Got a hunch he'll look for her, but if she left town, which seems likely, there's not much he can do. There's no point mentioning my theory that Zolanda was a blackmailer and that Leggett is now in possession of the extortion material, because I have absolutely no proof."

"If the police do find Leggett, they'll probably find the diary."

"Which means I have to find her first."

Adelaide regarded him with a thoughtful expression. "You're planning to look for Thelma Leggett yourself."

"I don't have much choice."

She nodded, accepting the statement. It occurred to him that a lot of women—hell, a lot of people, male and female—would have been more than a little uneasy with the idea of pursuing a private inquiry. But Adelaide didn't seem to have any difficulty with the plan.

Detective Brandon turned away from the body and walked toward them. Brandon was a solid-looking man with the face of a world-weary cop who did his best to do his job. His tie was badly knotted and his jacket was unfastened, revealing his holstered gun. He came to a halt, pushed his hat back on his head, and glanced up at the roof, squinting a little.

"Hard to believe she'd jump just to make her prediction come true," he said.

"Yes," Jake said. "That is hard to believe. "

Brandon switched his attention to Adelaide. "I find it interesting that the missing assistant called you this morning."

"Who else could be counted on to come rushing over here at such an early hour with an emergency packet of tea?" Adelaide said. "I think Thelma Leggett wanted me to find the body."

"Uh-huh," Brandon said. "That theory would seem to indicate that Thelma Leggett knows exactly how Madam Zolanda died."

"Yes, it does," Jake said. "She evidently didn't know if you would accept suicide as the cause of death. Leggett wanted a backup plan. She doesn't want you to look for her."

"Yeah." Brandon studied Adelaide again. "Good thing for you that you've got a real solid alibi, what with you and Mr. Truett having spent the night together and coming over here together this morning."

Adelaide gave him a cold look.

"I think we need to clarify a few things here, Detective," she said. "Mr. Truett and I went to see Zolanda's performance last night. Afterward, Mr. Truett took me home and then went to his cottage. I was getting ready for bed when I got the feeling that there had been an intruder in my house while I was out. I turned on every light. Mr. Truett noticed and came over to see if everything was all right. When we both decided that everything was not all right, Mr. Truett stayed until dawn."

Brandon narrowed his eyes. "Anything missing?"

"No," Adelaide said. "A window was open in the laundry room. I think there was an intruder but he didn't steal anything as far as I can tell."

Brandon nodded sagely. "But Mr. Truett here kept you company for the rest of the night because you were nervous."

"For your information," Adelaide said, "Mr. Truett and I spent the night chatting and playing cards."

"Is that so?" Brandon did not bother to hide his skepticism. He switched his cop glare to Jake. "And you were still at Miss Brockton's place when she got the call from Thelma Leggett?"

"When it got light, I decided to take a look around Adelaide's cottage before I went back to my place," Jake said. "Found a couple of cigarette butts and an empty matchbook out behind the garage. I think someone spent a good portion of the night watching Miss Brockton's house."

"There was a lot of fog late last night," Brandon countered. "Maybe some vagrant decided to spend the night inside a nice dry garage."

"In which case," Jake said, "the cigarette butts and the matchbook probably would have been left inside the garage. I found them on the outside, at the back. A man could have stood there smoking for a couple of hours, and no one inside the house would have noticed."

Brandon frowned at Adelaide. "You sure you had an intruder last night?"

"I can't be absolutely positive," she admitted.

"Yeah, well, let me know if you see anything else that makes you nervous. In the meantime I'll tell the night patrols to make a few extra trips past your place."

"Thank you," Adelaide said. "I would appreciate it."

The low growl of a car rumbled in the drive at the front of the mansion. The engine was shut down immediately. A car door slammed. Seconds later, rapid footsteps sounded on the garden path.

"Just what I needed," Brandon grumbled. "Meet the new crime beat reporter at the *Herald*."

A woman dressed in fashionable full-legged trousers and a pale yellow silk blouse trimmed with a silk tie raced into view. Her shoulder-length hair was set in the deep waves of the newest Hollywood style. She had a leather-bound stenographer's notebook and a pencil in one hand. She zeroed in on Brandon and came to a halt in front of him.

"A fine pal you are, Detective," she said, somewhat breathless. "If Sergeant Morgan hadn't called me, I'd still be eating breakfast out on the patio with Oliver. What's going on?"

Brandon waved a hand at Adelaide and Jake. "Mrs. Ward, allow me to introduce you to Adelaide Brockton. She's a waitress at the Refresh Tearoom. This is her neighbor out on Crescent Beach, Jake Truett."

Adelaide smiled. "No need for an introduction. Irene and I have met."

"Refresh has the best tea and pastries in Burning Cove," Irene said. She peered at Jake. "But this is the first time I've met you. I'm with the *Burning Cove Herald*. I cover the crime beat."

"Thought you didn't have much crime in this town," Jake said.

"You'd be surprised," Irene said. She looked at Adelaide. "Sergeant Morgan told me that you and Mr. Truett found the body. Are you sure it was Madam Zolanda?"

Adelaide waved a hand toward the scene on the patio. Dr. Skipton was getting ready to pull a sheet over the body. "Take a look for yourself."

Irene glanced at the body on the stretcher. "Oh, yes. I see what you mean. She really was a pretty woman, wasn't she?"

"Yes," Adelaide said.

"I wonder why she chose to become the psychic to the stars instead of trying to become a star herself," Irene mused. "Maybe she didn't have any talent."

"She had plenty of talent, if you ask me," Adelaide said. "Just think of how well she played the psychic role."

"You're right." Irene used a pencil to jot down some notes. "She was pretty enough and she had talent, but she didn't have that special something that stars like Vera Westlake have, did she?"

"If you'll excuse me," Brandon said. "I've got a job to do."

"I'll talk to you later," Irene promised.

"Lucky me," Brandon muttered.

He set off at a brisk pace and disappeared into the house.

Irene turned back to Adelaide. "Talk to me. What happened here?"

"It looks like Madam Zolanda may have jumped or was pushed off the roof of the villa sometime during the night," Adelaide explained. "That's really all we know. The only reason we're here is because I got a call from Zolanda's assistant, Thelma Leggett, early this morning. She claimed Zolanda was very upset and needed some of her special tea."

"Hmm." Irene glanced back at the door of the conservatory. "Is Leggett inside the house?"

"No," Jake said. "She seems to have disappeared."

"And Madam Zolanda is dead." Irene snapped her notebook closed. "Looks like I've already got my headline. *Psychic to the Stars Predicts Her Own Death.*"

"I had a feeling you wouldn't be able to resist that one," Adelaide said.

Chapter 19

"We should talk," Jake said.

Adelaide was seated in the passenger seat of the speedster, clutching the packet of Enlightenment tea and her handbag. She was very aware of the crystal perfume bottle stopper inside her bag.

She gave Jake a quick, uneasy glance. He did not take his eyes off the upcoming curve in Cliff Road. His driving, like everything else he did, had an easy, fluid, masculine grace.

"All right," she said. "What do you want to talk about?"

She was starting to feel as if she was ensnared in a spider's web. Intuition warned her that the safest course of action was to say as little as possible. Jake had his own priorities—he was after the missing diary. But she had priorities, too. At all costs she had to keep her history at Rushbrook Sanitarium a secret. She could not expect him to believe a word she said—not if he found out that she had escaped from an asylum for the insane.

Jake slowed the car, turned off onto a side road, and came to a stop overlooking a small, secluded beach.

With cool deliberation he shut down the engine and turned to face her. He rested his left hand casually on the wooden steering wheel. His right arm settled on the back of the seat, a position that put his hand directly behind her head.

"The situation is getting complicated," he said.

"You mean because Thelma Leggett has disappeared with that diary you're after?"

"It's not just that she's gone," Jake said. "Until this morning I've been assuming that I was chasing a blackmailer. I'm still sure that's the case but I don't think it's the whole story."

Her stomach knotted. "I don't understand."

"I'm starting to think that Zolanda and Leggett may have been involved in something more than garden-variety blackmail."

"What makes you suspect that?"

But she knew the answer.

"Your intruder last night," he said.

She almost stopped breathing. "How could there possibly be a connection?"

Her voice sounded thin. She was going to have to get better at playing the role of innocent tearoom waitress or she would find herself back at Rushbrook.

"I have no idea," Jake said. "But there must be one. Otherwise we are looking at an amazing coincidence."

"Coincidence?"

That sounded stronger, she decided, as if she was interested but not panicky.

"I'm told there's very little in the way of serious crime in Burning Cove, so what are the odds that someone breaks into your cottage and then hangs around outside to watch your place on the very same night that Madam Zolanda gets murdered?"

"I have no idea," she said. "What are the odds?"

"I'm not sure, either, but whatever they are, I don't like them. I have a hunch that one way or another, everything that happened last night and early this morning is connected."

She clenched her fingers around her handbag. "You sound very certain."

"I told you, I used to be in the import-export business."

"And you carried a gun because it was a dangerous business."

"Yes," Jake said.

He did not elaborate.

Adelaide sat quietly in the seat, trying to find logic in the chaos of the ominous currents that were swirling around her. She couldn't stop a force of nature like Jake Truett. The best she could hope to do was gain some control over his investigation. She reminded herself that recovering a diary filled with secrets was his primary objective.

"Thelma Leggett is the key to this situation," she said finally.

"One of the keys, yes."

"The police are looking for her, but as you pointed out, if she left town, there's not much they can do about finding her."

"No," Jake agreed. "And if Dr. Skipton rules Zolanda's death a suicide, Detective Brandon will have no reason to waste his time searching for a missing assistant."

Adelaide gathered her nerve. "Doesn't mean we can't look for her."

Jake looked intrigued. "Sounds like you've got a plan to do that."

"I told you, I've got a friend who just opened a detective agency here in town. Finding people is her specialty."

"The lady private investigator who checked into my background?"

"Yes, Raina Kirk. Do you have a problem with the idea of hiring a female investigator?"

"No," Jake said. "It's just that I've never met one before. Are there any other detective agencies in town?"

"Not that I know of. Raina is our only option. She needs the business and I think we can trust her."

"You *think* we can trust her?"

Adelaide gazed straight ahead through the windshield and contemplated the disaster that had enveloped her the last time she took the leap of faith that real trust always demanded. She had been very naïve. But this was different, she thought.

"You can't ever be absolutely positive that a person is trustworthy, can you?" she said. "People lie all the time. But, yes, I think that we can trust Raina. She is new in town and she is trying to establish a reputation here in Burning Cove."

"I see," Jake said.

She turned her head to look at him. He was watching her with a very intent expression. A shiver of dark awareness chilled the back of her neck.

"You're wondering if you can trust me, aren't you?" she asked.

He gave her a cold smile. "And you're asking the same questions about me."

"We don't know much about each other."

"No," he agreed. "But as you pointed out, we're stuck with each other. We are each other's alibi for last night."

"Assuming we might actually need alibis," she said.

"When you're dealing with murder, it's always a good idea to have an alibi, especially if you're the one who discovered the body. In my experience, cops are usually suspicious of the person who reports the death."

"You're convinced Zolanda was murdered?"

"Until proven otherwise, yes." Jake glanced at the gold watch on his left wrist. "We can't afford to lose any time. When can I meet Raina Kirk?"

"I'm sure there won't be any problem getting an appointment for today."

"Good." Jake took his arm off the back of the seat and turned around to start the car. "How do you feel about taking in a boarder?"

She went very still. "You?"

He put the speedster in gear. "Look on the bright side—I may be out of work but I can afford the rent."

"You're convinced that we're involved in something that might be very dangerous, aren't you?"

"A blackmailer is dead and her assistant is probably in possession of a lot of secrets, including a certain diary," Jake said. "Yes, I think we're involved in something dangerous."

"As of this morning, my reputation is in tatters and, as it happens, I have an extra bedroom," she said. "I wouldn't mind taking in a boarder. To be honest, I could use the extra money to help make ends meet."

Chapter 20

Raina drew on all of the cool composure she had cultivated in her career as a professional secretary at a prestigious New York law firm. She needed the business, but Luther Pell would be a dangerous client.

"Exactly what is it you want me to do, Mr. Pell?" she asked.

"Someone is stealing some of my most expensive liquor," Luther said. "The losses are never serious enough to warrant calling in the police. A few bottles of good whiskey one week, some French champagne the next. At first my manager and I attributed the missing items to inventory errors."

"I see." She opened her notebook and picked up a sharpened pencil. "I'm sure you go through a lot of liquor at your nightclub."

Luther raised his brows. "Do you disapprove of my business, Miss Kirk?"

"I have no problems with it unless you are engaged in some illegal activities on the side. I'm new here in town. I can't afford to take any case that might get me into trouble with the local police."

"No need to worry about that. If the cops give you any problems, I'll have a word with the chief." Luther smiled. "My relationship with the Burning Cove Police Department is excellent."

"Because you pay the cops very well to look the other way?"

Luther assumed a pained expression. "This isn't L.A., Miss Kirk, and I don't own a powerful movie studio. I don't buy and sell the local police. I'm just a businessman, one who, at the moment, happens to have a small but rather annoying inventory problem."

Luther Pell was certainly a businessman, but her intuition warned her that that was only one of many guises that he adopted to confront the world. There was a lot more going on beneath the surface of the man, and she was sure that some of it was profoundly complicated.

He was in his late thirties, maybe three or four years older than her, but his eyes were those of a man who had seen too much darkness. Someone had mentioned that he had served in the Great War. She did not doubt it. Violence, she reflected, always left its mark.

Tall and lean, he wore his fashionable drape-cut linen jacket and immaculately creased trousers with an air of casual sophistication. There was some interesting gray in his jet-black hair, which he wore parted on the side, lightly oiled and brushed straight back in the style made fashionable by stars such as Cary Grant.

Her plan had been to start her agency by attracting a female clientele on the assumption that women would feel more comfortable confiding in another woman than in a male investigator. She had been floored when the owner of the Paradise Club walked through her door a short time ago. She didn't count the phone calls to L.A. that she had made to confirm the identity of Jake Truett. Those calls were favors for a friend.

"Forgive me, Miss Kirk, but I'm getting the impression that you are not interested in taking my case," Luther said.

"I need the business," she said. "But I'll admit you aren't exactly the kind of client I was expecting to attract."

"Should I be insulted?" Luther asked a little too gently.

Alarmed, she sat forward very quickly. The last thing she needed was to make an enemy of Luther Pell. He and his very good friend Oliver Ward, the owner of the Burning Cove Hotel, exerted a great deal of influence in town. Individually, either one of them could destroy her business before she even got it going.

"I am well aware that you are a powerful figure in Burning Cove," she said. "But rumor has it that you are connected to certain individuals who operate casinos in Nevada. In addition, I understand you have an interest in at least one of the gambling boats anchored off of Santa Monica."

Luther nodded solemnly, taking the implied criticism in stride. "I'm impressed. You're well-informed for a newcomer."

"My business depends on knowing who controls what in Burning Cove."

"If it helps, I recently sold my interest in the gambling boat."

"Any particular reason?"

Luther moved a hand in a vague gesture of dismissal. "The gaming business is changing. Reno is where the action is these days, and now that the dam has been completed, Las Vegas may become even more profitable. The offshore casinos won't be able to compete."

"Why not?"

"Do you have any idea how hard it is to keep a large boat in good repair when it is sitting in salt water day in and day out?"

Raina blinked, a little taken aback. "I never thought about the upkeep problems."

"Trust me when I tell you that rust and salt corrosion are relentless forces of nature."

"I'll take your word for it."

"I assure you I am content with my nightclub here in Burning Cove," Luther continued. "I have discovered that there is no need to dabble in illegal sidelines, not as long as I'm selling a reliable fantasy."

She realized that, although she was still wary of Luther Pell, she was also fascinated by him.

"What, exactly, is the fantasy that you sell?" she asked.

Luther got to his feet and walked to the window of the office. He contemplated the shady plaza.

"When people walk into the Paradise Club, they do not merely get a glimpse of a glamorous world. For the time that they are in my club, they are inhabitants of that world."

"In other words, they participate in the fantasy?"

"Exactly. That's the secret of any form of successful entertainment. The audience must be completely involved. At the Paradise Club the patrons know that there is a very good chance that a Hollywood celebrity or a powerful studio executive is sitting in the adjacent booth. A lady can always hope that a famous movie star will ask her to dance. Gentlemen know that they are rubbing shoulders with some very important people, including the occasional mobster."

She suppressed a shudder. "I understand that a woman might be thrilled to dance with a leading man, but why would anyone want to rub shoulders with a mobster?"

Luther turned around to face her. He looked amused. "Organized crime is the dark side of the legitimate business world, Miss Kirk. The same powerful forces are at work. And power, regardless of the source, is always fascinating."

"Only to those who have not been burned by it," she said before she could stop herself. "Sensible people are cautious when dealing with powerful individuals."

"I take it you have been burned by someone who wielded a lot of power?"

"We are not here to discuss my personal life, Mr. Pell."

He raised one shoulder in an elegant shrug. "The point I am trying to make is that I do know what I am selling at the Paradise Club."

"A fantasy."

"A fantasy with just enough reality infused into it to make it seem very, very real."

"That is very insightful of you."

"You sound surprised."

"I am quite sure that you always know exactly what you're doing, Mr. Pell." She tapped the pencil on the notepad. "I do have a question for you."

"You want to know why I haven't taken this problem to my own security team."

"Yes. Can I assume that means you suspect one of your security people might be involved in the pilfering?"

"It's not exactly pilfering, Miss Kirk. We're talking about small but steady losses that, if they continue, will add up to a considerable amount of money over time. And, yes, there is a possibility that someone on my security force is behind the theft. It would explain how someone is managing to sneak the liquor out of the locked storage room without being detected." Luther glanced at his watch. "I have another appointment. I'd like to get this matter settled. Will you take my case or not?"

She hesitated only a couple of seconds. A successful conclusion to a case that had been brought to her by one of the most powerful men in Burning Cove would do wonders to establish her agency.

"Yes," she said. "I'll take the case."

"Excellent." Luther smiled a very satisfied smile. "You'll want a retainer."

"Of course." In spite of her uncertainties about Luther Pell, she got an odd little rush of excitement. She had landed her very first case. She was now a real private investigator. "I'll want to take a look around your club. I'll need to assess your current security arrangements so that I can analyze possible weak points."

"Whenever it's convenient for you," he agreed. "Just say the word."

She pretended to study her calendar. The only appointment on it was the one she had made a few minutes ago with Adelaide.

"I'm free tomorrow morning," she said, trying to make it sound as if she could just barely squeeze him into her busy schedule.

"I'll tell my men to expect you," Luther said. "Thank you, Miss Kirk. I'll look forward to working with you."

He wrote out a check and left with the air of a man who had accomplished his objective and now had other important things to do.

She sat quietly for a time, thinking about Luther Pell. She was pleased to have the business, but her intuition told her that something did not feel right. After a moment or two she realized what was bothering her.

Luther Pell had not tried to probe deeply into her previous investigative experience. He had accepted her carefully prepared cover story without so much as a single question. That should have been reassuring but for some reason it was not.

She had dealt with dangerous men in the past. If there was one thing she knew for certain, it was that such men did not do business with people whose backgrounds they had not thoroughly researched. She cast her mind back, recalling every aspect of her departure from New York. She had planned her exit carefully and paid attention to every detail. She was almost certain that there was nothing for Luther to discover that might make him question her story.

Almost certain.

Chapter 21

Thelma Leggett opened the trunk of the aging sedan and removed the hatbox containing the stash of secrets. It had been her idea, which she hadn't shared with Zolanda, to conceal the blackmail materials in the back of the limo. Her theory had been that it was a far more secure location than the villa. Anyone, including the housekeeper who came in daily, could search the big house while the occupants were out. But it was far less likely that a potential thief would look for a hatbox in the back of a car.

There had been another reason for storing the secrets in the limo's locked trunk. With rare exceptions the car was usually close at hand, where Thelma, in her role as chauffeur, could keep an eye on it. Early that morning when she had dumped the big car in favor of the old sedan she had stolen in a poor neighborhood, she had simply transferred the hatbox from one vehicle to the other. It had been a shame to get rid of the limousine but she had no option. It was far too memorable.

The shabby old cabin on the outskirts of the decaying seaside town had been deserted for a while now. It was filthy and in need of repairs.

There were indications that various rodents and a few transients had taken up residence from time to time. Definitely not the sort of classy accommodations she had become accustomed to during the three years that she and Zolanda had been running the psychic-to-the-stars game, Thelma concluded. But the one-room structure had a very big advantage—none of Zolanda's clients knew about it. No one could follow her here.

The cabin had belonged to her uncle. She remembered him as a cheerful, fun-loving man who had always arrived on his sister's doorstep with toys and candy for his niece. But he had come home from the Great War a changed man. He had retreated to the cabin, where he had done odd jobs around town while he proceeded to drink himself to death.

He had left the dilapidated structure to Thelma's mother, who had tried unsuccessfully to sell it. After her death, Thelma had inherited it.

There was a faded For Sale sign in the window. She had put it there a couple of years ago but no buyer had come along. In hindsight, that was a very fortunate turn of events.

She set the hatbox on the sagging bed and removed the lid with shaking fingers. She was consumed with a feverish excitement. What she planned to do was extremely dangerous, but she needed cash and she needed it quickly.

She studied the contents of the hatbox and considered her options. She had known that if she disappeared in the wake of Zolanda's so-called suicide, the cops would want to question her. She was reasonably certain that in the end they would have let her go for lack of evidence. But she did not dare hang around Burning Cove long enough to go through the formalities. She had more immediate problems to worry about.

She had called Adelaide Blake-Brockton that morning from a gas station, anticipating that no one would answer the phone. She had assumed that by dawn Adelaide would be dead or missing. But with Zolanda dead instead, the entire situation had changed. So she had placed the call in an attempt to find out if the plan to get rid of a certain tearoom waitress had been carried out successfully.

No one had been more surprised than she was when Adelaide herself had answered.

Sending Adelaide to the villa that morning to discover Zolanda's body had been an inspiration of the moment. At the very least it would muddy the waters and help make Brockton look like a suspect. But that plan, too, had gone awry. According to the radio, the tearoom waitress had not been alone when she discovered the dead psychic to the stars. A certain businessman from Los Angeles had been with her.

Adelaide Brockton was a problem for Gill and Paxton, Thelma decided. But Jake Truett was another matter. It was no longer safe to assume that his presence in Burning Cove was a coincidence. He was on the trail of the diary. She had to run as far and as fast as possible, but for that she needed money—a lot of it.

She reached into the hatbox and shuffled through an assortment of potentially damning photographs, letters, journals, and papers. All of the items were valuable, but the one that would be the easiest to cash in immediately was in an envelope at the bottom of the box.

She pawed through the pile of secrets until she found the one she wanted. She took it out of the box and replaced the lid.

The next step was to find a pay phone. There were a lot of people who would be willing to pay a great deal of money for the contents of the envelope, but she knew who would pay the most.

She put the lid on the box, crossed the room, and opened the door. She paused for a moment, thinking. She had another piece of time-sensitive information that was worth a lot to one individual. It could be used only once, and it would not hold its value for long. The smart thing to do would be to sell it first. Easy money and there was no danger involved.

After she had collected that payoff she would arrange to cash in the far more dangerous contents of the envelope.

She glanced at her watch. It was not yet eight o'clock. She was exhausted because she had been on the road since finding Zolanda's body early that morning and there had been the added stress of stealing the vehicle. But she could not rest. She had two phone calls to make.

Chapter 22

"Are you sure you want to hire me for this job?" Raina said. "According to the radio, the cops are already searching for Thelma Leggett. I hate to say this because I would dearly love the business, but I'm afraid that hiring me would be a waste of your money. The authorities will probably find her long before I do."

"Mr. Truett thinks the police are likely to conclude that Madam Zolanda's death was a suicide and that Thelma Leggett found the body, panicked, and fled," Adelaide said. "If they don't think they're looking for a killer, they won't look very hard."

She and Jake had discussed exactly what they would tell Raina. Now they were sitting in the plush office of Kirk Investigations, and already the conversation was veering off course.

"I get the feeling you think Leggett murdered her boss," Raina said. "Zolanda was the one who brought in the cash. Why would the assistant kill the goose that laid the golden eggs?"

It was a reasonable question, Adelaide thought. She looked at Jake, making it clear that it was up to him how much information he wanted to divulge. He was the one chasing a blackmailer.

He gave the matter some thought and then, to her surprise, he responded honestly.

"I have reason to think that Zolanda was running a blackmail business," he said. "She conned someone I know out of a certain item which, if it fell into the wrong hands, could prove embarrassing to the victim's family. I have a hunch that Leggett is now in possession of that item."

Raina looked satisfied with the response, even sympathetic.

"All right, now I understand why you are anxious to get to Leggett before the police do," she said.

"I'm a little irritated with Thelma Leggett, too," Adelaide said. "She tried to set me up to look like a suspect if the cops do decide Zolanda was murdered. Not that I'm one to hold a grudge."

"Of course not," Raina said. "Only very petty people hold grudges. Still, in your situation I'd be rather annoyed myself. It does occur to me that it is fortunate that you and Mr. Truett both have ironclad alibis, however."

Adelaide winced. "You've heard the gossip already?"

"Well, this is a small town and news travels fast," Raina said somewhat apologetically. "I'm afraid I also read the special edition of the *Burning Cove Herald*. It came out an hour ago."

She gestured toward the folded newspaper on her desk. Adelaide picked it up and opened it. The story carried Irene Ward's byline.

Psychic to the Stars Predicts Her Own Death

Early this morning a local tearoom waitress and a visiting businessman from Los Angeles discovered the body of Madam Zolanda, the famous Psychic to the Stars. Your cor-

respondent arrived in time to view the shocking scene and
interview the witnesses, who were clearly shaken. Readers
will recall that Madam Zolanda predicted blood and death
at the end of what proved to be her final performance . . .

Adelaide tossed the paper aside, grimly resigned to the inevitable.
"This story is going to go national."

"As we speak," Raina said.

"Will you take our case?" Jake asked.

"Yes," Raina said, "but I have to warn you again, you may be wasting your money."

"I doubt that the Burning Cove police have what you would call
extensive resources outside of this town," Jake said. "Adelaide tells me
that you, on the other hand, have some connections with investigation
agencies around the country. She said you were able to call someone in
L.A. to confirm my identity."

Raina switched her attention to Adelaide. "You told him?"

"Yes. Raina, I think an intruder entered my cottage while we were
at the theater. I was nervous. Mr. Truett kindly offered to stay with me
until morning."

Raina frowned. "What's this about an intruder?"

"We don't know anything about him except that he watched the
house for a considerable portion of the night and smoked a few cigarettes," Jake said. "Found the butts this morning. Evidently he was
waiting for me to leave."

Raina turned back to Adelaide, clearly troubled. "Did you notify
the police?"

"I mentioned it to Detective Brandon this morning," Adelaide said.
"He promised to increase the night patrols that go by my cottage."

"Meanwhile, Miss Brockton has been kind enough to allow me to
board at her place until the police find out who was watching her house
last night," Jake added.

"I've got an extra bedroom," Adelaide said quickly. "And I could use the money."

Raina looked both amused and satisfied. "That sounds like an excellent plan." She reached for a leather-bound notebook. "I'll start looking for Thelma Leggett."

Chapter 23

Conrad Massey put down the phone, stunned. If the woman who had just called him long-distance was telling the truth, it meant that Gill had been lying to him from the start.

He stared at the phone while he struggled to control the acid-hot rage that was threatening to take control of his senses.

"How stupid do you think I am, you double-crossing son of a bitch?" he said.

But there was no one to hear him. He was alone in his study. He shoved himself to his feet and stalked to the window. On a clear day he had a view of San Francisco Bay and the spectacular new bridge they had named for the strait that it spanned—the Golden Gate. But today the scene was locked in fog.

The weather suited his mood.

The woman who had just telephoned him wanted cash in exchange for the location of Adelaide Blake. Fine. He was happy to pay. The question was, why had Gill lied? They had made a deal.

It was possible that Gill simply didn't want him to interfere, but that didn't make any sense. Gill needed the cash that he was receiving for keeping Adelaide locked up at Rushbrook.

Conrad clenched one hand into a fist. He had to get control of the situation. He had worked too hard and sacrificed too much to watch his carefully planned future go up in flames. He was trying to rebuild an empire and he needed Adelaide Blake's inheritance to do it.

His grandfather had come to San Francisco along with the other great men who had made their fortunes in railroads. The old man had stayed to found the shipping business that had established the Masseys as one of the most respected families in the city.

The first Massey mansion had been built on Nob Hill, sharing the elegant neighborhood with the houses of the other tycoons of the day—Stanford, Huntington, Hopkins, and Crocker. The original Massey mansion had been destroyed in the 1906 earthquake and the fire that followed. But like his wealthy neighbors, his grandfather had rebuilt, albeit in a different area of town.

In due course the shipping business and the new mansion had passed into the hands of Conrad's father, Emmett. That transition had proven disastrous. The empire that had managed to survive the devastating impact of the earthquake and the fire, the empire that should have prospered during the Great War, could not survive inept management at the top.

Conrad had known, even as a child, that his father was weak. Emmett Massey had cared more about the details of his busy social life—his clubs and his mistresses—than he had about the business. Not wanting to be bothered with the day-to-day decision making and the long-range planning required to keep the firm going strong, he had dumped the responsibilities onto the shoulders of his managers, bankers, and lawyers. The finely tuned machine that was Massey Shipping had faltered. The crash had finished the job. The company plummeted into bankruptcy. Six months later, Emmett suffered a stroke and died.

Conrad was eighteen when he inherited the ruins of what had once been a powerful financial empire. He had been determined to rebuild, but the dark clouds of the depression that had settled on the country had blocked him at every turn.

No bank would touch him because of the bankruptcy, so in the end he had made the mistake of borrowing money at outrageous interest rates from a very dangerous tycoon. He had used the cash to relaunch Massey Shipping. There was hope on the horizon, especially given the fact that the world was surely falling into yet another worldwide conflict.

There were fortunes to be made when great nations went to war. The government would need ships and the crews that knew how to man them. It would require the expertise of captains who had sailed the treacherous seas of the Pacific Ocean and were well acquainted with far-flung ports of call. Massey Shipping would be ideally positioned to reap enormous profits when war was declared. The company would do its duty for the nation—for a price.

The future had at last begun to come into focus, Conrad thought. But now the man who had loaned him the money was demanding that the entire amount plus interest be paid by the end of the year. They both knew that was impossible.

Conrad had finally understood that his generous benefactor had intended that outcome from the beginning. The bastard planned to take over Massey Shipping and rake in the enormous profits generated by the war effort.

Conrad had been so desperate that he had contemplated murder. The only thing that had stopped him from making the attempt was knowing that the tycoon's equally ruthless sons would step into their father's shoes.

It had all seemed hopeless. The only thing that had kept him going was the fire of rage and ambition that burned within him. He was willing to sacrifice anything and anyone. Dr. Ethan Gill had offered up Miss Adelaide Blake, a sheltered, naïve librarian who had found herself alone in the world and in possession of a valuable inheritance. Gill had assured him that Adelaide was mentally unbalanced and that she was better off in the asylum.

The sacrifice had been performed, Conrad thought, but things had gone wrong. In the end it was necessary to tell some lies and forge some papers, but Adelaide had finally vanished into the Rushbrook Sanitarium. He did not know exactly why Gill had been so anxious to get hold of Adelaide, and Conrad had not asked. The truth was that he did not want to know.

But Adelaide had stunned them all by escaping the locked ward at Rushbrook. And now Gill was lying about her whereabouts.

Conrad reflected on the conversation he'd had on the phone a short time ago. The caller had been a woman who had refused to identify herself.

"I know where Adelaide Blake is. For a price, I'll give you the information. But you'd better move fast because Gill already knows where she's hiding out. The only reason he and his pal haven't grabbed her already is because they haven't figured out how to do it without drawing the attention of the local police. Miss Brockton—that's the name she's using these days—has friends now, you see. If she goes missing, people will start looking for her."

"I can handle Adelaide Blake or Brockton or whatever she's calling herself," he'd said. *"Just tell me how much you want for the information and where you want me to leave the money."*

The anonymous caller had named the price and given him the location where the transaction would take place. She had warned him not to be late. He had agreed instantly although it involved a long drive to the rendezvous point, a gas station outside a small rural town on Highway 101. He glanced at his watch. It was a little after eight in the morning. He would pack a bag and leave immediately.

Gill and whoever he was working with might not be smart enough to figure out how to get control of Adelaide without drawing the attention of the cops, but that would not be a problem for him, Conrad thought. He had been able to make her fall in love with him once. He could do it again.

Chapter 24

The following morning the Refresh Tearoom was packed.

"Business is certainly booming today," Florence declared. She set the teapot down on the counter and surveyed the packed tearoom through the kitchen doorway. "Maybe you should find dead bodies more often."

"Don't say that." Adelaide carefully measured tea into a pot. "I'm still trying to get the scene out of my head. It was awful, Flo. She was just lying there, all crumpled up on the patio."

The Refresh Tearoom had been busy from the moment it opened. The questions had been incessant but Adelaide came up with a standard reply: *Sorry. Can't talk about it. Police are still investigating.* When the investigation was concluded, she planned to rewrite the script: *Sorry. Can't talk about it. Too upsetting. I'm sure you understand.*

"I think you should know that it's all over town that Jake Truett spent the night at your place," Florence warned in low tones. "And that he was with you when you found the dead psychic."

"I told you, Mr. Truett is my new boarder. I need the money."

"I heard you the first time," Florence said. "But that's not going to stop the gossip. You might need the cash but Truett doesn't need the cheap rent. He could afford to stay at the Burning Cove Hotel."

"He prefers the privacy of a cottage on the beach."

"Not much privacy at your place, is there? You're sharing the same bathroom now."

Last night the shared bathroom had not been a problem, Adelaide reflected. She had been too exhausted to care that there was a man in her cottage. The sleepless night before the discovery of Zolanda's body followed by the long day spent talking to the police and hiring Raina had ensured her first solid night's sleep in months.

Jake had been a perfect gentleman. Knowing that he was sleeping just down the hall had given her the first real peace of mind she had experienced since the awful night when she was locked up at Rushbrook.

She had to admit she had been severely jolted that morning, however, when, still groggy from sleep, she opened the bathroom door and found Jake, nude to the waist, shaving in front of a steamy mirror. They both apologized and she backed out of the small space immediately. But once she recovered from the shock, she had concluded that she could quickly become accustomed to the sight of Jake without a shirt. He had a very nicely muscled back and excellent shoulders.

"There's plenty of room at my cottage," she said to Florence.

"Honey, you don't have to pretend, not with me. I'm your friend, remember? I'm glad that you and Truett are having a little summer fling. I just want to be sure you understand that when he goes back to L.A., that'll be the end of it. Do yourself a favor. Don't start dreaming of wedding gowns and gold rings."

Adelaide thought about the gold ring in the safe under her bed. A shiver of icy horror swept through her. "Trust me when I tell you that I am definitely not making wedding plans."

Florence eyed her closely for a few seconds and then nodded once, evidently satisfied with what she saw. "I can't help but notice that your new boarder has very conveniently managed to escape all the curiosity seekers. He hasn't been in for his usual cup of green tea this morning."

"Jake went into town to pick up a few things at the hardware store," Adelaide said. "He wants to do some minor repairs on my cottage."

There was no need to add that he had left with a shopping list that included new locks and the tools required to install them.

"Does he, now? Well, well, well. Wouldn't have thought a rich businessman from L.A. would make a good handyman."

"I think he's trying to make himself useful," Adelaide said.

That was no less than the truth, she decided.

Florence peered at her. "Speaking of Mr. Truett and his exhausted nerves, how did he handle the scene at Madam Zolanda's villa yesterday morning? Must have been a real shock for him. I gather he didn't faint or have hysterics."

Adelaide thought about how quickly Jake had approached the body, checked for a pulse, and then searched the villa.

"Nope," she said.

Florence chuckled. "Had a hunch that might be the case. I don't think there's anything wrong with his nerves."

"I agree," Adelaide said. "But he needs a job, Flo."

Florence got a speculative expression. "Heard he used to be in the import-export business. That covers a lot of territory, if you take my meaning."

Adelaide remembered Raina's comments on the subject of Jake's former line of business.

"Are you implying that Mr. Truett is a shady character?" she asked.

"Well, I'm told that he and Luther Pell are friends of long standing."

Startled, Adelaide set the kettle down on the stove with more force than she had intended. She spun around to look at Florence.

"Who told you that?" she demanded.

"A friend of mine whose son works as a valet at the Paradise Club said that Pell has invited Truett for drinks in Pell's private quarters above the club a few times since Truett arrived in town," Florence said. "Heard they've played a couple of rounds of golf together, too."

Adelaide wasn't sure why she was taken aback by that information, but for some reason it left her strangely disconcerted.

"I had no idea," she said. "Jake . . . Mr. Truett . . . never mentioned that he knew Luther Pell."

"Nothing to worry about, I'm sure," Florence said quickly. "It's just that everyone says Pell has connections in the gambling world, and that world is one hundred percent in the shade. And then there's the fact that Pell owns a nightclub here in town. A lot of folks would say that is another shady line of work."

"Yes, I know."

Adelaide told herself she had no right to be blindsided. Jake had a right to his secrets. Nevertheless, a long-standing friendship with Luther Pell probably ought to be cause for concern. Florence was right. Gambling and nightclubs were shady businesses.

Not necessarily illegal, she reminded herself, just . . . shady.

The bell chimed over the front door of the tearoom, distracting her. She glanced through the kitchen doorway in time to see Vera Westlake make an entrance.

An expectant hush fell over the tearoom. Unlike most celebrities who showed up at Refresh, Vera Westlake always arrived unaccompanied and she always sat alone at her favorite table. There was no assistant, no publicist, no gossip columnist, no male companion with her. Adelaide smiled to herself. Evidently, Westlake did not need an entourage to remind those in the vicinity that she was a star. She had the power to command every eye in the room. But, then, she had it all—elegance, glamour, talent, beauty, and that magical quality called presence. When she was in the room, it was hard to look away from her.

She had a few trademarks. One was her maroon lipstick. She also had a habit of appearing in public dressed in a single color from head

to toe. Today was no exception. Every item of clothing that she wore—
the flowing, high-waisted silk trousers, the silk blouse with its billow-
ing sleeves, the chunky-heeled sandals, and the little confection of a
felt hat—was in a rich shade of cream. Her dark hair was parted on the
side and fell in waves to her shoulders. Her eyes were enhanced with
mascara and eyeliner. Her brows were thin and gracefully arched.

She seemed utterly oblivious to the fact that everyone in the tearoom was staring at her.

"Movie stars," Adelaide whispered. "Not a subtle bunch, are they?"

"No, but they can sure sell tea," Florence said.

"True. There's an additional benefit to having Miss Westlake drop
in for tea this morning. Her presence will change the topic of conversation out there."

"Don't hold your breath." Florence wiped her hands on a towel. "I'll
get her seated while you fix her tea. Expect she'll be wanting her usual."

Florence bustled out of the kitchen. Adelaide got busy preparing a
fresh pot of Tranquility tea.

Florence hurried back into the kitchen. "She wants to talk to you."

Adelaide groaned. "You mean she wants to interrogate me about
what happened yesterday morning?"

"Probably. Apparently everyone, including some movie stars, is interested in the psychic who predicted her own death."`

"I'm going to stick with my story. As long as the cops are investigating, I can't say much."

"Good luck."

Adelaide set the teapot and a dainty cup and saucer on a tray. "I'll
be polite. I just won't give her any information."

"You could try changing the subject by asking her about the wonders of that diet drink she's always so eager to talk about."

Adelaide shook her head. "I can't understand how she could allow
herself to believe that diet tonic actually works. Paxton is nothing but
a snake oil salesman."

Florence chuckled. "If the rumors are true, she's having an affair with Dr. Paxton. Maybe she's in love with the man and just wants to do him a favor by helping him market his tonic."

"Maybe. But I'm telling you, the reason Paxton's tonic has been so successful is that fancy bottle. Packaging is the key. I need to work on our tea labels. Also, we need a catchy slogan."

"No need to fuss with the labels and such, not when we've got stars like Vera Westlake dropping in for a pot of one of your special tea blends."

Adelaide smiled. "You're right. Miss Westlake may be promoting Paxton's tonic, but she's also selling a lot of tea for us, isn't she?"

"Yes, indeed," Florence said.

Adelaide carried the tray with the pot of Tranquility tea out into the tearoom and set it down on Vera's table. She had to resist the urge to curtsy.

"Good morning, Miss Westlake," she said. "Thank you so much for stopping by Refresh today. I've got your special blend brewing in the pot. It will be ready in a few minutes. Would you care for some tea cakes or cookies?"

"You mustn't tempt me," Vera said with a languid smile. "When I crave sweets, I reach for a bottle Dr. Paxton's Diet Tonic. It works wonders. I wouldn't want to spoil the effects by snacking on cakes and cookies."

Vera had the smoky voice of a nightclub singer. She managed to make the sales pitch for Paxton's tonic sound like an invitation to an exclusive private party. Adelaide knew that everyone in the tearoom had just heard her praise.

"Will there be anything else?" Adelaide asked.

"I understand that you're the one who found Madam Zolanda yesterday morning." Vera visibly shuddered. "It must have been a terrible shock for you."

"Yes, it was," Adelaide said. "I'm afraid I can't talk about it. The police are still investigating."

"According to the local paper, you were not alone."

"No, I wasn't alone."

Vera sighed. "One shouldn't speak ill of the dead, but Madam Zolanda was a fraud."

Adelaide cleared her throat. "A lot of people are convinced that she had genuine psychic powers."

"Nonsense. There is no such thing as paranormal abilities."

"You were not one of her clients, then?"

"Of course not." Vera looked out the window, a faraway expression on her lovely face. "Still, it's all very sad, isn't it? She must have been planning to take her own life when she made that final prediction. She would have loved seeing herself in the headlines."

"You were at the Palace when Zolanda gave her final performance?"

"Yes. Dr. Paxton wanted to attend. He thought it would be amusing. He asked me to go with him, so I did."

"I'm surprised, given your opinion of Zolanda's talents."

Vera turned away from the view out the window and smiled a surprisingly wistful smile. "Don't misunderstand me. While I'm certain Zolanda had no real paranormal talents, I did find her act entertaining. You saw the audience. Everyone enjoyed the performance."

"Yes."

"I was not one of her clients but I was acquainted with her. She and I were both aspiring actresses at one time."

"I see," Adelaide said.

"We showed up at the same casting calls. Occasionally we had drinks together. But when I got the lead in *Dark Road*, everything changed. It's very difficult to maintain a friendship between two people who are competing for the same roles."

"I understand."

"Believe it or not, I was very happy for Zolanda when she came up with the psychic routine. It seemed to be working brilliantly. She must have been making a lot of money. She had all the publicity she could possibly want. Half the stars in Hollywood were clamoring for private consultations. I can't believe she took her own life. Suicide makes no sense."

"Perhaps the police will be able to find some answers," Adelaide said.

Vera's eyes narrowed a little. "If you ask me, they need to track down her assistant. I hear she went missing around the time of Zolanda's death. Sounds suspicious to me."

"I wouldn't know anything about that." Adelaide hoisted the empty tray. "If you'll excuse me, I should get back to the kitchen."

"Of course. I'm sure it's been very difficult for you and that businessman from L.A. who was with you when you found Zolanda's body. Thank goodness he happened along when he did, hmm?"

Adelaide went still. "I beg your pardon?"

"I just meant that it was a lucky break for you. After all, things could have been a bit awkward with the police if you had been alone when you discovered Zolanda's body."

Adelaide decided she'd had about enough. She fixed Vera with a steady gaze. "What makes you say that, Miss Westlake?"

Vera's eyes widened in an expression of pure innocence. "It just occurred to me that the police might have wondered why you happened to be on the scene of such an unusual death so early in the morning."

Adelaide managed what she hoped was coolly amused smile. "By any chance are you trying out for the role of a lady detective in your next film, Miss Westlake?"

Vera looked startled for an instant. Then she gave a throaty little laugh. "I admit that, like everyone else in town, I'm curious about the death of Madam Zolanda. She never became a star on the silver screen, but she was certainly a Hollywood celebrity. I know several of her clients. It was amazing how many people fell for her act."

This was getting dangerous, Adelaide thought. The tearoom was not very large. Although she and Vera had been conversing in low tones, Adelaide was quite certain that those who were sitting at nearby tables had overheard every word.

"I hope you enjoy your tea, Miss Westlake," she said. "Please excuse me. As you can see, we're quite busy today."

Vera's mouth twisted in a humorless smile. "Nothing like a mysterious death to bring out the curiosity seekers."

"Evidently," Adelaide said.

She hurried off to check on a nearby table before Vera could say anything else.

Florence emerged from the kitchen with a pot of tea and a sly expression.

"Your new boarder is waiting for you," she whispered when she passed Adelaide.

Adelaide hurried into the kitchen. Jake was there. She realized he had entered the tearoom through the kitchen door.

"Florence told me that Vera Westlake managed to snag you," he said. "I assume she was curious about the psychic's death?"

"Yes." Adelaide set the tray on the counter. "I didn't tell her anything more than what was in the *Herald*. Evidently she and Zolanda knew each other when they were aspiring actresses. Their lives went in different directions when Vera became a star and Zolanda . . . didn't."

"Huh." Jake looked interested. "Was Westlake one of Zolanda's clients?"

Adelaide raised her brows. "You're wondering if Vera Westlake might have been one of Zolanda's blackmail victims, aren't you?"

"The possibility crossed my mind. If so, she would have had a motive for murder."

"I asked Miss Westlake if she had ever consulted with Zolanda. The answer was a very firm no. Miss Westlake doesn't believe in psychic powers. But she did say she finds it difficult to believe that Zolanda took her own life. She suspects that Thelma Leggett had something to do with the psychic's death."

"She's not the only one holding that theory. A lot of people in town are convinced that Leggett murdered her boss."

"Why?

"The folks I talked to assume that Leggett murdered her boss in order to steal money or jewelry."

Adelaide frowned. "Where did you hear all this?"

"The hardware store. Where else? Women get their local news at the beauty shop. Men get it at the hardware store."

"I'll remember that."

"I learned something else about Zolanda today. While she was here in Burning Cove she was a regular at the Paradise Club. The night she died was the one night she did not go to the club."

"Who told you that?"

"Luther Pell."

Adelaide stilled. "Florence mentioned that you and Mr. Pell are acquainted."

"Pell and I met each other a few years ago."

"I see."

"Luther also mentioned that Thelma Leggett usually drove Zolanda to the club and escorted her inside. After seeing her boss settled into a booth at the Paradise, Leggett was in the habit of going to the Carousel, a club on the other side of town. But on the night of Zolanda's death, Leggett evidently took her boss straight back to the villa. Leggett showed up at the Carousel as usual. She left around three thirty in the morning. No one saw her after that."

"What does that tell us?"

"It could indicate that Zolanda expected to meet someone after the show."

"Maybe." Adelaide waved the issue aside. "But it could just as easily mean that she was exhausted from the performance. Either way, it still leaves Leggett as the chief suspect."

"After I talked to Luther it occurred to me that it might be interesting to go to the Paradise Club tonight."

"Why?"

"Because Luther also told me that Zolanda was not the only regular who did not show up at the club on the night that Zolanda died. Dr. Calvin Paxton has made a practice of appearing at the Paradise on most nights. He usually comes in around midnight and sits at Miss Westlake's table. They have a few drinks and a few dances together, and then they both leave in separate cars around three in the morning."

"So?"

"On the night Zolanda died, Vera Westlake arrived at the Paradise Club around midnight, as usual, but Paxton never joined her."

Adelaide gave that some thought. "Maybe Paxton decided to go somewhere else after Zolanda's performance. The bar at the Burning Cove Hotel is also very popular with the Hollywood set."

Jake shook his head. "Luther talked to his friend Oliver Ward, who owns the Burning Cove Hotel. Paxton is staying there but he called for his car around seven o'clock. He drove himself to the Palace Theater, where he met Vera Westlake. Following the performance, Paxton seems to have disappeared until he returned to the Burning Cove Hotel around four thirty that morning."

"Maybe Paxton went to one of the other nightspots in town."

"It's possible, but Paxton likes to hang out with celebrities. He's not the sort to spend a night at a joint like the Carousel. Look, under most circumstances I wouldn't have given Paxton's failure to show up at the Paradise or the bar at the Burning Cove on any given night a second thought. But Luther came up with one other interesting fact. A few days before her final performance, Zolanda and Paxton both left the Paradise Club together in Paxton's car. Evidently, Paxton offered to give her a ride back to her villa. But the valet said that when they got into the vehicle, they were arguing."

"What about?"

"The valet said that all he overheard was something about running out of time. He said he didn't hear anything else, but it was clear they were not on friendly terms."

"Hmm." Adelaide leaned back against the counter and folded her arms. "Paxton might be able to account for his whereabouts on the night Zolanda died but we can't ask him outright for the information. We're not the police."

"No, but it might be interesting to observe Paxton in his natural habitat, so to speak."

Adelaide raised her brows. "Meaning?"

"If he stays true to form, he'll be at the Paradise Club tonight."

"Which is why you'll be there, too."

"Correction. You and I are both going to the Paradise tonight."

Startled, Adelaide unfolded her arms and straightened away from the counter. "I don't think that's a good idea. It will look like we're out on a date."

Jake smiled. "That is more or less the whole point of the exercise."

"But we've been telling everyone that you're my new boarder." Adelaide realized she was waving her arms. She forced herself to stop. "People will get the wrong impression."

"Got news for you. The boarder story isn't working very well."

She winced. "You heard that at the hardware store?"

"I told you, hardware stores are hotbeds of local gossip."

"Apparently so. You do realize I haven't a thing to wear—not to a swanky place like the Paradise. I'll have to go shopping after the tearoom closes today."

"This is my idea, so I'll take care of the bill for the dress."

She narrowed her eyes. "No, you will not pay for my new dress. That will only add fuel to the gossip fire."

"You refer to the fire that is already burning?"

Adelaide beetled her brows. "Shouldn't you be installing locks or something?"

"Oh, yeah. Locks." Jake picked up the sack and headed for the kitchen door. "Let me know when you're ready to do your shopping. I'll drive you."

"Do you really think that's necessary?"

Jake paused, one hand on the doorknob. "We don't know a lot about what is going on here in Burning Cove, but we do know that someone was watching your cottage on the night that a famous psychic died. Until we get some answers, I don't think it's a good idea for you to be alone."

She almost blurted out the truth. She didn't know anything more than the police did about Zolanda's death, but she did have some idea of who might be watching her. The problem was that if she told Jake everything, there was a very real possibility that he would conclude she was crazy. What man in his right mind would trust an escapee from an insane asylum?

It wasn't as if he had been entirely straightforward with her, either, she reminded herself.

She focused on the immediate problem of obtaining an affordable dress that would get her through the exclusive doors of the Paradise Club.

"You don't need to go shopping with me," she said. She knew she sounded stiff and tense. "I've got a friend who knows all about the latest fashions and where to find them here in town."

"How long will it take?"

"Hours," she said with a cold smile, silently daring him to complain about the shopping process.

"Take your time. Luther invited me to play a round of golf this afternoon. I'll give him a call and tell him I'm free."

Chapter 25

"That's the gown," Raina announced. "It fits you beautifully and the deep turquoise blue enhances your eyes. You look sophisticated and mysterious. That's exactly the right impression to make at a place like the Paradise Club."

"Miss Kirk is correct," the saleswoman gushed. "She has an excellent eye for fashion."

Adelaide studied herself in the dressing room mirror. Raina and the saleswoman were right, she thought. The ankle-length gown was very flattering. The lustrous satin was cut on the bias so that it flowed effortlessly over the body and flared out below the hips. It would look terrific on a dance floor.

The front was styled with a demure, high neck but the back plunged to the waist with nothing more than a few decorative strips of fabric to secure it. It was a gown designed for a night of glamour and seduction.

She had purchased similar gowns in those first giddy weeks after Conrad Massey had moved into her life. And then one day she had awakened in a hospital gown in a locked room at Rushbrook. She shuddered at the memory.

Raina's brows snapped together. She leaned forward and lowered her voice.

"Are you all right?" she asked.

Adelaide pulled herself together. "Yes, I'm fine. Just dealing with the shock of the price tag on this little number, that's all."

"No need to worry about the price," the saleswoman said airily. "I'll give you a twenty percent discount because you'll be seen in the gown at the Paradise Club. That is excellent advertising for my shop. All you need now are a pair of smart shoes, a wrap, some earrings, and the right evening bag, and you're all set for a night on the town."

Reality struck Adelaide with staggering force. She could—just barely—manage to pay for the dress. The accessories the saleswoman suggested were out of the question.

"I'm sorry," she said. She reached around behind herself to find the hidden zipper. "The dress is lovely but you're right, it needs all the appropriate trimmings. I'm afraid I'm on a strict budget."

Alarmed, the saleswoman started talking very quickly. "I'm sure we can find a few things in your price range."

"The accessories will not be a problem," Raina said. "I think I've got a bag and a wrap that will go nicely with that dress. I also have some earrings that will work, as well. That just leaves the shoes. Unfortunately, mine will be too big for you, Adelaide, although we might be able to wad up some tissue to stuff into the toes."

The saleswoman smiled a mysterious saleswoman smile. "I'll be right back," she said.

Adelaide and Raina looked at each other.

"I've got news for you," Raina said quietly. "Not a lot but it might prove useful. I'll tell you when we're finished here."

"Does it have anything to do with Thelma Leggett?"

"Yes."

The saleswoman appeared as if by magic. A pair of strappy, high-heeled dancing sandals dangled from her fingers. The shoes were made of silver leather. They seemed to radiate starlight.

Adelaide gazed at them, mesmerized.

"Oh, my," Raina said softly. "Yes, indeed, I think those will do nicely."

"I'm sure they're too expensive," Adelaide began.

"I was going to put them on sale next week," the saleswoman said. "I'll let you have them for the sale price now."

"We'll take them," Raina said.

Adelaide looked at her. "I can't afford them, even if they're on sale."

"I'll loan you the money if necessary," Raina said.

Adelaide gave up. "All right. But only if they fit."

The shoes fit as if they had been made for her. Adelaide took a deep breath and opened her handbag to take out her wallet. At the rate she was going through money, she might have to take in a real boarder after Jake left town.

By the time she and Raina left the dress shop, she was feeling dazed by the amount of money she had just spent. It was not as if she still had access to her inheritance, she reminded herself. She was living on a waitress's wages.

"Don't worry about it," Raina said. "Think of the dress and the shoes as an investment."

"In what?" Adelaide said. "I'll probably never wear them again."

"You live in Burning Cove now. Trust me, you will have other opportunities to wear that gown and those fabulous shoes. Let's have coffee and then we can go to my place to pick up the wrap, the earrings, and the evening bag."

"I need something to help me get over the shock of spending all that money. I suppose it's too early for a martini."

"Save the martini for tonight when you're actually wearing the new dress and the shoes," Raina said.

They found a small, shaded table at an outdoor café in a busy shopping plaza. Smartly dressed women with bags from various nearby stores strolled past, chatting with friends and discussing the latest fashions.

She was not a huge fan of coffee—she preferred tea—but it was good to have coffee with a friend, Adelaide thought. It made her feel almost normal.

She and Raina were gradually working their way into a deeper friendship. One day they might even feel free to exchange their most closely guarded secrets. But that day had not yet arrived. How did you tell a new acquaintance that a few months ago you had been diagnosed as having suffered a nervous breakdown? That you had been used as a test subject in a secret experiment conducted in an insane asylum by a doctor who was later murdered?

A story like that would make even a very good friend question your sanity.

When the coffee was delivered, Raina raised her cup in a small salute.

"Here's to a great evening out," she said.

"You do realize this isn't a date." Adelaide fortified herself with a sip of the strong coffee. "Jake and I are curious about Dr. Paxton because he seems to have gone missing on the night Zolanda died. But I doubt that we'll learn anything useful. You said you had some news of Thelma Leggett?"

"Not a lot," Raina said. "Not yet. But I've been doing some thinking and there are a couple of things that bother me. The first is that Thelma Leggett was not a big or muscular woman. She was, in fact, shorter and more slightly built than her boss. So how did she manage to overcome Zolanda and push her off the roof? For that matter, how did she manage to convince Zolanda to go up to the roof in the first place?"

Adelaide lowered her coffee cup. "You don't believe that Thelma Leggett murdered Zolanda, do you?"

"Anything is possible and we still don't have many facts, but, no; the more I consider the question, the more I'm inclined to think that Leggett wasn't the one who pushed Zolanda off that roof—assuming she was pushed. Jake Truett seems convinced that Zolanda was in the blackmail business. If that's true, it leaves us with a lot of suspects."

"That's what Jake says."

"I am not convinced that Thelma Leggett murdered Zolanda but I agree with Truett—we need to find her. She's the only one who can shed some light on the death of her boss. I've done some research. Leggett and Zolanda both lived in L.A. but Leggett wouldn't dare go home. It's the first place the police would have looked."

"Then she's on the road? Maybe holed up in an auto court someplace?"

"Maybe, but there may be a more likely possibility. My contact in L.A. says he talked to one of Leggett's neighbors who told him that a few years ago Leggett's mother died and left her some property on the coast. The neighbor said there was a cabin on the property. I'm trying to find out where it's located."

"Do you think that Thelma might be hiding out there?"

"It's possible. When I worked as a secretary for a legal firm, I was frequently asked to locate individuals. In my experience, when people run, they tend to head for a place that feels familiar, a place that feels safe."

Adelaide tightened her grip on the coffee cup. That was exactly what she had done, she thought. She had run to Burning Cove because it felt somewhat familiar, somewhat safe. When she was a little girl, her parents had taken her there every summer for a vacation. Her father and mother had often talked about retiring in Burning Cove.

Her mouth went dry. In retrospect, taking refuge in the seaside town might have been a huge mistake. If the people who were looking for her had used the same logic that Raina was using, they might have already found her. It would certainly explain why someone had spent a night lurking in the fog, watching her house.

"Adelaide?" Raina leaned forward a little. "Are you sure you're all right?"

Adelaide forced herself to focus. "I was just thinking about what you said. You'll let us know right away if you track down the location of the property that Thelma Leggett inherited, won't you?"

"Of course. Meanwhile, do me a favor."

"What's that?"

"I know why you and Jake Truett are going to the Paradise Club tonight, but try to have a good time, anyway."

Adelaide managed a shaky smile. "I'll do my best."

They finished their coffee and walked back to Raina's convertible. They stored the shopping bags in the trunk, and Raina got behind the wheel.

Adelaide opened the passenger side door. She was about to make a comment on the very fine weather, when she felt a ghostly shiver of awareness on the back of her neck.

She paused and glanced back over her shoulder. The shopping plaza was still busy, still filled with shoppers and people enjoying the pleasures of the sidewalk cafés. But at the very edge of her vision she glimpsed a man in a fashionable dark blue linen jacket and tan trousers. She could not see his face because he was in the process of turning away from her. In addition, he was wearing a straw hat angled so that it concealed his profile.

She got only the briefest of glimpses before he disappeared around a corner, but that was enough to ice her blood.

She slipped into the passenger seat of the car and closed the door very firmly. She had not been hallucinating. The man in the blue linen jacket had carried himself and moved in exactly the same way that Conrad Massey did.

Chapter 26

"You're sure the psychic didn't jump," Luther asked.

"I'm sure," Jake said.

He selected his putter and positioned himself in front of the golf ball. He took a moment to absorb the feel of the green.

The great thing about a golf course was that two men could have a private conversation without worrying about being overheard. He and Luther were alone on the green. The caddies waited a respectful distance away.

It was an ideal day for a game of golf. The weather was perfect, sunny and warm, and the elegantly manicured course was in prime condition. The fairways were lush, the greens were smooth and fast and mostly true, but this one had an almost imperceptible slope to the right. His ball had landed a yard away from the hole.

He lined up the putt, compensating for the small slope and the fast green, and ushered the ball into the hole with a gentle tap. He straightened and saw Luther watching him with an amused expression.

"How the hell do you do that?" Luther said.

"What?"

"You make it look so damn easy."

Luther walked to where his ball lay some two yards away from the hole. He overshot the cup by about four inches.

"The greens are a little fast today," Jake observed.

"Thank you for that helpful observation."

"I sense sarcasm."

"Could be."

Luther took aim again and sank the putt.

The caddies noted scores, collected balls and clubs, and replaced the flag. They all headed toward the next tee.

"I take it you didn't find what you were looking for when you searched Zolanda's house," Luther said.

"No. I'm sure the assistant has the stash of blackmail material. Adelaide and I hired Raina Kirk to look for her."

"Miss Kirk is a very interesting woman," Luther said. "I hired her, too. I want her to look into a small security problem for me."

"Adelaide said Miss Kirk is new in town. How did you meet her?"

Luther smiled. "Ran into her at the library a few weeks ago."

"Yeah? What was she reading?"

"Old copies of the *Herald*," Luther said. "She explained that reading out-of-date newspapers was a good way to get to know a town."

"Huh. A private detective who reads and a nightclub owner who also reads. Sounds like a match made in heaven."

"Or somewhere," Luther said.

"Adelaide Brockton is an interesting woman, too."

"I'm getting that impression. Any idea how or why she ended up here in Burning Cove?"

"Judging by the fact that Miss Brockton keeps a gun under her bed and that someone was watching her house the night Zolanda jumped off that roof, I'd say she's running from someone."

"Wouldn't be the first time a woman tried to escape a mentally unbalanced man who became obsessed with her."

"Obsession is a dangerous thing," Jake said.

Luther shot him a quick, searching look. "It's over. They're both dead, Jake. It ended that night on the *Mermaid* when Garrick tried to kill you."

Jake thought about the violent evening on the gambling ship. He often relived the scene in his dreams. Garrick had come at him from behind with a knife, hoping for a quick, quiet kill, one that concluded with a body dumped over the side.

But Garrick had been the one who went overboard and drowned in the waters off Santa Monica. His body had washed ashore a few days later. If the authorities noticed the small wound in his throat, they had not mentioned it to the press. It was, after all, not the first time a dead gambler had turned up on the beach.

It had been a bad night, Jake reflected, but at the time he believed that it closed a dark chapter in the story of his life. Then Elizabeth's diary had gone missing.

"It's not over until I find that diary," he said.

"I understand," Luther said. "By the way, you might be interested to know that I sold the *Mermaid*."

"Getting out of the offshore gambling business?"

"That boat was starting to cost more than it made in profits. Besides, times are changing."

"You and I have undergone a few changes, too."

"Yes," Luther said. "But I'm settled here in Burning Cove. I like this town. It suits me. What are you going to do now that you've sold your business?"

"You're starting to sound like Adelaide. She thinks I need a real job."

"She may be right," Luther said. "We both know you've been drifting ever since Elizabeth died. You sold the business. You got rid of the big house in L.A. Damn it, you're living in a hotel in Pasadena. What kind of a life is that?"

"The Huntington is a very nice hotel."

"That's not the point."

"I've got a private bungalow. There's a pool. Room service. What more can a man ask for?"

"You can't live in a hotel forever."

"Why not? You seem to be doing just fine living on top of a nightclub."

"That's different. I own the place. You're living as if you were still in the import-export business, always prepared to pack a bag and travel halfway around the world at a moment's notice. Those days are over, Jake."

Jake exhaled slowly. "I know. But I've got to recover that diary before I can think about what I want to do next."

He lined up the tee shot and sent the ball sailing down the long fairway, straight toward the green.

"How the hell do you *do* that?" Luther said. "You should have become a professional."

"Too hard on the nerves," Jake said. "Mine are already exhausted, remember?"

"Yeah, I did hear something about that."

Chapter 27

The Paradise Club lived up to its reputation as an eternally midnight realm steeped in intimate shadows and dark glamour. The velvet-covered booths were arranged in semicircles that rose in tiers above the crowded dance floor. Small candles burned on each table, giving off a warm, flickering light that enhanced the drama and encouraged flirtation. Cigarettes sparked in the darkness.

The members of the orchestra wore white dinner jackets and black bow ties. A large, mirrored sphere hung over the dance floor, its faceted surface scattering light across the dancers, who appeared to be gliding and swaying through a storm of sparkling jewels.

The music blended with the hum of low-voiced conversations and the occasional ripples of laughter. The French doors that lined one entire side of the room were open, allowing the night air to cool the space and help dissipate the cigarette smoke.

"How will we know if Paxton is here tonight?" Adelaide asked.

She and Jake were seated at a table that was in the last tier of booths. She was well aware that it was not considered a prime location, but it had two major advantages: It provided privacy while simultaneously allowing a view of the dance floor.

She was sure they were the only ones in the club who were not drinking cocktails. They had both ordered sparkling water. They had a long evening ahead of them. Becoming intoxicated was not on the agenda.

"According to Luther, Paxton always sits at Westlake's table," Jake said.

"Yes, but what if she doesn't show up?"

"I was told that her assistant called earlier to make sure that Miss Westlake's table would be ready, as usual."

"All right. How will we know when she arrives? Will Mr. Pell send someone to inform us?"

Jake was amused. "You'll know when she arrives the same way you know when she enters the tearoom."

"In other words, she'll make an entrance," Adelaide said.

"Management will ensure that she does. The maître d' will escort her and whoever she's with to one of the booths at the edge of the dance floor."

Adelaide smiled. "Can I assume that this isn't your first visit to the Paradise?"

"I've spent some time here in Burning Cove over the years, so, yes, I've been in the Paradise. But I've also been in a few other nightclubs around the world. Take it from me, they all have a lot in common when it comes to how they treat their celebrity guests."

"The celebrities pretend they want to be incognito but of course what they really want is to be noticed," Adelaide said.

"Even if the stars don't want to be noticed, the studio publicists go to great lengths to make sure that they are."

"When you think about it, being an actor or actress must be a very stressful career."

"There's a price for everything," Jake said.

"Yes."

Jake studied her from the opposite side of the small booth. "What did you do before you became a tearoom waitress?"

She hesitated and then decided there was no harm in telling him some of the truth. "I was a librarian. I worked in a research library that specialized in the botanical sciences."

"Did you enjoy the work?"

She brightened at the memories. "Oh, yes. The library is very highly regarded. The collection is excellent. My colleagues and I conducted literature searches for scientists and medical researchers from around the nation. It was fascinating work."

"And now you're in Burning Cove working in a tearoom."

She tensed. "My parents died. I was alone. No family. I felt that I needed a change."

She held her breath, afraid that he would press her with more questions. *Should have kept my mouth closed,* she thought.

But Jake simply nodded in understanding. "I know the feeling."

She relaxed. "Some people think I've lived a sheltered life. They think I'm naïve. My parents were always afraid that some man would take advantage of me."

Which was, of course, exactly what had happened, she thought.

"Maybe a dose of naïveté is the price you pay to be a good, decent person," Jake said. "Seems like the only alternative is to become cynical like me. I can't really recommend it."

Adelaide picked up her sparkling water and looked at him over the rim of the glass. "I may be inclined to be naïve but I'm not stupid. Once I know for certain that I can't trust someone, I never make the mistake of trusting that person again."

"Sounds like a reasonable policy to me." Jake raised his glass and touched it lightly against hers. "To naïveté and lessons learned the hard way."

The orchestra launched into a slow, smooth dance number. Adelaide watched couples drift out onto the floor and into each other's arms. There was a time when she had danced with Conrad Massey in the same romantic fashion. Naïveté didn't begin to excuse the huge mistake she had made with Massey. She had been a fool.

The thought reminded her again of the man in the dark blue coat she had glimpsed in the shopping plaza that afternoon. She had been unable to get the memory out of her head. She tried to tell herself that she had imagined the similarity between Conrad Massey and the stranger on the street. *Paranoia is a sign of mental instability.* But she could not convince herself that she had not seen the bastard.

"Will you dance with me?" Jake asked quietly.

Jolted out of her grim thoughts, she turned away from the view of the dance floor and saw that Jake was watching her with a brooding intensity.

"What?" she said.

"I asked you to dance with me."

"Why not?" She summoned up what she hoped would pass for a bright, vivacious smile. "The damage has already been done, hasn't it?"

His ascetic face, illuminated in candlelight, became even more forbidding than usual.

"Damage?" he repeated in very neutral tones.

"I'm sure that by tomorrow morning what's left of our cover story will be in tatters, anyway. It's not exactly customary for boarders to go out to nightclubs with their landladies."

"Right," he said. "The damage has been done. Let's dance."

It sounded like an order, not a request.

She steeled herself. It wasn't as if he were asking her to marry him, she thought. He was simply suggesting that they dance together. Nevertheless, for some inexplicable reason, it felt as if accepting the offer was a risky venture.

"Yes," she said. "Yes, I would be delighted to dance with you."

She slipped out of the booth before she could change her mind.

Jake got to his feet, offered her his arm, and led her down the aisle to the dance floor.

Together they moved into the shower of sparkling lights cast by the mirrored ball. She caught her breath when she felt Jake's strong, warm hand on the bare skin of her lower back.

"Nice dress," he said. "What there is of it."

She nearly choked on a burst of nervous laughter. "Thank you."

Somehow it was easier to relax after that. She discovered she liked dancing with Jake. She liked it a lot. For a few minutes she was almost able to forget about the man in the straw hat and the blue linen coat. Almost.

A ripple of awareness washed across the room, dampening conversation and causing heads to turn.

"Vera Westlake has arrived," Jake said. "I told you we wouldn't be able to miss her entrance."

Adelaide turned her head and saw the maître d' escorting Vera down the aisle to the one booth at the edge of the dance floor that was still empty. The most beautiful woman in Hollywood was spectacularly elegant in a sultry gold gown covered in crystals that caught the light with every step. Her hair was rolled and pinned up in an elegant cluster of curls. The style emphasized her dramatic cheekbones and heavily made-up eyes. She was alone.

The hovering maître d' seated the star and summoned a waiter, who hurried forward to take Westlake's order. When the waiter scurried off again, Vera took out a gleaming cigarette case. The maître d' rushed forward to ignite the star's smoke and then discreetly withdrew.

"There goes a real movie star," Adelaide whispered.

Jake did not appear to be starstruck. "Here comes Dr. Calvin Paxton, right on schedule."

Adelaide peered around his shoulder and watched the maître d' seat Paxton at Vera's table.

"I can't understand why a famous movie star would hang out with a doctor who pushes a fake diet tonic."

"And here I thought we had just decided that you're the naïve one on this date." Jake sounded amused.

"I bought a bottle of Paxton's so-called diet tonic and tried it. It's nothing but sugar water and, I suspect, some caffeine."

"I'll take your word for it," Jake said. "Maybe Westlake is attracted to Paxton because, even though he moves in the same world, he's not in the same line of work. They aren't competitors."

"True, but if you ask me, Miss Westlake could do a lot better than Paxton. He's just using her to sell his phony diet drink."

"She doesn't seem to mind. Maybe she really believes that it works."

Adelaide watched as Paxton ordered a cocktail and lit a cigarette. He and Vera Westlake sat back in the booth and looked as if they were about to expire from ennui. They were not alone for long. A procession of people found reasons to pass by the booth and pay homage to the star. Vera was always gracious. Paxton leaned in a little closer to her, as if trying to steal some of the invisible glow of fame that enveloped his companion.

Jake swung Adelaide into another slow turn around the dance floor. When the music stopped, they were on the opposite side of the room.

"Let's go outside and get some fresh air," he said.

He took her hand and steered her toward the open French doors. The lush gardens that surrounded the Paradise Club were a wonderland at night. The footpaths were illuminated with small, low-level lamps. Tiny lights sparkled in the tall hedges. The air was fragrant with the scents of flowers and citrus. The grounds had been designed to provide privacy for couples. Adelaide heard soft laughter and low murmurs wafting on the evening air.

Jake drew her to a halt in the deep shadows of an orange tree.

"Would you mind telling me why you've been so tense since you returned from your shopping trip with Raina this afternoon?" he said.

She froze. It took her a few seconds to recover.

"Why shouldn't I be tense?" she whispered. "If your suspicions are correct, we may be hunting for a killer. At the very least we're trying to locate a blackmailer. I'd say I have a lot of reasons to feel tense."

"Take it easy. I agree with you. It's just that you seem a little different tonight. Distracted. Jumpier than usual."

So much for thinking that she had succeeded in concealing her emotions. Her temper spiked.

"Jumpier than *usual?*" she said.

"If you don't want to talk about it, that's fine."

"There is nothing to talk about," she said, careful to keep her tone very even.

Jake went preternaturally still. "Hush."

"Don't you dare tell me to—"

She closed her mouth because Jake had put one hand firmly over her lips. Before she could protest, he was easing her into the deep shadows of a nearby orange tree.

He took his hand away from her mouth and kissed her before she could catch her breath.

For a few seconds she was too astonished to react. And then a wild rush of excitement flashed through her. Some part of her had been anticipating the moment when Jake took her into his arms since the first time he had walked into the tearoom. She had sensed even then that his kiss would change her life, if only for one night.

She had been wrong.

Jake's kiss was cold and calculating. There was nothing thrilling about it. His mouth was hard on hers, devoid of any trace of warmth and passion. She was still reeling from the disorienting shock when she heard the approach of rapid footsteps on the graveled path.

Understanding crackled through her. The kiss was not real. It was a screen kiss designed to fool an audience.

The footsteps drew closer. Whoever was coming their way would pass them in a few seconds. Jake was faking the kiss because he wanted whoever was coming toward them to think they were just another romantically inclined couple that had slipped into the gardens for some privacy.

She wound her arms around Jake's neck and pressed herself very tightly against him, throwing herself into the role that he had assigned her. She knew how to play a part, she thought. Hellfire and damnation, did she know how to act. She had fooled a mad scientist, a couple of experienced nurses, some oversized orderlies, and the scheming bastard who ran the Rushbrook Sanitarium. When the occasion demanded it, she was as good an actress as any Hollywood star.

Her spirited response caught Jake off guard. It was his turn to freeze in surprise. She tightened her arms around his neck. The hurrying footsteps drew closer.

Jake lost control of the kiss. He groaned and crushed her against his chest. The clinical embrace went from ice-cold to red-hot and out of control between one heartbeat and the next.

The footsteps passed by and faded into the distance, but Jake did not relax his grip. Adelaide was just starting to realize that the storm of passion had become shatteringly real when it ended as suddenly as it had begun.

Jake ripped his mouth off hers, closed his hands around her forearms, and very carefully, very deliberately set her a short distance away.

Fingers as cold as the grave touched the back of her neck, just as they had earlier that afternoon. The heat of passion evaporated instantly. Panic churned in her stomach.

She opened her eyes and found herself looking past Jake's broad shoulder. A tall, elegantly thin man in a white dinner jacket was just disappearing around a hedge. The light of a nearby garden lamp gleamed briefly on his oiled dark hair. He didn't give any indication that he had noticed the couple embracing in the shadows of the orange tree. He moved like an angry, impatient, or, perhaps, very frustrated man.

He moved exactly like the man she had glimpsed in the shopping plaza that afternoon—exactly like Conrad Massey.

She realized that Jake was watching her with a disconcerting intensity. It was, she thought, almost as if he was suddenly a little wary of her.

"My apologies," he said. His low voice was rough around the edges. "I was just trying to keep him from seeing you."

She took a shaky breath. "I understand. I think you were successful."

Jake searched her face.

"Did you get a look at him?"

"No, not really." That much was true but it was not the whole truth. She needed time to think, but the panic rising inside her told her that time had run out. "I only saw him from the back. He was wearing a white evening jacket. Dark trousers. Dark hair."

"That describes half the men in the Paradise tonight, including me."

"No," she said before she could stop herself. "It doesn't describe you."

"Are you sure?" He sounded wryly amused.

"You move . . . differently." She waved her hands, struggling to explain. "Like a very large cat. A leopard or a mountain lion or . . . something. The man I saw did not walk the way you do. Never mind, I can't explain it. You'll have to take my word for it."

"That's not terribly helpful. Did you notice anything else about him?"

"He was walking very quickly. I got the impression that he was angry."

"I think he followed us out here. But he didn't see us in the shadows."

"Why would he follow us?" she asked. She knew her voice sounded weak.

Jake gave her a searching look. She knew he didn't believe her but he did not comment. Without a word, he took her arm.

Unable to think of anything else to do, Adelaide allowed him to steer her back into the nightclub. The first thing she noticed was that Vera Westlake was once again sitting alone.

"Paxton is gone," Jake said. "That's interesting. Any sign of the other man?"

"No, but I can't be positive he's not in here somewhere," she said. "It's just too dark. The only people I can see clearly are the ones seated in the booths around the dance floor and the couples who are dancing."

"Luther's security people will have a list of everyone who is in the club tonight. I'll ask to take a look at it tomorrow."

Would Conrad Massey—assuming it was Massey she had seen—use his real name? Adelaide wondered.

Jake escorted her to their booth. She looked at the sparkling water in her glass. What she really needed was a martini, she thought.

She picked up the glass of water and tried to decide what to do. She finally came to a decision. She set the glass down abruptly.

"There are some things about me that you should know," she said, choosing her words very carefully. "I was hoping I would never have to explain my life to you, but I don't think I have a choice now. You deserve the truth."

Jake had just swallowed some of his sparkling water. He lowered the glass. His eyes never left her face.

"I'm listening," he said.

"I don't want to talk about it here."

Jake got to his feet. "Let's go home."

She wanted to tell him that she didn't have a home, that in a very real sense she did not even exist. That she was just Patient B and, as far as some people were concerned, she had vanished.

But it was not the kind of story a woman told a man while sitting with him in a candlelit booth in a nightclub.

Chapter 28

She had not lied, Jake thought, but she had not told him the full truth about the man who had passed them in the garden. Once again he reminded himself that she had a right to her secrets, but whatever she was not telling him was definitely complicating the problem of keeping her safe.

They stood silently together in front of the big wrought iron gates at the front of the Paradise Club, waiting for the valet to fetch the car. He was very conscious of Adelaide's nearness but he had no clue as to her thoughts. It was obvious that she had been badly shaken by the events in the gardens, but he did not know if it was the kiss that had rattled her or the sight of the man who had walked past them. He was starting to wonder if it was both of those things.

One thing was certain—the kiss that had flashed like lightning between them had definitely left him feeling shaken. It wasn't that he hadn't known there was some risk involved in kissing her. But he had been so damn sure he could control the situation.

He had been wrong, and not for the first time when it came to Adelaide, he thought.

The valet brought the speedster to a stop in front of the gate and got out. Jake opened the passenger side door to allow Adelaide to slip into the front seat. A silver sandal gleamed briefly in the moonlight, allowing him a glimpse of one elegantly arched foot. The heat that had slammed through him when he had taken her into his arms a few minutes ago stirred his senses again.

He closed the car door very quickly and took a couple of deep breaths while he walked around the long hood of the vehicle. By the time he got behind the wheel, he thought he was back in command of himself.

He put the car in gear and drove down the lane and onto Cliff Road. The moon was still out but a light fog was starting to coalesce over the night-darkened ocean.

"Why don't you start by telling me what it was about that man who passed us in the gardens that is worrying you?" he asked.

Adelaide had been concentrating on the view of the narrow strip of pavement unspooling in the car's headlights. She turned her head and gave him a very brief, very sharp look. For a moment he didn't think she was going to answer.

"I'm almost positive that I saw him earlier today while I was shopping with Raina," she said finally. "But I only caught a glimpse of him then, too, so I can't be absolutely certain."

"You thought you recognized him?"

"He resembled a man I knew in San Francisco. We . . . dated for a time."

Jake remembered the golf course conversation with Luther. *Wouldn't be the first time a woman tried to escape a mentally unbalanced man who became obsessed with her.*

"Do you think that a man you once dated has followed you to Burning Cove?" he asked, needing to be sure.

"Maybe. The story is complicated. I'd prefer to wait until we get home. I could use a drink—something stronger than water or tea."

He wanted to keep pushing her for answers but it was obvious that she needed time.

"All right," he said. "Meanwhile, I think it might be a good idea for me to have a look around Calvin Paxton's villa at the Burning Cove Hotel. Luther can probably get his friend Oliver Ward to let me inside."

Alarmed, Adelaide turned quickly in the seat. "Are you talking about breaking into Dr. Paxton's villa?"

"No, I'm talking about asking a friend to get me a key to the villa so that I can take a look around while Paxton is out. Got a better idea?"

"Not yet, but I'll think of something," Adelaide vowed. "Give me thirty seconds."

"Why are you so concerned about me going into Paxton's villa?"

"Because if you're right, if he did have something to do with Zolanda's death, he's dangerous."

"Thank you for your concern but I can take care of myself, Adelaide."

"Yeah, yeah, I know—you used to be in the import-export business. You have a gun. I've got one question for you."

"What?"

"Where is that gun tonight?"

"Locked inside the glove compartment of this car. Luther doesn't allow guests to carry guns into the club. I could have asked for special permission, being his friend and all, but I didn't think it was necessary. Luther's security people are well armed. There's probably no safer place in Burning Cove than the Paradise."

"Oh," Adelaide said.

She studied the glove compartment in front of her as if she had never seen one before.

"I assume you were going to point out that owning a gun isn't much use if it's not available when you need it," he said.

She sighed. "Something like that. I didn't bring my gun, either, so I'm in no position to lecture on the subject. Moving right along, has it occurred to you that Paxton might also own a gun. If he surprises you while you are searching his villa, he would have every reason to shoot you first. He would be able to claim he thought you were an intruder. Which would be more or less the truth."

"Huh."

"Now what are you thinking?"

"It strikes me as rather interesting that you would leap to the conclusion that Paxton might have a gun," he said.

"Why wouldn't I think that? I've got one and so do you. And someone in this situation is already dead."

"Madam Zolanda was not shot."

"True," Adelaide said. "But if she was murdered, I think I may know how."

"What the hell are you talking about?"

"I'll tell you when we get back to the cottage. You're driving at the moment. You shouldn't be distracted."

"And what you're going to tell me will probably distract me?"

"Probably."

Adelaide fell silent. He realized that he was starting to enjoy the view of Cliff Road. The pavement was lengthening and unwinding in front of the car—all the way into infinity. It occurred to him that he could drive forever and never arrive at the end. He would have Adelaide beside him all the way.

The moonlight splashed silver on the night-darkened ocean. The glow was becoming more intense. It was beckoning him, drawing him deeper into the night. It was a spangled highway that until now he had never known existed. There were secrets at the end of the gleaming silver road. All he had to do was follow the radiant trail.

"Jake?"

Adelaide's voice came from another dimension.

"There's nothing to worry about," he said. "We're going to find all the answers when we get there."

"Where are we going?" Adelaide asked.

She was concerned. He did not want her to worry. He would protect her.

"Everything will be all right," he said. "Can't you see the moonlight highway? We can follow it to the truth."

"Jake, listen to me. You must stop the car."

"But we're not there yet. Look at all the colors around us. Who knew there were so many shades of night?"

"I said, stop the car."

She leaned toward him. For a few seconds he thought she was going to kiss him. Instead, she yanked the key out of the ignition. The roar of the engine ceased abruptly. The car began to slow.

Adelaide grabbed the wheel.

"Let go," she ordered.

He obeyed, letting his hands drop to his knees. She was climbing over him now, taking control of the wheel.

He laughed. "You should have told me you wanted to drive."

"Move your foot out of the way," she said. She kicked the side of his leg with one silver sandal. "Do it now, Jake Truett."

Obediently he moved his foot. Adelaide was half sitting on his thigh. He could feel the lush curve of her hips. Filled with wonder, he raised a hand to touch her bare back.

"You're so soft," he said. "And warm."

She got one silvery foot on the brake and steered the car onto the side of the road. It came to a full stop. The glorious night closed in around them.

"Are we going to make love now?" he asked.

"No," she said. "We're going to get out of the car."

"Good idea," he said. "We can make love on the beach."

"No," she said again. She scrambled back to her side of the seat and used his keys to unlock the glove compartment. He watched with interest as she took out his gun and a flashlight.

"Do you want to do some target practice on the beach?" he asked.

"Pay attention, Jake, and do exactly as I say."

"All right. Are we going to follow the moonlight road?"

"Yes. But it will be easier to do that if we get out of the car."

"Are you sure?"

"Positive."

"The car is faster."

"But it will take us in the wrong direction."

That made sense, he concluded. He opened his car door and climbed out. The colors of midnight grew ever more dazzling, swirling around him like an old-fashioned magic lantern show. No, not a magic lantern show; a kaleidoscope. That was it—he was inside a giant kaleidoscope and he was perceiving the secrets of the universe. He could watch the brilliant, shifting waves of light forever as long as Adelaide was there.

She rounded the car to join him. She had his pistol in one hand and the flashlight in the other.

"The end of the moonlight highway is down on the beach," she explained.

"You're sure?" he asked.

"Absolutely."

"Why are we taking my gun?"

"Because I think someone is trying to kill us."

Chapter 29

This is my fault, Adelaide thought. She had brought this danger down on Jake.

Later there would be time enough to contemplate the enormity of her guilt. First, she had to keep them both alive and safe.

"Don't worry," Jake said. He came to a halt in the sand. "If someone tries to hurt you, I'll kill him."

She was relieved to see that her words had succeeded in penetrating some of Jake's drug-induced delirium. But if he had been poisoned with Daydream, as she suspected, the hallucinatory effects were nothing if not unpredictable. His mood was already undergoing a one-hundred-and-eighty-degree turn. He was switching from goofy but harmless to potentially dangerous and uncontrollable. If he turned on her, he would easily overpower her.

"You can kill him some other time," she promised.

"Now would be better," he insisted. "Then we can follow the moonlight to the answers."

"Jake, you must listen to me very carefully. You've been drugged."

He shook his head, as if trying to clear it. "I'm not drunk. I didn't have even one martini."

"Not drunk, *drugged*. Never mind. Follow me and stay very close."

The drug had hypnotic properties and, heaven help her, she'd had enough experience with it to know that anyone under the influence was highly suggestible. The trick was to get inside the person's delirium dream and try to shape the otherworldly reality of the visions.

"Can you see the moonlight highway now?" Jake asked.

"Yes," she said. "It will take us someplace where we'll both be safe. But we must hurry."

"I'll take you to the safe place, and then I'll come back here and kill anyone who tries to hurt you."

"We'll talk about that plan later."

"Sure," Jake said.

She was familiar with the beach and the path that led down to it. During her time in Burning Cove she had walked most of the local beaches.

"The moonlight highway leads this way," she said.

Jake concentrated for a beat and then became riveted by something only he could perceive.

"Oh, yeah," he whispered. "It's beautiful."

"I've been here before," she said. "When the tide is out like it is now, there are some caves above the waterline. We can hide in one of those if someone decides to look for us."

Fortunately, Jake did not seem inclined to argue. He shook his head again, as if trying to clear it.

"Caves at the edge of midnight," he said.

"What? Never mind."

"I'm hallucinating, aren't I?"

She was astonished that some part of his rational brain had managed to break through the delirium. But that was exactly how she had survived, she reminded herself. The trick was to cope with the real world and the hallucinations simultaneously. It took an enormous amount of willpower. The experience was disorienting. It was also exhausting. Ultimately the desperate attempt to steer a logical path through the strange inner cosmos of the Daydream-drugged mind led to a growing sense of panic that could easily slide into full-scale paranoia.

"Yes," she said. "Just remember that nothing you see is real."

"Except you."

It was not a question.

"Except me," she agreed. "Concentrate on sensations you can feel. Rely on your sense of touch because you won't be able to trust your eyes."

She switched on the flashlight. The descent to the beach wasn't very steep, but it was a tricky maneuver at night because of the loose pebbles and rocks. When they reached the bottom, they would have to move carefully to avoid the tide pools.

Jake followed close behind her. Even in his delirium he had no trouble keeping his balance.

Adelaide heard the roar of a car engine in the distance just as she and Jake reached the rocky beach.

"The person who drugged you might be in that car," she warned.

"There's still time for me to kill him."

"It might also be an innocent motorist who will stop to try to help. You don't want to kill an innocent person, do you?"

"Nope. Just the bastard who wants to hurt you."

"Right, so we will stay out of sight until whoever it is gives up and goes away."

"You look like a fairy-tale princess," Jake said matter-of-factly.

"It's the shoes."

"I like the shoes. They're made of moonlight."

"They'll never be the same again after this little hike." She aimed the flashlight toward the far end of the beach. "The caves are in that direction. Hurry. Whoever is driving that car might stop, and if he does, I'll have to turn off this light."

They wouldn't be able to trust any stranger who stopped, she thought. She was still trying to come to grips with the fact that Conrad Massey was in Burning Cove. If he was there, maybe Gill was, too.

With his easy, natural coordination and sensible masculine footwear, Jake did not have any problem navigating around the tide pools. She was the one who was in constant danger of slipping and falling. The silver dancing shoes and the turquoise evening gown were not made for beachcombing.

Jake caught her twice when the heels of her sandals skidded on wet, seaweed-draped rocks. When it happened a third time, he scooped her up in his arms and tossed her over his shoulder.

"What are you doing?" she yelped, startled.

"Faster this way," he explained.

There was no time to argue. He was moving much faster now that he no longer had to steer her around the treacherous tide pool rocks.

"The caves," she said. "That's where we want to go."

"Right. The midnight tunnels."

She realized she was still gripping the flashlight and that the beam was aimed straight down.

"You'll need the flashlight," she said.

"No. The moonlight from your shoes is all I need to see where I'm going."

"What are you talking about?"

"Hush. The monster will hear you. We're supposed to hide."

He was right. The vehicle she had heard a moment ago was coming to a halt up on Cliff Road. She switched off the flashlight. Sure enough, the beach was flooded with moonlight, although none of it was coming from her shoes.

"Here," Jake declared. "The tunnel of midnight is the secret entrance to the moonlight highway. The monster can't find you there."

He lowered her to her feet, steadying her. She saw the black mouth of a cave. There was a pale glow of moonlight emanating from inside. But that was impossible.

It took her a couple of seconds to realize she was looking through a narrow tunnel that had been carved into the rocks by the sea. The light she saw was the moon splashing on the beach on the far side of the passage.

"Right," she said. "Let's go find the answers."

Jake was already moving inside the tunnel, turning sideways so that his broad shoulders would fit. She could tell that he was transfixed by the moonlight on the other end.

She was small enough to slip easily through the entrance. Once inside, she could see that the passage widened. The rocky walls dripped with moisture and the pounding of the surf reverberated through the tunnel. When the tide was in, the cave would be flooded.

She fought the claustrophobia that threatened to engulf her. Not much farther, she told herself. Just a few more feet.

"We're going down under the sea," Jake announced. "It's all right. We can breathe there."

"That's good to know," Adelaide muttered.

It was a relief to reach the exit of the cave tunnel but the patch of sand on the other side was very small, almost nonexistent. A jumble of large rocks littered the beach. They would provide cover if anyone came looking for them, Adelaide thought.

Jake had stopped at the water's edge. He stood looking out at the moonlit ocean, once again mesmerized by something only he could see.

Afraid that in his delirium he might decide to wade into the water, she put the flashlight on a nearby rock and grabbed Jake's arm.

"It's all right," she said. "We're safe now."

"I can't see the answers yet," he said.

"You will," she said.

"No answers, but I can see the monsters now." Jake's voice hardened abruptly. "They're hiding behind the rocks. Give me my gun."

There was no fear in his voice. He was the hunter who had spotted prey.

"I don't think that's a good idea," she said.

She did not dare give him his gun, not when he was in the grip of the drug. He was already seeing things in the shadows. The hallucinations were getting worse.

"All right," he said, agreeably enough. "You keep the gun. I'll use this."

He reached inside his dinner jacket and took out his fountain pen. She realized that to his hallucinating mind it probably appeared to be a knife.

"Excellent choice of a weapon to use against monsters," she said, trying to sound enthusiastic.

She tightened her grip on the pistol. She knew how to use the weapon, thanks to Raina, but she had never shot any living creature in her life, let alone a human. The thing that scared her the most was that she might kill some hapless individual who had stopped to help. But unless the new arrival was Conrad Massey or Dr. Gill, how could she tell the difference between an innocent passerby and one of the real monsters? And what about Paxton? How did he fit into the situation? She decided that, for now, at least, she would have to classify him as a bad guy.

With luck, an innocent person would be easily frightened off. Who, in his or her right mind, wouldn't run from a certifiably crazy woman holding a gun?

She listened closely, hoping to hear the muffled rumble of an accelerating car engine telling her that whoever had stopped had left the scene. A Good Samaritan would likely take off once he realized the occupants of the car were gone. But if the driver of the car was the person who had drugged Jake, he might decide to conduct a search of the beach.

A searcher looking for a hallucinating man and an escaped mental patient would probably use a flashlight, she thought.

She peered back through the narrow tunnel. She glimpsed the weak beam of a flashlight sweeping back and forth. The searcher was still up on Cliff Road.

She knew the roar of the surf would drown out the sound of their voices; nevertheless, she went up on tiptoe and spoke directly into Jake's ear.

"The person who drugged you is searching the beach. He's looking for us."

"For you," Jake said with great certainty. "The monster is looking for you, isn't he?"

"Yes, I think so. I'm hoping he won't come down to the beach. If he does, we must be prepared. He might have a gun."

"Doesn't matter," Jake said, blithely unconcerned now.

He held up the fountain pen. The handsome barrel gleamed in the moonlight.

"Let's hide behind those rocks," she whispered.

The boulders offered some concealment, she thought. They were the only hope if the searcher came through the tunnel.

"No," Jake said.

"Jake, please, this is important."

"I'll take care of you," he said.

Without another word he turned and walked to the mouth of the rock tunnel.

"Jake, where are you going?" she hissed.

"Stay here," he said. "I'll be right back."

"What are you going to do?"

"I'm going to kill the monster."

"Jake, no. We can talk about killing the monster later. Right now we have to stay here on this side of the tunnel. You might get hurt."

"Nope," he said. "The monster can't see me. The moonlight makes me invisible."

"Damn it, Jake, come back here."

She rushed forward and grabbed his arm again, but he gently pried off her fingers and disappeared into the tunnel. She reminded herself that she was the one with the gun. All Jake had was a fountain pen.

Unable to think of anything else to do, she followed him.

When they reached the far side of the opening in the rock, there was no sign of a flashlight beam. She heard the rumble of an accelerating car engine. Up on Cliff Road headlights lanced the darkness. The vehicle drove off in the direction of Burning Cove. Relief left her feeling oddly weak.

"It's all right, Jake," she said. "The monster is gone."

"Good." He put the fountain pen back inside his jacket. "Now we can follow the moonlight road and find the answers."

"The answers are at home," she said.

"Are you sure?"

"Yes," she said. "I'm sure."

He didn't argue. She took his hand and led him up to the road. Jake's speedster was the only vehicle in sight.

He contemplated the car with a thoughtful air.

"You should drive," he said.

"That is a very good idea."

Chapter 30

The most dangerous time in a blackmail operation was the moment when the transaction took place, Thelma Leggett thought.

It was two o'clock in the morning. She stood inside a deserted hot dog stand, Zolanda's pistol in one hand, and watched the darkened ticket booth at the entrance of the old seaside amusement park.

The park had closed a few years earlier, one more victim of the lousy economy. It had never been as grand as the boardwalk amusement park farther up the coast in Santa Cruz, but when she was a kid, it had seemed like a magical place. Tonight the moonlight shone down on the hulking skeletons of the great wheel and the roller coaster. The rides and arcades that lined the old midway were now deserted ruins. The wooden boardwalk was rotting into the sand.

She had chosen the ticket booth for the drop point because she knew the territory. When she was a little girl, her mother had often taken her to the amusement park in the summer when they came to the small town to visit her uncle. Tonight she had left her car parked a couple of blocks away on a dark side street where it was unlikely to be noticed. She had spotted the opening in the fence at the back of the park that morning when she had set out to choose a safe location for the payoff.

She and Zolanda had developed a variety of secure payoff strategies. The ticket booth had the single most important advantage that they had considered necessary for success in the extortion business—it could be observed from a safe distance. The old hot dog stand in which she stood was just one of a sprawling jumble of tumbledown shacks and arcades that littered the grounds of the amusement park.

A car cruised slowly past the sagging gates at the front of the park. It was the first vehicle to drive down the street in the nearly two hours that she had been waiting. Arriving early to ensure that there were no surprises was another important element of the payoff procedure.

Her nerves, already strained to the breaking point, threatened to shatter. She had collected blackmail payments before but always in Los Angeles, a city that was big enough to allow her to remain hidden.

Tonight was different. It was very possible that tonight she was doing business with a killer.

She could have used a couple of cups of the Enlightenment tea that Adelaide Brockton had concocted for Zolanda. Luckily she had a bottle of whiskey waiting back at the cabin.

A sedan stopped at the end of the street, did a U-turn, and drove back to the entrance of the amusement park. The driver brought the vehicle to a halt a short distance away. A figure wearing a trench coat with the collar pulled up and a hat angled low to conceal the profile got out from behind the wheel.

Thelma's pulse skittered with excitement. Her first solo extortion payoff was going like clockwork. She didn't count the deal that she had done with Conrad Massey yesterday. That had been a straightforward financial transaction.

She had been careful to conceal herself behind a large pair of sunglasses and a big hat when she met Massey at the gas station, but there was no reason to fear him. All he wanted was the information she had to sell—the location of the woman who was currently calling herself Adelaide Brockton—and he had been willing to pay for it. Massey had burned rubber when he floored the accelerator of his speedster and headed off down the highway toward Burning Cove.

But tonight's business was very different and a lot more dangerous.

The figure in the trench coat and hat pushed open the rusty gates and stopped briefly. A flashlight sparked. Thelma realized the target was looking for the ticket booth that she had described on the phone. She had made certain that it could be easily spotted.

The target hurried toward the ticket booth and pushed a bulky package over the counter. It fell inside the small structure and disappeared.

It was all over in less than two minutes. The target rushed back to the sedan and drove off down the street.

Thelma waited until the rumble of the vehicle's engine had faded into the distance. And then she waited a little longer, just to be sure. The thrill of success threatened to steal her breath. Her pulse was kicking up like crazy now.

Hardly daring to believe how easy it had been, she left the shadows of the hot dog stand and went quickly to the ticket booth. She opened the rear door. The interior of the small structure was steeped in darkness. She couldn't see a thing and she didn't dare use her flashlight for fear that a passerby might notice it.

She took two cautious steps inside. The toe of her shoe nudged an object on the floor. She reached down and grabbed the envelope. It was thick and reassuringly heavy. Small bills bound up in large quantities weighed more than most people expected.

Clutching the envelope in one hand and the pistol in the other, she left the ticket booth and started back through the amusement park. The fog was rolling in fast but there was still enough moonlight to allow her to find her way.

It had all been so easy.

She heard a sound behind her. Panic jolted her nerves, even as she told herself there was nothing to worry about. She had probably surprised a transient who had decided to bed down in the shelter of the old carousel.

A cat meowed in the shadows. A few seconds later the creature darted past her, gliding briefly through the moonlight before disappearing again.

She started breathing again but she could not squelch the panic entirely. She went quickly toward the exit, clutching the gun. She did not stop until she reached her car. She used the flashlight then, aiming it through the back seat window to make sure no one was concealed on the floorboard.

She got into the Ford and slipped her gun back into her handbag. She was shaking so badly it took two tries to turn the key in the ignition, and she had to concentrate hard just to get the car in gear. The fog was rolling in heavily now. She drove slowly through the dark streets and out onto the road that would take her back to the cabin.

A short time later she walked through the front door, flashlight in hand. Dropping the handbag and the envelope onto the cot, she crossed to the small kitchenette and lit the lantern on the counter. The glary light flared, illuminating the small space. The bottle of whiskey was sitting next to the cracked, chipped sink.

She poured herself a large glass and gulped down a fortifying swallow. She'd taken a risk tonight but it had paid off. The score was a big one. She was in business. She had enough secrets to last for years. She did not need Zolanda.

In spite of the whiskey, a chill whispered through her. For some reason the cabin no longer felt like a safe place to hide. She would head for San Francisco in the morning. It would be easier to disappear in a city.

Satisfied with that decision, she drank some more whiskey and contemplated the thick envelope on the cot. A rising sense of hot exultation burned away the uneasy sensation that she had experienced a moment ago.

She lit a cigarette, stuck it in the corner of her mouth, and crossed the small space to the cot. Seizing the envelope, she tore it open and upended it, dumping the neatly bound packets onto the stained quilt.

So much money. Maybe she should have asked for more. But tonight had been only the first of what would become a steady stream of payoffs.

She picked up one of the packets and startled to riffle through it.

Seconds later, she paused, horrified. The bill on top was real but the rest of the packet was nothing but a stack of neatly cut newspapers. She tossed it down onto the cot, rage splashing through her. Quickly she checked the other packets. They were all the same—only the bills on the top were genuine.

The target had dared to cheat her. Why do such a thing?

The answer came in a dizzying rush. She had been set up.

She had to get away. Now. Tonight.

Hauling the grip out from under the bed, she threw her things into it and slammed the lid closed. She hoisted it and set it on the floor near the door. She would take the hatbox out to the car first. It was very heavy. She could not manage it and the suitcase at the same time.

She yanked open the front door and confronted a seemingly impenetrable wall of fog. The lantern light spilled through the doorway behind her. It would be a tough drive but she had to get away.

She carried the hatbox down the front steps, set it inside the trunk, and rushed back into the cabin to pick up the grip. Once again she started down the steps to the Ford.

She froze halfway to the car because things were moving in the mist. Horrifying, snake-headed creatures twisted and writhed end-lessly, their iridescent scales glowing with bizarre colors. Fangs dripped with blood.

Somewhere in the back of her mind she realized that she was hal-lucinating. The whiskey, she thought vaguely. But she wasn't drunk. She had taken only a couple of swallows.

She gave up trying to make sense of what she was seeing because the colors of the snakes were too hot and painfully bright. One of the monsters swam toward her through the mist. Its eyes blazed with a terrible radiance.

A flashlight, some remote part of her brain tried to tell her. Just a flashlight. But she could not hold on to the rational explanation.

She started to turn around, intending to flee into the safety of the cabin. But it was too late.

The killer came up behind her and plunged the needle into the curve of her shoulder, close to her neck. She staggered over the thresh-old and made it as far as the bed before she collapsed. Her last con-scious thought was that the target had double-crossed her.

The killer took out a gun. The occasion called for another suicide but it was time to change the method. The nearest house was half a mile away. The roar of the ocean would muffle the shot.

The next order of business was locating the stash of blackmail ma-terials. The hatbox containing the secrets that Madam Zolanda and her assistant had collected during the past three years was in the trunk of Leggett's car.

Chapter 31

Jake opened his eyes and was vaguely annoyed to see the dull gloom of a foggy morning. Something important had happened during the night, he thought. But for a moment he could not remember what it was. Fragments of dreams whispered through his mind.

He recalled standing on a moonlit beach with Adelaide and seeking answers at the end of a highway paved in silver moonlight. A monster had lurked in the shadows. It had threatened Adelaide.

He was trying to focus on the memory when Adelaide herself appeared, hovering over him. She was no longer wearing the satin gown and silver shoes. Instead she had on a pair of wide-legged trousers and a snug-fitting sweater. Her hair was pinned in a severe knot at the nape of her neck. She had a mug in one hand.

"I gave you the antidote as soon as we got back here last night," she said. "I managed to get you up the stairs to your bed before you collapsed. Otherwise you'd have awakened on the floor downstairs. I made some strong coffee for you. Trust me, it will help."

"If you say so."

He sat up slowly and swung his legs over the edge, planting both feet on the floor. He was still wearing the trousers and the white shirt that he had worn to the Paradise Club. Somewhere along the line he had lost his jacket, his tie, and his shoes.

He wrapped one hand around the mug and took a cautious swallow. It tasted very good. He took another swallow.

"What did you say about an antidote?" he finally asked.

"I think that you were drugged with a dangerous hallucinogen called Daydream. My parents discovered it. As soon as they realized its dangerous properties, my mother created an herbal antidote. I did the research in the botanical literature for her so I know the ingredients."

"This is going to be a very complicated story, isn't it?"

"I'm afraid so," Adelaide said. "How do you feel?"

He considered the question closely. More memories trickled back.

"I'm not sure," he said. "All right, I think. Did I have too much to drink last night?"

"No. You didn't have anything to drink except sparkling water. You were drugged and it's my fault."

He eyed her closely. "You didn't drug me, did you?"

"No, of course not. Look, I hate to say this, believe me, but I think you should leave as soon as possible."

He contemplated her for a long moment. She looked anxious, stricken with guilt, and quite desperate.

"Let me get this straight," he said. "You're kicking me out?"

"I think it's for the best."

"For me or for you?"

"For you. It's clear now that I've put you in terrible danger."

"Believe it or not, I figured out at the start of this thing that you were running from something or someone. It's too late to ditch me. We're in this together."

"You don't understand."

"No, but I will just as soon as you explain it to me. What time is it?"

"What? Oh." She glanced at her watch. "It's just going on six thirty. Why?"

"That means we've got plenty of time before you have to go to work at the tearoom."

"Time for you to pack?"

She sounded almost hopeful, he thought.

"No," he said. "Time for you to tell me what's going on."

Adelaide hesitated. "All right. After what happened, you have a right to some answers. I was going to tell you some of it last night but then you started hallucinating—"

He held up a hand to stop her. "Not so fast. I am going to clean up, shave, and put on some fresh clothes. Then we'll talk."

She hesitated. "All right. I'll make breakfast while you're getting ready."

"That sounds like a very good plan."

She took a deep breath and visibly steeled herself. "I think you should know that I didn't tell you the whole truth last night when I said I didn't recognize the dark-haired man who walked past us in the gardens."

"I figured there was more to the story. Who was he?"

"I can't be absolutely positive because I didn't get a good look at him, but I think it may have been my husband," Adelaide said.

She turned and walked out of the bedroom before he could think of a reasonable response.

He sat on the edge of the bed for a moment, contemplating what she had just told him.

There was a husband. Damn.

He collected his shaving kit and went into the bathroom. He set the kit on the pink tiled counter and put the coffee mug next to it. Then he looked at his reflection in the mirror. He was not an inspiring sight, he decided. His face was shadowed with dark stubble, his hair was standing on end, and his eyes were those of a man who had spent an exhausting night fighting demons.

He drained the last of the coffee and set the empty mug back on the counter.

"I knew it was going to get more complicated," he said to the man in the mirror.

Chapter 32

He went downstairs a short time later, feeling remarkably improved. It was amazing what a quick bath, a brisk shave, and a cup of strong coffee could do for a man.

Adelaide was at the stove frying eggs and slathering butter on thick chunks of toast. When she saw him, she handed him another mug of coffee without saying a word.

He sat down at the scarred table and hoisted the mug.

"I'm listening," he said.

She concentrated on the eggs in the skillet.

"You're probably going to think I'm delusional," she warned.

"Is that why you haven't told me the whole truth until now?"

"Yes." She used a spatula to lift one of the eggs out of the pan and slipped it onto a plate. "I didn't want to have to tell you the truth because I liked the way you looked at me—at least, the way you looked at me until last night."

"How, exactly, did I look at you?"

"As if I was normal. That's the way everyone else here in Burning Cove looks at me, too. It makes me feel good."

"Are you saying you're not normal?"

"I think I'm fairly normal. But it's going to be hard to convince you of that after I tell you my story."

"Let's hear it."

"All right."

She dished up the second fried egg, added the toast, and set the plate in front of him. She poured a large glass of freshly squeezed orange juice for him, got a mug of tea for herself, and sat down on the opposite side of the table.

"I told you that my mother was a botanist," she said. "And that my father was a chemist. They were both dedicated scientists who spent their lives searching for new drugs that could be used on patients who suffered from very severe forms of depression and other mental illnesses. My father came from a wealthy family. He built his own private lab. A year ago they discovered a drug they thought had the potential to revolutionize the treatment of the mentally ill. It has a long chemical name but they called it Daydream."

He nodded and forked up a bite of eggs. "Go on."

"Shortly after they made their discovery, my parents were both killed in an explosion in their lab. I was devastated. I didn't have any brothers or sisters and no close family. I found myself alone in the world."

He tore off a chunk of toast. "Alone in the world with a lot of money."

She paused in the act of taking a sip of tea. "Yes. My father left me a sizable fortune."

"Uh-huh."

"You sound as if you know where this story is going," she said.

"It's obvious it doesn't have a good ending. You're no longer rich and it's starting to look as if someone from your past is hunting you. Presumably that individual does not have good intentions."

"You're right, except that I think several people are looking for me. As I was saying, I was still reeling from the loss of my family when Conrad Massey came into my life. He was witty, charming, very handsome, and very understanding. I was sure he wasn't a fortune hunter because he is descended from an old San Francisco family. He inherited the family business."

Jake paused in the acting of forking up a bite of fried egg. "Are you talking about Conrad Massey of Massey Shipping?"

"You've heard of it?"

"Sure. I used to be in the import-export business, remember? I'm aware of all the major shipping companies on the West Coast. Never had any dealings with Conrad Massey himself, though. I don't know the man. I seem to recall hearing rumors that his company was facing some serious financial problems."

"All I can say is that, in hindsight, I should have known Conrad was too good to be true."

"Mr. Perfect swept you off your feet?"

"Yes. For a time." Adelaide glanced down at her left hand as if there had once been a ring on one finger. "He asked me to marry him. But that's where things get murky."

"How murky?"

"Conrad wanted to elope. He claimed he was so passionately in love with me that he could not go through a long, formal engagement. Because I was still grieving the loss of my parents, the last thing I wanted was a big society wedding. I admit that, at first, I was dazzled by Conrad. But I started to get the feeling that I was being rushed. It was as if I could hear my parents' voices in my head, telling me to slow down and be very sure of what I was doing. So I told Conrad that I wanted time to think about it. He agreed but he insisted on giving me a ring."

"An engagement ring?"

"He said no, that it was just a token of his affection, something to make me think of him whenever I looked at it. I wore it for a while but the more I thought about a future with Conrad, the more uneasy I got. I just couldn't see myself married to him. I had inherited money, but my parents had never moved in the social world. I didn't feel comfortable at the nightclubs and restaurants that Conrad enjoyed. I think he must have realized that I was about to end things, because he invited me to a private dinner in his town house one evening. That night I told him that I couldn't marry him and I gave him back his ring."

"How did he react?"

"He said he was disappointed but that he would wait for me to change my mind."

"What happened next?"

"I drank some of the champagne that he had poured for me, and about twenty minutes later I went crazy. I started hallucinating wildly. I was consumed by panic and paranoia. I was convinced that I was falling through the floor of the dining room into hell. The devil himself came toward me. He was wearing a surgical mask. He gave me an injection. I was locked in a delirium nightmare. I didn't come out of it for nearly three days. When I woke up, I was in a locked room in an insane asylum named Rushbrook Sanitarium."

Jake put his fork down with great precision. He had to work hard to control the searing fury that burned deep inside him.

"Sounds a lot like what happened to me last night," he said.

"Yes. Fortunately you didn't drink all of that water. You got a fairly light dose. I'm sure that the drug they used on you was the same one they used on me while I was locked up at Rushbrook, the one my parents discovered."

"Daydream."

"Yes. When I slowly came back to my senses, I tried to explain to everyone at Rushbrook, including Dr. Gill and the director of his private lab, Dr. Ormsby, that I was all right. I told them I was convinced that Conrad had drugged me and that someone had helped him."

"The man in the surgical mask."

"Yes."

"How did Gill and Ormsby react?"

"They gave me another dose of Daydream," Adelaide said.

Jake realized he was gripping something in his right hand. He looked down and saw that he had picked up the knife. Very deliberately he put it down on the table.

"Some monsters are real," he said quietly.

"I finally realized that Gill and Ormsby had been conspiring with Conrad from the start. In fact, I'm quite sure that it was Gill's idea to use me."

"Use you?"

"They needed another test subject, you see. I was Patient B. Evidently, Patient A died. The people housed on ward five told me that one day Gill and Ormsby would kill me with the drug and I would become a ghost, just like the other patient who had been locked in my room."

"Gill and Ormsby conducted experiments on you?"

"They had other patients they could have used, of course, but those people were all locked up at Rushbrook in the first place because they had been diagnosed as suffering from some type of severe mental illness. Gill and Ormsby wanted a research subject who was . . . normal."

"They didn't just want a subject who was normal," Jake said. "They wanted someone who was alone in the world. Someone who didn't have any family members who might ask awkward questions."

"They could have kidnapped some poor soul off the street if that was all they wanted," Adelaide said. "But they also needed money. They had a nice little sideline going with the sales of some drug that they packaged in perfume bottles, but they didn't have the capacity to produce and market large quantities of the stuff. And, as it happens, experimental research is expensive."

"Massey agreed to give Gill a share of the money he got from your inheritance."

"Yes."

"How did Conrad Massey get involved in this?"

Adelaide's smile was both cold and sad. "He wanted to marry me for the oldest reason in the world."

"He needed money."

"Yes."

"But to get control of your inheritance, he would have had to marry you," Jake said. "Not only that, he would have had to be your husband in order to have you committed against your will. You said you decided not to marry him. You gave him back his ring."

"I told you, that's where things get murky. You see, when I woke up in the Rushbrook Sanitarium, everyone insisted on addressing me as Mrs. Massey. I had a gold wedding band on my left hand."

"The bastard claimed he had married you? Dr. Gill believed him?"

Adelaide shrugged. "I think it was Gill's idea from the start. But here's the problem—it might be true. I don't know if I'm actually married to Conrad."

"You don't know?"

"I don't have any clear memories of the time between the night of my so-called breakdown in Conrad's dining room and the morning I finally started to recover from the delirium. I lost three days of my life to a nightmare. I was told that during those three days, Conrad and I had eloped to Reno. I was also informed that it was the stress of my wedding night that had caused my nervous breakdown. Gill said that I was suffering from amnesia."

"Even though you collapsed in Massey's town house shortly after you drank some drugged champagne?"

"I was advised that I could not trust any of my memories of events that took place during those three days."

"You said that they were using Daydream, the drug your parents discovered, for the experiments. How did Gill and Ormsby get hold of it?"

"Gill was well aware of my parents' research. He's in the business of operating a psychiatric asylum, after all. My father had said Gill was especially interested in a drug that would cause patients to become highly suggestible. Gill claimed he wanted a drug that would induce a trancelike state so that a doctor could use hypnosis in a therapeutic way to stabilize a patient's unbalanced mind. To some extent Daydream accomplishes that goal—it certainly has hypnotic properties. But as you discovered, it has some very serious side effects."

"The hallucinations?"

"Yes. It is also very unpredictable. It can make you extremely paranoid, for example. In the end my parents concluded that it was simply too dangerous. They informed Gill that they were closing down the research into Daydream." Adelaide paused. Her eyes tightened at the corners. "Coincidentally, my mother and father were killed less than a week later in a mysterious explosion in their laboratory, and all of the research files on Daydream disappeared."

"But you doubt that?"

"Supposedly my parents' notebooks were destroyed in the blast, but I'm very sure that Gill and Ormsby stole them."

"You think Gill and Ormsby murdered your parents."

"At the time I was convinced that the explosion really was an accident. But I stopped believing that when I woke up in a room at Rushbrook." Adelaide made a face. "As I said, I may be a little naïve, but once I know the truth about someone, I learn my lesson."

"What about the antidote?"

"Gill and Ormsby never knew about it. In hindsight, I think my parents may have been starting to get concerned about Gill. There must have been a reason why they did not record the formula for the antidote in the notes that they kept in their laboratory."

"But you knew the ingredients because you had done the research for your mother."

"Yes. Once I realized what was happening to me, I set about collecting them. Some of the herbs were actually growing in the hospital gardens. The rest of the ingredients were smuggled in by my friends."

He set his mug down hard on the wooden table. "You had *friends* in that asylum?"

"I was there for two months," Adelaide said gently. "I had time to get to know a few people—the janitors, one of the guards at the front gate. A nurse. A member of the kitchen staff. I was also friends with some of the patients, especially the woman everyone called the Duchess. I owe them all more than I can ever repay. It took a while but eventually they helped me collect the ingredients that I needed for the antidote."

"How did you manage to make it without attracting the attention of Gill and Ormsby?"

"I kept the herbs under my mattress. After each session in the lab, a friend in the kitchen made sure to send a pot of hot tea to my room. I added the herbs. I was terrified that, in my drugged state, I would accidentally give myself away. But some of the effects of the drug can be ... managed ... once you've had experience with it. Thanks to Gill and Ormsby I got a *lot* of experience."

Jake sat back in his chair. "What happened to the wedding ring?"

"I've still got it. I keep it in a box under the bed, the same place I keep my gun. I've been afraid to sell it for fear someone would ask questions. I didn't want my new friends here in Burning Cove speculating about my husband."

"What about a marriage license?"

"I don't have a copy of it but that doesn't mean I didn't sign one in my hallucinatory state. I've thought about it a lot, though, and I doubt that one exists. It's very possible there never was a marriage. There was no need for one, you see. It's extremely rare for someone to actually demand proof of a marriage."

"Good point. Which is why bigamy is a surprisingly common crime. It usually comes to light only when someone dies and another spouse steps forward to claim an inheritance."

"But I wasn't dead. I had been declared mentally ill. There was no reason that the New York bankers who handle my father's estate would question Conrad's claim that he had married me. I told you, he's the descendant of a very distinguished family. Why would they doubt his word?"

Jake nodded, thinking about it. "It was a risk, but one Massey and Gill were willing to take. And you haven't dared to contact the people handling the estate, have you?"

"I've practiced all sorts of ways to try to explain what happened to me, but I'm terrified that they'll think I really am crazy."

"Even if a marriage license does exist, it's entirely possible that it was forged," Jake said. "It would be a fairly simple thing to do. I think you're right; the most likely explanation is that there never was a marriage."

"What makes you so sure?"

"Because none of them—not Gill or Massey or Ormsby—have let on that you escaped."

"Gill and Conrad have kept quiet about it," Adelaide said. "There never was a risk that Ormsby would tell anyone about my escape. He's dead."

"How?"

"I saw him the night I left Rushbrook. Someone used the drug on him. He was hallucinating wildly. The killer deliberately frightened him so badly that he jumped out one of the windows in the laboratory at Rushbrook."

"You saw the murderer?"

"I saw him twice that night," Adelaide said. "The first time was when he chased Ormsby through the lab and again in the hallway a short time later. But I didn't get a good look at him either time because he wore a surgical mask and a doctor's coat and cap."

Jake reached for his coffee mug. "You saw Ormsby go out that window?"

"Actually, I heard him go out the window. I was in his office in the lab at the time. I wanted to get my patient file before I left. I was afraid that Gill and the others could use it to convince a judge to send me back to Rushbrook."

"Did you find the file?"

"No, because the killer chased Ormsby into the lab just as I was searching for the key to the file cabinet. After the murderer left, I dared not take the chance that he might come back. I ran."

"You said you saw the man in the surgical mask again that night?"

"The second time I saw him he was just leaving the hallway where my room was located," Adelaide said. "He had a syringe in his hand. I was the only patient housed in that particular corridor. I think he intended to kill me."

"Sounds like it. No wonder you were so shaken by Madam Zolanda's death. It looked too much like Dr. Ormsby's death, didn't it?"

Adelaide put her mug aside and folded her arms on the table. "It's not just the fact that both appear to have been suicides. Remember that cut crystal perfume bottle stopper that you found under the liquor cabinet?"

"You know something about that, don't you?"

"I told you that, in addition to Daydream, Ormsby and Gill were brewing up some illicit drugs in their laboratory. I'm not sure of the purpose of the drugs but I am certain that they were not legitimate medicines. Every couple of weeks Ormsby complained because he had to take time off from perfecting Daydream in order to make up a batch of the other drugs. He bottled the stuff in crystal perfume bottles that he stored in a velvet jewelry case. Usually, Gill stopped by the lab to pick up the bottles. But on the night I escaped, the killer, not Gill, took the drugs."

"You're sure the killer was not Gill?"

"Positive," Adelaide said. "Gill is a short man. The killer in the surgical mask was tall."

"You saw him take the perfume bottles?"

"Yes. I was hiding behind Ormsby's desk at the time. I was terrified that he would find me. I had a couple of jars of chemicals that I planned to throw into his eyes if necessary."

Jake swallowed the last of the coffee and put the mug down.

"That," he said, "is one hell of a story."

Adelaide closed her eyes as if absorbing a physical blow. When she raised her lashes and looked at him, he could see the fear she was struggling to control.

"You don't believe me, do you?" she whispered. "I was afraid you wouldn't. I've been lying low, living under a new name here in Burning Cove while I try to figure out what to do. I haven't dared to go to the police because I've been afraid they would find out that I was an escapee from a lunatic asylum. The first thing they would do is contact my so-called husband."

"Who would then call the head of the Rushbrook Sanitarium."

"Yes."

He got to his feet and rounded the end of the big table. Reaching down, he grasped Adelaide's arms and hauled her gently out of the chair.

"One thing we need to get straight before we discuss anything else," he said. "No one is going to take you away. No one is going to send you back to Rushbrook. No one is going to lock you up again. I will not allow it."

"But what if Conrad really is my husband?"

"Then you and I will go to Reno and we will stay there for the necessary six weeks until you can file for divorce. Trust me, Conrad Massey won't be a problem. A nuisance, maybe, but not a serious problem. Do we understand each other now?"

She watched him with her shadow-filled eyes for what seemed like an eternity. And then she threw her arms around him, rested her head on his chest, and held him as if he had just saved her from drowning. He folded her close.

"Thank you," she mumbled into his shirt. "I'm so sorry I dragged you into this situation."

"You didn't drag me into it. I came to Burning Cove to look for Madam Zolanda. Now she's dead and that perfume bottle stopper we found at her villa indicates she may have had a connection to the bastards at the Rushbrook Sanitarium. If that's true, it's all tied up together and we might finally be able to figure out what is going on here."

Adelaide sniffed a couple of times and raised her head with obvious reluctance. There were tears running down her cheeks. She stepped back and used the hem of her apron to dab at her eyes.

"I knew that, sooner or later, I was going to have to find a way out of this mess, but I figured as long as Gill and Conrad were pretending that I was still a patient, I was safe. But last night everything changed."

"Yes," he said. "Until now you've been worried that someone would drag you back to Rushbrook. But it looks like we've got an even bigger problem."

"I know. Someone tried to kill you."

"And you, as well. Whoever drugged me last night had to know there was an excellent chance that I would drive straight off Cliff Road into the ocean. If that had happened, we would probably both be dead. The original plan may have been to kidnap you and take you back to Rushbrook, but obviously that has changed. Whoever is after you is evidently willing to murder you."

"But I'm no good to Conrad unless I'm alive. Under the terms of my father's estate, if I die with no offspring, my inheritance goes to some very distant relatives."

"Massey might want you alive but it doesn't look like the others do. I think they've decided that if they can't grab you, they have to try to silence you."

"But who would believe my story?" Adelaide said.

"I believe it. Trust me, that's enough to create serious problems for Gill and Massey and the guy in the surgical mask. I've got one more question."

"What is it?"

"What made you pick that particular night—the same night that a killer was prowling the halls of Rushbrook—to try to escape the sanitarium?"

Adelaide smiled a watery smile. "The Duchess warned me that something terrible was going to happen that night. She said that if I didn't leave, I would not survive until morning. She said I would become the next ghost."

Chapter 33

Adelaide was washing teacups in the big sink in the tearoom kitchen when the phone rang. She wiped her hands on her apron and crossed the pea green linoleum floor to pick up the receiver.

"Refresh Tearoom," she said.

"Adelaide, it's Raina. I have a possible location for Thelma Leggett."

"That's great."

"No guarantees but here's what I've got. I located the property that Leggett inherited. I made a phone call to a local real estate firm and pretended that I was looking for a place to rent for a week. I mentioned that I had seen an empty cabin the last time I drove through the town. I gave them the address of the property that Leggett owns. The secretary who took my call said that the place has had a For Sale sign in the window for about two years but the day before yesterday a woman moved in. Her car is still sitting in the driveway."

"Raina, you are absolutely brilliant."

"It might be a huge coincidence that a woman moved into Leggett's cabin a couple of days ago," Raina warned.

"It must be Leggett."

"That's what I'm assuming. I checked a map. Looks like the town is about a two-hour drive from Burning Cove."

Adelaide glanced at the wall clock. "It's a little after ten. I've got to call Jake. He's talking to Luther Pell. If we leave now, we can be there before one o'clock."

"What about your job?"

"Flo will understand when I tell her I need the day off. She'll probably assume that Jake and I are sneaking off for an afternoon tryst at some unnamed auto court."

"When nothing could be further from the truth, right?"

"Right. Got to go, Raina. Thanks."

"I'll send my bill to Mr. Truett."

"No, that wouldn't be right. Send it to me."

"You can't afford me, pal. Drive carefully."

Raina hung up the phone.

Chapter 34

The shot to the temple had done a lot of damage but there was enough left of Thelma Leggett's face to identify her.

"Another suicide," Jake said. "What an amazing coincidence. But this time the victim used a gun. Someone evidently decided to rewrite the script."

Adelaide turned away from the sight of Thelma Leggett sprawled on the thin, blood-soaked bed. For a moment she was afraid that she would be sick.

"Are you all right?" Jake asked.

"Yes. No. But I'm not going to faint, if that's what's worrying you."

Jake rounded the end of the cot and put an arm around her shoulders.

"Why don't you wait outside?" he suggested, his voice gentling.

She shook her head and stepped away from the comfort he was offering. She forced herself to take another look at the cot. Thelma had evidently been sitting on the edge of the bed when she put the pistol to her temple and pulled the trigger. She had fallen backward across the quilt. Her fingers were still wrapped around the gun.

"What is going on here?" she said.

"It would be easy to assume that someone was after the stash of blackmail secrets. But now, given what happened to Zolanda and what you told me about Ormsby's death, I'm wondering if we're looking at something a lot more complicated."

"Such as?"

"You described a drug ring operating out of the Rushbrook Sanitarium. People engaged in that business tend to be vicious and ruthless. Maybe the killer has concluded that it's time to leave the old gang behind and strike out on his own."

"Why murder Ormsby, the person who concocted the drugs?" Adelaide asked.

"Whoever is behind this may have concluded Ormsby had become a problem. Or maybe Ormsby was no longer needed. There are other chemists in the world."

"Where do Zolanda and Thelma Leggett fit in?" Adelaide asked.

"The drug business is a business like any other. In addition to a manufacturing facility it requires distributors and sales reps who know how to target a certain market, in this case a very exclusive market."

"Zolanda and Leggett had access to some of the most important people in Hollywood. Talk about an exclusive market."

"This is all speculation but things are starting to come together," Jake said.

"What do we do? Contact the FBI?"

"No," Jake said. "Not yet."

"You're right. It's too soon. We don't have any proof. We're leaping to conclusions, aren't we? Maybe Thelma Leggett really did kill herself. The gun is still in her hand."

"Which is one of the reasons I don't believe she took her own life,"

Jake said. "She would have been sitting on the side of the bed when she pulled the trigger. The gun would have fallen from her hand and most likely landed on the floor or close to the edge of the mattress. She certainly wouldn't have kept her grip on it as she fell onto her back."

Adelaide wanted to ask him how he could be so sure of that analysis, but this was not the time.

"You said that was one of the reasons you don't think this is suicide," she said. "What else?"

"The suitcase," Jake said.

They both looked at the grip sitting on the floor near the door.

"What about it?" Adelaide asked.

"It looks like Thelma was getting ready to leave. Why would she bother to pack her bag if she was about to kill herself?"

"Maybe she never unpacked in the first place."

Jake shook his head. "She was here for a couple of days. There are dishes in the sink, a loaf of bread and some cheese on the counter, and that bottle of whiskey is empty."

"You're right. At the very least, she would have opened the suitcase to take out a nightgown and a change of clothes." Adelaide looked at the door. "She was on her way out of town, wasn't she?"

"I think she got scared and decided to run again. But the killer got here before she could escape."

"If we're right, she didn't put up much of a struggle."

"She probably didn't have a chance." Jake started opening and closing cupboards and drawers. "Most people do exactly as they're told when someone aims a gun at them."

Adelaide looked at the empty whiskey bottle. "Most people are also highly suggestible when they are under the influence of Daydream."

"Don't remind me." Jake closed the last cupboard. "Nothing here. I'm going to take a look at her car. Maybe she left something in the trunk. While I'm doing that, check the suitcase and her handbag. Use a handkerchief. When we've finished searching the place, we'll find a pay phone and call the cops to report the body. They'll know we were in here but there's no sense leaving any more fingerprints around than necessary."

"All right," Adelaide said. She opened her handbag and extracted a neatly folded linen handkerchief. "What am I looking for?"

"I have no idea. I just hope that we'll know it when we see it."

Jake let himself outside, leaving the door open behind him.

She crouched beside the suitcase and got it open. There was a jumble of clothes inside and some toiletries but no envelope containing a blackmailer's secrets and no journal with a list of potential victims.

She got up and went to the front door.

"Looks like Leggett packed in a hurry," she said. "But I didn't see anything that looked like a clue. No tickets. No money. No papers. Definitely no blackmail secrets. How do you transport extortion secrets, anyway?"

"Depends on the secrets." Jake closed the trunk of the Ford and came back up the steps. "If I'm right about Madam Zolanda having collected blackmail materials for some time, she must have had a sizable stash. She probably also had a journal with names, dates, addresses, phone numbers, and incriminating details. There might have been photos and documents, as well. I'd say we're looking for something the size of a small suitcase."

"Looks like whoever murdered Thelma now has that suitcase," Adelaide said. "I'll check her handbag."

She was about to head for the leather bag when she saw two oblong slips of paper in the shadows under the cot.

"Who would leave money behind?" she asked.

She went down on one knee and retrieved the two slips of paper.

"Just cut-up newspapers," she announced. "So much for finding a couple of dollar bills lying around at the scene of the crime."

"Let me see those," Jake said.

She got to her feet and gave him the papers. He examined them with a thoughtful expression.

"This is very, very interesting," he said.

"Why?"

"These papers were cut to precisely the same size and shape as dollar bills."

"I can tell that you don't think that is a coincidence," Adelaide said.

"No. Got a hunch our blackmailer got conned."

"With just two pieces of paper? That doesn't sound likely."

"There were probably a lot more of these," Jake said. He surveyed the room. "I think the killer cleaned up the scene. A pile of fake dollar bills might have forced the cops to pay too much attention to what was supposed to pass as a suicide."

Adelaide went to the end table, opened the brown leather handbag, and surveyed the interior.

"Just the usual things a woman keeps in a purse," she reported. "A wallet, a compact, a lipstick, a comb, and a hankie."

She paused when she saw the folded paper at the bottom of the handbag. A little rush of excitement splashed through her. She took out the paper and unfolded it.

A split second later her excitement metamorphosed into shock.

"What is it?" Jake asked.

"A phone number," she said, trying to keep her voice even.

"Los Angeles? Burning Cove?"

"No. I think it might be a San Francisco number. Douglas 4981."

"Sounds like you recognize it."

"It's been a while since I had a reason to call this particular number, so I may be wrong. But I'm almost positive it's Conrad Massey's home number."

"Write down the number. We'll call it later, after we deal with the police."

"Why are we going to call it?"

"Because if Massey answers, we'll know he's home in San Francisco."

"And if he doesn't answer, we'll know he's probably the man I saw in Burning Cove."

"Exactly," Jake said.

Chapter 35

By the time they finished with the police, the fog that had been hovering offshore most of the day had begun to move inland. The winding coastal highway was rapidly being flooded with a gray mist.

"I thought we'd have enough daylight for the drive back to Burning Cove," Jake said. "But it will be dark soon and the fog is getting heavy. There aren't any hotels around here. We'd better try to find an auto court for tonight."

Adelaide contemplated the scene through the windshield. She had been so consumed with thinking about their conversation with the local police that she had not been paying much attention to driving conditions. They were deteriorating rapidly.

Jake had put up the top of the convertible, but the damp chill of the fog succeeded in penetrating the interior of the vehicle. Or maybe that was just her imagination, she thought. Regardless, it would be reckless to try to make the drive back to Burning Cove tonight.

"I agree we should stop for the night," she said. "We don't know this road, and even if we did, we'd have to drive so slowly it would take half the night to get back to Burning Cove. We passed an auto court on our way into town this morning."

"I remember. It should be coming up soon. Let's hope they've still got a vacancy. Wouldn't be surprised if they're full, though. Anyone with common sense will be pulling off the road to avoid the fog."

"We could turn around. There might be a place in town where we can put up for the night."

But even as she made the suggestion, she realized she really did not want to return to the town where Thelma Leggett had been killed. The conversation with the police had gone reasonably well. Surprisingly, the detective in charge had not leaped to the conclusion that Leggett's death was a suicide. He had questioned them in depth about their reasons for pursuing Leggett, and he had made them cool their heels at the station while he phoned the Burning Cove police department to confirm their identities. He had even gone the extra mile and verified their departure time from Burning Cove. That had been easy enough to do because they had stopped to fill up the gas tank before leaving town that morning. The attendant had recognized them and remembered servicing the car.

The good news, Adelaide thought, was that she and Jake were not suspects in Thelma Leggett's death. But that was the only good news so far. The San Francisco phone number she had copied was still burning a hole in her handbag.

A sign advertising an upcoming gas station loomed in the mist.

"There will probably be a pay phone there," she said. "Let's stop so that I can call that San Francisco number."

"I'm sure there will be a phone at the auto court," Jake said.

"Maybe. But if there isn't one or if it's out of order, I'll have to wait until tomorrow to find out if Conrad is still in San Francisco. I need to know, Jake."

"All right," Jake said. "Got to admit, I'm pretty damn curious myself."

He turned off the highway onto a side road and pulled into the closed gas station. A faded sign on the wall pointed to a telephone booth around the corner of the garage.

Jake brought the car to a halt but he left the lights on and the motor running.

"We need to hurry," he said. "The fog is getting bad fast. Bring the flashlight."

Adelaide already had the glove box open. Jake's gun was no longer inside. He was wearing it in a shoulder holster. She grabbed the flashlight and got out of the car. Jake climbed out from behind the wheel and joined her. He took the flashlight and switched it on.

They walked around the corner of the building. The flashlight picked out the darkened phone booth a few feet away from the entrance of the closed garage.

Jake opened the door of the booth and aimed the beam at the front of the telephone so that she could see the dial. She took the little notebook out of her purse and found the number.

Jake handed her some coins. She dropped them into the slot and dialed the operator.

"Long distance, please," she said.

"One moment. I'll connect you," the operator said.

There was something reassuring about the very professional, very efficient, very competent female voice on the other end of the line. It was the voice of the modern era, Adelaide thought, the voice that was associated with the latest developments in communications technology. She liked the fact that it was a woman's voice.

The operator asked for some additional coins. Adelaide fumbled them into the slot.

She was vaguely aware of the distant rumble of a car engine. Headlights glared in the fog. The vehicle turned off the highway and onto the farm road that went past the gas station. Jake turned to watch the car motor slowly down the side road, but he seemed to relax when the vehicle did not pause.

"Just some farmer trying to get home before the conditions get worse," he said.

The wait for the long-distance operator to establish the connection seemed an eternity but Adelaide knew that it was probably no more than a minute and a half or two minutes. Finally the phone rang on the other end of the line. Once. Twice. Three times. At last someone picked up.

"Douglass 4981."

The voice on the other end was that of a middle-aged woman. The housekeeper, Adelaide thought.

"Long-distance calling for Mr. Massey," the operator said.

"Mr. Massey isn't home," the housekeeper said. "He's away on business. May I take a message?"

"Yes, I'll leave a message," Adelaide said quickly.

"Go ahead," the operator said.

"It's very important that I get in touch with Mr. Massey," Adelaide said to the housekeeper. "Would you please tell me where he is?"

"I'm afraid I don't know," the housekeeper said. "He got a long-distance phone call from a woman the day before yesterday. He had me pack his suitcase and then he left. He said something about a business emergency. If you'll give me your name—"

"No, that won't be necessary," Adelaide said. "I've decided not to leave a message."

She hung up quickly.

"I take it you were right?" Jake said. "The number belongs to Conrad Massey?"

"Yes. The housekeeper said he's away on business. She doesn't know when he'll be back. She said he left the day before yesterday, immediately after receiving a long-distance call."

"And yesterday afternoon he turned up in Burning Cove," Jake said. "I think we can assume that the phone call he got was from Thelma Leggett. She probably offered to sell him information about your current whereabouts."

"Maybe he's the one who murdered her."

"I'm not so sure," Jake said. "We've got plenty of suspects to go around at the moment. Let's get back on the road. We need to place another long-distance call but it can wait until we find an auto court."

"What other call do you want to make?"

"The Rushbrook Sanitarium. It will be interesting to find out if Gill is also away on a business trip."

"Why don't we call right now? The secretary will have gone home for the day but one of the night orderlies might answer."

"If we don't get back on the road now, we'll be spending the night in the car," Jake said.

He wrapped a strong, sure hand around her arm and eased her out of the phone booth.

"The auto court is only a couple of miles from here," Adelaide said.

The low rumble of a slow-moving car made her glance toward the farm road. The beams of the headlights shot through the fog. The vehicle was coming from the rural area beyond the gas station, heading toward the highway.

"I think that's the same car that pulled off the road a few minutes ago," Jake said.

"The driver must have realized he took a wrong turn in the fog."

"Maybe."

Jake switched off the flashlight. The fogbound night enveloped them like a dark, incoming tide.

"Why did you do that?" she asked.

"Come with me," he said.

His hand tightened around her arm but he didn't propel her toward the speedster. Instead he drew her in the opposite direction, deeper into the shadows, well out of range of the convertible's headlights.

The rumble of the approaching car was louder now. Adelaide watched as it turned off the farm road and pulled into the gas station. A dark-colored sedan rolled slowly toward Jake's vehicle.

Jake drew her a few more feet into the dense darkness, halted, and put his mouth close to her ear.

"Don't move," he said. "Don't say a word."

She went very still beside him. She could not see the figure behind the wheel of the other car but she saw what appeared to be the flame of a cigarette lighter. Something sparked and caught fire.

Not a cigarette, Adelaide realized.

The shadowy figure behind the wheel of the sedan tossed what appeared to be a stick out the window. The flaming object was attached to it by a string or a cord.

There was a soft *thunk* when the stick landed on the concrete and rolled under the speedster.

The sedan roared out of the gas station, tires shrieking.

Jake moved suddenly, pushing Adelaide against the side of the building. He crowded in close, crushing her against the wall.

She heard a muffled *oomph*. An instant later the explosion ripped apart the night. Glass shattered.

For a few seconds, Jake did not move. Finally he stepped back, freeing Adelaide. She realized he had been shielding her. They both turned to look at the convertible.

At first Adelaide could not see anything. The vehicle's headlights had been knocked out by the force of the blast. The engine had stopped.

An unnatural silence descended. It did not last long.

The fire roared out of the guts of the speedster. The wildly flaring light revealed the broken hulk of the car. Adelaide gazed at the scene in disbelief and then turned to Jake. The flames glinted on the gun in his hand. Until that moment she had not realized that he had taken the pistol out of the holster.

"Dynamite?" she whispered.

"Why not?" Jake said. His voice was flat and grim. "Very handy stuff. You can get it anywhere, especially in rural communities like this one. Farmers use it to clear fields."

"Whoever threw that stick of dynamite under your car must have assumed that we were—" She broke off. She did not want to finish the sentence.

"Yes," Jake said. "The lights were on and the engine was running. The driver of the sedan assumed that we were still in the car."

Chapter 36

"Car broke down, eh?" The grizzled proprietor of the auto court peered at Jake over a pair of spectacles. "Bad night to end up hitchhiking. Not surprised no one stopped to pick you up. Only a fool would be out driving in this pea soup."

He'd introduced himself as Burt and he had seemed pleased to see a couple of customers walk through the door.

"Have you got a cabin for us?" Jake asked.

"Well, now, let me take a look," Burt said. He lounged against the counter and gave Jake a knowing wink. "We're a mite busy tonight, what with the fog and all."

Jake took out his wallet. "I understand."

He put a couple of bills down on the counter.

He sounded remarkably patient, Adelaide thought. Too patient. She'd had it with the disasters of the day. She was exhausted from the damp, miserable trek along the deserted highway. On top of that, she was struggling to cope with the fact that someone had tried to murder them with a stick of dynamite. She was very short on patience.

She gave Burt a fierce look. "When we arrived a few minutes ago, we noticed that one of the cabins is empty. There's no car parked in front and no lights on in the windows. Also, I can see a key hanging on the wall behind you. Looks like it goes to number six."

"Yep, you're in luck." Burt chuckled, scooped the money off the counter, and turned around to reach for the key. "Number six is available. Say, did you two hear a loud boom about an hour or so ago?"

"Yeah," Jake said. "Figured it was a car crash but we didn't pass any wreckage."

Adelaide glanced at him, impressed with his ready answer. He ignored her slightly raised eyebrows.

"If some poor soul went off the road in this fog, they won't find the car until morning," Burt said.

A stern-looking woman, her gray hair pinned in tight curls, appeared from the kitchen. She wiped her hands on her apron and peered suspiciously at Adelaide's left hand.

"Here, now, are you two married?" she asked. "We've only got the one cabin. Can't rent it to a couple that isn't properly married. Got standards here. This isn't some flophouse. Tell 'em, Burt."

"Take it easy, Martha." Burt winked at Jake as he handed over the key. "I'm sure this nice young couple is married."

"If that's the case, why aren't they wearing wedding rings?" Martha demanded.

Adelaide decided she'd had enough. "For your information, we just eloped. We haven't had a chance to buy rings."

Jake put his arm around her shoulders. "You'll have to forgive my bride. She's a little upset, what with having to walk for a couple of miles after our car broke down. The flashlight died just before we got here. This is our wedding night. As you can see, things haven't gone exactly as planned."

"Honeymooners, eh?" Martha's severe face abruptly softened. She smiled at Adelaide. "I can understand why you're in a bad mood, what with having to walk all that way on a night like this. Your nerves are probably a little on edge."

"You have no idea," Adelaide said.

"I understand. I reckon you probably didn't get any supper, right?"

"No," Adelaide said.

"I've got some leftover stew and corn bread. Go on over to number six and get settled. I'll send Burt over with the food in a bit."

"Thank you," Adelaide said. She suddenly felt guilty about her churlish behavior. "Sorry about snapping at you. It's just that it's been a very long day."

"I can imagine. Weddings are always stressful—even when things go like clockwork. Run along now. I'll get the stew and the corn bread ready. Burt will be over shortly."

"Number six is at the end of the row," Burt said helpfully. He handed a flashlight to Jake. "Here, take this. You'll find a lantern in the cabin. There's also a fireplace. Plenty of wood and kindling. Watch your step out there in the fog."

"Thanks," Jake said.

He kept his arm around Adelaide's shoulder and steered her toward the door. When they were outside, he released her and switched on the flashlight. Lantern light glowed behind the curtains of the five occupied cabins. Number six was so dark it was nearly invisible in the fog.

Jake aimed the beam of the flashlight briefly at each vehicle parked in front of a cabin. Adelaide realized what he was doing and shivered.

"You're wondering if the guy who tried to murder us ended up stopping here for the night, aren't you?" she said.

"It was a possibility," he said. "Not a lot of auto courts between here and Burning Cove. But none of these cars look like the one the guy with the dynamite was driving. He probably didn't dare stop so close to the scene of an attempted murder."

"What on earth would you have done if we had stumbled across him here?"

"I'm sure I would have figured out something," Jake said.

They found the front steps of number six. Jake opened the door. Adelaide moved past him into the small, shadowy confines of the one-room cabin.

"I can't believe it," she said.

"What?" Jake closed the door and threw the bolt. "That we finally found the auto court in that fog?"

"No," she said. "I can't believe that for the second time in my life I'm a fake bride. What are the odds?"

"Probably not good," Jake said.

Chapter 37

"Where do you suppose the person who tossed that stick of dynamite under your car ended up spending the night?" Adelaide asked.

She was feeling better now, she concluded. Not exactly normal—she was no longer sure how normal felt—but she was definitely calmer and more clearheaded.

The chicken stew had been hot and filling. The corn bread had been perfect—a lovely golden brown with a crispy crust on the bottom and the sides, courtesy of the cast-iron skillet in which it had been baked. There was a fire going in the brick fireplace. She and Jake were relaxing in a couple of wooden rocking chairs positioned in front of the hearth. The light from the lantern on the small table cast a warm glow over the one-room cabin.

Best of all she was not alone.

It occurred to her that she should not allow herself to get too comfortable with Jake's companionship. He would not stick around forever. Nevertheless, she was sure that he would remain at her side until they figured out what in the world was going on. He did not doubt her story, and for now that was the most important thing. They were partners, at least for a while, bound together by a web of murder, drugs, and blackmail.

Jake lounged back in his rocker and propped his feet on a hassock. He contemplated the flames in the fireplace.

"Best guess," he said, "is that the bastard ended up doing what we were planning to do if the fog got heavier—pulled off the highway and is now sleeping in his car. It will be interesting to see what he does when he finds out that we're still alive."

"Maybe he'll panic and run," Adelaide said.

"I think we have to assume that he'll head for Burning Cove. That seems to be the center of this spider's web."

Adelaide tightened her grip on the arms of her rocking chair. "Because I'm there?"

"Yes." Jake met her eyes. "And because I'm there, too."

"Partners," she said.

"Yes."

The single word was diamond hard.

A short time later Jake turned down the lantern and banked the fire. He cracked one window partially open for ventilation and then he looked at the two narrow cots.

"Which one do you want?" he asked.

The cots were identical, as far as she could tell. There was one positioned against the wall on each side of the cabin.

"The one on the left," she said.

She waited for him to suggest that they hang a couple of blankets between the cots for privacy purposes.

"It's all yours," he said.

He unfastened his shirt and draped it over the back of one of the chairs. His snug-fitting undershirt revealed the strong line of his shoulders and back. He must have sensed that she was staring because he gave her an inquiring look.

"Something wrong?" he asked.

She flushed and quickly averted her gaze.

"No, of course not," she said.

She winced. Her voice sounded strained and unnaturally high.

It wasn't the first time she had seen him shirtless, she reminded herself. She wondered if he would strip off the undershirt, as well. She could not decide if she was relieved or disappointed when he left the garment firmly tucked into the waistband of his trousers.

He picked up the wool blanket at the foot of his cot and unfolded it with a short snap.

"Don't hesitate to wake me if you hear or see anything that makes you uneasy," he said.

"I won't," she croaked.

He settled down on his side, politely turning his face to the wall to give her some privacy.

She perched on the edge of her cot and contemplated the outline of his lean, nicely muscled body under the blanket for a moment.

Maybe she was the one who was supposed to suggest that they hang some blankets between the cots. On the other hand, there were no extra blankets—just one for each narrow bed. As the fire died down, the damp chill of the foggy night was going to penetrate the cabin. They would each need their blankets.

Partners, she reminded herself. True, there had been that one memorable kiss in the gardens of the Paradise Club, but a single kiss did not a romantic relationship make. Jake certainly showed no signs of staging an assault on her virtue.

That realization was oddly depressing.

She unfolded her blanket, tugged it over her shoulders, and curled on her side, facing the wall. She hoped sleep would come quickly but she had a bad feeling that would not be the case. She was probably doomed to replay the events of the day in her mind for the rest of the night, searching for answers and a path forward. The mix of questions and the accompanying anxiety made for a toxic brew. She wished she had brought some of the tea that she used for the bad nights.

After a while she realized that one question in particular kept rising to the surface.

She stared, wide-eyed, at the shadowed wall until she couldn't stand it any longer. She had to know.

"Jake?" She kept her voice to a whisper, telling herself she wouldn't wake him if he had managed to fall asleep. The man needed his rest.

"Yeah?" he mumbled.

"Are you asleep?"

"Not now. What's wrong?"

"Nothing. It's just that I've been wondering about something ever since we found Thelma Leggett's body today."

"What have you been wondering about?" he asked patiently.

"How could you be so certain so quickly that she probably didn't take her own life? You were almost as quick to conclude that Zolanda hadn't intentionally jumped off the roof of her villa. How do you know things like that?"

There was a long silence from the other cot. When Jake spoke again, he sounded fully awake but his words lacked all trace of emotion.

"I suppose I'm predisposed to assume murder until proven otherwise because of my wife's death," he said. "She was murdered but the killer staged the scene to make it appear that she had taken her own life."

"Someone killed her?" Stunned, Adelaide sat up on the edge of the cot. "When Raina looked into your background, she didn't find anything to suggest that your wife was murdered."

"That's because I did a very good job of keeping the truth out of the press," he said. "It wasn't difficult because the L.A. cops and the medical examiner did not question the conclusion."

"Was there an investigation?"

"No, but I knew who murdered her."

"Who?"

"A man named Peter Garrick. Among other things, he was her lover."

Adelaide absorbed the implications of that statement. "I see. Raina did say that there had been rumors of an affair."

Jake was quiet for a time. She was starting to think that was the end of the conversation. But after a moment he began to talk. It was as if he had decided to unlock the door of a very dark room to allow the light to reveal what was stored inside.

"Elizabeth was beautiful, charming, and smart," he said. "She spoke a couple of languages in addition to English. She was well-traveled. Her family was from the East Coast. They had moved in New York society for generations. There were a lot of very distinguished names dangling from her family tree, including a couple of ambassadors, a state governor, and a senator. I met her while she was vacationing on the West Coast. Her family was not thrilled at first when she accepted my offer of marriage. After all, I wasn't a product of their world."

"Did they try to forbid the marriage?"

"No. I was more than a little surprised when they did not try to stand in our way. Initially I assumed that was because they believed that Elizabeth truly loved me and that they wanted her to be happy. In a sense, that was true. Elizabeth told her family that she didn't want a big society wedding. Looking back, it's clear they were very relieved. We were married three months after we met. It wasn't until after the wedding that I slowly began to realize that she was . . . unbalanced."

"Mentally unbalanced, do you mean?"

"Yes," Jake said. "It's hard to explain. She could be as euphoric and excited as a child at a birthday party one day, depressed and withdrawn the next. She lost her temper easily, and when she did, she would scream or throw things. From one day to the next, I never knew what to expect."

"There were some patients like that at Rushbrook. It was very unsettling to be around them."

"I found out later that her family had hoped that marriage would calm her wild temperament, but of course that didn't happen. If anything, marriage made her more unstable."

"When did you discover that she had taken a lover?"

"Elizabeth didn't take a lover after our wedding," Jake said evenly. "She already had one. Peter Garrick. In fact, he was the one who introduced Elizabeth to me. Garrick was a successful lawyer in Los Angeles. He had a lot of wealthy, influential clients including some studio heads, tycoons, and politicians. Garrick and I moved in the same business circles."

"It must have come as a terrible shock when you discovered that your wife and Garrick were lovers."

"The fact that she was having an affair with Garrick was certainly disturbing," Jake said. "But the real shock was finding out that Garrick was a spy for a foreign power. It made me realize what a fool I'd been."

"Believe me when I tell you I know the feeling."

"Yes, but you are a naturally trusting person, Adelaide. I am not so inclined to trust. I never thought I could be deceived. To say I learned a lesson is putting it mildly. Con artists will tell you that anyone can be tricked if you promise the target what he or she wants most. They are right."

"You wanted a wife and a family."

"Like you, I was alone in the world. I was growing weary of the constant traveling and my work abroad. Yes, I wanted to start a family of my own. Elizabeth seemed perfect."

"Too good to be true."

"Yes."

Adelaide gripped the edge of the cot with both hands. "How did you discover that Garrick was a spy for a foreign power?"

"I was convinced from the start that Elizabeth had not hanged herself. After the funeral I went through her things. I found some letters in the bottom of her jewelry box. They were from Garrick. There were also photos of him and mementos of the times they had spent together. I finally understood that my marriage had been a lie from the start. She had married me to please Garrick. Once I started looking into his background, it didn't take long to realize that from the very beginning of their relationship he had planned to use her."

"How?" Adelaide asked. "I don't understand."

"Soon after I took over my father's import-export business I was approached by a man who works for a certain government agency. I was asked to do some favors."

"What kind of favors?"

"I told you that my business took me to some dangerous places. The whole world is preparing for war, Adelaide. I was often in a position to observe and photograph the construction of fortifications of various foreign harbors and airports. In the course of my business I met many of the people around the globe who are engaged in the manufacture and shipment of weapons and military equipment. I learned who is stockpiling fuel and other essential materials and where those things were stored."

"You were a secret agent? A spy?"

"I was never on the government payroll. But, yes, I did favors for that agency I mentioned. Garrick knew that."

"How did he find out?"

"When it was all over, my contact at the agency told me that they had discovered a freelance spy working at the very heart of the agency. He was selling secrets to anyone who came up with the money."

"How did you discover that Garrick was working for a foreign power?"

"It wasn't until I concluded that he had murdered Elizabeth that I began to realize what had happened. Garrick had used her and manipulated her. In his letters he swore he would marry her when he had the information he needed. He made her think that I was the foreign spy and that she was doing her country a service by reporting on my contacts overseas. I think that Elizabeth believed him. She would have believed anything he said. She was obsessed with him. At first, she seemed to have thought that it would be exciting to be a spy. But she soon became bored and frustrated with the task. She wanted out. Garrick killed her to keep her quiet."

"What happened to Garrick?"

There was a short, brittle pause from Jake's cot. For a moment she did not think that he would answer the question. But eventually he spoke quietly into the darkness.

"About a month after he murdered Elizabeth, Garrick died," he said.

"How did that happen?"

"He spent an evening on a gambling ship anchored off Santa Monica. He had too much to drink, fell overboard, and drowned."

The lack of even a nuance of emotion in his voice told her that there was probably a lot more to the story. She also knew that she was not going to get the rest—not tonight.

"That was certainly convenient from the government's point of view," she ventured.

"No, it wasn't convenient for the government," Jake said. There was a cold, sharp edge on the words. "The agency rather liked the idea of leaving Garrick in place so that they could watch him."

"But that would have meant letting him get away with murder."

"The spy game is a game that is played outside the rules. Those who take part do not allow themselves to be distracted by questions of legality or right and wrong, let alone justice. All that matters is information."

She heard the bleak resignation in his voice and understood.

"It sounds as if you had your fill of that game," she said.

"I will admit that it was thrilling for a time. I was young and up for adventure and risk. I told myself that I was doing my patriotic duty."

"You were."

"I like to think so. But I got weary of living in the shadows."

"Trust me, no one understands that better than me."

"I know that now," he said.

"Is Elizabeth's family aware that she was murdered?" Adelaide asked. "Or do they believe the suicide story?"

"At first they were convinced that Elizabeth took her own life. They knew all about her strange temperament. At the funeral her father told me that she had attempted suicide on more than one occasion in the past. But, yes, now they know the truth."

"What happened?"

"After Garrick fell off that gambling ship, someone contacted Elizabeth's father anonymously to tell him that his daughter had been having an affair with a foreign spy and that she had been actively engaged in espionage against her own country. The blackmailer claimed to be in possession of Elizabeth's diary."

"How did you come to suspect that it was Zolanda who had it?"

"When I went through Elizabeth's appointment calendar, I found the dates and times of her sessions with Zolanda. On one of them she had jotted down a reminder that the psychic had requested her to bring her diary to the appointment. There was some nonsense about using it to analyze the energy of Elizabeth's dreams."

"Elizabeth's family will be ruined if the contents of that diary land in the headlines," Adelaide said.

"Yes. An illicit liaison can be dealt with by a powerful clan like the New York Bentons. Affairs are routine in that world. But accusations and insinuations of espionage and treason would destroy the family."

Adelaide caught her breath. "That's why you're so determined to recover the diary. You're trying to protect Elizabeth's family from scandal."

"That's part of it, but the truth is I have an obligation to do everything I can to find that damned diary. I was her husband. I didn't protect her."

"Stop it." Adelaide shot to her feet, clutching the blanket at her breast. "Listen to me, you are not responsible for what happened to Elizabeth. You cannot save someone who does not want to be saved or who cannot muster the willpower to save herself. You could not fix her unstable temperament. Obviously she was obsessed with Peter Garrick. She was doomed because of that obsession. That was not your fault."

Jake was quiet for a long moment. "I have to find that diary."

"I know. Believe me, I do understand. Your sense of duty and honor and responsibility won't allow you any other option. But you must not blame yourself for the situation that Elizabeth and Garrick created. That is another matter entirely. You are simply trying to clean up the mess they made. It's a task you have undertaken and you will see it through because that is the kind of man you are. But you are not at fault."

Jake fell silent again for a short time.

"I have never thought of things in quite that way," he admitted after a while. "It's all been tangled up in my mind from the moment I walked down those basement steps and found Elizabeth. I was planning to tell her that I wanted a divorce, you see. I knew it would look as if she had hanged herself because she was so unhappy in her marriage."

"So you blamed yourself for that, as well. What did happen there at the end?"

"Elizabeth was not a very good spy. She simply wasn't interested in me or my business connections. All she cared about was Garrick, but she never managed to give him anything that he considered useful. When she got bored and restless with the role he had assigned to her, she became a liability as far as he was concerned. He finally concluded that she was more of a liability than an asset."

"It's all so sad," Adelaide said. She became aware of the chill in the room. She pulled the blanket more securely around her shoulders and moved to stand in front of the dying fire. "Thank you for telling me about Elizabeth and the diary. It makes it easier to understand what we're dealing with."

Jake got to his feet and came to stand behind her. "You have a right to the whole story. I should have told you sooner."

"You had every reason to be careful about confiding in me. After all, I'm an escapee from a lunatic asylum."

"No," Jake said. "You escaped from a gang of criminals holding you against your will and using you in experiments that involved dangerous drugs."

Adelaide watched the flames. "It's as if we are stuck in a spider's web. Everyone who blunders into it gets caught: you and me, Madam Zolanda, Thelma Leggett—even Dr. Ormsby."

"The doctor who worked in the Rushbrook lab?"

"Yes. I hated him but I honestly don't think he cared about selling the drug—he was obsessed with his research."

"Did he or the others ever figure out that you had made an antidote to Daydream?"

"No. Believe me, I kept that secret."

"Good."

"What are you thinking?" Adelaide said.

"That antidote may be your one ace in the hole if someone succeeds in grabbing you," Jake said.

"What do you mean?"

"It gives you something to trade."

"For what?"

"Your life."

She made a face. "Thanks for the cheery thought. But even if that strategy worked, I'd end up back at the Rushbrook Sanitarium. I'd rather be dead."

"Don't talk like that. We're going to get through this."

"All right, but promise me one thing."

"What?"

"If I end up back at Rushbrook, promise me that you'll find a way to get me out."

Jake gripped her shoulders and turned her around to face him.

"Last night on the beach I told you that I would kill anyone who tried to hurt you," he said.

"Yes, I know. And it was very sweet of you." A wistful sensation whispered through her. She smiled a little. "But you were hallucinating."

"I remember every word and I meant every word. If you end up back at the asylum, I will come and get you and I will destroy anyone who stands in my way."

She believed him. She could not explain why, but she did. There was a sharp, fierce edge to his words that told her he would keep the promise or die trying.

"Jake," she said. "You cannot know how much that means to me."

"Maybe not, but I do know how much you mean to me. The world."

His mouth came down on hers in a kiss that sealed the vow.

Chapter 38

For a heartbeat she did not—could not—respond. There was heat and power and promise in his embrace but there was also risk. She was very sure now that she could trust him to try to protect her, but there was nothing he could do to shield her heart. She was falling in love with him. That was her fault, not his.

Nevertheless, there was an unshakable bond between them, a bond forged by the forces that threatened them both. They needed each other if they were to have any chance of surviving the nightmare that had enveloped them.

That bond was enough, at least for tonight. She craved the raw thrill of abandoning herself to the desire that flared between them. She was desperate for a sensation strong enough to free her from the past, even if the escape was only temporary.

With a soft, muffled cry, she wrapped her arms around Jake's neck and gave herself up to the embrace.

"Adelaide."

He said her name in a hoarse, urgent growl infused with hunger and a need that resonated with something deep inside her.

His hands moved from her shoulders to the buttons of her blouse. He did not release her mouth as he got the garment open. The kiss bound them together as securely as any lock and chain.

She fumbled to tug the hem of his undershirt out of the waistband of his trousers. She had no practical experience in the business. Before Conrad she had enjoyed a few light flirtations with young men who were as shy and uncertain as herself. None of the relationships had progressed beyond stolen kisses and some illicit fondling in the shadows of a porch swing or the front seat of a car.

She had hoped to discover passion with Conrad but he had not encouraged her. His kisses had been nothing if not restrained. At the start of their relationship she had assumed it was because he was determined to be a gentleman. Toward the end she had concluded that she was one of those unfortunate women the doctors labeled frigid. She had been wrong on both counts.

She might be inexperienced but she applied herself to the task of pulling Jake's undershirt free of his trousers with diligence and determination. The result was that by the time he got the zipper of her trousers down, she was threading her fingers through the crisp, curling hair of his chest. The feel of firm, masculine muscle beneath warm skin was beyond exciting. It was intoxicating.

He finally set her mouth free, albeit with obvious reluctance. He peeled off her blouse and tossed it down on the cot. Her rayon-and-silk knit bra was next. When his palms closed gently over her breasts, she heard him draw in a sharp breath.

"You are so beautiful," he said.

She wasn't beautiful, not in the way of a star like Vera Westlake, she thought. But, damn, it was exactly the sort of thing a woman needed to hear at a time like this.

He got her loose, flowing trousers open and pushed them down over her hips. They tumbled into a pool on the floor. She kicked the fabric aside, wanting to get it out of the way so that she could get closer to him.

When she was left in only her panties, he picked her up and set her down gently on his cot. He straightened just long enough to get rid of his own trousers and undershirt. In the low light of the fire she could see that he wore the latest in men's undershorts, a pair of close-fitting briefs. She had seen the ads for them in the newspapers but she had never viewed them in person on a man. As she watched, fascinated, he stepped out of them.

Her mouth went dry. She was the daughter of two scientists and she was a professional librarian. She knew far more about biology than most sexually inexperienced women. Nevertheless, this was the first time she had ever seen a naked, heavily aroused man.

She managed to conceal her shock, but not without considerable effort. She was grateful for the deep shadows in the small cabin.

Instead of coming directly to the cot, Jake picked up his jacket, reached into an inside pocket, and took out a small tin.

"You're going to smoke a cigarette?" she asked. "Now?"

He laughed. "I don't smoke."

"I'm glad to hear that. My father always said that smoking was very bad for the health."

"Getting pregnant at the wrong time is not a good idea, either. This is a tin of condoms."

"Oh."

Talk about naïveté, she thought. She was probably beet red from head to toe. It would probably be a good idea to keep her mouth shut for a while. She did not want to sound any more unworldly than she already did.

Jake sheathed himself and then, very carefully, very deliberately, lowered himself alongside her, gathering her close. She was amazed that the cot did not collapse under their combined weight.

The furnace-hot warmth of his body was far more effective than the blanket when it came to warding off the chill of the damp night.

He touched her the way he might have touched a rare and extremely valuable vase—as if he could not believe he was holding her, as if he was afraid he might drop her. His hand skimmed lightly across her, exploring her with exquisite care, easing his way into the forbidden places.

When he bent his head to kiss the tips of her breasts, she could barely catch her breath. Her lower body clenched. An urgency built deep inside her. She felt like a tautly strung bow in the hands of a skilled archer.

Jake's fingers went lower and suddenly she was melting. His touch became increasingly intimate. When he stroked between her thighs, she gasped, startled and astonished. He penetrated her gently with one finger, and for a few seconds she could not breathe at all. She curled her fingers into his shoulders and buried her face against his chest.

"Jake."

"You're so tight," he grated against her ear. "Wet and tight and hot. I'm not going to last long once I'm inside you, so we're going to make damn sure you come first."

She was shocked all over again. No man had ever talked to her that way. She couldn't find the words to respond verbally so, feeling very daring, she reached down between them and tentatively wrapped her fingers around him. She was alarmed and excited by the size of his erection.

He groaned again and drove himself deeper into her grasp. She got the message. She tightened her hold on him.

"That feels so good." He lowered his head and kissed her throat. His words were a feral growl against her skin. "Much too good. But I told you, your turn first."

He began to work the incredibly sensitive nub of firm flesh between her legs. The sense of urgency became overwhelming. After a while she released him to clutch at his shoulders. She moved her lower body against his hand, wanting—needing—something more.

"Jake."

The release swept through her, a storm of sensation unlike anything she had ever experienced. The little waves of energy convulsed her entire body.

She did not realize she was trying to scream until she discovered that he had covered her mouth with his own, effectively muffling a shriek of pleasure that would no doubt have been audible in the neighboring cabin.

She wanted to laugh, to cry, to sing. She had never known that her body was capable of such a response. She was still marveling at the wonder of it all when Jake fitted the blunt tip of his erection to her still-quivering body and drove relentlessly into her.

It was too much. He was too big. She was too sensitive. Pain and the remnants of recent pleasure twisted together. She gasped and flattened her palms against his shoulders, instinctively trying to push him away.

Jake froze.

"Adelaide. What the hell—?"

"It's all right," she managed. "Just give me a minute."

"Why didn't you tell me?"

He started to withdraw.

She dug her fingers into his back. "No. It's all right. I want this. I want you."

"Are you sure?"

"Yes, damn it."

He waited. She knew how much it cost him to restrain himself because his shoulders and back were wet with sweat.

Finally, cautiously, she urged him deeper. He braced himself on his elbows and sank slowly into her body.

A moment later his climax crashed through him. She caught his head between her hands and pulled his mouth down to hers so that she could kiss him. She swallowed his roar of masculine satisfaction.

She had never been so aware of her feminine power, never felt so strong, so free. The thrill was intoxicating.

Chapter 39

J ake opened his eyes and contemplated what was left of the fire. He should get up, stir the embers, add a couple of sticks of kindling and another small log. But he was feeling very good at the moment. The last thing he wanted to do was move. Adelaide was cradled spoon-fashion against him. It was the only way the two of them could fit on the cot. She was soft and warm and delightfully curvy. The primal scents of the recent lovemaking infused the atmosphere.

He knew then that in the future, whenever he thought of this night—and he was certain that he would think of it often—it would not be just the intensity of his own physical release that he would recall. It would be the intoxicating kaleidoscope of sensations created by the raw elements of passion that would sear his memories. He would remember how the small rivulets of perspiration between Adelaide's delicate breasts had mingled with the sweat on his chest. He would recall how the dampness had pooled between her thighs. He would have wet dreams about her tight body and the way she had clutched at him when he tried to withdraw. Most of all he would remember the way she had found her release in his arms.

No, he really did not want to get out of bed to prod the fire, but the chill of the night would only get worse if he stayed where he was. Reluctantly he eased himself off the cot and got to his feet. He reached down to tuck the blanket around Adelaide's bare shoulders. She stirred then, turning onto her back and stretching her arms over her head in a luxuriously sensual way.

A jolt of lightning shot through him, and suddenly he was aroused all over again. Minutes ago he had concluded that he had never been so satisfied—so thoroughly relaxed—in his life. But just watching Adelaide made him want to climb back onto the cot.

"Is it morning yet?" she asked.

"No." With a determined effort he forced himself to turn away from the sight of a very naked Adelaide and crossed the small space to the hearth. He grabbed a poker and prodded the embers. "I just got up to put another log on the fire."

There was a short silence behind him. He heard movement on the cot. He glanced over his shoulder to see if Adelaide was stretching again. But she was sitting up on the edge of the narrow bed. The blanket was pulled securely around her, covering the entire front of her body. Her hair tumbled around her shoulders. She no longer looked luxuriously sleepy. Instead there was a new tension about her. He could sense her uncertainty. His good mood started to evaporate. Damn. She was already having regrets.

She cleared her throat. "This is rather awkward, isn't it?"

"The fact that someone wants to kill us? Yeah, I'd say that definitely qualifies as awkward."

"I wasn't talking about that," she mumbled. "I meant this." She waved one hand. "Us."

He tossed some kindling onto the fire and watched the flames leap. "Why didn't you tell me that you were inexperienced?"

"Because it didn't matter, not to me. Did it matter to you?"

"Yes. No. I probably would have gone about things more slowly if I had known."

Then again, maybe not, he thought. The realization that she wanted him had made him ravenous.

"I thought it all went quite well," Adelaide said.

She sounded so smug, so pleased with herself. He smiled.

"I thought it went rather well, too," he said.

"Don't worry, I won't read too much into what just happened," she added quickly.

He stopped smiling. Straightening, he gripped the mantel and concentrated on the flames.

"What the hell does that mean?" he asked.

She exhaled softly. "I'm just trying to get things back on track between us."

"We are not a couple of trains passing in the night, Adelaide."

"I didn't mean to imply that. The thing is, we're partners. Two people caught up in a dangerous situation. We were thrown together by circumstances. You mustn't worry that I will now think of us as . . . as lovers, simply because of what happened tonight."

He had told himself that he would be patient. Sensitive. She had been through a lot lately. But a man could only take so much.

He turned around to face her. "We are partners. We are in a dangerous situation. And we were thrown together by circumstances. But like it or not, as of tonight, we are also lovers. Even if we never sleep together again for the rest of our lives, you cannot claim that we are not lovers."

She watched him with a startled expression. "Are you angry?"

He thought about it. "'Angry' may be too strong a word. I'm irritated. Annoyed. Exasperated. If we pursue this argument much longer, I may get angry."

"What argument?" She got to her feet, clutching the blanket at her throat. "For your information, I wasn't arguing. I merely made what I consider to be a very reasonable observation. I thought describing what happened as 'awkward' was a lot more genteel than some other terms that spring to mind. After all, it's not as if we're in love and planning to marry. We're a couple of people who are stuck together until we figure out who is trying to murder us."

"You can call our relationship whatever you want—just don't call it awkward." He crossed the room in three long strides and gripped her shoulders. "Because it doesn't feel awkward to me."

"Really?" She paused, frowning a little. "How would you describe it?"

"Damned if I know. And damned if I care. Just remember that whatever happens in the future, we are now lovers."

She started to separate her hands in a gesture of exasperation. At the last second, evidently remembering that she was nude, she tightened her grip on the blanket instead.

"This is ridiculous," she said. "I can't believe we're arguing about something as trivial as how to label our relationship when we've got much bigger problems."

"You're absolutely right." He raised his hands from her shoulders and cupped her face. "Our heated discussion sounds a lot like a lovers' quarrel to me."

Her eyes widened. For a few beats he thought he had pushed her too far and that she was really going to explode. Instead she grimaced. She followed that with a rueful smile.

"I refuse to admit that it was a lovers' quarrel," she said. "However, I do appreciate your attempt to lighten the mood."

"I was dead serious, but never mind. As you said, we've got other problems. As soon as the fog starts to lift we're going to have to hike back to that gas station and explain my wrecked car to the owner and, no doubt, the local cops. Not that they'll be able to do anything."

"Why not?"

"Whoever tossed that stick of dynamite under my convertible will be gone at first light, assuming he decided not to risk the fog last night. Meanwhile, we need to figure out how to get back to Burning Cove."

"I suppose we could always hitchhike," Adelaide said.

"That would take hours, maybe the rest of the day. I've got some cash. With luck the proprietor of the gas station will know one of the locals who will be happy to sell us a used car."

"You're right about the hitchhiking," Adelaide said. "With our luck the one car that would stop to give us a lift would be the one that was driven by the killer."

"I doubt it. I think it's far more likely that, until proven otherwise, he'll assume we're dead. He will certainly hope that's the case."

☙

Adelaide hung up the pay phone and moved out of the booth. "Gill is away on a fishing trip. That means he could have been the one who murdered Thelma Leggett."

"We've got enough suspects to go around," Jake said. "What we need now is a motive."

They walked to the battered Oldsmobile sedan. Jake opened the passenger side door. "It's not a speedster," he said. "But with luck it will get us back to Burning Cove."

He closed the door and walked around the front to get behind the wheel.

"Did you get the feeling that the local police are very glad that we are leaving town?" Adelaide asked.

Jake fired up the Oldsmobile's engine and put the car in gear.

"Yes, I did get that impression," he said.

Adelaide smiled.

Jake gave her a quick, searching glance before he pulled out onto the road.

"What are you thinking?" he asked.

"Nothing. It just occurred to me that my nerves are evidently strong enough to survive a real wedding night," she said.

He surprised her with a wicked smile. "Yeah, I think it's safe to say that you can handle the physical demands of married life."

Chapter 40

Adelaide was back at work in the tearoom by three o'clock, just in time to help with the afternoon rush. The last customer departed an hour and a half later. She collected the empty cups and carried them into the kitchen. She was running water into the sink in preparation for washing the dishes when she heard the bell chime over the front door. Florence bustled across the tearoom to respond.

"I'm so sorry, sir," she said. "We close at four thirty. I can sell you some packaged tea to take with you and I believe I may have one or two pastries left, but if you would like full service, I'm afraid you'll have to return tomorrow. We open at nine."

"I'm not here for tea," Conrad Massey said in a stone-cold voice. "I came to find my wife."

The cup that Adelaide had been about to wash fell from her fingers. Fortunately there was enough water in the sink to cushion the landing. The cup did not break. She gripped the edge of the counter with both hands and reminded herself to breathe.

You knew that sooner or later you would have to confront the bastard, she reminded herself. *You're not alone now. You've got friends. He's not going to try to kidnap you in broad daylight—not when there are witnesses.* And there were certainly a lot of those around. In addition to Florence, there were a number of shoppers on the sidewalk outside. That should have been reassuring but it did nothing to slow her heart rate.

Should have brought my gun, she thought.

"What on earth are you talking about?" Florence said, her voice sharpening with suspicion.

"I don't know what she's told you, but the woman who is calling herself Adelaide Brockton is my wife," Conrad said.

"You're out of your mind," Florence said. "I insist you leave immediately or I will call the police."

"I'm afraid it's poor Adelaide who is not mentally stable," Conrad said. "She suffered a nervous breakdown on our wedding night. I had to have her committed to an asylum. But she escaped. I'm here to take her back to the hospital, where she can continue receiving proper treatment."

Florence said, "Adelaide isn't married. You're the crazy person. Go on, get out of here."

"You can't stop me from seeing my wife."

Adelaide finally managed to take in some oxygen. A fierce anger burned through the shock and panic that had struck her when she heard Conrad's voice. She pushed herself away from the sink, wiped her hands on her apron, and strode across the kitchen. She picked up a large bread knife before she went through the door.

Conrad, fashionably dressed in a pair of light-colored, crisply pleated trousers, white shirt, tie, and blue coat, looked at her. He started to assume an expression of deep concern. Then he noticed the knife.

"Adelaide," he yelped, "what do you think you're doing? Put that down."

"Stop trying to intimidate my boss," she said. "You're wasting your time."

"Damn right, he's wasting his time," Florence said.

Conrad recovered his air of husbandly concern. "Adelaide, my dear, thank goodness I found you. I've been so worried about you."

"Stop right there." Adelaide aimed the knife at him. "You lied to me, you conned me, you cheated me, and you had me locked up against my will. If you think I'm going to believe anything you say, you're the one who is crazy."

"I just want to talk to you, sweetheart. If you put the knife down, we can go somewhere quiet and have a cup of coffee together."

"So that you can slip some Daydream into my drink the way you did the night you arranged for me to be kidnapped?"

"You weren't kidnapped," Conrad said. "You had a nervous breakdown that was followed by amnesia. The stress of our wedding night was too much for your delicate nerves."

"There was no wedding night, certainly not one that resulted in the consummation of our marriage. I happen to know that for a fact now."

Conrad's eyes widened. "What?"

"Forget it," Adelaide said. "It's none of your damned business."

"Sweetheart, you're delusional. That's why you had to be committed. But you were getting better at the sanitarium. I was planning to bring you home. Now you've undone all the benefits of the medication you were receiving. You need to return to Rushbrook for more treatment."

"I've got news for you, Conrad, I'm as stable as I'm ever going to get."

Florence glared at Conrad. "I told you to leave."

"Don't you dare threaten me," Conrad said. "I'm here to take my wife back to the sanitarium. She is dangerously ill. Just look at that knife she's holding if you don't believe me."

Adelaide raised the knife in a deliberately threatening manner. "Stop calling me your wife."

"It's the truth," Conrad said. But he took a step back, putting a little more distance between them. "Surely you remember our wedding in Reno. You were so happy. I gave you a gold wedding band. You were wearing it when you went into the sanitarium."

"I know a private investigator who can discover the truth. If it turns out that you actually managed to bribe some Reno judge to marry us while I was under the influence of the drug, I'll go back to Reno to file for divorce. Oh, wait, I can get the marriage annulled on the grounds that it was never consummated."

"There was a wedding," Conrad insisted. "That gold ring is proof."

There was a slight movement in the kitchen doorway. Adelaide turned her head and saw Jake. He was not looking at her. Instead he watched Conrad with ice-cold eyes.

"If Adelaide ends up on the train to Reno, she won't be alone," he said. "I'll be with her to make sure she gets there safely. The judges in Nevada don't ask a lot of questions. She'll get her divorce—assuming she actually needs one, which I doubt. I can personally testify to the fact that your marriage, if it ever took place, was never consummated."

Conrad's face reddened with fury. "You must be Jake Truett. I've heard all about you. You took advantage of my poor wife's delusional condition to seduce her. You're after her inheritance. Admit it."

Jake fixed Conrad with an intense curiosity that Adelaide decided could only be described as predatory. It was the expression of a wolf that was about to go for the throat.

"Is that right?" he asked very softly. "Who told you that?"

Conrad took another step back. "Dr. Gill, the head of the Rushbrook Sanitarium, phoned to tell me that Adelaide had been located here in Burning Cove. He warned me that there were rumors that a businessman from L.A. was trying to seduce her. You obviously figured out who she is. You know she inherited a fortune."

"Dr. Gill told you that, did he?" Jake said. "And just how did Gill discover that Adelaide was here in town?"

"How the hell should I know?" Conrad shot back.

Adelaide did not wait for Jake to respond. "Speaking of my inheritance, Conrad, I'll be hiring a lawyer soon. He'll explain things to the bankers who are handling my money. They will probably prosecute you for fraud and embezzlement."

Conrad was seething now. "Don't you understand? Truett is the one who is trying to con you. He wants to marry you for your money."

"Who said anything about marriage?" Adelaide shot back. "I have every intention of controlling my own money and my own future. Now go away and leave me alone."

Florence gave Conrad a steely smile. "You've got to the count of ten before I call the cops and have you locked up for trespassing. One . . . two . . ."

Adelaide gestured toward the door with the knife. "Get out of here."

Jake folded his arms and lounged against the doorjamb. "You heard the ladies."

Conrad looked as if he wanted to commit murder but he did not say another word. He swung around and stalked back across the tearoom and outside onto the sidewalk. He slammed the door so hard the glass rattled.

An eerie silence descended on Refresh. No one moved for a few beats. And then Adelaide realized that she suddenly felt very light—excited and thrilled.

"Thank you," she said softly. She did not take her eyes off the front door. "Thank you both."

"You don't have to worry about the likes of him," Florence said. "You've got friends here in Burning Cove."

"For the past two months I've been terrified that Conrad would find a way to make me vanish again, just as he did the first time," Adelaide said.

"That trick may have worked in San Francisco," Jake said. "But this is Burning Cove. The rules are different here."

Florence peered at Adelaide. "Did that man really have you committed to an asylum so that he could get his hands on your inheritance?"

"Yes," Adelaide said.

Florence shuddered. "It's like something right out of the movies. Thank goodness you escaped."

Adelaide gave her a shaky smile. "You mean, thank heavens I've got friends like you."

Jake looked thoughtful. "That brings up a question I've been meaning to ask you. You do have friends here in Burning Cove. You must have had friends in San Francisco, too."

"I did," Adelaide said. "Most of them were my colleagues at the botanical library."

"Why didn't they ask questions when you suddenly vanished?" Jake said.

"I wondered the same thing," Adelaide said. "A few weeks ago I finally worked up my nerve to place an anonymous phone call to the library. I asked for Adelaide Blake. I was told that she had moved back east to live with relatives."

"Huh," Jake said.

Adelaide looked at him. "What?"

"I'm wondering exactly when Gill located you."

"I can tell you one thing for sure," Adelaide said. "You can't believe anything Conrad Massey says."

Chapter 41

Conrad lit another cigarette and contemplated the martini on the table in front of him. The glass did not look clean.

It was Gill who had insisted that they meet at the Carousel. It was a dark, grimy, smoke-filled dive. He figured it had probably been a speakeasy during Prohibition. Not his kind of place, he thought. He would have much preferred the swanky bar at the Burning Cove Hotel or the Paradise Club. But Gill wanted to stay out of sight.

It was early evening. The Carousel was still empty except for the handful of customers hunkered down on the bar stools. The bored cocktail waitress was making idle conversation with the bartender.

A shadow fell across the table. Conrad looked up.

"I take it your plan did not go well," Gill said. He lowered himself into the booth on the opposite side of the table. "I warned you that it wouldn't be so easy this time. She's on guard now and Truett is keeping an eye on her."

"He wants to control her inheritance."

"Certainly. His motive is the same as your own. The problem is that possession is nine-tenths of the law and, for the moment, at any rate, he's got possession of her."

"All I need is ten minutes alone with Adelaide," Conrad said. "Just long enough to slip the drug into her drink. Ten lousy minutes. Once she's under the influence, I can make her trust me, at least long enough to get her back to Rushbrook."

"That's certainly where she belongs. She is a very fragile patient. She never recovered from the shock of her parents' deaths."

"You told me back at the start that she was unstable. She needs help."

Somehow that had made the scheme seem almost all right, he thought. Gill had succeeded in making him believe that he would be doing Adelaide a favor by marrying her and then sending her to Rushbrook for treatment.

When he realized that she was going to refuse his offer of marriage, he had panicked. The plan had been to slip just enough Daydream into her champagne to make her highly suggestible. Gill had assured him that the stuff had strong hypnotic properties and that once she was under its influence he could convince her to marry him.

But everything had gone wrong. In hindsight he wondered whether Gill had deliberately miscalculated the dose or if the drug was inherently unpredictable. Maybe a little of both. Whatever the case, after drinking the drugged champagne, Adelaide had plunged into a delirium. Gill and Ormsby had taken charge of her that night.

"As her doctor, I can tell you that she's liable to suffer another nervous breakdown at any moment," Gill said. "But I doubt very much that you're going to get another shot at trying to convince her you are passionately in love with her. Truett would be a fool to let her out of his sight now that he knows you're in the picture. Adelaide is worth a lot of money."

"I know." Conrad snorted in disgust. "Truett doesn't need her inheritance. I'm the one facing bankruptcy."

"I understand," Gill said. He lowered his voice. "There may be another way to rescue poor Adelaide from Truett's clutches and return her to the sanitarium where she belongs."

One last chance to save Massey Shipping, Conrad thought. He downed the last of his martini and lowered the glass.

"I'm listening," he said. "How do we get Adelaide back to Rushbrook?"

Chapter 42

"Are you crazy?" Adelaide said. "It's a trap. You can't possibly be serious about meeting Conrad alone. He told you it was a matter of national security? Surely you don't believe that."

It was nearing midnight. The phone had rung a short time ago. When Adelaide had answered, she was at first startled and then outraged to hear Conrad's voice. He had pleaded with her to let him speak to Jake. She was about to hang up but Jake had taken the phone out of her hand.

Now she and Jake were in the middle of her kitchen, arguing. She was dressed in a robe and slippers. Jake had pulled on a pair of trousers.

"I'm starting to wonder if Massey is right," he said. "This may be an issue of national security."

"What on earth are you talking about?"

"You said Gill and Ormsby were determined to make Daydream work as a truth serum and a hypnotic. A drug with those properties would be worth a lot to certain people in the government. Hell, it would be worth a lot to foreign governments, too."

"Yes, but that doesn't mean you can trust Conrad."

"Don't worry, I don't trust him."

"He's a desperate man. I wouldn't put it past him to try to murder you."

"Give me some credit," Jake said. "I do realize he sees me as an obstacle in his path and that he would very much like to get me out of the way. But he does have information we need—it may be information that he isn't even aware he possesses."

Adelaide had been pacing the kitchen. She paused at the far end and whipped around to face Jake.

"You said the spy game was always about information," she said. "That nothing else mattered. But you are no longer a secret agent."

"Sometimes you need information in order to survive. I think this may be one of those times. I've got a feeling that whatever is going on at Rushbrook, it involves something much larger and potentially more dangerous than a scheme to market drugs to celebrities and gain control of your inheritance."

"Excuse me?" Adelaide folded her arms and narrowed her eyes. "You make it sound like I simply got conned out of my money. That's not what happened. I was deceived, kidnapped, and used in a drug experiment. And to top things off, someone tried to murder me. I didn't just get fleeced by a fast-talking con man, damn it."

"That's my point," Jake said in his infuriatingly unruffled manner. "It's clear that the drug, Daydream, is at the core of this situation—not your inheritance. I think that was just a bonus for Gill—something he could offer Massey to get him to cooperate with the scheme. I doubt that Massey knows much, if anything, about the drug and probably couldn't care less."

"He just saw an easy way to get his hands on my money."

"Yes."

Adelaide drummed her fingers on her forearms. "I agree that the drug is the key here. But it's Conrad you're planning to see tonight, and he's dangerous because he's desperate. I'm telling you, he will do anything to save Massey Shipping. It's an obsession with him."

"Trust me, I understand the nature of obsession," Jake said. "It's obvious Massey did a deal with Gill in order to get his hands on your inheritance. But he may know something about Gill's plans for Daydream."

She frowned. "If you're right, it means Gill is manipulating him."

"Massey went into the arrangement with his eyes open."

"I know."

"Huh."

Adelaide eyed him. "What now?"

"You told me that Conrad Massey breezed into your life one day and tried to sweep you off your feet. But you never explained exactly how the two of you met."

"Conrad and I met in an antiquarian bookstore. My mother collected old herbals. After her death I inherited her books. I wanted to continue the tradition."

"Is Massey interested in antiquarian books?" Jake asked.

Adelaide unfolded her arms and raised one shoulder in a small shrug. "He told me that he collects old books related to the maritime industry. It wasn't a complete lie. When we were dating, he showed me his library. He did have a lot of volumes on the subject. He mentioned that his grandfather had started the collection."

"Do you really think it was a coincidence that he walked into that bookshop the same day you did?"

"In hindsight, I'd have to say probably not."

Jake nodded. "Someone, most likely Gill, arranged for Massey to meet you in that bookshop. After the first encounter, it was up to Massey to deliver the goods."

"Me."

"You," Jake agreed. "Why did you choose that particular afternoon to go to that particular antiquarian bookshop?"

Adelaide summoned up the memories of that fateful day. "I got a telephone call from the proprietor of the shop. He told me that he had just found an eighteenth-century herbal that he knew I might want for my collection."

"You were set up."

"Good grief. Do you really think the proprietor of the bookstore was in on the scheme? That's ridiculous. Mr. Watkins did have the herbal. I bought it that day."

"I doubt if the bookshop owner had even an inkling of what was going on," Jake said. "I suspect that Gill made sure the herbal got into his hands and suggested that Watkins telephone you to arrange a time for you to come into the shop."

Adelaide shivered. "You really do think like a professional spy."

"I've had some practice." Jake's jaw tensed. "Any idea how Gill might have discovered that you were interested in old herbals?"

"It was no secret. I told you, Gill knew my parents rather well because he followed the results of their research. He would have been aware that my mother loved old herbals and he may have known that I shared her interest in them."

"The next question is, how did Gill know that Massey would agree to become part of the conspiracy?"

Adelaide stopped abruptly.

"The Duchess," she whispered. "She's the patient who insisted that I did not belong at Rushbrook. She helped me escape."

Jake went very still. "Tell me about her."

Adelaide turned to face him. "I never found out her real name. Everyone called her the Duchess because she claimed to be descended from an exclusive San Francisco family. It was probably true. Rushbrook was in the business of locking up the mentally ill relatives of wealthy families. The Duchess was not dangerous, but it was obvious that she was delusional."

"In what way?"

"She acted as if Rushbrook was her own private country house. The other patients were houseguests. Because she was considered harmless, she had the run of the place and the grounds. She never left her room unless she was wearing a hat and gloves. In the dining room her manners were impeccable." Adelaide smiled. "I loved that she referred to the orderlies and the nurses as servants. In her mind Gill was the butler. Ormsby was a handyman."

"That explains why everyone called her the Duchess."

"She was crazy but harmless. For the most part she lived in her own world and she seemed happy. She didn't cause any trouble so the staff humored her. For some reason she took a particular interest in me right from the start. I often met up with her in the gardens when the orderlies escorted me on my daily walks. She would invite me to have a cup of tea with her. The orderlies didn't care. They were bored with their jobs. I looked forward to those invitations to tea more than you can possibly know. When I had tea with the Duchess, I felt almost normal for a while."

"Tea with a crazy woman in the gardens of an insane asylum." Jake shook his head. "Sounds like a scene out of *Alice's Adventures in Wonderland*."

Adelaide smiled ruefully. "Yes, it does. But I considered the Duchess a friend. She, on the other hand, was convinced that I was a member of her family. A cousin. Once I tried to explain that we weren't related but she got very upset so I never mentioned it again."

"Did she realize that she couldn't leave the mansion?"

"Oh, yes. In her own way she had arrived at a very clear understanding of her situation. She said that she could never leave the mansion because she was crazy. She explained that respectable families like ours had to keep their mentally unbalanced relations hidden away. *It wouldn't do to have other people knowing that there's a streak of insanity in the bloodline.*"

"Did she think that she had other relatives besides you at the asylum?"

"I asked her that from time to time. She always said no, that it was just the two of us. But she insisted that I didn't belong there. She said it was fine for me to visit occasionally but that I must not stay there forever because I wasn't crazy like her. She told me that it was high time I did my duty by the family."

"What was your duty?"

Adelaide smiled. "I was supposed to go out into society and entertain on a proper scale. I was also instructed on my responsibility to beget a few heirs to the family fortune."

"Did she ever say which family the two of you were supposedly descended from?" Jake asked.

"No. I asked that, too. She just winked and told me that I knew the answer and that we mustn't mention the name of the family because the servants might overhear us. I'm sure her family came from San Francisco, though. She talked a lot about her past. It was clear she had grown up in the city."

Jake turned thoughtful. "Conrad Massey's family would certainly qualify as an old, established San Francisco family."

Adelaide looked at him, startled. "You're thinking that maybe I wasn't the first person the Massey family had tucked away at the Rushbrook Sanitarium, aren't you? That maybe the Duchess is a Massey relation?"

"That would certainly explain how Gill and Conrad Massey knew each other and how Gill might have been aware that Massey was desperate for money."

"Yes, it would. It also explains why the Duchess took such a personal interest in me. She knew me as Adelaide Massey."

"Massey is headed for bankruptcy, so it's very likely that he was thinking of cutting a few corners in his financial affairs. Keeping a crazy relative tucked away in a high-class asylum is expensive. Maybe Massey told Gill he was going to stop paying the bills for the Duchess."

"And Gill suggested a way that he could solve his financial problems?" Frustrated by the unknowns, Adelaide swept out her hands. "It's all speculation at this point."

"Which is why I agreed to meet Massey tonight," Jake said. "We need whatever information he can provide."

"I'm terrified that you'll be walking into a trap."

"Knowing it's a trap gives me an edge."

"How?"

"It allows me to set a trap of my own," Jake said.

"Did you learn that sort of thing in the import-export business?"

"I'm afraid so."

"In that case, I'd say it's a very good thing you got out of that line—except that now you're back in the business, aren't you? All because of me."

He crossed the room to where she stood, and closed his powerful hands very firmly around her. His eyes were no longer enigmatic. They were very fierce.

"We're in this thing together. Don't ever forget it."

"Right. We're partners. I should come with you tonight."

"No," Jake said. "I'm going to take you to the safest place in Burning Cove."

"Where is that?"

"The Paradise Club," Jake said. "Luther has a small army working for him. You'll be well protected there."

"Hah, the last time we were there you were drugged."

"Trust me, Luther's security people are on guard now."

The tone of his voice told her there was no room for argument.

"Jake," she said. She stopped because she could not think of anything else to say.

He covered her mouth with his own. The kiss was as fierce as his eyes.

Chapter 43

The pier was located in a sheltered cove a few miles outside of town. It had been built for the owner of the summerhouse perched on the low bluff above the beach. The owner was not in residence, however, so the house was dark.

There were no lights, but the night was clear and the moon was still nearly full. There was a boathouse and a shed designed for hooks, nets, ropes, and other boating gear.

Jake waited in the shadow of the boathouse.

"Think he'll show?" Luther asked from the darkness beside the shed.

"He sounded desperate," Jake said. "He'll show."

They had arrived by boat an hour earlier because they knew that Massey would expect Jake to come to the meeting point in a car. The first rule when rendezvousing with a contact who promised to provide important information was to change the rules. That was especially true when you had a reason to think that the person who had set up the meeting was probably planning to kill you, Jake thought.

It occurred to him that he was feeling remarkably good considering that he was there to meet with a man who might try to murder him. Adelaide had changed everything, he thought. He had stopped drifting through life. He had a sense of purpose. He was starting to think about his future. For the first time since the nightmare of his doomed marriage had ended, he felt as if he was no longer trapped in a bad dream.

He had the feeling that he was not the only one who might be slowly surfacing from an old nightmare.

"I was surprised to see Raina Kirk with you at the club tonight," he said.

"I told you, she's investigating a small problem for me," Luther said.

"At midnight?"

"Well, I do operate a nightclub. Most of the action happens around midnight or later."

"I couldn't help but notice that the two of you were sitting in your private booth."

"The location provides an excellent view of the bar. My problem involves the theft of liquor."

"Yeah?"

"Look at it this way: Adelaide won't have to spend the evening alone while she waits to hear what happens here at the pier tonight. Raina is keeping her company."

Before Jake could think of anything else to say, headlights lanced the night. A vehicle lumbered down the rutted dirt road that led to the dock. He couldn't see beyond the glare of the beams but he knew from the rumble of the car's engine that Massey had not driven a speedster to the late-night meeting. It sounded as if he had borrowed an unremarkable Ford for the occasion, the sort of car that no one would remember later.

"We've got company," Luther said.

The Ford was nearly at the bottom of the access road. In another few seconds the headlights would illuminate the pier.

The vehicle came to a halt but the driver did not turn off the engine or the headlights.

A few more seconds passed before Jake heard a car door open and close.

"Truett? Are you here? You're supposed to be here, you bastard. Where are you? It's all gone wrong because of you, but I'm not going to let you destroy me. Do you hear me? You can't have her. She's mine."

Massey sounded as if he'd had a few martinis to work up his courage for the meeting. His voice was too loud and very blurred around the edges. It was probably sheer luck that he hadn't driven into a ditch or gone over the edge of Cliff Road on his way to the pier.

"I'm here, Massey." Jake did not move out of the shadows behind the boathouse. There was no way Massey could see him.

"Where are you?" Massey shouted. "Show yourself, you son of a bitch."

Jake put his back to the wall of the boathouse and took a quick look around the corner. Massey was a dark silhouette against the glare of the headlights that now illuminated the pier. The object he gripped with both hands was not a flashlight. It was a gun.

So much for the faint possibility that Massey really had come to make a deal.

Massey might have been drunk, but he wasn't so far gone that he couldn't see Jake briefly revealed in the headlights.

"Damn you, you're not going to stand in my way," he yelled.

He lunged forward, firing wildly. The thunder of the pistol shattered the unnatural stillness of the night. Again and again he pulled the trigger. Most of the shots went wild but Jake heard a couple plow into the wooden boathouse.

"Adelaide is mine," Massey shrieked. "You stole her from me. Everything will be all right again if I get her back."

"Who told you that, Massey?" Jake said.

"Gill explained everything. He needs her, too. It's a matter of *national security.* Top secret. Very hush-hush. There's a war coming. Gill says the government will need the drug. It will pay a fortune for a truth serum that works."

Massey advanced another couple of paces and pulled the trigger again. Jake heard wood splinter in the dock.

"Gill already has the drug," Jake said. "He can sell it to the government. He doesn't need Adelaide."

"The drug isn't right yet. Gill needs to run some more experiments. Adelaide has to go back to Rushbrook. Don't you understand? It's a matter of *national security.*"

"If you want me to get out of the way," Jake said, "you've got to answer a few more questions."

"No more questions. You're trying to trick me. You have to die."

"That's going to be a problem," Jake said.

Massey responded by pulling the trigger again.

There was a faint but distinctive *click.* The gun was empty.

Massey screamed.

"No," he shrieked. "Stay away from me. Stay back."

He sounded like a man who was fighting a waking nightmare. Jake heard a car door open. There was another volley of gunshots. Someone had accompanied Massey to the pier.

Massey screamed again, this time in pain as well as fear. But he was still on his feet. He fled down the pier. When he went past the boathouse Jake was using for cover, he did not pause. He was a man fleeing demons.

He reached the end of the pier. Jake saw him silhouetted in the moonlight. He teetered for a moment at the edge, as if trying to stop himself from going over, but he had too much momentum.

Panic-stricken, he yelled one last time and then he was gone.

The screaming didn't stop until he sank beneath the surface of the black waters of the cove.

Jake leaned around the edge of the boathouse again just in time to hear the door of the Ford slam. The vehicle made a tight turn and rocketed off into the night, heading back to the main road. It disappeared in the direction of Burning Cove.

There was a short silence before Luther emerged from the shadows of the shed. He slipped his gun into the holster he wore beneath his jacket.

"Well, that didn't go according to plan," he said.

Jake holstered his own gun and took his flashlight out of the pocket of his jacket. "I'm starting to think that the plan wasn't a good one. I don't suppose you got a look at the driver of the Ford?"

"Sorry, no. Too busy trying to dodge stray bullets. You'd be amazed how many people get killed by stray bullets."

Jake switched on the flashlight. "It's a damn shame we lost Massey. He could have answered at least a few questions."

"Yeah, after he sobered up."

"I don't think he was drunk," Jake said.

The screaming started again. Hysterical shrieks echoed up from the water below the pier.

Jake moved to the edge and aimed the flashlight beam downward. Luther came to stand beside him. Together they looked at Massey, who was clinging to one of the pier uprights. He stared up into the light, his eyes wide with terror. He screamed again.

"Demons," he yelled. "Stay away from me."

"He's still alive," Luther observed. "But I'm not sure he's going to do us any good. Sounds like he's lost his mind. He's hallucinating."

"Got a hunch someone slipped him a drug before putting a gun in his hand and pointing him at me."

"A human weapon, huh?" Luther sounded intrigued. "It's an interesting method for committing murder, but obviously a little unpredictable. One thing's for sure. Massey will never make it to shore on his own."

"I doubt that he was intended to survive tonight. I think the plan was for him to kill me and then make it appear that he took his own life by jumping into the cove. When things veered off course, the guy in the Ford tried to adjust the details of the scheme."

"If we don't get him out of the water, he'll drown," Luther observed.

"He won't be any use to us dead." Jake peeled off his jacket and unbuckled his shoulder holster. "It was my plan that went wrong. My job to clean up the mess. If he recovers from the delirium, we still might have a shot at getting some information out of him."

"I'll give you a hand." Luther shed his coat and gun. "I've seen men panic like this when the firing starts. That kind of fear gives them an unnatural strength. Massey won't even realize that we're trying to save him. He'll fight you."

"I'd appreciate the help." Jake picked up a coiled rope and a boat hook and started down the wooden steps. "This job just gets crazier and crazier."

"Job?"

"Adelaide says I need to find a job. For now, this is it."

"Sort of similar to your old line of work, isn't it?"

"Sort of."

"You were good at it, as I recall."

"It got old," Jake said. "Or maybe it was me who got old."

"You and me both. Burning Cove is a good place to start something new."

"Yeah, I'm getting that feeling."

Chapter 44

"In the end I had to clip him one on the jaw just to get him out of the water," Jake explained. "We got him tied up and the bleeding under control while he was groggy. But when he came to, he was in this weird state."

Adelaide gripped the bars of the jail cell and studied Conrad. She and Raina had arrived a short time earlier, escorted by two of Luther's security people. Jake and Luther were standing nearby. Detective Brandon and one of his police officers were also present. So was the doctor that Brandon had first summoned to examine Madam Zolanda's body.

Dr. Skipton had managed to get Conrad's shoulder bandaged while officers restrained the patient. He had offered to inject Conrad with a strong sedative to try to quell the hallucinations, but he had warned them that it might not work. He had no idea how the sedative would react with the unknown drug. That was when Jake had telephoned the Paradise Club, where Raina and Adelaide had been anxiously waiting.

Conrad was huddled in a corner of the cell now, whimpering. His wrists were secured with handcuffs. His shoes and belt had been removed. Detective Brandon had explained that it was for Conrad's own good. Dr. Skipton had said that if they set Massey free, he might try to harm himself or anyone who got close.

At the moment he did not appear to be a threat, Adelaide thought. Conrad murmured softly and rocked back and forth. He seemed oblivious of his injured arm as well as what was going on around him.

"He's trapped in a nightmare," Adelaide said quietly. "He's almost paralyzed with fear. He's making himself as small as possible, trying to hide from things that only he can see."

Raina watched Conrad with a grim expression. "It would serve him right if he gets permanently trapped in that other world."

Adelaide tightened her grip on the jail bars. "I know what it feels like to be lost in a nightmare. I wouldn't wish that on my worst enemy."

"Unfortunately, you seem to have a number of enemies," Raina said.

"Hard to figure out which of them is number one," Jake added.

"I've done all I can do for him," Dr. Skipton said. He looked at Adelaide, who was standing next to him. "You're sure you don't want me to give him a sedative?"

She shook her head. "You're right, there's a good chance that it would make things worse. The drug he took is very unpredictable. A sedative might not be effective at all, or it might put him into a coma that could last for days. It might even kill him. There's just no way to know."

"If he goes into a coma or dies, we'll never get any information out of him," Jake said.

"I'll try to get him to drink the antidote," Adelaide said. She glanced at Brandon. "I brought the herbs with me but I'll need hot water to make the tisane."

"We've got a kettle in the lunchroom," Brandon said. "I'll be right back."

He disappeared down the hall.

An officer appeared at the door. "Call for you, Dr. Skipton. It's your wife. She says Mrs. Ortega has gone into labor."

"Tell Betty I'm on my way," Dr. Skipton said. He hoisted his black satchel and turned to leave. He paused to give Adelaide a stern look. "Promise me you won't take any chances. There's no telling what Massey might do in his current state. You heard what Mr. Pell and Mr. Truett said. He lashed out at them when they tried to save him. He might lash out at you, too."

"I'll be careful," Adelaide said.

Jake looked at Skipton. "Don't worry, I'll make sure Massey doesn't get his hands on her."

"I'll be off, then," Skipton said. "Good luck with that tisane, Miss Brockton. Do let me know if it works."

"I will," she said.

Detective Brandon returned with a steaming teakettle and an empty mug. "Will this do?"

"Yes," Adelaide said.

She went to a nearby table, opened her handbag, and took out the small packet of herbs that she had brought with her. She emptied the packet into the mug and added the hot water.

"Now to see if I can convince him to drink the antidote," she said. "I'm going to try to get into his nightmare."

She carried the mug back to the cell and looked at Conrad through the bars.

"Conrad, can you hear me?" she said softly.

He flinched at the sound of his name but he did not respond. He did not make eye contact, either. He appeared transfixed by the shadows under the bunk.

"Where are you, Conrad?" she asked

He jerked again. "Hiding. I have to hide."

"You don't have to hide from me. I'm very naïve, remember? I trust you. Remember how easy it was to make me fall for you? I really believed you loved me."

Adelaide heard Jake swear softly under his breath. She shot him a warning glance and mouthed the word *quiet*.

He subsided but his expression was grim.

In the corner of his small cell, Conrad was struggling to focus on something other than whatever he saw under the bunk.

"You tricked me," he said at last.

"We were both tricked by Dr. Gill," Adelaide said. "He lied to both of us, didn't he?"

"Yes," Conrad said eagerly. "Gill insisted that you had to go to Rushbrook. He said it was for your own good. He tricked both of us. That's exactly what happened. The bastard tricked me."

Conrad's face contorted with sudden rage. The drug was an emotional roller coaster, Adelaide reminded herself.

"Did he tell you that you should pretend to love me?" she asked.

Conrad straightened to a sitting position. "I had to do it. You understand that, don't you? I had to do it for the sake of my family. And for reasons of national security. I had a duty to make you fall in love with me."

He was pleading now.

"Yes, I understand," she said. "You did what you had to do to save the family business. You have a responsibility to the Massey name. I met your relative at the Rushbrook Sanitarium. She explained things to me."

"You met crazy Aunt Eunice?"

"She was kind to me."

"They had to have her committed when she was eighteen. She's insane, you know. Family secret. Don't tell anyone."

"I won't."

"Can't have any rumors about a streak of insanity in the bloodline, you see. That kind of thing can destroy a family."

"Yes, your aunt explained that."

Conrad nodded solemnly. "I did what I had to do when I let them take you to Rushbrook. Future generations of Masseys will be grateful to me for saving the family business. My grandfather would have been proud of me."

"You're just like him, aren't you?"

"Yes." Conrad nodded several times in an agitated way, as if trying frantically to convince himself. "Just like my grandfather. Not like my father. He was weak. But I'm not."

Jake spoke quietly. "Ask him if he knows Paxton."

Adelaide looked at Conrad. "Did Calvin Paxton trick you, too?"

Conrad scowled. "Who's Paxton? I don't know anyone named Paxton."

"Why did you go to the Paradise Club the other night?" Adelaide said.

"Because I saw you shopping that afternoon," Conrad said. "I talked to the saleswoman after you left. She said she had just sold you a gown that you planned to wear to the nightclub. I thought if I could find you at the club, I could talk to you. Make you understand that you had to go back to Rushbrook. But Truett never let you out of his sight."

"You went into the gardens."

"I saw you go out there with Truett. I followed you. But I couldn't find you. I went back inside. I was going to ask you to dance when you came back into the club. You loved to dance with me, remember? But you and Truett left a short time later."

"Did you put a drug in Mr. Truett's glass that night?" Adelaide said.

"No." Conrad sounded irritated, almost petulant. "I don't have any drugs. Gill is the one with the drugs. Listen, you have to protect me, Adelaide. Truett wants to kill me. You have to stop him. I was only doing what I had to do for the sake of national security."

"You're safe behind these bars," Adelaide said. "Mr. Truett won't kill you."

"Truett's not the only one who wants to kill me."

"Who else wants to kill you?" Adelaide asked.

"Gill. He said that everything would be all right again if we met Truett at the dock. He said Truett was a businessman. That we could do a deal with him. But when we got there, Gill gave me a gun. He said I had to kill Truett. He said it was the only way to get you back."

"So it was Gill who drove you to the dock tonight and put the gun in your hand?" Adelaide asked.

"Yes. He said that after I killed Truett, everything would go back to the way it was." Conrad broke off. He shivered violently. "But he lied. I remember now. I was supposed to put the gun to my own head after I killed Truett. Gill lied to me."

"Everything will be fine once you have some tea," Adelaide said.

"Are you sure?"

"Yes," she said. She handed the mug through the bars. "Here you are. You'll feel much better after you drink this."

Conrad hesitated and then lurched awkwardly to his feet. He crossed the cell and took the mug from her fingers. He drank some of the tea and then looked at her with frantic eyes.

"You understand, don't you?" he said. "I didn't want to put you in that place but I had no choice. I had to save the family business."

She did not answer. She waited in silence until he had finished the tea.

"Give me the mug, Conrad," she said.

He handed it back to her. "You understand, don't you?"

"No," she said. "I don't understand. I might have understood if you had done what you did to me in order to save the life of someone you love. But to save a company and your family name? No. I don't understand that at all."

He looked stunned. "You said you understood."

"I lied."

"You can't lie to me," Conrad raged. He seized the bars in his cuffed hands and shook them with a drug-enhanced strength. "You're too naïve, too trusting, too dumb to lie."

Adelaide sensed Jake moving. In the blink of an eye he was at the cell door, key in hand.

She grabbed his arm.

"No," she said. "Please."

Jake glanced down at her fingers on his arm and then raised his burning eyes to look at her.

"Don't you see?" she said quietly. "He's like a maddened bull right now. Let the tisane take care of the situation. When it wears off, he'll be facing bankruptcy and charges of fraud and kidnapping and who knows what else. He'll be ruined. That's all the revenge I need."

The brew was working quickly. Conrad gripped the bars and stared at her. He made a visible attempt to focus his eyes.

"You lied to me," he mumbled. "You said it was tea but it was poison."

He released the bars, stumbled to the bunk, and collapsed on the thin mattress.

Adelaide became aware of the acute silence around her. She turned, walked across the room, and set the empty mug on the counter.

"I gave him a very heavy dose," she said, keeping her voice expressionless. "He'll probably sleep for a few hours."

She stared at the wall in front of her and wondered why she felt numb.

Jake came to stand beside her. He turned her gently in his arms.

"I'm sorry," he said.

"I almost let you go into that cell," she whispered. "But you might have killed him. I couldn't allow you to do that. Not for me."

"There's no one I would rather kill for than you." Cold steel underlined the words.

She managed a teary smile. "Thank you but it's not necessary. I'm not alone now. I don't have to hide any longer. I've got friends here in Burning Cove."

"Damn right," Raina said.

Chapter 45

Everything had gone wrong. Again.

Gill flung the last of his clothes into the suitcase, wiped cold sweat off his forehead, and swung around to examine the hotel room. He must not leave anything behind that would lead Truett and the police back to him. Truett was the one who worried him the most. The bastard should have died tonight, the victim of a jealous husband who had gotten drunk and then gone to a midnight rendezvous with the intention of killing his rival.

The plan had included Conrad Massey's death, as well. At least that part of the scheme worked. One of the bullets had struck Massey. He went off the end of the pier. There was no way he could have survived.

No possible way.

Gill forced himself to check the bathroom cabinet and the closet one last time to make certain he had not left anything behind. He had been careful to register under another name when he had checked into the cheap, run-down hotel. Truett and the police would not be able to use the guest records to identify him. Not that they were ever likely to trace him to this dump, he thought.

He closed the suitcase, hauled it off the bed, and headed for the door. He hurried downstairs to the dimly lit lobby. There was no sign of the night clerk at the front desk. The sound of snoring came from the inner office. One piece of good luck at last—there would be no one to witness the late-night departure of the mysterious Mr. Smith.

Gill opened the door, hurried across the porch, and went down the front steps. He walked quickly along the sidewalk and around the corner. Earlier, when he had returned from the debacle at the pier, he had parked on an empty side street. There was only one streetlamp at the end of the block. The light it cast did not reach far into the darkness. He did not think anyone would notice the Ford.

He tossed the suitcase into the trunk, closed the lid, and started toward the driver's side door. A figure emerged from the shadows of a long row of bushy oleander trees. Calvin Paxton moved into the moonlight. He had a gun in his hand.

"I always knew that you were too weak to stick with the plan if things got complicated," Paxton said. "Figured you'd lose your nerve and run."

"What are you going to do?" Gill opened the driver's side door. "Shoot me here on the street outside my hotel? If you really think that's a smart move, you're as crazy as any of my patients at Rushbrook. The cops will investigate. Once they identify me they'll start asking questions. Sooner or later they'll find a connection between us. It's over, Paxton. The operation is crumbling. If you had any sense, you'd run, too."

"There's no need for me to run," Paxton said. "No one knows that I'm involved with you and the drug business that you and Ormsby were running out of Rushbrook. Zolanda and Leggett are dead. They are the only ones who could have pointed the finger at me. I'm in the clear, unless, of course, you decide to talk to the police or the FBI."

"I'm not going to talk to anyone," Gill said. "Massey's dead. As long as you and I keep quiet, we'll be all right."

"You don't know, do you? Of course not. How could you know?" Paxton lowered the gun. "Massey survived."

Gill felt as if he'd taken a punch to the gut. For a second or two he could not catch his breath.

"The hell he did," he said. "I saw him go off the end of that pier. He was alive but he was bleeding. I shot him, Paxton. In addition, he was in a full-blown delirium. If he didn't bleed to death, he must have drowned."

"I watched Truett and Pell take him into the police station. From what I could tell, Massey was only semiconscious, but you're right, he was hallucinating wildly. That means we've got some time. You gave him a big dose of Daydream, so it will take at least a couple of days before the effects of the drug start to wear off. But when they do, he'll talk. He'll tell the police that you drove him to that pier to meet Truett. He'll say that you were the one who set him up—that you drugged him and put the gun in his hand."

"The key is that he was on drugs," Gill said urgently. "Hallucinating. Don't you understand? Nothing he says will stand up in court—especially when they find out that I was at home in Rushbrook when the shooting happened here in Burning Cove."

"It's a long drive back to Rushbrook. A good three hours, maybe longer if you run into fog."

"That's why I have to get on the road. It's after one. If I leave now, I can be there by four or five. The staff at Rushbrook believe I'm away on a fishing trip. I'll go into the office at my usual time tomorrow morning and tell everyone that the fish weren't biting so I returned sooner than planned."

"What are we going to do about Massey?" Paxton asked. "He knows too much."

"If the police question me, I'll tell them that there's a streak of insanity in the Massey family. I've got his crazy aunt tucked away at Rushbrook to prove my point, remember? But I'm telling you, it won't come to that, not if I get back to the sanitarium before the night is over. In fact, with a little luck we can still salvage the plan. Think about the money, Paxton. Daydream is worth a fortune."

"Even if you convince the police that Massey is insane, what about Truett and Adelaide Blake?"

"I've been thinking," Gill said. He spoke slowly, feeling his way as the new plan began to take shape in his head. "Adelaide Blake is crazy. Hell, she escaped from an asylum. The police won't believe a word she says. But it occurs to me that if she were to poison her lover, Jake Truett, it wouldn't be the biggest surprise in the world. After all, she was locked up for a reason."

"Huh." Paxton sounded intrigued. "That is not a bad idea."

"It will take a little planning but I think we can come up with something that might work. But I need to get out of town first so that I can establish my alibi."

"All right."

"You're safe. You were nowhere near the pier tonight."

"True." Paxton slipped the gun inside his jacket, took out a gold lighter, and lit a cigarette. "You're right. I'll be fine. Go on, get out of here."

Gill did not need any urging. He climbed behind the wheel and turned the key in the ignition. Just as he was about to put the car in gear, Paxton materialized at the passenger side window. He rapped on the glass.

"Hang on," Paxton said loudly. "Your trunk is open. I'll close it for you."

Gill waited while Paxton moved behind the Ford, raised the trunk lid, and slammed it firmly closed. He waved once, signaling that the problem had been taken care of, and then he turned and swiftly disappeared into the shadows of the oleanders.

Gill put the Ford in gear and pulled away from the curb. He started to breathe again. There had been a time when he was jealous of Paxton and Paxton's glittering, star-studded life, envious of the fact that Paxton was fucking the most beautiful woman in Hollywood.

Now I'm afraid of the bastard, Gill thought.

No question about it, he would have to find a way to get rid of Paxton. Maybe he could figure out how to kill Paxton as well as Truett with Daydream and blame both murders on crazy Adelaide Blake. Maybe he could salvage the original plan. Maybe he could survive the mess.

The more he thought about it, the more it seemed obvious that he did not need Paxton. He promised himself that by the time he got back to Rushbrook, he would come up with a scheme to ensure that he was the last man standing. He and he alone would control Daydream.

He got as far as Cliff Road before the explosion erupted, shattering the silence of the night. He died instantly.

The intense fire crackled to life a short time later.

Paxton stood in the shadows and watched the Ford burn. It had been so easy to light the fuse on the stick of dynamite he had hidden under his coat, so easy to toss the explosive into the trunk of Gill's car.

The thrill of satisfaction was intoxicating. They were all gone now—Ormsby, Madam Zolanda, Thelma Leggett, and finally, tonight, Gill. The drug ring had been shut down—except for him, of course. He was the last man standing. Now he and he alone controlled the powerful hallucinogen called Daydream.

Unlike Gill, he had no intention of selling it to a foreign government or anyone else. The potential was too promising. A few refinements were all that was needed to make Daydream more predictable. He could use derelicts and transients for the final phase of development.

Once he was sure that the drug was reliable, he would be able to control the most powerful people in the nation: industrialists, newspaper magnates, politicians—hell, maybe even the president.

Paxton envisioned his destiny with a sense of wonder. Soon he would become the most powerful man in America.

There was no reason to worry about Conrad Massey. It was true that he knew too much but everything he knew was connected to Gill and Ormsby, and both of them were now dead. Massey had never been aware of the drug ring that had been operating for years out of the Rushbrook Sanitarium. He had never known that Zolanda and Thelma Leggett had been dealing drugs to celebrities in Hollywood or that Gill's old pal from medical school had been involved from the start.

Gill had been right about Adelaide Blake. No one would take her seriously once it became known that she had escaped from an asylum. Jake Truett was the only unpredictable element in the equation. He was evidently the kind of man who would keep asking questions until he was satisfied. Gill's idea to have Adelaide Blake poison her lover was not a bad one. It had been easy enough to slip some Daydream into Truett's drink at the Paradise Club. It was just a fluke that Truett had survived the first dose. He would not survive a second.

The front door of the hotel slammed open. The night clerk rushed out onto the porch to view the fiery scene at the end of the street. A few startled guests raised their windows to see what was going on.

The night clerk hurried back inside, no doubt to telephone the fire department.

Sure enough, a short time later sirens sounded in the night. By now the night clerk was back outside on the porch. He was accompanied by a handful of guests in their bathrobes.

Paxton waited a moment longer before he left the shadows of the oleanders and entered the hotel through the back door. There was no one in the lobby. The registration book was open on the front counter. It showed that a Mr. Smith had been staying in room five. The key was still on the counter where Gill had tossed it on his way out.

Paxton grabbed it and headed upstairs. It wouldn't take long to set the stage.

He left the crumpled receipt in the trash basket and then he hurried back downstairs. His car was waiting on the street behind the hotel. Time to return to the Paradise. The most beautiful woman in Hollywood was waiting for him. Vera would start to worry if he didn't get back to her soon. She got very anxious when he was not around.

Chapter 46

Luther hung up the phone on the wall of Adelaide's kitchen. "Oliver Ward says that Paxton left the Burning Cove Hotel earlier this evening and has not yet returned. My manager told me that Paxton showed up at the club a short time ago. He is currently seated with Miss Westlake. They are both enjoying martinis."

"That leaves a lot of Paxton's time unaccounted for," Adelaide pointed out.

"He's involved in this thing," Jake said. "I know he is."

It was going on two thirty in the morning. She was at the kitchen counter making coffee. Jake, Luther, and Raina were gathered around the big table. It had been a night of shocks and surprises, she thought, but at long last they were getting some answers. Things were falling into place.

"Well, we know one thing for sure," Raina said. "Paxton is alive and having cocktails with Vera Westlake, so that tells us he's not the dead man in the Ford. It must be Gill."

"There's no way to know for certain until that car cools down enough to allow the authorities to pull the body out of the front seat," Luther said. "And even then we might never know for sure."

"That fire was very intense," Jake said. "I doubt if there will be enough left for a positive identification, but unless Gill shows up alive at Rushbrook, I think it's safe to assume he was the one behind the wheel of the Ford."

Luther looked at him. "I agree with you, Jake. Paxton is closing down the drug ring that was operating out of Rushbrook."

"All we've got at this point is that receipt for three sticks of dynamite," Adelaide said.

"Dynamite is not exactly a subtle method of getting rid of people," Jake said, "but it does have one very useful side effect."

"It doesn't leave much in the way of evidence," Raina observed.

Adelaide turned around, coffeepot in hand, just in time to catch the expression on Luther's face. He was watching Raina with an interesting mix of speculation, curiosity, and admiration.

"You make an excellent point," he said.

When news of the explosion reached the police station, they had all piled into cars and followed Brandon and his officers to the scene. There was enough left of the burning vehicle to identify it as a Ford, but the warped and twisted metal was still too hot to allow the fire department to extract the remains of the body in the front seat. The hotel desk clerk said that one of his guests had driven the Ford.

Detective Brandon had not argued when Jake, Adelaide, Raina, and Luther accompanied him up the hotel stairs to number five. Gill had done a thorough job of packing but he had missed the crumpled receipt for three sticks of dynamite in the small trash basket. Jake was the one who had noticed it.

"What we know for certain is that someone, presumably Gill, purchased three sticks of dynamite from a hardware store in a small town about halfway between Burning Cove and Rushbrook," Jake said. "If we assume that one of the sticks was used to blow up my car, that means Gill might have had two more in the Ford."

Adelaide poured coffee into the four mugs on the table. "If Gill was the one who purchased the dynamite sticks, the explosion tonight must have been accidental."

Jake picked up his mug and cradled it in two hands. "A stick of fresh dynamite is not particularly unstable, but old dynamite is very dangerous. The stuff degrades over time. The nitroglycerin seeps out and that, of course, is highly volatile. Wouldn't take much to set it off."

"Dynamite purchased in a small-town hardware store might be old," Luther observed. "A careless match or even a strong jolt could cause it to explode.'"

"Gill smoked," Adelaide said. She sat down in the empty chair next to Jake. "He always had a cigarette in his hand. I remember Dr. Ormsby complaining about it whenever Gill came up to the lab. Some of the chemicals were highly flammable."

Raina's eyes narrowed a little. "If Gill tossed a match or a half-smoked cigarette out the window and it blew back into the car and landed on the dynamite, that would certainly account for the explosion."

"Maybe," Jake said.

Adelaide looked at him. "What's worrying you?"

Luther studied Jake from the opposite side of the table. "He's thinking that this whole thing seems to be ending a little too neatly."

"Neatly?" Raina said. "It all seems very bizarre to me."

"Not if you consider that everything that has happened somehow revolves around the drug that Adelaide's parents discovered," Jake said.

Adelaide shuddered. "Daydream. They should have called it Nightmare."

"Let's assume that Gill and Paxton had been running a profitable little drug ring and marketing their wares to Hollywood celebrities,"

Jake said. "They used Madam Zolanda and Thelma Leggett as distributors. Then Gill realizes that Adelaide's parents have discovered a new hallucinogen with hypnotic properties."

"A drug that could be used to implant hypnotic suggestions could be worth a fortune not only on the private market but also to certain government agencies in every country in the world," Raina mused. "The potential would be huge."

"But only if Gill and Paxton can have exclusive control of the drug," Jake continued. "So they decide to get rid of everyone who knew too much about the original drug ring and about Daydream. Patient A evidently died from the effects of the drug. That left Ormsby, Zolanda, Thelma Leggett, and Patient B."

"Me," Adelaide said.

Jake looked at her. "But Patient B vanished the night they planned to murder her. That left Gill and Paxton with a serious problem because Adelaide was the one person who knew all about the secret experiments at Rushbrook. They had to find her before they continued dismantling the ring. They finally tracked her down here in Burning Cove."

"Madam Zolanda and Thelma Leggett were sent here to get a handle on the situation," Luther said. "If Jake's right about Paxton, that explains his presence in town."

"They knew that I wouldn't recognize any of them," Adelaide said. "But by the time they found me, I had settled into life here in Burning Cove. I had a job. Friends. People would have noticed if I simply vanished. They needed a plan to kidnap me or maybe murder me without drawing attention to themselves."

Raina nodded. "Do you think the original scheme involved Madam Zolanda making that final prediction about someone dying before morning?"

"Maybe," Jake said. "It wouldn't have been a bad plan, when you think about it. If Adelaide had been killed or if she had vanished that night, the press would have gone wild. Zolanda could have added to her fame by helping the police find the body."

"Instead, it was Zolanda who was killed," Luther said. "If her plan was to predict Adelaide's death, it backfired."

"Gill and Paxton obviously had a different outcome in mind," Adelaide said.

"One thing seems certain," Raina said. "If we're right about all of this, Paxton is the last member of the drug ring who is still alive. How do we go about proving he is not only a killer but also in possession of a dangerous new hallucinogen?"

Jake put down his coffee mug and got to his feet. "We need more answers and there's only one place left to look for them."

"Where?" Adelaide asked.

"Back where it all started, the Rushbrook Sanitarium." He glanced at the wall clock. "If I leave now, I can be in Rushbrook by dawn. Luther, look after Adelaide until you hear from me, all right?"

"Of course," Luther said. "She can stay in a guest room at my place. There's plenty of security around the Paradise."

"No," Adelaide said. She got to her feet and looked at Jake. "I'm coming with you."

"I don't think that's a good idea," Jake said.

"You'll need me. You don't know your way around Rushbrook. I know every inch of it. I know where the keys are kept. I also know some of the patients and the staff. You'll be able to search the place much more efficiently if I'm with you."

"She's right," Raina said.

Luther nodded. "I agree with Raina. It would be helpful to have someone with you who knows her way around the sanitarium. Raina and I can keep an eye on Paxton while you're gone."

Jake hesitated and then surrendered to the logic.

"All right," he said.

"You'll need a good, fast, reliable car," Luther said to Jake. "I wouldn't trust that secondhand Oldsmobile you picked up when you tracked down Thelma Leggett. Adelaide's Ford isn't in great shape, either. You can take my car."

"Thanks," Jake said.

Adelaide headed for the stairs. "I'll get my gun."

Jake groaned. "I was afraid you were going to say that."

Chapter 47

The Rushbrook Sanitarium loomed in the dawn fog, a monstrous gargoyle frozen in stone. Adelaide had spent the past three hours trying to fortify her nerves, but when she saw the asylum, she knew that nothing could have prepared her for the cold shock. The Duchess's words rang in her ears. *You should not return to this place. You don't belong here.*

Jake brought the car to a halt near the front gate and shut down the engine. He sat quietly for a moment, his hands resting on the steering wheel, and contemplated the sanitarium.

"Looks like a movie set for a horror film," he said.

"According to the Duchess, the house has a very odd history," Adelaide said, trying to distract herself with facts. "It was built by a man who made a fortune in oil. He set out to construct a Gothic castle that he thought would please his East Coast bride. The story is that when she saw it for the first time on her honeymoon, she was horrified. She announced that she would never live in such an ugly place. There was a quarrel. The husband went mad and pushed his bride out one of the tower room windows. She was killed, of course."

"Just like Ormsby," Jake said.

Adelaide looked at him. "Yes, just like Ormsby."

"I can see someone inside the guardhouse at the front gate."

"That will be Oscar," Adelaide said. "He works the night shift. The day man, Pete, won't arrive until seven."

"Not a lot of security for a secret drug manufacturing facility."

"I don't think there was much need for security, at least not until recently. Most people aren't even aware that Rushbrook exists. There are two orderlies on every floor and they are all hired for their muscle. But I'm quite sure they aren't involved in the drug ring."

"What makes you so certain?"

"For the simple reason that none of them is getting rich," Adelaide said. "They grumble constantly about the low pay. The only real security is on ward five, where the most insane patients are housed. That ward is locked twenty-four hours a day. The entrance to the tower room lab is on that floor."

"You said you know where the keys are kept."

"Yes. They are in Gill's office on the second floor."

"But you think the files we want are kept upstairs in the lab."

"That's where they were when I was—" She broke off because she refused to label herself a patient. "When I was here."

"You mean when you were involuntarily in residence?" Jake asked with a wry smile.

For some reason the grim attempt at humor buoyed her spirits.

"Yes," she said.

"But you escaped," he said. "Don't ever forget that. You saved yourself."

She took a breath. "Right. I escaped. So, how do we do this?"

"The easy way. We walk through the front door."

They got out of the car. Jake paused to put on his coat and collect an official-looking briefcase from the trunk of the car.

They went toward the guardhouse. A stocky man with thinning red hair peered out at them. He glanced briefly at Adelaide, started to switch his attention to Jake, hesitated, and then looked back at Adelaide. His eyes widened in astonishment.

"Adelaide? Mrs. Massey? Is that you?"

"Hello, Oscar."

"I was afraid Dr. Gill would find you," Oscar said. He glared at Jake. "Are you the hired gun Gill sent to track down Mrs. Massey? You ought to be ashamed of yourself. She doesn't belong in this place."

"I agree. I'm Jake Truett. You could call me a hired gun but I'm working for Adelaide, not Gill. And by the way, she isn't Mrs. Massey. Her last name is Blake."

Oscar looked skeptical. He turned to Adelaide. "That true?"

"Yes, it is," Adelaide said. "I was never married."

"Dr. Gill said—"

"Dr. Gill lied," Adelaide said. "The only reason I'm here now is because I left something behind. I came back to get it. Mr. Truett accompanied me to make sure I don't have any problems with Gill."

Oscar grunted. "No need to worry about running into Gill. He's off on a fishing trip. He's not due back until the end of the week."

"So you haven't seen Gill recently?" Jake asked.

"Not since he took off in his old Ford. Heard he left his sharp new Lincoln behind. It's in the garage at his house. He told someone he didn't want to get it muddy on the back roads in the mountains."

"Who did Gill put in charge of the sanitarium while he's out of town?" Adelaide asked.

"That's the weird thing—he didn't leave anyone in charge. He just took off real sudden like. Nurse Conner is looking after things." Oscar glanced at his watch. "But it's just going on five thirty. She won't arrive until eight o'clock."

"That means we'll be dealing with the orderlies," Adelaide said.

She gave Oscar a bright smile. "I don't think Mr. Truett will have any problem handling them."

Oscar eyed Jake with a considering look. "Not sure what's going on here, but if you're a friend of Adelaide's, I can give you some advice that might save you a whole lot of trouble."

"I'm always open to good advice," Jake said.

"If any of the orderlies tries to make trouble for you, just slip him ten or twenty bucks. That will make him look the other way."

"Thanks for the tip," Jake said. He took out his wallet and removed some bills. "Sound advice is worth a lot to me."

Oscar raised his bushy brows and palmed the money. "Not necessary. Happy to help out Mrs. Massey—I mean, Adelaide. But thanks. I can buy that new radio Nancy's been wanting. We get a real chuckle out of that *Fibber McGee and Molly* show and we never miss *The Shadow*."

"How is you wife's insomnia these days?" Adelaide asked.

Oscar smiled. "Much better, thanks to you. She brews up some of those herbs and flowers you told me about and drinks a cup or two before she goes to bed. Sleeps real good. I've started drinking some of the stuff myself."

"It was one of my mother's recipes. I'm glad it worked for your wife. Take care, Oscar. And thanks for your kindness to me when I was here."

"You were in real bad shape the night Dr. Gill brought you here. He said you'd had a nervous breakdown and that he and Ormsby were going to give you some special medicine that would help you. But as far as the staff could tell, it made things worse, just like it did the first patient they treated with it. Except you survived. After you disappeared, a lot of folks here, including me, said you were better off away from this place."

"You and the others were right," Adelaide said. "I've been doing great since I left the Rushbrook Sanitarium."

"Glad to hear it. Run along now and fetch your things. Reckon one of the orderlies can show you where they stored your belongings."

"I wasn't able to carry much with me the night I left," Adelaide said. She turned to Jake. "Are you ready to see the place where I was involuntarily in residence for nearly two months?"

Jake's eyes got the cold, expressionless look that she was coming to know so well.

"Yes," he said.

They walked through the deceptively serene gardens and went up the stone steps to the massive wooden door. Jake tried the handle. When he discovered it was locked, he leaned on the bell button.

An attendant dressed in a white uniform opened the door. He looked rumpled and annoyed—a man at the end of a long night shift. Adelaide didn't need the name tag on his shirt to identify him. Harold Baker liked the night shift because he could doze through most of it. He did not immediately recognize her.

"Visiting hours are three to four in the afternoon," he announced. "Dr. Gill is very strict about that. Upsets the patients if people come and go at any time of the day."

"We're not here to visit any of the patients," Jake said. He pulled a leather case out from under his jacket and flipped it open and closed very fast. "Special Agent Jake Truett, Federal Bureau of Investigation. Dr. Gill has been doing some clandestine work for us. There's been a breach of national security."

"Huh?"

"I need to confiscate some files immediately."

Befuddled, Harold looked at Adelaide as if seeking clarification. Belated recognition sparked in his eyes.

"Hey, aren't you Patient B?" he demanded.

"Good news, Harold. My mental health has vastly improved since I left the Rushbrook Sanitarium," Adelaide said. "By the way, we'll need the keys to ward five."

"I can't give you those keys," Harold said, alarmed. "Dr. Gill would be real upset."

"Unless you would like me to take you in for questioning concerning a serious breach of national security, you'll give Miss Blake the keys," Jake said.

"Miss Blake? Her name's Mrs. Massey."

"I'm not Mrs. Massey," Adelaide said. "You had better give Special Agent Truett those keys before he arrests you."

"Damn it, I don't get paid enough to take this kind of grief," Harold growled. "The keys to the fifth floor are in Gill's office. Help yourself."

Adelaide started toward the grand staircase. "Follow me, Special Agent Truett."

"Right behind you, Miss Blake," Jake said. "I can assure you that the Bureau is very grateful for your cooperation in this vital matter."

Harold watched, mouth agape, as Adelaide and Jake went quickly up the stairs.

When they reached the landing, Adelaide looked at Jake. "Is that a real FBI badge?"

"Real enough," Jake said.

"Meaning?"

"Meaning it worked."

"I guess that makes it real enough," Adelaide said.

Gill's office was locked.

"We'll have to make Harold give us the key," she said.

"Let me try my skeleton key," Jake said.

"You have a skeleton key?"

"Technical term."

Jake took his gun out from under his jacket and used the handle to tap the glass pane in the door with judicious force. The glass shattered. He reached inside and turned the knob.

"Right," Adelaide said. "A skeleton key. Very handy piece of equipment."

"Yes, it is," Jake said.

The iron ring containing the key to the fifth-floor ward was on a hook on the wall. Adelaide grabbed it.

No one tried to stop them until they reached the locked ward on the fifth floor. At that point they were confronted with another thick wooden door and an old-fashioned lock. Adelaide got the door open with the key.

She thought she was braced for the return to the ghastly place where she had spent a two-month-long nightmare, but when she moved into ward five, a wave of panic hit her. She froze. She wanted to turn around and run for her life.

She was vaguely aware that Jake had stopped beside her. He surveyed the ward with its sterile white walls, white tile floor, and twin rows of locked rooms.

"Don't worry," he said. "You're never coming back to this place."

She pulled herself together. "But if I do end up back here, you'll come and get me."

"Yes."

"I'm all right now," she said. "The staircase that leads to the lab is at the far end of this hall. Whatever you do, don't look through the grills into any of the rooms. Don't make eye contact with any of the patients."

"I understand. The patients deserve some privacy."

"Of course, but it's not just a matter of privacy. Only the most troubled are housed on this floor. Some of them can become quite violent. If they weren't paranoid before they were committed to this place, they became paranoid soon after they were locked up here. I did."

"You had good reason to become paranoid."

A face appeared at one of the grills. Adelaide was careful not to look at the patient but she could not ignore the moaning cry.

"It's the ghost," he rasped in anguished tones. "She's back."

Another face appeared at the grilled opening in the door across the hall.

"You shouldn't be here," a woman keened. "Go away. Run. They'll kill you again."

"She's back," someone shouted. "The ghost is back."

There was a face at every grill now. One of the patients uttered an anguished howl. The rest took up the cry.

"It's the ghost . . ."

"The ghost is back . . ."

The glass-paned door of the nurses' station opened. A large, heavily muscled man with straggly hair emerged from the small room. Adelaide recognized him immediately. His name was Buddy. He ignored her and fixed his attention on Jake.

"Who are you and what are you doing here?" Buddy snarled. "This is a locked ward. No visitors allowed."

"Government business," Jake said. He flipped open the leather case and snapped it shut in one smooth motion. In the process he made sure that the holstered gun under his jacket was briefly visible. "There's been a breach of security concerning the research that is being conducted here at the Rushbrook Sanitarium. I have been sent to collect any and all files pertinent to that research."

A second orderly charged out of the room. He was as big as Buddy and he was almost completely bald, but there was more intelligence in his eyes.

"Dr. Gill didn't say anything about letting someone take the files," he growled.

"Hello, Victor," Adelaide said. "Remember me?"

Victor stared at her. "Say, you're that crazy Patient B—I mean, Mrs. Massey. What's going on?"

"Guess what," Adelaide said. "I'm no longer Patient B, I'm not Mrs. Massey, and best of all, I'm not crazy. I'm Adelaide Blake. Don't bother to offer tea or coffee. We won't be staying long."

"Where did you get the key to this floor?" Victor demanded.

"As Mr. Truett was just explaining to Buddy, we're here on government business," Adelaide said.

Jake looked at her. "You said the lab is at the end of the hall?"

"That's right."

Adelaide started forward. But Victor stepped in her path.

"Hang on, Mrs. Massey, or Patient B, or whoever you are. Only authorized personnel are allowed in that lab."

Jake opened the edge of his coat just enough to reveal the gun again. "We have authorization from the appropriate authorities." He let the coat fall closed.

"Oh," Victor said. His jaw hardened. "I should probably call someone to confirm it."

"You'll have to call long-distance, Washington, D.C.," Jake said. "Meanwhile, we'll be in the lab."

He fell into step beside Adelaide. Together they went briskly along the hall to the glass-paned door marked *Laboratory: Authorized Personnel Only*.

The keys shivered on the iron ring as Adelaide tried one after another.

"None of them work," she announced. "Looks like we'll need your skeleton key again."

Jake took out his gun and tapped the glass pane with just enough force to shatter it. Holstering the gun, he reached through the opening and turned the knob.

Adelaide moved into the stairwell and flipped a switch on the wall. The sconces came on, illuminating the twisted stone steps. She tried without much success to repress a shudder.

"I hate this place," she said.

She didn't realize she had spoken aloud until Jake answered.

"After we leave here today, you'll never have to come back again," he said.

She put one foot on the first step. "The lab is at the top."

She went up the stairs. Her shoes echoed on the stone. Jake was right behind her. The mad cries and moans of the patients on ward five followed them, echoing in the stairwell.

"You were right," Jake said. "I did need you to guide me around this place. Whoever designed this mansion must have been as crazy as any of the patients."

"You can understand why the owner's bride was not thrilled with her new castle," Adelaide said.

She came to a halt at the top of the stairs. The early morning light streaming through the tall, arched windows that lined one wall did little to alleviate the invisible miasma that seethed in the space.

The panic welled up out of nowhere again. This time it threatened to choke her.

"Are you all right?" Jake asked.

"Yes," she managed. "Yes, I'm all right."

She made herself take a detached look at the laboratory. The arched window that Ormsby had shattered when he leaped to his death had been boarded up, but aside from that it was all horribly familiar. She would never be able to forget it, she thought. The workbenches were littered with laboratory glassware of all shapes and sizes. Gauges, Bunsen burners, weighing machines, and various kinds of instruments lined the shelves.

The wooden upright chair where the orderlies had restrained her while Gill and Ormsby forced her to drink the Daydream drug sat in one corner. It looked so very ordinary now.

This time is different, she thought. *This time you're in charge. This time you're not alone.*

"I thought of it as the electric chair," she whispered.

She was speaking to herself but Jake heard her. He came up behind her and touched her shoulder.

"It's over," he said. "You fought them and in the end you escaped.

You beat the bastards. Gill and Ormsby are both dead. Conrad Massey is facing bankruptcy and prison. We're going to find a way to make sure Paxton ends up behind bars. If you ever decide that's not enough justice and you want him dead, too, that can be arranged."

She touched Jake's hand on her shoulder. "There's been enough death."

"Just be sure to let me know if you ever change your mind."

"Thanks. I'll do that. We'd better get busy. I wouldn't be surprised if Victor is on the phone now, telephoning the local police. I'm not sure he bought your FBI agent act."

"And here I thought I played the part so well," Jake said. He angled his chin toward the office at the back of the lab. "I assume the files are kept in there?"

"Yes. I just hope Gill or Paxton didn't move them for some reason."

"Why would they do that? They would have considered this the safest possible place for the files because they assumed they had complete control over the Rushbrook Sanitarium."

Jake went down the aisle formed by two workbenches and once again used the handle of his gun to shatter the glass pane set into the door. He turned the knob and went into the room.

Adelaide hurried after him. They both looked at the wooden file cabinets arranged against one wall.

"The files relating to the Daydream experiments are in the last cabinet," Adelaide said, "the one that's locked. Ormsby used to keep the key in his desk drawer, but I couldn't find it the night that I escaped so I had to leave my file behind."

"No problem," Jake said. "It's just a small, standard-issue drawer lock."

He took a firm grip on the drawer handle and yanked hard. Adelaide heard something metallic snap inside the cabinet. The drawer popped open.

Together they looked down at the neatly arranged row of folders.

She searched quickly for her own file. The one in front was marked *Patient B.* She seized it and opened it.

"This is it," she said. "This is my proof that they were running experiments on me."

"Is there a folder for Patient A?"

Adelaide closed her own file and riffled quickly through the remaining folders. She shook her head.

"No," she said. "I recognize some of these other files, though. They are the records of my father's research, the files that went missing after he and my mother were killed in that explosion."

"We'll take your file and anything else we can carry out in this briefcase," Jake said. "I want to know what the hell was going on here."

Adelaide scooped out an armful of files and gave them to Jake, who stuffed them into the briefcase. When the drawer was empty, he fastened the case, straightened, and went to the desk.

"What are you looking for?" Adelaide asked.

"I have no idea." Jake snapped the lock on the center desk drawer. "Here we go. This might be interesting."

He took out a leather-bound notebook.

"What is it?" Adelaide asked.

"Looks like Ormsby's appointment book and daily calendar." Jake opened the book and flipped rapidly through the pages. He stopped. "Here's the last entry. It's a note about the need to prepare a dozen vials of Daydream. The date is the same day you escaped."

"The perfume bottles that I saw on this desk that night," Adelaide said. "The killer took them. They were full of Daydream, not the usual drug."

"That's how Paxton came by the Daydream he's been using in Burning Cove." Jake did not look up from the appointment book. "Damn," he said very softly. "It's all here, Adelaide. Names, dates, all the details of the drug operation they were running out of this place. This is everything we need to tie Paxton to the ring."

The howls and moans on the floor below escalated sharply. The eerie, mournful chorus reverberated up the stone staircase. Adelaide shivered.

"The patients are becoming more agitated," she said.

She knew the dreadful cries would only get worse before the orderlies managed to calm the wretches in the cell-like rooms.

Jake closed the appointment book with an air of grim triumph. "Ormsby's note says that Paxton ordered the dozen vials of Daydream. It's all clear now. I've been trying to figure out the link between Rushbrook and Madam Zolanda and Thelma Leggett. I couldn't understand how they came to know each other. Gill worked here at the asylum. Zolanda lived in Hollywood. It's not as if they would have moved in the same worlds. Paxton is the connection."

"That makes sense," Adelaide said. "He's a Hollywood doctor. He would have known about Zolanda's psychic business. I wonder how Paxton and Gill met."

Paxton spoke from the top of the laboratory staircase.

"I'll be happy to answer that question," he said. "Gill and I met in medical school."

Startled, Adelaide swung around. Paxton took a few steps into the laboratory. He had a gun in his hand. It was aimed at her but he spoke to Jake.

"The orderlies told me that you were armed," he said. "Put the gun on the floor. One false move and I'll shoot Adelaide."

Chapter 48

"Take it easy," Jake said. "My gun is in a shoulder holster. I'll have to reach inside my coat."

"Get it," Paxton said. "Slowly. Put it down on the floor. One false move, Miss Blake dies first."

Jake took out his gun and crouched to set it on the floor. Adelaide caught a flash of lapis blue in his hand. She realized he had palmed his fountain pen when he reached for the pistol.

Paxton looked at Adelaide. "Kick it over here, out of Truett's reach."

She used the toe of her shoe to nudge the gun out of the office doorway. Her handbag containing her pistol was sitting on the edge of the desk. The weapon might as well have been a thousand miles away.

"Good girl," Paxton said approvingly. "Now, both of you, come out of the office where I can get a clear shot if I need one."

"Do as he says," Jake said quietly. He did not take his eyes off Paxton.

Adelaide moved first. Jake followed. Together they faced Paxton.

"You're the reason the patients suddenly got so agitated a few minutes ago," Adelaide said. "They recognize you. They know you're a murderer, don't they? You were the man in the surgical mask who frightened Ormsby so badly he jumped out the window."

"I spiked Ormsby's coffee with some of the drug," Paxton said. "When he started hallucinating, I followed him up here, lit a Bunsen burner, and aimed it in his direction. His mind did the rest."

"You killed all of them," Jake said. "Ormsby, Madam Zolanda, Thelma Leggett, and, last night, Gill."

"I can take credit for all of them except Zolanda," Paxton said. "Leggett is obviously responsible for that. She evidently was tired of playing second fiddle to the psychic to the stars."

"You tried to murder us, too," Jake said. "Where did you get the expertise with dynamite?"

Paxton gave him a thin, icy smile. "Don't you know? I'm a hero of the Great War. Dynamite was everywhere on the battlefields."

"You murdered all those people because you wanted to control Daydream," Adelaide said. "But how will you produce it without Ormsby and a lab?"

"In my own lab, of course. The drug is still in the experimental stage, but I'm sure I can perfect it. I'll use transients and vagrants for my test subjects this time—people no one will miss."

"You're a fool," Jake said. "And you're too late."

"What are you talking about?" Paxton demanded.

"Didn't the orderlies tell you? I'm with the FBI. Special Agent Jake Truett."

"Yeah, the orderlies said something about that, but you lied to them," Paxton said. "You're not a government agent. You're just a retired import-export businessman who is pals with Luther Pell, a guy with mob connections. Somehow the two of you found out about Daydream. You're after the formula. Admit it."

Paxton was trying to sound sure of himself but Adelaide thought he looked uneasy. She wondered if the unholy din of the screaming, howling patients was starting to affect him. The cries of a ward full of doomed souls were enough to rattle anyone's nerves.

She took her attention off Paxton long enough to look at Jake. He appeared far too relaxed. He was almost lounging in the doorway of the office. She realized he was watching Paxton's eyes, waiting for something—anything—to distract the doctor. The dark tide of wails and shrieks from the ward was having an impact, but more was needed.

"I'm on the trail of the drug," Jake said, "but I'm working for the government. Ormsby tipped off the FBI months ago. We've had agents watching Gill ever since, but things got complicated after Miss Blake escaped. Like you, we had to find her. That took time."

"I'm not buying that story," Paxton said. "Not for a minute. Why would Ormsby go to the FBI?"

"That's easy," Jake said. "He traded the information about Daydream and the illicit drug operation here at Rushbrook in exchange for the promise of his own lab. It's all right here in this appointment calendar. Evidently he was tired of being at the beck and call of what he termed a couple of shady doctors who had no respect for serious science."

"Stop lying," Paxton raged.

But Adelaide could tell that Paxton was starting to believe Jake's story.

"By the way," Jake continued, "the FBI is going to be the least of your problems. If anything happens to Adelaide and me, Luther Pell will be on your doorstep long before the government men get there. Or maybe he'll just send someone to deal with you. As you said, he's got connections with some very dangerous people. He can contract out that kind of work."

"You're making this up as you go along," Paxton hissed. "Give that appointment calendar to Adelaide."

Jake hesitated.

"Do it now," Paxton said. "Adelaide, bring that calendar to me. Now, you stupid bitch."

Jake held the calendar out to Adelaide. At the same time he let her catch another glimpse of the elegant fountain pen he held in his other hand.

She tried to signal that she got the message, but she was not sure if he understood. She took the calendar and started down an aisle formed by two long workbenches.

Jake needed a distraction.

Paxton barely looked at her as she moved toward him. She realized that as far as he was concerned she was not important, certainly no one he needed to worry about. She was just Patient B.

She stumbled as she went past a workbench, and lurched to the side. She put out a hand as though to grab the edge of the counter. Instead she swept everything within reach off the bench.

A storm of glass beakers, flasks, test tubes, and instruments crashed onto the tiled floor.

Paxton flinched in reaction. Instinctively he turned toward Adelaide, aiming the gun at her. She dropped to the floor behind the workbench just as the pistol roared, shattering more glass.

Paxton turned back around to confront Jake but he was too late.

Jake had already thrown the lapis blue fountain pen as if it were a small knife.

Paxton reacted violently, reeling back a couple of steps. He screamed and clawed wildly at his throat. Simultaneously he squeezed the trigger in a reflexive action. A window in the office exploded. The screams from ward five rose in a muffled roar.

Moving very fast, Jake charged toward Paxton, who got off one last shot before losing his nerve. He swung around and ran for the stairwell.

Jake went after him.

The Duchess appeared in the shadows at the top of the stone staircase. Paxton shoved her aside. The Duchess reeled back against the banister, shrieking in dismay.

Paxton tripped over the long skirts of her old-fashioned gown. They both started to fall. Jake grabbed the Duchess's wrist and hauled her into the safety of the laboratory.

Paxton screamed and toppled headfirst down the stone staircase. Adelaide heard a series of sickening thuds, and then it was over.

The moans and wails on ward five ceased very suddenly. An ominous silence fell.

Jake went down the stairs. Adelaide followed. She stopped midway and looked over the iron railing. She could see Paxton sprawled on his back on the bottom steps. His head was twisted at an unnatural angle. Jake's fountain pen was sticking out of his neck.

Jake reached the body, crouched, and checked for a pulse. He looked up at Adelaide, his eyes burning hot with the aftereffects of violence. He shook his head once.

He retrieved his fountain pen, wiped it clean on Paxton's white linen jacket, and got to his feet. He looked up at Adelaide again.

"Are you all right?" he said.

"Yes," she said. "Yes, I think so. What about you?"

"I'm all right," he said.

The Duchess appeared at the top of the stairs.

"One of the servants told me that you had returned to pick up something that you had left behind, dear," she said to Adelaide. "That was a very risky thing to do."

"Yes, I know," Adelaide said. "That's why Mr. Truett accompanied me. Don't tell anyone but he's a government agent who is on a secret mission. That man on the floor is a criminal who came here to steal some drugs."

"The deliveryman?" the Duchess said. "I'm not surprised to hear that he's a thief. I never did trust him. Whenever he showed up a few valuables always went missing. He was here the night you left, my dear. He was wearing a surgical mask, of all things, but I recognized him. A very rude man."

The orderlies appeared at the bottom of the staircase. They were disheveled and flushed.

"We thought we heard gunshots," Buddy said. "We took cover."

"Gosh, that was quick thinking," Adelaide said. "I don't suppose it occurred to you to come to our rescue instead of cowering in the nurses' station?"

The Duchess tsk-tsked. "So hard to get good staff these days."

Victor eyed Paxton's body. "What the hell happened to him?"

"Isn't it obvious?" the Duchess said in regal tones. "He fell down the stairs."

Buddy and Victor both eyed Jake with suspicion.

"He fell, huh?" Victor said.

"Obviously," Jake said. He didn't offer anything else.

Sirens sounded in the distance.

Adelaide looked at Victor. "Did you call the police?"

"No," Victor said. "We couldn't get to a phone."

"Oh, right, because you were taking cover in the nurses' station," Adelaide said.

"Who called the cops?" Buddy asked, bewildered.

"I think I know," Jake said. He looked at Adelaide. "Come with me. There's something we need to do before the police get here."

"All right," Adelaide said.

The Duchess looked at Jake. "You'll take good care of her, won't you? Wouldn't want her to end up back in that dreadful room at the end of the hall."

"Trust me," Jake said, "I'll make certain that Adelaide never returns to the Rushbrook Sanitarium."

The Duchess smiled in approval. "She doesn't belong here."

Jake looked at Adelaide. "I know. She belongs with me."

⚜

The car Paxton had driven to Rushbrook was parked behind the sanitarium's kitchen. There was a large hatbox in the trunk. It was stuffed with envelopes and packets of photographs, diaries, letters, and assorted papers.

"That must be the stash of blackmail material that Zolanda and Thelma Leggett collected," Adelaide said.

"Looks like it," Jake said. He hoisted the hatbox out of the trunk. "With luck the diary will be inside this box."

"What are you going to do with the rest of the extortion materials?" Adelaide asked.

"The police don't need to know about this hatbox," Jake said. "We'll take it back to Burning Cove and destroy the contents."

The first of the police vehicles rolled up to the guardhouse and stopped just as Jake closed the trunk of Luther's maroon speedster. A man in a Rushbrook Police Department uniform climbed out from behind the wheel.

"Got a message for Special Agent Jake Truett," he shouted. "Anyone here by that name?"

Jake walked toward him. "I'm Jake Truett."

"Just got a long distance-call from someone named Luther Pell in Burning Cove. He said you might be in real trouble here at the sanitarium. Something about a dangerous man named Calvin Paxton having pulled a fast one. Evidently this Paxton fellow managed to sneak out of Burning Cove without anyone noticing until about half an hour ago. Pell seemed to think this Paxton guy might be on his way here and that he was after you and a lady."

"Paxton won't be a problem for anyone now," Jake said.

Chapter 49

"It's a version of a throwing weapon called a shuriken," Jake said. He looked down at the lapis blue fountain pen in his hand. "A few years ago a man I did business with in the Far East taught me how to use one. They come in a variety of shapes and are meant to be easily concealed. This one was designed to my specifications. Here in the States no one thinks twice about a man carrying a fountain pen."

"It's so small," Adelaide said. "I'm amazed it made such an impact on Paxton."

It was early evening. She was exhausted but her nerves were still on edge. She wished she had some of the tisane that she used for the bad nights. She had been obliged to make do with regular tea.

She and Jake were sitting in a cabin in an auto court halfway between Rushbrook and Burning Cove. Shortly after they had finished with the police and started the long drive back, the fog rolled in over the coastal highway. Driving had become hazardous. As Jake had pointed out, they had taken enough risks for one day.

They had pulled off the road to spend the night at the first establishment that appeared clean and comfortable.

There was a fire going on the hearth. The hatbox was on the floor beside Jake's chair. The briefcase containing the files they had taken from Ormsby's office sat next to it.

"A shuriken is not designed to kill," Jake said, "although it can be used that way at close range. It is, after all, a very sharp blade. But it's primarily a weapon of distraction. You use it to startle and, with luck, frighten your opponent. The idea is to gain a little time to move in on him."

"Which is exactly how it worked," Adelaide said. "Something to be said for all that traveling you did while you were in the import-export business. But I'm glad you're out of that line of work."

"It was time. I'm not much use to our government now, anyway. Thanks to that spy in the agency I mentioned, too many people abroad know who I am. I no longer have a useful cover."

"What about Luther Pell? You said the two of you were introduced by a mutual acquaintance. Was it the same man who recruited you as a spy?"

"Yes. Luther occasionally does favors for the FBI now. The Bureau finds his underworld connections useful from time to time."

"That's how you got the fake Bureau ID?"

"Uh-huh."

Adelaide watched the flames in silence for a time.

"You'll need to find another job," she said finally.

"You are certainly anxious to see me employed." Jake smiled. "I promise you, I won't starve. I made a lot of money in the import-export business."

"I don't doubt that, but you still need gainful work."

"Something will come along. But first things first."

Jake leaned down and removed the top of the hatbox. They both contemplated the wealth of materials stuffed inside the box. There was a small, leather-bound appointment journal on top.

Jake took out the journal, opened it, and turned a few pages. "Looks like Zolanda kept detailed records of her victims and their secrets. She used initials for names but there are also dates. Beside each entry there's a number."

Adelaide picked up one of the sealed envelopes. "There's a number on each packet, too."

"Each one probably corresponds to an entry in the journal."

"It will take hours to sort through all those papers and photos and journals," Adelaide warned.

"Thanks to Elizabeth's father, I know exactly what I'm looking for and I also know the approximate dates when Elizabeth consulted with Zolanda."

It didn't take long to find Elizabeth's diary. It was very close to the top.

"Elizabeth was one of Zolanda's most recent victims, wasn't she?" Adelaide said.

"Looks like it," Jake said.

He paged through the diary, pausing here and there to read a passage more closely. "It's all here. The things Garrick demanded that she do in exchange for his promise to marry her. He used her, or tried to use her." Jake turned another couple of pages. "In the end it looks like he got angry because she never gave him any substantial information about me. He told her that he would never see her again. She threatened to tell me about him."

"That's why he murdered her, isn't it?"

Jake turned another page and stopped. "Looks like he had a change of heart. Declared that he could not live without her. He told her that they would run off together. Told her that she should pack a bag. He said he would come by the house to pick her up and that they would go to Reno so that she could get a divorce. He told her that she must make certain no one saw them. She writes that she will give the housekeeper the day off."

"That's the day Garrick went to your house and murdered Elizabeth, isn't it?"

"Yes." Jake closed the diary. "I knew something was wrong, right from the start. But it never dawned on me that Elizabeth was being manipulated by a spymaster until after I found her in the basement."

"I told you once before, you couldn't save her because she did not want to be saved. But you can save her family. You can destroy the diary."

"Yes, I can do that." Jake opened the diary again. One by one he fed the pages to the flames. When he was done, he sat back in his chair. "I'll telephone Elizabeth's father tomorrow and tell him that the diary no longer exists and that the blackmailer is dead."

"We should burn the rest of these secrets," Adelaide said.

"Not tonight. I need to go through them first to make certain there is nothing in the box that might affect national security. That will take time. We'll take the rest of the items back to Burning Cove with us and deal with them there."

"It's over," Adelaide said quietly.

"Not yet." Jake looked at her. "There's one more thing you should know before we close the door on my past. It's about the manner in which Garrick died."

"Are you going to tell me that it wasn't an accident?"

Jake exhaled slowly. "He followed me out to the *Mermaid* that night. I was sure that he would. He came at me with a knife. But I was expecting him to do just that."

"Believe it or not, I had already figured out that Garrick's convenient drowning was not an amazing coincidence."

Jake watched her for a time. "I just wanted you to know."

"I understand. What happens now?" she said. "Will you contact someone in the FBI? After all, we just uncovered a drug ring. But if we try to explain things to the authorities, they'll want to know all about Daydream. They'll demand that we turn over the formula. And then they'll question me and they'll find out about the experiments and they'll think that maybe I really am crazy—"

Jake leaned forward and put his fingers on her lips, silencing her. "No one is going to question you. The drug ring no longer exists. There is nothing in this case that the police in Rushbrook and Burning Cove can't handle. No need for the Bureau to get involved." He took his hand away from her mouth. "Trust me."

Adelaide breathed a sigh of relief and then tensed. "What about Conrad Massey?"

"Massey knows he's lucky to be alive. He'll keep his mouth shut because he's aware that he'll go to jail for kidnapping, fraud, and attempted murder, among other things, if he tells his story to the police—assuming he survived long enough to stand trial."

Adelaide shot him a severe look. "You don't really mean that."

Jake looked at her. He did not say a word.

"All right, you do mean it."

"Oh, yeah," Jake said. "But you can relax. Massey isn't in a position to make trouble for us. He's going to have his hands full dealing with the financial disaster that is about to overtake him. That will be followed by a social disaster. For all intents and purposes, he is a ruined man."

"One of the first things he'll do is stop paying for the Duchess's care at Rushbrook."

"With Gill out of the way, perhaps a new, modern-thinking doctor will take over the asylum," Jake said. "Or maybe it will be closed."

"Regardless, I will keep an eye on things and make certain that the Duchess is settled someplace where she'll be comfortable."

Jake smiled. "We will both keep an eye on her." He looked at the briefcase. "I want to go through the files on Daydream before we destroy them. I need to find out if there was any connection to foreign agents or someone in our own government. But we can burn your patient file tonight. It's up to you."

She contemplated the briefcase for a moment.

"No," she said at last. "I think I want to read that file. I need to know exactly what they did to me. And then I'll destroy it."

"And afterward?" Jake said. "What do you want to do when you're finally free of the past?"

"Florence says my teas have been great for business. I like blending them for people so I'll keep doing that. But I would also like to use my mother's collection of old herbals as a foundation for a new botanical research library in Burning Cove."

"That," Jake said, "is an excellent plan."

Adelaide braced herself. It was time to face the future. "What about you? You've accomplished your objective. You recovered the diary. Now you're free, too."

He rose, reached down, and tugged her to her feet. He cupped her face in his hands. There was a lot of heat in his eyes.

"I'm thinking of moving to Burning Cove," he said. "Life by the seaside has done wonders for my nerves."

Her laughter bubbled up out of nowhere. She put her arms around his waist.

"Mine have certainly improved since I took up residence there," she said.

"How do you feel about taking in a permanent boarder?"

"I like the idea," she said. "I like it a lot. I could put you to work in my library, although probably not at the reference desk. I don't think you would be good at dealing with the public."

A rare flash of warm laughter lightened Jake's avenging-angel eyes. "Living with you and having a steady job sounds like the perfect future," he said.

"Yes, it does," she said. "And just think, you will have a convenient supply of your favorite green tea."

"I hoped that would be part of the deal." His amusement faded. He tightened his grip on her face. "I know it's too soon to say this, but I love you, Adelaide. You should know that sooner or later I will ask you to marry me. In fact, I will beg you to marry me."

"In that case, I would suggest that you ask me sooner rather than later. One thing I have learned recently is that life can be unpredictable. One should not put off until tomorrow what one wants very much to do today."

"You can say yes today?"

She smiled. "Yes."

There was a new emotion in his eyes now. She could have sworn that she caught the glint of tears. But that was impossible, she told herself. A man like Jake would not cry.

Concerned, she raised her fingertips and touched the corner of his eye. "Jake?" she said.

He did not answer. Instead, he kissed her with an aching tenderness that let her know the tears were real. It was a kiss that promised a soul-stirring love.

She wrapped her arms around his neck and gave herself up to the embrace.

"Adelaide," Jake said against her mouth. "Adelaide."

The kiss became more intense. The thrill of shared desire consumed them. Jake started to undress her but soon they were fighting each other for the embrace.

They made it to one of the two narrow beds, leaving a trail of discarded clothing behind. Jake yanked the quilt aside and stretched out on his back. He pulled her down so that she sprawled on top of him. They were still very new at the business of making love together, Adelaide thought. There was so much to learn about each other.

She could have sworn his hand shook a little when he touched her breasts, as if he could not quite believe that she was real.

She trailed her fingertips down the length of him, from his sleek, strong shoulders to his thighs. She explored his lean, muscled body with a sense of wonder and satisfaction. He was her lover and she was his.

When she reached the hard, rigid evidence of his desire, he exhaled on a harsh groan and fitted his hands to her waist. He positioned her so that she straddled him, and drove himself slowly, relentlessly into her welcoming body.

"I need you," he rasped. "I need you so much. Come for me, sweetheart. I want to feel you come while I'm in you."

She loved knowing that he wanted her so desperately, loved knowing that she could thrill him, loved knowing that he thrilled her.

He reached between her legs and found the exquisitely sensitive spot. She caught her breath.

Moments later her climax struck in cascading waves, carrying her away.

"*Jake.*"

"Yes," Jake said. "Yes."

He watched her with half-closed eyes, enthralled. She sensed that he was trying to hold back but his formidable willpower failed him. The storm of his own release crashed through him.

When it was over, she collapsed on top of him. He held her very close and very tight.

❦

She felt him stir a long time later.

"There's something you should know about me before we get married," he said.

"Something else besides the fact that once upon a time you were a secret agent?"

She was lying on top of him, her head pillowed on his chest. The cabin was getting cold but Jake's body was warm enough to melt a glacier. She did not want to move.

"I do have a job," he said.

"What?" She raised her head so that she could look down at him. "Why didn't you tell me?"

"Because it's not a very secure job. I could be fired at any time. The pay is erratic and uncertain. The hours are sometimes very odd. But on the positive side, I can do my work in Burning Cove just as easily as in Los Angeles."

"I don't understand. Do you sell real estate or stocks?"

"No." Jake threaded his fingers through her hair. "I write the Cooper Boone spy novels under the name Simon Winslow."

"You're joking."

He shook his head.

She eyed him warily. "You're not joking."

"No. I haven't been writing for long, just a couple of years. I've only had two books in the series published. I can't assure you that I'm going to be a success in that line of work."

She thought about the yellow legal pad and the sharpened pencils that he kept in his briefcase. She wrinkled her nose.

"Does Luther Pell know about your writing career?" she asked.

"He's one of the very few people who does know."

She groaned. "You must have been very amused by my efforts to get you to concentrate on finding a new job."

"No," he said. He twisted a lock of her hair around his fingers and tugged her gently down on his chest. "I was touched that you cared enough to be concerned. I can't remember the last time someone worried about me."

She glared at him. And then she started to laugh. He watched her, bemused for a moment, and then he grinned.

"You're not mad?" he said.

"No. Why should I be mad? I'm going to marry the author of the Cooper Boone novels. I won't have to wait for the next one to be released. I'll get to read it before anyone else."

"Yes," he said. "You will."

She widened her eyes. "Gosh, could I have your autograph?"

It was his turn to laugh.

"How about something a little more useful?" he said.

"Such as?"

"Such as this."

He released his grip on her hair, cupped his hand around the back of her head, and drew her down so that he could kiss her.

"This is all right," she said against his mouth. "But I still want you to sign my copy of your latest book."

"Fine. I'll sign anything if you'll promise to stop talking and kiss me."

"I can do that."

Chapter 50

The following morning Raina opened the drawer of her desk and took out the slender file folder that contained the flawlessly typed report she had prepared. She put the folder on the desk but she did not open it. Instead she folded her hands on top, anchoring it securely in place.

"I have the names of your liquor thieves, Mr. Pell," she said. "But we need to discuss this situation before I give you the report."

Luther lounged back in the client chair and eyed the folder. When he looked at her again, his expression was perfectly neutral. He gave nothing away.

"What is there to discuss?" he asked. "I hired you to find out who was stealing liquor from my club. You say you were successful. Now you are going to give me the names of the thieves and I will pay you for your time. That does not sound complicated."

"Actually, it is somewhat complicated. You see, there are nuances."

"Nuances." He made it sound as if it were an unfamiliar word.

"The people involved in the theft are not expert thieves," she said.

"That, by the way, is probably why your security people didn't identify them. They were looking for professionals."

"Then we aren't talking about an organized ring."

"No, Mr. Pell, we are dealing with a couple of young people."

"Kids?"

"Not exactly. They are working for you, after all. But they are young and in love and planning to marry."

Luther's expression was no longer neutral. He looked deeply pained.

"Spare me any excuses that involve romance," he said. "If you think that I'm going to overlook the thefts because you imagine that the two crooks are modern-day versions of Romeo and Juliet—"

"They aren't stealing the liquor to pay for a honeymoon," Raina said. "One of the thieves has a mother who is quite ill. Her doctor has told her that her only hope is an operation. Unfortunately the family can't afford to pay for it."

"Before we go any deeper into this subject, are you telling me that you actually believe the tale of the poor, sick mother?"

"Yes. I verified the facts of the situation. Before I give you the names of the two young people, I want your word that you won't do anything to them."

"*Do* anything?"

"I realize you'll probably feel you must fire them. That will be devastating to both, I promise you. Losing their jobs will be ample punishment, especially because in a small town like Burning Cove it will be very hard for them to find new jobs. Once the word gets out that you let them go, other employers won't want to hire them."

"Maybe they should have considered the consequences before they started stealing from me," Luther said.

"I told you, they are very young."

"And in love. And trying to pay for an operation. Stop right there. If you give me any more details, you'll have to provide me with a hankie."

She relaxed a little. "There's an extra charge for hankies."

Luther's mouth kicked up a little at the corner. "All right, let me get this straight. You'll give me the names of the thieves if I promise to do nothing more than fire them."

Raina cleared her throat. "I don't want you to make an example out of these kids by doing something . . . harsh."

Luther tapped one long finger on the arm of his chair and watched her with unreadable eyes.

"Do you really think I'd have a couple of kids beaten up, or worse, just because they stole some liquor from me?"

Raina exhaled deeply. "No. But I had to be sure. You have a certain reputation, Luther. I'm told you have connections to some very dangerous people. That makes you dangerous, too."

He gave her a considering look. "You know a little something about dangerous people, don't you, Raina?"

She froze, fighting to keep her face expressionless.

"One meets a few in my line," she said carefully. "A hazard of the investigative profession, I'm afraid. Take yourself, for example."

"Or, perhaps, your previous employer? I believe you were a secretary for the firm of Enright and Enright in New York."

She forced herself to breathe. "How did you figure it out?"

Luther raised one shoulder in a casual shrug. "A lot of little things. Your East Coast accent, your rather vague employment history, your connections with other private investigation agencies. And then, of course, there was the matter of your timing."

She tightened her folded hands. "What about my timing?"

"You showed up here in Burning Cove a couple of weeks after the death of your former employer."

"Why did that make you suspicious?"

"As I said, it was just a lot of small things that started to add up. What clinched it, though, was the day that we met in the Burning Cove Library. You were reading some month-old newspapers. The headlines involved certain incidents that took place here in town, including a fatal car crash."

She exhaled softly and nodded, resigned. "I was afraid that you had noticed the articles I was reading. Are the circumstances of my arrival here in Burning Cove a problem for you?"

Luther smiled. "Not in the least. I do find them intriguing, however."

He was telling the truth, she decided. She got to her feet and walked across the room to the window. The morning fog had burned off. The warm, golden sun filtered through the leafy palms, dappling the courtyard.

She had not been in town very long, she thought, but she was already in love with Burning Cove. It felt like home in a way that New York never had.

"I'm not sure why I decided to come here," she said.

"I know why." Luther rose and came to stand behind her. "You had to see the place for yourself. You had to read the papers. You wanted to know what happened to your employer's son."

"Yes. And after I got here, I decided to stay. I like it here."

"Welcome to California. And welcome to Burning Cove."

She had the impression that he was about to put a hand on her shoulder, perhaps turn her around to face him. They were standing very close together. Anticipation made her a little light-headed. Luther Pell was a dangerous man but he had the hands of an artist.

"Thank you," she said.

"Stop worrying," he continued. "I won't fire Romeo and Juliet. And, yes, I'll pay for the surgery."

She turned around and smiled. "I thought you would say that once you were familiar with the nuances of the case."

"You know, until now, I never realized that I was a man who appreciated nuances," Luther said.

"How odd." Raina could not stop smiling. "I knew from the moment I met you that you were exactly the kind of man who appreciated nuances."

Chapter 51

That afternoon Adelaide sat with Raina in the offices of Kirk Investigations. They were drinking coffee that Raina had made. Jake and Luther were meeting with Detective Brandon to give him the carefully packaged news that Paxton, Gill, Zolanda, and Thelma Leggett had been dealing drugs and that it looked like Leggett had murdered her boss. Paxton had decided to get rid of the other members of the gang and had pursued Jake and Adelaide to Rushbrook hoping to stop them from collecting evidence.

The hatbox full of celebrity secrets was presently concealed in the trunk of Adelaide's car. Neither she nor Jake had wanted to risk leaving the box unattended at the cottage, and they had decided that no one else needed to know about the contents. Hiding a large container of blackmail materials had proven to be somewhat awkward, however. The trunk of her car seemed as safe a place as anywhere else. The plan was to burn the contents of the hatbox and her patient file that evening.

"I still can't understand why Madam Zolanda predicted a death at the end of an otherwise routine psychic act," Adelaide said. "She had no history of adding such a dramatic touch to her show."

Raina set her teacup down with a thoughtful air. "I realize I'm supposed to be the cynical private eye here, but what if Madam Zolanda really was psychic?"

Adelaide almost laughed. "Are you serious? Do you mean to tell me that you actually believe that she really did have some paranormal power?"

"No, but the only other viable explanation is that the prediction was somehow supposed to tie in with your disappearance or murder."

"That's what Jake says but I'm not sure I buy that explanation. Why would Zolanda risk calling attention to herself in that way? Yes, it would have been good publicity for her but she had to know that the police would immediately suspect her. And if that was her plan, why didn't she at least set up a solid alibi for herself for the hours following the end of her performance? As far as we know, she was home alone."

"Except that it looks like she had a visitor who murdered her. You said Paxton denied killing Zolanda, so obviously it must have been Leggett who did it. After all, she's the one who ended up with the stash of blackmail secrets."

"Paxton was convinced Leggett murdered Zolanda. That makes sense but it still leaves me with my question—what did Zolanda think she was doing when she gave that final prediction?"

"I have no idea. Let me know if you come up with any good theories." Raina put down her cup and opened a desk drawer to take out a notebook. "Meanwhile, I'm going to start work on my new case."

"You said you solved Luther Pell's missing liquor problem."

"I did." Raina looked pleased. "There wasn't much to it, really. But it turns out that handling Luther's case made for some excellent word-of-mouth advertising. I got a call from Mr. O'Conner. He's the head of security at the Burning Cove Hotel. He asked me to make some inquiries into the background of someone the hotel is considering for employment."

Adelaide smiled. "You did it, Raina. You got your investigation business up and running. Congratulations."

"What about you? Now that you've got access to your inheritance, surely you're going to stop working at the tearoom."

"I dropped in at the tearoom before I came here to see you. I wanted to let Florence know that I was back in town and that all was well. I told her I could work for her as long as she needed me and that I would continue to blend teas for people."

Raina's eyes widened. "What will you do when you're not blending teas and tisanes?"

"I plan to establish a private library of herbals and other books on the medicinal uses of plants. It will be open to scholars and researchers."

"Sounds like you've got a lot of new dreams," Raina said. "What about Jake?"

"As it happens, he does have a job."

Raina laughed. "Yes, I know, Luther told me that he writes those Cooper Boone spy novels. What I meant was, will he be staying here in Burning Cove?"

A sense of happiness sparkled through Adelaide. "Yes. He plans to stay in Burning Cove."

"With you?" Raina asked.

"With me."

"That is very good news," Raina said. "We must get together soon and celebrate."

"Great idea."

"But not tonight," Raina said. She smiled a small, secretive smile. "I've got plans for tonight."

"Jake and I have plans for this evening, too, but maybe tomorrow ... Wait. What do you mean you've got plans for tonight? Something to do with your new case?"

"No. I've been invited to the Paradise Club for cocktails and dinner."

Adelaide raised her brows. "With Luther?"

"Yes."

"I didn't know the Paradise Club served dinner."

"It doesn't. Dinner will be in Luther's private quarters above the club. He is sending a car to pick me up."

"That," Adelaide said, "sounds very interesting."

Raina's smiled widened. "I certainly thought so."

Adelaide cleared her throat. "I'm sure you know what you're doing, but as your friend I feel obliged to point out that Pell has a reputation for being connected to some dangerous people."

"Look who's talking. You're not exactly dating a Boy Scout, are you?"

Adelaide laughed. "All right, you've got me there. And, to be fair, Luther and Jake aren't dating Girl Scouts, are they? Look at us. We're not the sort of high-class ladies that nice guys take home to meet their mothers. I'm an escapee from an insane asylum and you're a private detective who investigates people with shady pasts."

"The way I look at it, what we lack in polish and refinement we more than make up for with a quality that, I do believe, is highly valued by men like Luther and Jake."

"Ah, yes." Adelaide smiled. "We are *interesting* women."

"Precisely. I doubt that they will ever find us dull or boring."

"We can say the same about them, can't we? They may be complicated at times. And stubborn. Even difficult."

"But if either of us ever vanished, they would both walk into hell to find us."

"Yes," Adelaide said. She smiled. "Yes, they would."

Chapter 52

She drove back to the cottage, parked in the small garage, and took the hatbox out of the trunk. It occurred to her as she went up the front steps that she could afford a larger place now. But she had grown oddly attached to the little house. *Because Jake moved in with me,* she thought. It was his presence that made the cottage feel like home.

Taking the key out of her handbag, she let herself into the small, cozy house. She headed for the kitchen, set the hatbox on the table, and put the kettle on the stove. Next she spooned her strongest tea into a pot. She needed to do some serious thinking.

While she waited for the water to boil, she lounged against the counter, folded her arms, and contemplated Madam Zolanda's final prediction.

So many things had been explained, yet the circumstances of the blackmailer's death remained murky. Why the melodramatic ending to her final performance?

Melodramatic performance.

Zolanda had been a very skilled actress but she had failed to become a Hollywood star.

On the night of her last show, Zolanda had held a crowded theater spellbound with her last psychic prediction. It was as if she had been trying to prove that she really was psychic.

Or trying to prove that she could act the role of a powerful psychic.

Adelaide unfolded her arms, pushed herself away from the counter, and grabbed the phone book. She looked up the number and reached for the receiver.

"*Burning Cove Herald*. How may I direct your call?"

"Irene Ward on the crime desk, please," Adelaide said. "Tell her Adelaide Blake is calling. No, wait, she knows me as Adelaide Brockton."

Sounding distracted, Irene came on the line.

"Hi, Adelaide. I just heard that Dr. Paxton, the diet doctor to the stars, died under suspicious circumstances. I also heard you were on the scene. I was about to call you for details."

"I promise I'll tell you all about it, but first I have a question about Madam Zolanda's final prediction."

"Dr. Skipton finally ruled Zolanda's death a suicide. I think Detective Brandon has his doubts but he's got no way to prove murder."

"Yes, well, it looks like Thelma Leggett killed Zolanda. But that's not what I wanted—"

"Hang on, let me get a pencil."

"I'll tell you everything later. Right now I need to know who was in the crowd at the Palace Theater that night when Zolanda predicted a death before morning."

"Are you kidding? There must have been a couple of hundred people at the Palace that night."

"Yes, but many were locals. I'm talking about Hollywood people. I'm sure that's a relatively small number. I'm wondering if there were any directors, producers, or talent scouts in the audience."

"Is it important?"

"I think it may be, yes."

"Hang on, I'll check with Trish. She covers celebrity news. She'll know if there were any studio executives in the audience that night."

Adelaide heard the telephone receiver clatter on the desk. She listened to the background din of the small but busy newsroom—typewriter keys clacked and a man shouted something about a deadline.

Irene came back a short time later.

"Trish says that there were a couple of actors who were staying at the Burning Cove, including Miss Westlake, in the audience. Douglas Holton was also there."

"The director?"

"Yes. No one knew he was in town until he showed up at the Palace. Trish says he's rumored to be looking for a new face for a key role in a film he's going to be directing."

"Does Trish know what the film is about?"

"Hang on, I'll ask her."

When Irene came back on the line a short time later, she sounded breathless.

"You're not going to believe this," she said. "Trish tells me it's a very hush-hush project but there is a rumor that it involves a psychic who predicts murders."

Adelaide stared at the wall, understanding washing through her with such certainty that she felt a little dizzy.

"Zolanda thought she was auditioning for a role in that movie."

"Do you really think so? Well, anything's possible when it comes to actors. They've been known to do some very strange things if they believe that it will land them a role in a film. Still—"

"If I'm right, Zolanda was conned into setting the scene for her own murder."

"In that case, it must have been Paxton who set her up," Irene said thoughtfully. "He was the one with Hollywood connections, not Gill. Maybe he told her that a famous director was in the audience and that he was looking for someone to play the role of a psychic. Zolanda fell for it."

"He promised her what all successful con artists promise their marks—a shot at something they want very, very much."

"But she was a con artist herself."

"That doesn't matter," Adelaide said. "If anything, it made her even more vulnerable. She was probably convinced that she couldn't be conned because she knew all the tricks. But logic and common sense go out the window in a heartbeat if the deceiver offers you something you want very badly."

"You're right. And it does answer the question of why Zolanda gave that creepy final act. Do you realize what this means?" Excitement sparked in Irene's voice. "I'll get one more front-page headline out of the dead psychic story. My pieces on Zolanda have all gone national. Wouldn't be surprised if this one does, too."

"That's great," Adelaide said. "Listen, I've got to run. I'll call you later."

"Promise you'll call me immediately if you come up with any more interesting theories about Zolanda's death."

"I promise."

Adelaide hung up the phone and stood quietly for a moment. Knowing that a powerful director was in the audience and that he was in the process of casting a new picture that involved a psychic went far toward explaining why Zolanda had given that last shocking performance. But something didn't feel right. Why had Paxton gone to such dramatic lengths to set the scene for Zolanda's death? Why not simply drug her, push her off the roof, and let the authorities conclude that she had taken her own life?

Why make Zolanda believe that her dreams might come true, that she had an opportunity to showcase her talent for a powerful director?

Zolanda's carefully staged death had all the hallmarks of a carefully plotted act of revenge.

Adelaide contemplated the hatbox.

The kettle was whistling. She crossed the kitchen and took it off the stove but she did not bother to pour the water into the pot. Instead she went to the table, opened the hatbox, and took out the journal.

Each entry listed only a set of initials, a date, a note about the form of the blackmail material—letter, photo, diary—and a number that corresponded to a particular sealed envelope. The night before, Jake had quickly discovered the packet containing Elizabeth's diary because he had recognized her initials and the date when she had given the extortion materials to Zolanda.

The remaining initials and dates meant nothing at first glance. Adelaide realized that she would have to go through the journal line by line and open each corresponding packet to see if there were any clues to the identity of the killer.

She decided to start from the most recent entries and work back toward the oldest. She was prepared for several hours of work, but in the end the answer leaped off the page.

The third most recent entry was annotated with a cryptic abbreviation: *Pt. File.* The accompanying initials meant nothing—J. T. But the date was approximately four months before she had been kidnapped and locked up at Rushbrook.

The Duchess had mentioned that Patient A had vanished a few months before Adelaide arrived at the asylum.

A rush of dark energy flooded through her. She went through the envelopes in the hatbox until she found the right one. Ripping it open, she dumped the contents on the table. She picked up the first one. And nearly stopped breathing when she realized she was looking at the sanitarium record of Patient A. There were several pages of Ormsby's detailed notes.

Patient A lapsed into another delirium following the third dose . . .

Patient A experienced strong hallucinations again today . . .

Patient A was cooperative for a time and then abruptly became hysterical . . .

Orderlies report that Patient A hallucinated all night again. Can't
risk giving her a sedative because of the chance of inducing a
coma . . .

There was far more information on the first test subject. She was a
female. She had signed the commitment papers voluntarily. She had
been hospitalized for nervous exhaustion. When she had arrived at
Rushbrook, she was accompanied by a friend who insisted that the patient be admitted under an assumed name.

And just to complete the blackmail file there were some photographs of Patient A in a Rushbrook Sanitarium gown. Her face was
disconcertingly slack, as if she had been drugged, but Adelaide could
see the helpless rage in the woman's eyes.

In one of the photos, she was sitting on the edge of a hospital bed.
The gown was hiked up to her waist. She was not wearing anything
underneath. Her legs were spread wide. Calvin Paxton, his trousers
down around his ankles, stood between her thighs.

In the next photo Gill was the one who had been photographed
raping the helpless, drugged woman.

Adelaide dropped the files on the table, jumped to her feet, and
rushed across the kitchen to seize the phone.

There was no dial tone. The line had been cut.

She had to get out of the house.

She grabbed the car keys and yanked open the kitchen door.

Vera Westlake emerged from the shadows at the side of the doorway. She had a gun in her right hand.

"Not another step," Vera Westlake said. "I can't miss. Not at this
distance."

Chapter 53

For some bizarre reason, Adelaide's first thought was that Vera looked like the movie star she was, as if she was acting the role of a desperate woman who was prepared to kill. But the gun in her hand was all too real.

She was fashionably dressed in a pair of trousers, a snug-fitting sweater, and a pair of blue and white oxfords. For once she was not wearing her trademark monochromatic color scheme. Her hair was mostly concealed beneath a scarf that was knotted under her chin. She wore a pair of dark glasses that were probably designed to make her appear anonymous but which only called attention to the profile of the most beautiful woman in Hollywood.

Adelaide stared at the gun, transfixed for a couple of heartbeats.

"I always wondered what happened to Patient A," she said. "Why don't you come in and have some tea. We have a lot to talk about, don't we?"

Vera moved through the doorway and stopped. She glanced at the hatbox.

"You found my Rushbrook files, didn't you?" she said.

"Yes. Zolanda had them."

"That bitch. After I drugged her, she said she wanted to tell me a secret. I asked her what that was. She laughed hysterically and said that she had my Rushbrook files. She said she had planned to hold them until my career was at its height and then demand a fortune for them. I was stunned. I had assumed the files were still safe at Rushbrook. I asked her where she kept them but by then she was no longer making sense. She told me the truth but only part of it. She said the files were in a hatbox, but she never said where the damned hatbox was located."

"Daydream is very problematic when used as a truth serum," Adelaide said.

Vera made a small sound of disgust. "Evidently that's especially true when it's combined with booze, because I sure couldn't get a straight answer out of Zolanda that night. After she went off the roof, I searched the villa. When I didn't find the files, I dared to hope that they had been a figment of Zolanda's hallucinations. I was wrong, obviously."

"Zolanda had help going off that roof, didn't she?" Adelaide said. "You told her that an important director was in the audience and that he was looking for a fresh face to play the role of a psychic."

"I wrote the whole damned script for her last prediction," Vera said softly.

"How did you convince her that you were going to make her big dream come true? She had no reason to trust you. After all, she had betrayed you in the worst possible way."

Vera smiled a humorless smile. "Zolanda was a good actress but I'm better. I allowed her to think that I was grateful to her for taking me to Rushbrook. I let her believe that I didn't remember the rapes and the hallucinations, that I was sure the drug had actually cured me. I even convinced her that I was obsessed with Paxton. When I told Zolanda that I wanted to repay her by arranging for a famous director to see her act onstage, she bought the whole story."

"You're right," Adelaide said, "you really are a brilliant actress. But you also had one big advantage, didn't you? Zolanda desperately wanted to believe you."

"It was pathetic, really. After the performance I called her to tell her that I had some good news but that I needed to give her the details privately because everything about Holton's next film is a secret. I told her that she should make sure her assistant was not around."

"When Leggett was out of the way, you went to the villa."

"Zolanda was thrilled," Vera said. "I told her that the director had left the theater looking for a phone. He wanted to call his secretary immediately and tell her to make an appointment for a screen test for the psychic to the stars."

"Zolanda believed every word you said because she wanted to believe that she was going to become a star."

"We grew up in the same small town. We traveled to Hollywood on the same train. We stayed in the same shabby boardinghouses while we tried to get those first screen tests. I made it but Zolanda didn't. Yes, I was offering her the one thing she craved more than anything else in the world."

"She was jealous of you."

"You could say *insanely* jealous." Vera's eyes were bleak. "But it took me a while to realize that. As I told you, she was a good actress. I'll give her that much. She just didn't have the look the directors want. I knew she was making money with her psychic routine. I thought she was content. I never understood the depths of her hatred and jealousy until the night she took me to the Rushbrook Sanitarium and handed me over to those two monsters, Gill and Paxton."

"The paperwork says you signed the voluntary commitment papers."

"I was on the verge of a nervous breakdown," Vera said. "The gossip magazines had declared me the most beautiful woman in Hollywood.

Thanks to *Dark Road* I was an overnight star. I should have been on top of the world. I had everything I could want, but I was more depressed and anxious than I had ever been in my life. I was contemplating suicide."

"But you didn't want the studio to know."

"I didn't dare let them think that I was mentally unstable. I couldn't see a doctor in Los Angeles, let alone check myself into a hospital for treatment. There are no secrets in that town. So I called the woman I believed was still my best friend from the old days, the one person I thought I could trust."

"You called Zolanda."

"She picked me up at my home and drove me all the way to Rushbrook."

"She knew all about the Rushbrook Sanitarium because she was dealing drugs for Paxton and Gill," Adelaide said.

"Yes, but at the time I didn't know about the drug connection. When we got to Rushbrook, that bastard, Gill, was waiting for us. I was admitted under an assumed name. At the time I really believed that Zolanda was doing me a great favor. Gill gave me an injection, a strong sedative. I woke up in a room at the end of a long hall on ward five."

"That's almost exactly how I got to ward five, except that it was my fake husband who had me committed."

"I still remember the screams at night," Vera said.

"So do I. Nights were always the worst."

Neither of them spoke for a moment. Eventually, Vera continued with her story.

"I'm not sure what they had in mind when I first arrived, but it didn't take long for Gill and Ormsby to decide that I was an ideal test subject for Daydream. I wasn't insane like the others on that floor," she said.

"That's how you became Patient A."

"Gill planned to sell the drug to anyone who could pay the price for it. But Paxton had even greater ambitions. He hoped to use the drug to control powerful people—wealthy industrialists, senators, maybe the president."

"Talk about hallucinating."

"They weren't altogether wrong about the drug, were they?" Vera said. "It does work as they thought, at least to some extent. In addition to being a strong hallucinogen, it makes a person susceptible to hypnotic suggestion. How do you think I got Zolanda up on that roof?"

"Did you push her off the parapet?"

"No," Vera said. "There was no need to go that far. She started seeing things in the darkness. She panicked and fell. But in the end I made certain that she understood exactly why I was there."

"What about the others? Ormsby, Leggett, Gill. Even Paxton is dead now. They went down like dominoes. In the end the entire drug ring was destroyed. That was not a coincidence, was it? You wanted revenge on all of them. You succeeded in destroying them."

"I admit I owe you and Jake Truett for Paxton's death. I had other plans for him but you took care of that problem for me. As for Ormsby, Gill, and Leggett, it wasn't hard to convince Paxton that he didn't need any of them. He was so sure that I wasn't very bright. He was also convinced that the Daydream had left my nerves in a very fragile state. I let him think that I needed him in order to survive the stress of Hollywood."

"He believed you."

"Yes.

"Paxton was convinced that he was controlling you," Adelaide said. "He never realized that you were manipulating him."

"He was only too happy to get rid of the others. He had his own grand plans for Daydream."

"I know what happened to Ormsby," Adelaide said. "Tell me about Thelma Leggett."

"Leggett called me after she went into hiding. She told me that she had my Rushbrook records. She said she would release them to the press if I didn't pay blackmail. I agreed. She ordered me to leave the first payment in an amusement park in a small town on the coast." Vera gave an elegant shrug. "I sent Paxton, instead."

"You knew he would probably kill her."

"Yes, of course. I also knew that he would grab the stash of blackmail materials, including my records. But I knew he would keep quiet because he had as much to lose as I did if those records hit the headlines."

"I assume it was also Paxton who talked Gill into drugging Conrad Massey and sending him to that pier to murder Jake," Adelaide said. "Massey was supposed to shoot Jake and then use the gun on himself."

"That was the plan. But I knew it would probably go badly for Massey and Gill."

"Because the drug is inherently unpredictable?"

Vera smiled. "And because I had a hunch that Jake Truett was too smart to get himself killed at a late-night rendezvous with a drug-crazed man."

"You were right," Adelaide said. "But why did Paxton want to murder Conrad Massey?"

"Massey didn't know much about Daydream but he knew enough to be dangerous. He could be counted on to keep quiet as long as he had control of your inheritance. But it had become clear that he had lost you to Truett, and that meant he would soon lose your money. That made Paxton very nervous. He became frantic when he found out that Massey had survived the meeting with Truett. He knew that if Massey pointed the cops at Gill, Gill would, in turn, point them at Dr. Paxton, diet doctor to the stars."

"So Paxton got rid of Gill that same night."

"And then he joined me at the Paradise," Vera said. "He wanted to establish an alibi in case he needed one. After he left the Paradise I went back to my villa. I assumed Paxton had gone back to the Burning

Cove Hotel. But I got an uneasy feeling early this morning. I telephoned his villa at the hotel. When there was no answer, I suspected
that he was up to something. I was worried that he had gone after you
again."

"What did you do?"

"I tried calling you here. When neither you nor Truett answered, I
did the only thing I could think of—I telephoned the Paradise Club.
Luther Pell was not there but whoever answered the phone said he
would get a message to him."

"That explains why Luther telephoned the Rushbrook police early
this morning," Adelaide said.

"I know it probably doesn't matter to you, but I never wanted you
to get killed. I didn't know that Paxton intended to murder you the
same night he killed Ormsby at Rushbrook. I didn't realize at first that
you were the reason Paxton and Zolanda and Thelma Leggett had all
made the sudden decision to travel to Burning Cove. But I realized that
the location offered a perfect opportunity for me to set my plans in
motion. You may not believe it, but I didn't even know that you were
Patient B, let alone that you had escaped Rushbrook—not until the
morning after Zolanda jumped off that roof."

"You didn't know that Paxton planned to kidnap me or kill me that
same night?"

"No," Vera said. "Not until the next day. Up to that point I had been
obsessed with my revenge. It was all I could think about. But the day
after Zolanda went off that roof, I overheard some of Paxton's phone
call to Gill. That was when I realized exactly who you were. By then it
was obvious that Jake Truett was more than he seemed—he was friends
with Luther Pell, after all. It was also clear that Truett was going to
keep a close eye on you. I hoped he could keep you safe."

"You knew there had to be some reason why a man like Jake Truett
would take a personal interest in a tearoom waitress."

Vera smiled a cool smile. "Truett is not the only one with hidden depths. You are a very brave, very resourceful woman, Adelaide. You have no idea how much I admire you for pulling off that escape from Rushbrook. I understand why Mr. Truett is so interested in you."

"If you admire me so much, why are you holding that gun on me?"

"Because I am well aware that you have no reason to trust me or help me. Where is my patient file?"

"It's there on the table."

Vera did not lower the gun, but she moved to the table and used her free hand to riffle through the contents of the file. She froze when she saw the photos.

"Those bastards," she whispered.

"Don't worry, the negatives are there as well," Adelaide said. "Gill and Paxton raped you while you were on the drug."

"Night after night. Back at the start they considered the photos trophies. They were having sex with a famous star. But they also realized they could use the pictures as blackmail to control me." Vera looked up from the file. "Did Gill and Paxton rape you, too?"

"No."

"I wonder why not."

"I realized right away that I dared not sleep at night," Adelaide said. "I wasn't afraid of Gill and Paxton. They didn't have any interest in me, not in that way, probably because I wasn't a star and, therefore, not a potential blackmail target. But I was terrified of the night orderlies so I stayed awake while they were on duty. Every time they came near my door I pretended to hallucinate wildly. To be honest, it wasn't always an act. The drug did cause me to hallucinate. The orderlies thought I was insane. I think they were afraid of me. Maybe Gill and Paxton were, as well. After all, they had no way of knowing exactly how the drug was affecting me."

"I'm glad you were spared that much, at least," Vera said. "Unfortunately, the drug left me in a sort of waking dream at night. I knew what was going on but I could not react."

"But in the end you were the one manipulating Paxton and you used him to get your revenge on the others," Adelaide said. "How did you get control of him?"

"Gill and Paxton took turns with me at first. They were thrilled to know that they were getting away with raping the most beautiful woman in Hollywood—and that the next morning she never seemed to remember that they had abused her. She thought she was hallucinating."

"But you did remember."

"Oh, yes," Vera said softly. "I remembered everything."

"How did you get released?"

Vera shrugged. "Paxton became obsessed with me. He also saw me as great advertising for his awful diet drink. That gave me all the power I needed to manipulate him. I pretended that I was equally obsessed with him. He wanted to believe that he had seduced the most beautiful woman in Hollywood. In any event, they had to let me go eventually. I was a famous movie star. I couldn't just vanish. If I did, I wouldn't have any value as a blackmail target."

"How did Zolanda get your file and those pictures?"

"I asked Zolanda that after she laughed about her plans to blackmail me. She said it had been very easy. She contacted one of the orderlies who worked on ward five and offered him a thousand dollars for the file. He told her that Gill also had some pictures in his safe that might interest her. She said she would pay him another thousand for those as long as he got the negatives, too. I understand he took the money and quit his job."

"Jake and I found Zolanda's stash of blackmail material in the trunk of Paxton's car. We are going to burn everything that is in that hatbox."

Vera glanced at the hatbox. "Do you know, I actually believe you."

"Well, that's the plan—assuming you don't kill me first. But you aren't going to do that, are you? There's no need to take the risk of getting arrested for murder. After all, at this point there is nothing to connect you to Zolanda's death or the drug ring operating out of Rush-brook."

The gun in Vera's hand wavered a little. After a few seconds she lowered it.

"No, I'm not going to kill you," she said. "I just wanted to find that damned file."

"And now you've got it. What will you do with it?"

"Burn it, as you suggested. And then I'm going to disappear."

"Why? You're a famous movie star. You've got a brilliant future ahead of you in Hollywood."

"Don't you understand?" Vera said. "It was Hollywood that nearly destroyed me. Hollywood is the reason I ended up at the Rushbrook Sanitarium. I just want to be free. The only way to do that is to vanish."

"If you succeed, you'll become a legend. People will never stop looking for you. You'll spend your life hiding from the press."

Vera smiled at that. "You don't know Hollywood as well as I do. I'll give the press one last good story, a suitably dramatic ending for a sadly troubled movie star. In a few months the gossip magazines will declare another actress to be the most beautiful woman in Hollywood. Within a year no one will remember my name."

"How will you survive financially?"

"I've been planning this for the past few months," Vera said. "I've made three very successful films. I didn't get paid much for the first two, but I got better terms on the last one, *Lady in the Shadows*, so I wouldn't have starved in any event. But I'll let you in on a small secret—Paxton kept a fortune in cash in a safe in L.A. He didn't entirely trust the banks. I found the combination weeks ago when I searched his study. I cleaned out the safe before we left for Burning Cove because I knew I would be disappearing after my plans were complete here."

"Will you stay in California?"

"No. I'm going to move to Seattle. Who would think to look for a faded movie star there?"

"If you ever do decide to return to Burning Cove, will you promise to come and see me?"

Vera's eyes widened. "You're joking. You really want to see me again? After all the trouble I've caused you?"

Adelaide held out her hand. "You're the only other person on the face of the earth who really understands what I went through at the Rushbrook Sanitarium."

Vera hesitated and then, cautiously, she put the gun on the table and held out her own hand. Tears glittered in her eyes.

"You're the only person who understands what I went through at that damned asylum," she said in a choked voice. "I suppose that is a bond of sorts, isn't it?"

Adelaide grasped Vera's hand and squeezed gently. Vera returned the silent gesture. They let their hands fall to their sides.

"Tea?" Adelaide asked. "A cup of Tranquility before you leave to find your new life?"

"I'd like that," Vera said. "I'd like that very much. It has been a long time since I've had tea with a friend."

❦

Jake came through the doorway, a gun in his hand, just as Adelaide was pouring a cup of Tranquility for Vera. He stopped and looked at both women.

"What the hell?" he asked.

Vera ignored the gun in his hand. She smiled her enigmatic smile. "Hello, Mr. Truett."

"We were just having tea," Adelaide said. "Would you care for some? I've got your favorite green."

Jake glanced at her. "I tried to call you. Your phone was out of order. I was . . . concerned."

"No need to be," Adelaide said. "Sit down. Why did you try to call?"

Jake did not take his attention off Vera. "Luther told me that the reason he found out that Paxton had stolen a car and slipped out of town was because someone on his staff received a mysterious phone call from a woman. When Luther got the message, he immediately phoned the Rushbrook police. Can I assume it was you who made that call, Miss Westlake?"

"Yes," Vera said. "I owe you a debt of gratitude, by the way. I am very glad that Calvin Paxton is dead."

"It was an accident," Jake said without expression.

Vera smiled. "Of course."

"Sit down, Jake," Adelaide said. "We'll all have tea, and Miss Westlake can tell you her story."

Jake hesitated and then he put the gun back into the holster. "I assume Miss Westlake's story in an interesting one?"

"Oh, yes," Adelaide said. "You see, she was Patient A, the other one who vanished."

Chapter 54

"She'll be gone by morning," Adelaide said. "Soon there will be a headline in the press about a brilliant actress who took a sailboat out alone and never returned. She will be presumed lost at sea. It's rather fitting that her last film, *Lady in the Shadows*, was about a woman who vanishes under mysterious circumstances."

"The nation will be distraught for a couple of weeks and then a new Hollywood scandal will hit the papers," Jake said.

Adelaide nodded. "Yes."

She and Jake were sitting in front of the fireplace, feeding blackmail secrets to the flames. Before they began the ritual, Jake had opened a bottle of champagne that Luther and Raina had dropped off earlier.

We've all got something to celebrate, Luther had said. Adelaide had noticed that he was looking at Raina when he said it.

"I still can't believe you invited Westlake to stay for tea and then sent her off with two large packages of her special blend," Jake said. He tossed some letters into the fire. "You even told her to telephone you when she ran out so that you could put some more in the mail for her."

"For the bad nights," Adelaide said.

Jake exhaled. "I get it." He fed a photograph of two men engaged in a sexual act into the fire. One of the subjects was a famous star. "For the bad nights."

"Everyone has them occasionally," Adelaide said.

"True," he said. "But you and I have each other now."

She smiled. "For the good nights and the bad nights."

"Yes." He looked down into the empty hatbox. "That's the last of it. Ready for your file?"

"Yes."

She opened the file marked *Patient B* and fed the contents to the flames. It was good to watch the papers go up in smoke. By the time the file was empty, she felt free.

She reached across the short distance between the chairs and took Jake's hand.

"It's nice to know that the next time we check into an auto court I won't be a fake wife," she said. "It will make a pleasant change of pace."

Jake laughed. He got to his feet and pulled her into his arms.

"It's good to be home," he said.

She framed his face with her hands. "Yes. It's very good to be home."

Author's Note

The hallucinogenic drug Daydream is fiction, but I took my inspiration from the fact that lysergic acid diethylamide—LSD—was discovered by a Swiss scientist in 1938. Over the years many researchers have been convinced that it has genuine medicinal properties. Others believed that it could be used to brainwash captured soldiers, implant hypnotic suggestions, or function as a truth serum.

Several sources claim that decades ago some famous Hollywood celebrities used LSD in conjunction with psychotherapy. And, of course, legends of secret government experiments abound . . .

Photo by Marc von Borstel

Amanda Quick is a pseudonym for Jayne Ann Krentz, the author of more than fifty *New York Times* bestsellers. She writes historical romance novels under the Quick name, contemporary romantic suspense novels under the Krentz name, and futuristic romance novels under the pseudonym Jayne Castle. There are more than 35 million copies of her books in print. She lives in Seattle.

CONNECT ONLINE

amandaquick.com
facebook.com/jayneannkrentz
twitter.com/JayneAnnKrentz